ILLUMINATION

Also by Matthew Plampin

The Street Philosopher
The Devil's Acre

ILLUMINATION

MATTHEW PLAMPIN

HarperCollins*Publishers*

HarperCollins*Publishers*
77–85 Fulham Palace Road,
Hammersmith, London W6 8JB

www.harpercollins.co.uk

Published by HarperCollins*Publishers* 2013
1

A catalogue record for this book
is available from the British Library

ISBN: 978-0-00-747908-5

This novel is entirely a work of fiction.
The names, characters and incidents portrayed in it,
while at times based on historical figures, are the
work of the author's imagination.

Set in Meridien by Palimpsest Book Production Limited,
Falkirk, Stirlingshire

Printed and bound in Great Britain by

For my mother

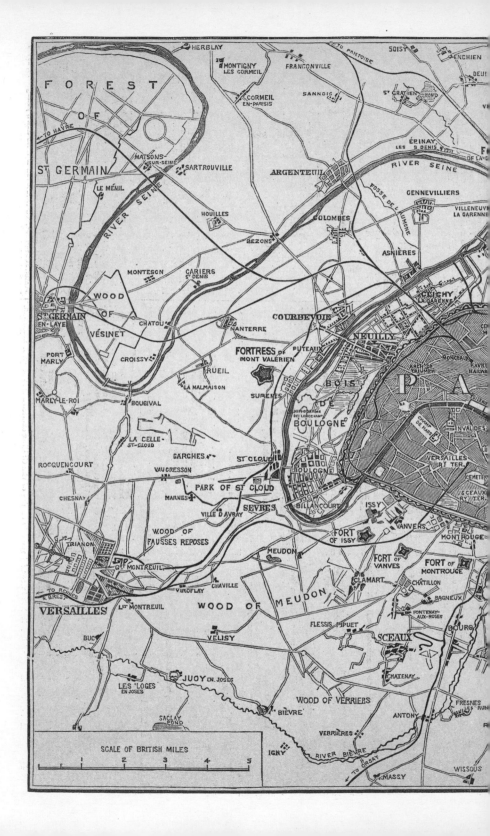

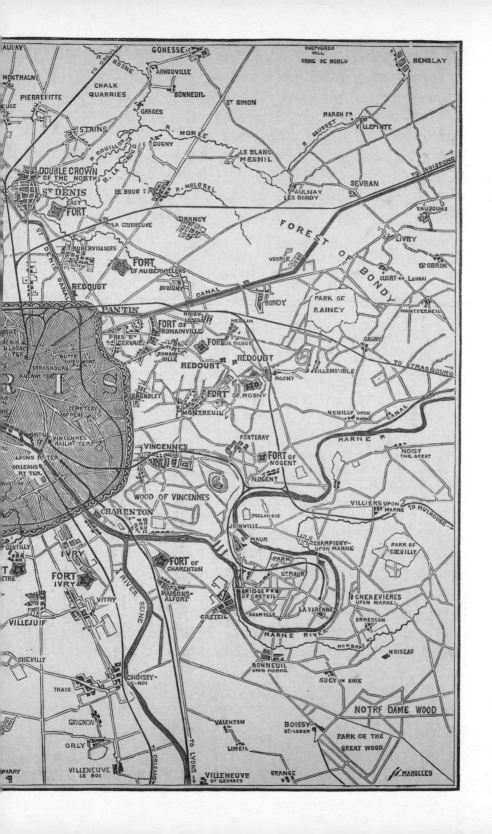

I no longer remember what Bakunin said, and it would in any case scarcely be possible to reproduce it. His speech was elemental and incandescent – a raging storm with lightning flashes and thunderclaps, and a roaring of lions. The man was a born speaker made for the revolution. If he had asked his hearers to cut each other's throats, they would have cheerfully obeyed him.

The Memoirs of Baron N. Wrangel

It is not enough to conquer; one must also know how to seduce.

Voltaire

PROLOGUE

Venus Verticordia
London 1868

Hannah entered the drawing room and froze: what appeared to be a miniature kangaroo had climbed up onto a chair and was nibbling at a vase of lilies. She stared at it for a few seconds – the black lips pulling delicately at the petals, the elongated toes rubbing mud into the satin upholstery – and wondered what she should do. Creatures both strange and familiar were everywhere at Tudor House. Caged parakeets shrieked in the hall; racoons and marmots scuttled beneath the furniture, their claws tapping on the floor tiles; and at dinner, a huge, sad-eyed dog (an Irish deerhound, they were told) had loped in and laid itself by the hearth without even glancing at the assembled guests.

'My apologies, Miss Pardy,' said her host, who had arrived at her side, 'the little buggers are always escaping from their pen and finding their way indoors. There is nought so bold, so precious clever, as a greedy wallaby. Do excuse me – excuse *us*.'

He edged forward with his arms outstretched, repeating the beast's name (which was Freda) in the tone of a doting father. The wallaby slipped from the chair, bounding sharply to the right and then to the left – a technique developed to foil the predators of the Australian desert that proved more than a match for a rotund painter-poet in a Chelsea drawing room.

The other guests had started to drift in. Instead of helping their host they gathered like spectators around a street show, cheering as Freda dodged another lunge. Most of them were writers or artists, or those who live off writers or artists; before long they were spouting poetry again, something about a knight's quest this time, bellowing the verse in good-humoured competition. Hannah didn't recognise it. She scratched her elbow through the sleeve of her gown. The evening was not going to plan.

Freda made it to the French doors, one of which had been left ajar, and hopped out into the cool April evening. Her owner was close behind, followed in turn by eight or nine chortling gentlemen. Among them was Clement, lighting a cigarette whilst recounting a joke he'd heard in an alehouse. He was doing rather better with these people than Hannah, despite knowing as much about art as the butcher's boy. *Opposite twins*, that was Elizabeth's favoured description: siblings born together who were different in every possible regard. This phrase had always made Hannah wince, but she could not deny the truth in it. Her brother had an easy amiability that she would never possess. Clem could bob along quite happily on the surface of almost any society – whilst she sank down into its depths, growing restless and irritable, longing to be away.

A finger prodded Hannah's hip. Elizabeth was smiling, but her eyes were hard with purpose. She nodded after their host. 'Follow him.'

'He is not interested, Elizabeth. Not in the least.'

'What rot. He'll soon be finished with that ridiculous pet of his and then you must act. This opportunity may not be repeated.'

'It is futile. You were at the table. You heard their conversation.'

'They are unconventional. I warned you of this, Hannah. They are artists. They think differently, even by our standards.'

Hannah sighed. 'They talked of money and their love affairs – gossip, Elizabeth – and recited a great long bookshelf's worth of poetry at one another. What is so unconventional about that?'

Elizabeth's smile vanished. It pleased her to think that these friends of hers were outrageous, an affront to propriety, and she did not appreciate Hannah suggesting otherwise. 'Perhaps, then, you should have done something to make yourself worthy of their notice. But once more you insist upon surly silence, coupled with a scowl that spoils you completely. How much do you suppose that will achieve, you impossible girl?'

Hannah would not be scolded. 'And what exactly was I to say? Their only care was the extent of my resemblance to you. None of them so much as mentioned my work. You said that they were curious – that you'd prepared the ground.'

This was a significant understatement. Back in St John's Wood, Elizabeth had declared that the evening would be nothing less than an *initiation*, launching Hannah into a vibrant world rich with possibilities. An alliance with the Cheyne Walk circle could lead to contacts, to sales, to an arrangement with a picture dealer – to an artistic career. Hannah had actually been excited, despite everything she knew about Elizabeth's promises and predictions; this, at last, had seemed like a real chance. Within a half-hour of their arrival at Tudor House, however, all hope had been dispelled. There was nothing for her here. Elizabeth had done it again, and Hannah had cursed herself for relaxing her usual scepticism.

'You must show some blessed *backbone*,' Elizabeth said. 'You have the matter in reverse. You are allowing him to overlook you.'

Hannah frowned at the floor. An oriental rug was laid across it, stained and faded by the passage of dirty paws. She decided to stay quiet.

Elizabeth pointed to a spot beside the grand piano. 'Stand there,' she instructed, starting for the garden. '*I* will follow him.'

The last of the party came in from the dining room – three young women, the only other females present that evening. All were unaccompanied, but this drew no notice at Tudor House. They'd been seated at the far end of the dinner table from Hannah; they hadn't been introduced, and had said and eaten very little. The three of them were oddly alike, pale and slender with their auburn hair worn down, clad in loose dresses so white they appeared to glow softly in the gaslight. Hannah wasn't easily intimidated, yet couldn't help re-evaluating her own garment; what at home had been a subtle celestial grey now seemed as drab as a day-old puddle.

The three women fell among the cushions of a long sofa, settling into each other's arms. This casual grace was undercut by their twanging accents, those of ordinary Londoners, which placed them some distance beneath the artistic gentlemen out whooping in the garden. Was this a harem, kept in a similar manner to the painter-poet's private zoo? Hannah didn't suppose that such an arrangement was beyond these people. One of the women was looking over at her, she realised, making an assessment then whispering to her friends; they leaned in, heads touching, to share a wicked giggle. Hannah turned away abruptly, searching the drawing room for a distraction. This wasn't difficult. Every surface was crowded with statuettes and vases, unidentifiable musical instruments or items of exotic jewellery – a collection as vast as it was haphazard. She went to a cluster of jade figurines on a sideboard, suddenly fascinated.

There was laughter in the garden, and Elizabeth re-appeared through the French doors with the painter-poet. The taller by two clear inches, she was leading him along as if escorting a convalescent. He was fretting about Freda, who remained at large; she was offering reassurance, telling him that his walls were high and his gardener well prac-tised in dealing with escapees. They drew to a halt a few feet before Hannah.

'And here she is, Gabriel,' Elizabeth announced, 'the reason I ventured out among the menfolk to claim you: my Hannah. Is she not a dove? A skylark, like that of dear Shelley: *a star of heaven in the broad day-light*?'

Hannah managed a feeble smile; she thought this a peculiar way to broach the subject of her paintings. Their host remained distracted, his small, sunken eyes twitching between the room's various doorways. He looked as if he was prey to many maladies, of both mind and body – a man locked into an inexorable decline. The three women on the sofa were waving, trying to coax him over, but he paid them no notice.

'Oh I agree, madam, a skylark, yes,' he answered, running a hand through his thinning hair. 'I'm afraid you must excuse me, though. Another crucial matter requires my attention – one quite unrelated to wallabies. It's my block-headed errand boy, you see. I have given him instructions, very *specific* instructions, but the clod is so extraordinarily slow that I cannot tell if he—'

'People have claimed,' Elizabeth continued, 'that she is the picture of me when I was her age; a duplicate, if you like. My feeling, however, if I am quite honest, is that she has a quality I did not. A Renaissance quality. A note of Florence, perhaps, in the late Cinquecento; the beautiful purity one sees in the maidens of Ghirlandaio. It must come from Augustus's side.'

Mention of Hannah's father, dead a decade now, was designed to pin their host in place. Augustus Pardy had been a poet of renown, author of the 'Ode to Dusk', the verse-play *Ariadne at Minos* and a number of other commended pieces. He was held in some esteem at Tudor House; Hannah suspected that it was largely for his sake that Elizabeth continued to be invited to these dinners. She held her own, naturally, with endless tales of her foreign travels and the celebrity they had once brought, but her late husband's name still served as her foundation.

The painter-poet, for the moment at least, was snagged. 'Your husband was certainly a striking fellow,' he murmured.

'She fits so very well among these treasures, does she not? Why, it is like she *belongs* here, in this enchanting haven of yours.' Elizabeth brought them closer. 'And she has a question for you, Gabriel. About your art.'

Hannah attempted to hide both her surprise and the utter blankness that followed it. Seconds passed, piling up; their host cleared his throat; Elizabeth's expectant gaze glared against her.

'I do envy your position here beside the river,' she said eventually. 'I am sure that if I lived at Tudor House I would be out on the embankment with my easel every morning. Might I ask how often you avail yourself of its sights?'

This made him laugh. 'Heavens above, I could never work *outside!* I trade in *beauty*, Miss Pardy, not coal-smoke and low-hanging cloud! What could there possibly be for my brush out on the Thames? And there are the flies, you know, and the dust, and all the blessed *people* . . . It's a French idea really, this outdoor painting, and results only in the most beastly slop.' He fixed Hannah with a quizzical expression. 'But I believe you mentioned an easel, miss. Do you paint?'

There was another brief silence.

Hannah looked back to the jade figurines. She imagined herself smashing them one by one in the fireplace. 'Our host,' she stated, 'is asking if I paint.'

Elizabeth ignored her. 'You can see something there though, Gabriel, can't you? As we discussed in the Garrick?' Her voice was brisk; she was attempting to close a deal. She nodded towards the women on the sofa. 'Her colouring is lighter than that of Miss Wilding and these others, but then variety is so often the key to success. Perhaps a blonde would—'

'*See something?*' Hannah interrupted. 'Elizabeth, what on earth are you—'

The painter-poet was growing uncomfortable. 'Now look here, Bess,' he said, tugging at his neat little beard, 'I have told you that I don't want it. I don't want the bother or the notice it will bring. I have decided upon my course and will not waste time with second thoughts.'

'What is he talking about?' Hannah demanded – although a couple of good guesses were forming in her mind. 'What doesn't he want?'

As always, Elizabeth refused to acknowledge defeat. 'For goodness' sake, Gabriel, you must not be so damnably stuck in your ways. Hannah may not be quite your normal type but without change, without development, we become *stagnant*, do we not? Such a painting would serve as the ideal culmination for my account of your career. It would bind author and subject, don't you see, in a most compelling manner. Interest is sure to be *enormous*. I predict a serialisation – in the *Athenaeum* at the very least – and a volume on the stands by the end of the year. Come now, don't be such a confounded mule. Give your consent and I can promise—'

Tudor House's errand boy, a gangling youth in cap and braces, filled the doorway that led out to the hall, torn between hailing his master and gaping at the women on the sofa. Provided with the excuse he needed to escape them, their host backed away, reeling off an apology before snapping a reprimand at his boy. Elizabeth watched him go; there was nothing she could do. She shook a crease from her lilac dress, taking care not to meet her daughter's eye.

'Explain this,' Hannah said. *'Now.'*

Elizabeth was unrepentant. 'If you cannot grasp it for yourself, Hannah, then I have truly failed.'

The artistic gentlemen were filing in from the garden. A spotless mahogany easel was carried through and erected by the piano; the painter-poet fiddled nervously with the gas fittings, opening valves to illuminate the room as much as possible; and finally, at his signal, the canvas was brought before them.

Hannah had never seen an example of their host's work. She knew about his central role in the Pre-Raphaelite controversy, of course, but that was two decades old; and furthermore, the major paintings it had produced all seemed to be by other hands. He'd become a mysterious figure, enjoying reputation without scrutiny, believed to be selling his startling canvases to a network of buyers across the British Isles yet shunning any form of public exhibition or exposure. Accordingly, although determined to extract a confession from Elizabeth, Hannah could not resist glancing over.

Unframed, unvarnished even, the painting had come straight from the studio upstairs. It depicted the head and shoulders of a young woman, roughly life-sized and quite naked. Her skin was flawless, suffused with warmth, free from the faintest wrinkle or blemish. Flowers crowded around

10

her, the colours unearthly in their richness – honeysuckle blooms rendered in curls of burning orange, roses that ranged from blushing cerise to the ruby blackness of blood. This woman's beauty had been refined somewhat, but Hannah recognised her immediately. The wide-set green eyes, the slightly heavy jaw, the red, pouting mouth: it was the girl from the sofa, Miss Wilding, who'd mocked her a minute earlier. Indeed, with the unveiling of the picture its model had shifted to the front of her cushion and was preening like an actress at her curtain-call. A cold thought struck through Hannah: *that is what my mother had planned for me*.

This was no straightforward portrait, however. Allegorical items were jammed into every corner. Behind the woman hung a gold-leaf halo, fringed unaccountably with buttery moths; off to the right was a bluebird, spreading its wings for flight. In one slender hand she held the apple of temptation, of original sin, and in the other Cupid's arrow, angled so that it pointed directly at her left nipple – this was Eve and Venus combined, a fleshy goddess neither pagan nor Christian.

To Hannah the result was absurd, overripe and weirdly lifeless, but the artistic gentlemen could scarcely contain their delight. Flushed with wine, they proclaimed the composition to be masterful in its simplicity, the brushwork consummate, and the overall effect so intoxicating that it almost brought one to a swoon. Miss Wilding was showered with compliments and joking avowals of love, and told that she had been captured precisely.

'The title is *Venus Verticordia*,' announced the painter-poet with a flourish, bolstered by his friends' flattery, 'the heart-turner, the embodiment of desire – the divine essence of female beauty.'

'And that she is!' exclaimed a notable novelist, moving in for a detailed inspection. 'Dear God, Gabriel, that she dashed well is!'

11

Hannah resolved to leave. She walked away from the sideboard and cut through the middle of the company. Clement said her name; others laughed and swapped remarks, assuming that her exit was provoked by a fit of feminine jealousy. She didn't care. Let these idiots think what they pleased. She wanted only to be gone.

Elizabeth caught her on the chequered tiles of the hall. 'Go no further, Hannah. We are not finished here.'

'No, Elizabeth,' Hannah replied, remaining steady, 'we most certainly are.'

'The *Venus* has upset you.' Elizabeth was perfectly calm. Hannah's stormings-out didn't offend her; she would usually applaud them, in fact, as evidence of her daughter's fighting spirit. 'It is a crude specimen, I grant you, but you must see that if you were to sit for Gabriel the two of you would be alone for many hours. There would be ample time for you to explain your ideas and win his support.'

This was too much; Hannah's composure deserted her. 'Skylarks!' she spat. '*Ghirlandaio!* You were trying to *sell me*. Is that where we stand, Elizabeth? Am I merely an object for you to bargain with?'

Elizabeth looked towards the front door; her profile, once featured on the cover plate of a dozen bestselling volumes and still formidably handsome, was outlined against the deep crimson wallpaper. 'I am disappointed that you choose to take such a naïve view.'

'What in blazes is *naïve* about it? Your plan was to deliver me to this Chelsea hermit of yours – to have him fashion me into a bare-breasted fancy for some banker to pant over in his study – so that he'd permit you to write a book about him and breathe life back into your wretched career!'

Hannah was shouting now. Parakeets flapped and squawked in their cages; a stripe-tailed mammal scurried into a rear parlour. All conversation in the drawing room

12

had ceased somewhere around 'bare-breasted fancy'. Gentlemen's shoes thudded across the faded rug; they were acquiring an audience. Aware that their host would be in it, and had probably heard her daughter's pronouncements, Elizabeth rose to his defence.

'The *Venus* may not be to your taste, Hannah – and you are, let us be honest here, very particular – but you must surely appreciate the thinking behind it. *Beauty*, that is Gabriel's creed: the creation of an art that is independent from religion, from morality, from every conventional form. An art that exists only for itself.'

'An art, you mean, that has been entirely severed from reality – that exists only in a perverse, febrile dream! At least the French painters he so disdains engage with *life*, with what is around them, whereas that daub in there – it's like this damned house. It is a retreat from the world, an evasion, a refusal to—'

A loud snort of amusement from the drawing room knocked Hannah off her stride. Elizabeth seized the chance to retaliate, asking what her daughter would have instead – pictures of pot-houses and rookeries, of dead dogs in gutters? – but Hannah found that her will to argue had been extinguished, shaken out like a match.

'You lied to me,' she said bluntly. 'You told him nothing about my painting. You brought me here only to serve your own ends.'

Elizabeth came nearer, lowering her voice. 'Oh, spare me that injured tone! It was a harmless manipulation that might ultimately have yielded results for us both. You must not be so damnably sensitive, Hannah.' Her manner softened very slightly. 'There is hope yet, I believe, if we work in concert. Something can always be salvaged.'

Hannah almost laughed; she took a backward step, then two more. Elizabeth's grey eyes had grown conspiratorial, inviting her daughter to join with her as an accomplice – a standard strategy of hers when things went sour. Hannah would not accept.

The front door was weighty, and its hinges well oiled; the slam reverberated through the soles of Hannah's evening shoes as she ran down the painter-poet's path. Elizabeth had insisted she wear her hair up, to show off the line of her neck. The real reason for this was now obvious; once out on Cheyne Walk she took an angry satisfaction in pulling it loose, the pins scattering like pine needles on the pavement as the ash-blonde coil unravelled across her back. The night was turning cold. Ahead, past the road, a barge chugged along the black river, its bell ringing. Hannah paused beneath a street lamp and considered the walk home: seven miles, eight perhaps, through several unsavoury districts. It was the only bearable option.

Before she could start, Clement emerged from Tudor House. She watched her twin approach, a cigarette in the corner of his mouth, moving from the gloom into the yellow light of her street lamp. His costume bordered on the comical. The formal suit he wore was several years old and cut for a rather more boyish frame; the necktie was escaping from his collar and threatening to undo itself altogether. It invariably fell to Clement to serve as the Pardy family's mediator, a role that fitted him little better than his suit; he was an awkward peacemaker, prone to vagueness and the odd contradiction, but there was simply no one else to do it. His grin, intended to mollify, looked distinctly sheepish.

'The woman is a monster,' he began. 'It cannot be denied.'

Hannah wasn't taken in. The aftermath of her ructions with Elizabeth followed a well-established pattern. She crossed her arms and waited.

'I do think she's embarrassed, though. These people really appear to mean something to her.'

14

'They are ludicrous. A gang of reptiles.'

Her brother, unfailingly decent, could not let this pass. 'I say, Han, that's hardly fair. A couple of them are pretty remarkable, in their way. There was this one little chap with the most gigantic head, a poet he said he was, who claimed to have—'

'I suppose she is apologising for me?' Hannah broke in. 'Begging our host's forgiveness?'

Clement tossed away his cigarette. 'Actually, when I left she was laughing it off – telling them that she had no idea that her daughter had grown so conventional, and asking for suggestions as to how it might be corrected.'

Hannah made a disgusted sound and walked off towards Westminster.

'Come now, Han,' pleaded Clement, trotting behind her, 'hold here for a minute more. You've got to look at it from her side. Every one of those fine gentlemen in there knows what she was, how famous and rich and so on. And every one of them knows where she is now. It's a terrible humiliation for her, really it is.'

This was his regular line of reasoning and it had worked on many occasions. Elizabeth's slide from glory, after all, had defined their lives. It had determined their transition to ever smaller houses, in less and less fashionable areas; the slow diminishment of their stock of valuables; the whittling of their domestic staff to a single elderly Irishwoman who washed the linen every other Wednesday. That evening, however, was different. Hannah felt it with unsettling clarity. Her brother's appeals were not going to win her around.

'I have been waiting for so very long for something to happen, Clem.' The words came out heavily, slowing her to a stop. 'She calls herself my best and closest ally. She loves to talk it up as a great cause – a battle waged for the whole of womankind.' A hot tear collected

15

against her nose. 'And yet all she does are things like this.'

Clement put a hand gently on her shoulder. He did his best, telling her that she must not lose heart and that her persistence was bound to bring rewards, but he couldn't begin to understand. He had no wind driving him – no desired destination in life. Clem was content merely to coast through a seemingly random series of projects that were often adopted and abandoned within the same week. His present fascination, for instance, was with the electric telegraph, leading to obscure experiments with currents and lengths of wire. This mechanical inclination was unprecedented among the Pardys. Knowing nothing of such matters, Elizabeth had left her son more or less alone – a lack of attention that had shaped his character as profoundly as her interference had shaped Hannah's.

'You must come back, Han, at any rate,' he concluded, 'to reclaim your cloak and hat.'

Hannah shook her head, wiping her eye on the cuff of her gown. Even this was unthinkable. Returning to her mother's side was a certain return to disappointment, to antagonism and dispute. It was reducing her, wearing her thin. She could not go on with it; she refused to. In her bookcase, between Mrs Trollope's *Domestic Manners of the Americans* and Mrs Jameson's *Sacred and Legendary Art*, was an envelope containing nearly fifteen pounds, scraped together over the past few years. The purpose of this sum, only half-perceived before that evening, came to her with sudden force. Hannah looked along the river, away from London and everyone in it. She had to act.

PART ONE

City of Light
Paris, September 1870

I

The platform was packed with people, well dressed and wealthy for the most part, jostling for places on a train that was about to leave for the provinces. They yelled and shoved, hitting at one another with fists, canes and umbrellas. Banknotes, bribes for the attendants, were being waved in the air like a thousand tiny flags. To Clem, fresh from the Calais express with a valise in each hand, the scene was positively apocalyptic. He stopped and tried to get his bearings.

'Head left,' Elizabeth shouted in his ear, pushing him forward. 'We want the rue Lafayette.'

The cab smelled of rice powder and a sickly citrus perfume. Clem heaved the bags up on the luggage rack and flopped into a corner, reaching inside his pocket for a cigarette. Opposite him, his mother had arrayed herself in her customary fashion: perched in the exact centre of the seat so that she had a clear view from both windows, with a notebook in her lap to record her observations. She began to write, lips slightly pursed, the pencil scurrying from one side of the page to the other and then darting back. Clem pulled open the window next to him and lit his cigarette.

His ribs were sore, bruised most likely; he'd been elbowed a good few times as he struggled across the seething concourse.

'Deuced keen to get off, weren't they? One would think the city was already burning.'

'Those who grew fat under the Empire,' declared Elizabeth, 'who benefited the most from all that corruption and carelessness, are scattering like geese now that something is being asked of them in return.'

'Well,' said Clem, 'that's certainly one way of looking at it.'

A vast military camp had been established in the streets around the Gare du Nord. Once-elegant avenues were choked with tents and huts, their trees stripped bare to fuel the fires that dotted the promenades, blackening the stonework with smoke. Soldiers sat in their hundreds along the pavements; peering down at them, Clem saw teenaged farmhands in ill-fitting blue tunics, their grubby faces vacant, rifles propped against their shoulders.

'Lord above,' he murmured, 'there must be an entire division out here.'

Elizabeth glanced at the mass of infantry for a couple of seconds and then resumed her note-taking. 'Efficiency must be our watchword,' she said as she wrote. 'We'll meet with Mr Inglis, we'll go to Montmartre to find her, and then we'll bring her straight home. Do you hear me, Clement? The three of us will escape this city together.'

'How much does your Mr Inglis know?'

'Simply that I have some urgent business to attend to before this situation with the Prussians comes to a head.' Her brow furrowed. 'He isn't someone I would necessarily choose to place my trust in, but the streets of Paris have been quite transformed since I last numbered among its residents. I doubt I could even find my way from the

Madeleine to Notre Dame after Louis Napoleon's barbaric interferences.' She finished a page and flipped it over, the flow of words barely interrupted. 'Mr Inglis, however, has lived on the rue Joubert for longer than anyone cares to remember. His assistance can only speed things along.'

The cab turned a corner, wheeling from sunlight into shadow; a detachment of field artillery clattered past, the crews shouting to each other from their positions on the mud-encrusted guns.

Clem had lost the taste for his cigarette. 'Whatever's best for Han,' he said, leaning forward to drop it out of the window.

They carried on into the heart of fashionable Paris. Clem marvelled at the crisp geometry of the streets, the monumental ranks of six-storey buildings, the endless rows of tall, identical windows; to one used to the crumbling muddle of London, the effect really was staggering. A neat enamelled sign, its white letters set against a peacock blue ground, informed him that they had reached the boulevard des Capucines, generally considered to be among the most splendid of the emperor's recent redevelopments. It had been kept free of soldiers, but in their place was an atmosphere of singular desolation. The magnificent shops had their shutters down and their awnings rolled; the gutters were clogged with mud and litter; the strolling, stylish crowds had long since fled. Hardly anyone at all could be seen, in fact, and Clem searched about in vain for a porter when they alighted before the Grand Hotel. Elizabeth went inside directly, pushing apart the heavy glass doors, leaving him to pay their driver and carry the bags.

Clem had friends who swore by the Paris Grand, waxing lyrical about its delightful society and many modern luxuries. That afternoon, though, it was like stepping into the atrium of a failing bank, the air charged with impending disaster. The crystal chandeliers were turned down low to conserve gas. Several of the public rooms had been roped off, the main bar was closed and a sign in front of the lifts informed guests in four languages that they were out of use until further notice. Only a handful of people were passing time there; exclusively male, soberly dressed or in uniform, they conversed quietly over their coffee cups.

Elizabeth was standing by the reception desk with a tallish man at her side. Some way past forty, with a sandy beard, he was wearing a green yachting jacket and shooting boots. He'd just kissed her hand and had yet to release it; she'd adopted a classic, much-employed pose, angling her head carefully to display her nose and jaw-line to their best advantage. Both were smiling.

'Mr Montague Inglis of the *Sentinel*,' Elizabeth said as he arrived before them. 'Mont, this is Clement Pardy, my son.'

Clem knew the *Sentinel*. A popular, rather frivolous paper with pretensions to being upmarket, it catered to those who aspired to a life of dandified loafing. He studied Mr Inglis more closely. The journalist's practical costume was belied by the costly gloss of his boot leather, the expert barbering of his beard and the diamond in his tiepin: the size of pea, this stone was surely worth more than the Pardy family had to its name. Clem set down the bags and the two men shook hands. Inglis's oar-shaped face was strangely vicarish, but weathered by fast living; his probing, watery eyes appeared to be running through some unknown calculation.

'Heavens,' he said, his voice low and slightly hoarse, 'the last time I saw this young buck he was still messing his britches. First trip to *La Ville-Lumière*, Clement?'

'It is, Mr Inglis.'

'Damn shame – it'll very probably be your last as well.' The journalist switched his attention back to Elizabeth. 'My dear Mrs P, I must insist that you tell me more about why

22

you've picked this moment for a visit. You are aware, I take it, that my poor Paris is doomed?'

He said this casually, as if confirming a dinner arrangement. Elizabeth's response was equally light-hearted; she twisted a dyed curl around her finger as she spoke, resting her elbow against the reception desk.

'That would seem to be the case, Mont, would it not? Why, in all my travels I have never seen so many blessed soldiers!'

'Yes, the boulevards have been quite defaced by that godforsaken rabble. Awfully depressing. And the Grand! My God, look at the place! A brilliant company used to assemble here every evening for champagne, billiards, some gossip before the theatre; now they're all either on the wing or in uniform, out filling sandbags by the city wall.' Inglis clapped his hands, raising his voice in sardonic triumph. 'Another capital result for the new republic! *Vive la France! Vive la liberté!* Bless my soul, I hope that villain Favre and the rest are pleased with what they've accomplished.'

Elizabeth's smile had grown strained. They were political opposites, Clem realised, despite the show of friendship; Inglis was a supporter of the Empire whose collapse at the beginning of the month had brought his mother such satisfaction. This flirtatious performance would only withstand so much before she felt compelled to strike out. Clem decided that he would change the subject.

'What news of the Prussians, Mr Inglis?' he asked. 'How close do the latest reports put them?'

Inglis ignored him. 'Madam, I do believe that you have yet to answer me. Why *are* you in Paris? Is it a new project, a new Mrs Pardy volume after all these years of inaction, so tormenting for your public? An account of my city's final hours, perhaps?'

Elizabeth was being goaded; her laugh had an edge.

'Goodness no, this is not a writing expedition. I am here for my daughter, Mont. Hannah, Clement's twin. She lives in Paris – has done so for nearly two and a half years.'

Inglis was unconvinced, but he let the matter go for now. 'Is she married to a Frenchman? An Englishman with business interests over here?'

'No, she is not.'

'A school, then – some manner of ladies' college?'

Clem dipped his head, squinting at his boots; they looked scuffed and cheap against the Grand's patterned marble floor. This Mr Inglis knew very well that Han had run away to Paris and was feigning ignorance so that Elizabeth would have to recount the details for him. For all his sociability he was trying to embarrass her.

Elizabeth, however, refused to be embarrassed. 'Hannah is a painter,' she said, her nose lifting, 'of quite extraordinary ability. She came here because she felt that female artists are taken more seriously in France than in England. She had – she *has* my complete support.'

Inglis took this in. 'And she wishes to return home, does she, to escape the coming trials?'

'I honestly don't know,' Elizabeth replied, remaining matter-of-fact. 'She hasn't contacted us for some months now. But we did receive this.'

She nodded at Clem, who reached inside his jacket for the letter – a single sheet covered on both sides with measured handwriting, making its case, in English, with eloquent directness. Both of them knew it almost word for word. Hannah was out of money, it claimed, friendless and destitute, trapped in Paris as the city faced a devastating ordeal that it might not survive. Her nationality would be no guard against a rain of explosive shells, or the lances of the Uhlans as they charged along the boulevards. They were her last and only chance; if they had any love for her they would go with all haste to No. 34 rue Garreau, Montmartre, Paris. It was unsigned, and offered no clues as to the author's identity.

'That is what brought us to Paris, Mont,' Elizabeth said. 'That is why we're taking this risk.'

Inglis skimmed the letter, a corner of the page pinched between his immaculately manicured fingertips. 'She is in Montmartre,' he said.

'A recent change. The address we had for her was in the Latin Quarter. I don't know why she has moved.'

The journalist handed the letter back to Clem, as one might to a butler. 'Dear lady, you're in luck. I'm well acquainted with the 18th arrondissement and would be happy to accompany you on this mission of yours. I was up there only yesterday afternoon, in fact, to pay a call on a photographer I know – an associate,' he added, 'of the great Nadar.'

Clem had been hoping that Mr Inglis would reveal himself to be of no use, allowing them to dispense with him and get on with their search alone. Now, though, he regarded the *Sentinel*'s correspondent with new curiosity. Photography was among his keenest interests; he'd even thought for a while last winter that he might have a proper go at it, until he'd discovered the prohibitive cost of the materials. Still, Nadar was a big beast – among the very biggest.

'Have you met Nadar, Mr Inglis?' he enquired, trying not to sound too impressed. 'Have you been to his studio?'

Again, Inglis acted as if Clem hadn't spoken. He turned towards the reception desk. No clerk could be seen. There were signs of neglect; dust was gathering in the pigeonholes and the brass counter-bell was dappled with fingerprints.

'Do you have a reservation?' he asked Elizabeth.

'We do, but I doubt we will sleep here. We are intending to be on the early-morning train back to Calais. With Hannah.'

25

'Wise, Mrs P, very wise. The Prussians will soon be blocking the railway lines. I understand that it's an initial stage in the process of encirclement.' Inglis straightened up. 'I'm rather surprised, actually, that it didn't happen this afternoon.'

Clem stared over at Elizabeth. She'd predicted confidently that it would be two more days before the invaders reached Paris. He felt sick, his collar tightening. This was a mistake of epic proportions. What on *earth* did they think they were doing?

Elizabeth remained composed. 'Is that possible?' she asked, sounding only mildly irked by the journalist's revelation. 'Can a city that is home to millions really be placed under siege? Is this some kind of joke, Mont?'

Inglis was grinning. 'No joke, Mrs P, upon my honour. All the experts are agreed. The Prussians are more than capable of organising such an operation. That is why the French have been crushed so absolutely – why their best legions have been knocked to bits in a matter of weeks. This is the modern way, you see. Valour and courage have been displaced by planning and logistics.'

'It seems improbable, to say the very least.'

'Perhaps, madam, but the strategies are well established. Roads will be barricaded, batteries built, trenches dug. They're going to lock us in, starve us down to nothing, and deliver a final humiliation so complete that the new republic will submit to whatever peace terms they propose.' Inglis struck the counter-bell, its sharp chime cutting through the lobby. 'The siege of Paris is about to begin.'

Evening had arrived whilst they'd been in the Grand. Ornate cast-iron lampposts lit expanses of empty pavement; a soft autumn mist was drifting down through the denuded trees. Inglis hailed them a cab, stopping to give the driver his instructions as Clem and his mother climbed inside. Elizabeth had entrusted Clem with her notebook; he went to draw it from his pocket and pass it over to her.

'No, Clement,' Elizabeth said, 'I fear that would only provoke him. Lord above, I'd forgotten how trying the man can be. Memory is too forgiving at times.'

'He isn't easy to like, I have to say.'

'Liking him isn't necessary. He might be able to help us locate Hannah. All we have to do is put up with him until then.'

Inglis folded his long limbs into the cab, settling himself at the opposite end of Clem's seat. The journalist was in high spirits, glad to have been liberated from the dullness of the Grand. He took a squashed-looking cap from his jacket and stuck it on his head. It was a kepi, he informed them, headwear of choice for partisans of the new republic – which made it an essential item for any man who wished to walk about the city and not be lynched either as a Prussian spy or an Imperialist.

'The latter,' he confided, 'for the shabbier class of Parisian, is by far the more grievous offence.'

They went north, passing through yet more roadside army camps, the fires now casting tangled shadows over the fine buildings behind. Inglis held forth on the incompetence of the new republic, the destructive savagery of the masses, the immense wrongs done to the noble, fallen emperor; Elizabeth stayed very still, gazing out of the window.

Entering Montmartre felt abrupt, like walking behind a section of stage-set. The scale and precision of the boulevards disappeared, the cab creaking its way up into a web of crooked, sloping lanes. No one had fled this district; Montmartre was truly alive that night, crammed with its inhabitants. The mood was oddly jubilant, the erratically lit streets resounding with songs and laughter. Every man was in uniform, but not one worn by any of the regular troops; their simple blue outfits were halfway between those of soldiers and policemen, topped off with a kepi just like Inglis's. The majority were drinking hard. They dominated the cafés and restaurants, debated on corners and lounged around shop fronts. Countless flags and banners were on display. The tricolour was the most popular – but another, plain red, was so common that it could easily have been mistaken for the standard of a new army, separate from that of France.

'National Guard,' Inglis said, his voice loaded with disdain. 'The Parisian militia. Louis Napoleon had the good sense to suppress them, but they're back with a vengeance now, claiming that they're the ones to save the city.' He pointed at a particularly large red flag, propped above the door of a bar. 'And as you can see, in humble districts such as this, the units are already thoroughly infected with socialistic doctrine.'

'The International?' Elizabeth asked.

'Among others. Reds of every stripe were all over Paris the moment the emperor was captured, spreading their sedition – sowing disinformation and slander.' Inglis smiled bitterly. 'Disaster piled upon disaster.'

The cab became caught in a herd of goats that was being driven into the city from the surrounding countryside. Inglis opened the door, leaned out to survey the brown, bleating backs, and suggested that they continue on foot.

'I know the way from here, Mrs P,' he said. 'It ain't far.'

Skirting the herd, he led them up a steep alley and across a courtyard. A good deal could be seen of the hilltop village Montmartre had been before it was swallowed by the expanding capital. Many of the houses were little more than cottages; whitewashed walls hemmed in gardens and orchards. Between a butcher and a tool shop Clem caught a glimpse of a broken-down windmill, the sails silhouetted against the darkening sky.

The rue Garreau lay a short distance beyond the courtyard. No. 34 was one of the larger buildings upon it, standing at the junction of two quiet backstreets, its floors stacked untidily like books on a scholar's desk. A portly, middle-aged woman in a grey dress was climbing down from a stool, having just lit the gas lamp above the door. Noticing their purposeful approach, she wiped her hands on her apron and prepared to meet them. Inglis began to speak, assuming command, but Elizabeth stepped smartly in front of him. They had arrived at Hannah's address; his usefulness was almost at an end.

Elizabeth bade the woman good evening and launched into a double-time explanation of their presence in Montmartre. Her French had remained remarkably fluent – whereas Clem's, only ever schoolroom level, had rusted to the point of uselessness. Following the conversation was a struggle, but he managed to grasp that this woman was Hannah's landlady – a Madame Lantier. Utterly overawed by Elizabeth, she was listening closely to what she was being told, her eyes open wide. She'd realised that they were relations of Hannah's due to the family resemblance, the blonde hair and so forth, and that they had travelled to Paris to effect a reunion; Elizabeth's talk of her tenant being in some kind of distress, however, came as a complete surprise.

'*Les Prussiens, oui, c'est très grave, mais Mademoiselle Pardy . . .*' Madame Lantier shrugged. '*Mademoiselle Pardy est la même.*'

Elizabeth shot Clem a glance; this was not the author of their mysterious letter. She asked another question and an agreement was reached, the landlady nodding as she turned to open her front door.

'She'll show us Hannah's room,' Elizabeth said. 'The blessed girl isn't there, of course – she's off in the city somewhere. But Madame hasn't noticed anything wrong at all.'

Clem considered this as they followed Madame Lantier into her hallway. It made sense that she was unaware of his sister's troubles. Who would want their landlady to know that they were out of cash, if they could possibly help it?

They were taken past the main staircase, through a pristine parlour and outside again, into the walled garden at the rear of the house. The air smelled of autumnal ripeness, of fat vegetables and soil; an abundance of tall plants thronged around a brick pathway, their leaves turning blue in the fading light. Madame Lantier had already started up this path, pushing through the press of vegetation. A little bemused, Elizabeth, Clem and Inglis went after her, holding onto their hats to stop them being dragged from their heads. After a few awkward yards they were back in the open. In front of them, set against the garden's rear wall, was a small wooden outbuilding. The landlady was at the door, fumbling with keys.

'Good Lord,' Elizabeth exclaimed, 'Hannah is living in a shed.'

The interior reeked of linseed oil, acrid and disagreeable after the sweet scents of the garden. It was dark; the single high window had been firmly shuttered. Clem could just discern a table, a stove, several easels and a number of black rectangles he took to be canvases.

'Stay where you are, Mrs P,' instructed Inglis. 'Madame has found a lamp.'

An oil flame flared, illuminating the modest room and the hoard of paintings it contained. There were views of sunlit boulevards, of cafés buzzing with people, of skiffs on the Seine – of Paris in 1870. The compositions were irregular, lop-sided, done with apparent disregard for both the conventions of picture-making and the symmetries of the remade city. Clem took a few steps towards one of the larger boulevard scenes. The image grew less precise the nearer he got to it. He saw how little detail there was, and how few definite lines; its forms were on the verge of coming apart, of dissolving into each other. Brush marks had been left openly visible throughout. Buildings were pale tracks of grey; trees feathery flurries of green and yellow; the crowds on the pavements nothing but a profusion of intermingled smears. Madame Lantier carried the lamp to the table. The light glistened across the surface of the canvases, catching on tiny beads and ridges of pigment.

'My dear Mrs Pardy,' Inglis said, 'I am so very sorry. Your poor daughter has obviously gone mad. The seedier side of Paris has corrupted her completely.'

Elizabeth had been making an initial survey of the paintings; now she turned on Inglis, dropping all pretence of amity. She would never permit anyone to criticise her children. That right was hers alone.

'This blinkered response does not surprise me, Mont. How could someone like you possibly appreciate such boldness and originality?'

Inglis appeared unconcerned by this shift in her attitude. He was well used to hostility, Clem perceived – welcoming it, even, as a sign of the merciless veracity of his observations. 'What is so original, pray, about painting like a drunk with a broom?'

'This is the *real world*, not the finely finished fakery of your beloved Empire, with its voluptuous come-hither nudes and slave-market scenes. This is art swept into the present.' Elizabeth looked over at her son, inviting him to rally to his sister's defence. 'Don't you agree, Clement?'

Clem's interest in painting was pretty casual, and inclined towards its technical aspects. The only time he'd become

31

truly enthusiastic had been a few years previously when he'd developed a fascination with the actual manufacture of the paint – how the stuff was mixed and squeezed into those metal tubes. He'd even taken a couple of cautious steps towards setting up his own factory, an artisanal operation catering only to the first rank of painters, but the finances had quickly become impossible and he'd been forced to abandon it.

'They're very fresh,' he said.

Elizabeth liked this. 'Aren't they? Why, the effect is like a spring breeze – a ray of living sunshine.' She paused significantly. 'Pass my notebook, would you?'

Inglis was clearly the sort who picked his battles carefully; sensing a disadvantage, he produced a cigar and pointed to the door. 'I think I'll wait outside, Mrs P – all this churning paint is making me nauseous. I'll be ready when you wish to resume the search.'

Clem handed the notebook to his mother. She started writing straight away, angling the page towards the lamp. 'I mean they're recent,' he enlarged. 'Not wholly dry. Some are less than a week old, I'd say.'

The room was clean and as orderly as an office. Sketches were stored away in folders, brushes and palette knives in jars, paint tubes heaped in a large cardboard box. A bookcase held a select library – works on art mostly, but also histories and a couple of slim volumes that looked like political tracts. There was no trace either of the corruption Inglis had mentioned or the miserable poverty described in the letter. Off to the side was a Japanese screen printed with a pattern of swooping swallows; behind it Clem could see a mattress, the corner of a battered chest and two winter coats, one black and the other blue, hanging from a nail in the wall. The black one, he realised, was made for a man.

'Elizabeth,' he said, 'I don't believe that Han is the only person living here.'

His mother followed his gaze. Such a discovery would have left any normal parent mortified, furious, raving about scandal and disgrace. Elizabeth, however, merely blinked; then she turned to study the paintings again.

'This is how artists are,' she said. 'It has always been thus, in Paris especially. Perhaps this friend is the reason she has moved out here, to Montmartre – although of course such a contrary step is typical of her.'

Their eyes met. For all Elizabeth's offhand tolerance, the same questions were occurring to them both. Was it this other resident, this man, who had written to them? Or was he the true source of danger?

Elizabeth resumed her grilling of Madame Lantier, rather more intently than before; Clem, meanwhile, walked further into the outbuilding, hunting for clues. Several unfinished works were propped away in a corner. Two were portraits: a young woman dressing, and a man sitting beside a window. The style was strikingly intimate and informal. The woman was perched on a wicker chair, a satin ballgown hitched up to her knees. She had an angular, impish face that hinted at an appetite for pleasure of all kinds; her tongue poked out between her lips as she reached for a stocking that lay crumpled on the floorboards. The skin of her bare shoulders had been painted in broad, butter-like strokes, the different tones left unblended beside one another. Just two shades of orange had been used to render her short coppery hair, and the bunched fabric of her gown was but a mesh of purple-pink diagonals.

The portrait of the man had a more considered effect. Clean-shaven and gravely handsome, he was sitting forward on a bench, his thick black hair brushed back from his brow. His coat was black as well, and his gloves; this austere figure, equal parts preacher, lawyer and soldier, had been set against a stretch of plain cream wallpaper, a contrast that fixed the eye upon him completely. In his hand was a slim green tome that Clem recognised as one of the political volumes from his sister's bookshelf. He was looking out at the viewer, his expression resolute but also reassuring, caring even, as if he was alone with a close comrade-in-arms.

Clem crouched to examine the picture further. Something he had taken to be a flaw, a crack in the paint, was no such thing. A dark scar ran down the left side of the sitter's face, running like a tear-track from his eye socket to the line of his jaw.

Over by the door, Elizabeth's voice was growing louder and more impatient. Clem stood up, thinking to go to Madame Lantier's aid, when he noticed a black strip on one of the other paintings in that corner, behind the two portraits. He pulled it out. Little more than a sketch, largely uncoloured, it depicted what looked like the inside of a small common theatre. An audience had gathered in the murky atmosphere, faces and hats and jackets blurring into an indistinct mass. Before them was an imposing, black-coated orator – the man from the portrait. He'd struck a simple pose, chin raised and right arm extended; his glove was a black V in the middle of the canvas, rendered with a single mark of the brush. Someone, Hannah it looked like, had scrawled a date along the bottom: *12th Septembre, 1870.*

Clem held it up for his mother and the landlady to see. *'Madame,'* he called, *'où est ça, s'il vous plaît?'*

The landlady told them that it was the Café-Concert Danton, a place of indifferent reputation only a few streets away. She pointed to another café scene, saying that it showed the Danton also; and another, over on the far side of the room.

'We should go there,' Clem said. 'Han's clearly a regular. If we don't find her we can come straight back.'

Elizabeth agreed. Madame Lantier provided directions and they left the shed at once. Inglis claimed to have heard of the Danton; he slowed his pace, though, dropping to the rear. His usefulness had expired, they all knew it, but he plainly had no desire to return to his lonely table in the lobby of the Grand. Clem suspected that they were stuck with him until they departed the city.

Once on the busier lanes they soon began to attract attention. Clem and Elizabeth's travelling clothes, although hardly ostentatious, were enough to draw unfriendly stares from nearly everyone they passed. Insults were hissed, the word *bourgeois* spat out as if it was the worst curse imaginable; children trailed behind them, sniggering and asking rude-sounding questions. Inglis wasn't nearly as comfortable in Montmartre as he'd implied. His proletarian disguise, with its various quality touches, was largely ineffective; Clem saw him remove the diamond tiepin and secure it inside his jacket.

Madame Lantier's directions brought them to the place Saint-Pierre, the square at the heart of the district, and on past the derelict merry-go-round in its centre. The northern side of the place had been left empty of buildings, a chain of gas lamps tracing a path up the last stretch of the hill to the signalling tower at its summit. An electric searchlight was trained on this structure; as Clem watched, a soldier stepped into its white beam, waved a series of semaphore flags and then withdrew into the darkness.

The Danton lay to the east, on the rue Saint-André. It was mean and rather dingy – nothing much to look at. Clem felt the deadening cramp of nerves, his breath catching in his throat. He hadn't seen Hannah for more than two years now, but that wasn't the reason for his unease. It was more like an intimation of doom – a profound sense that things weren't going to go as planned. This bothered him. He really wasn't the sort for such hand-wringing; indeed, he tended not to have the slightest inkling of doom's approach until he was sunk in it up to his neck. Nothing could be done, at any rate. Elizabeth was steaming past the gaudy street women sitting around the pavement tables and in through the doors. There was no time to reconsider.

Conditions inside were very close to the undignified crush represented in the paintings. The theatre itself was shut, the customers restricted to the narrow bar. A large proportion were National Guard, red flags and all; the rest were clerks, shop assistants, off-duty waiters and waitresses, with a scattering of trollops and pickpockets. Everyone was laughing, singing, arguing at the tops of their voices. Elizabeth jabbed a finger towards one end of the room and then started in the opposite direction, worming between the swaying guardsmen.

Clem pushed on along the bar as politely as he could manage. His ribs, still aching from the Gare du Nord, were barged anew; sour, boozy breath washed over his face as unpleasant comments were muttered; tobacco ash was flicked on his coat and wine splashed on his shoes. Ten minutes passed and he saw no one who looked remotely like an artist, or even like they might know an artist. He'd almost finished his search when a fight broke out nearby among a group of shrieking laundresses, forcing him against the marble bar-top. There was a mirror behind the rows of bottles: Clem contemplated himself as the brawling women were bundled into the street. How bloody *wrong* I am here, he thought, in my brown flannel and my squat English hat – wearing trimmed whiskers in this land of beards and drooping moustaches. He closed his eyes, sorely tempted to marshal his French and order a large brandy.

Upon opening them he saw someone familiar in the mirror, past his shoulder – a young woman. The image was itself a reflection, he realised, caught in a glass door panel and made especially sharp by the darkness outside. An arm nudged against this panel; it moved very slightly and the woman disappeared. He glanced around, judging the angles. By his estimation she was in a small area beyond the end of the bar. He worked his way towards it.

The woman from the painting was sitting at the edge of a candlelit booth, watching the barroom with an air of total boredom as a cigarette burned between her velvet-gloved fingers. She was almost as alien to the Danton as Clem – a more natural inhabitant of flash dancing halls than the drinking dens of Montmartre. Her dress was dark blue, extremely tight above the skirts and cut low to put as much of her pale flesh on show as possible. The copper hair, longer than in the portrait, was gathered up and adorned with black ribbon and lace. Her legs were crossed carelessly, revealing patent leather ankle boots and a few inches of silk stocking. She noticed Clem, acknowledging him with a beat of her turquoise eyelids. There was sly recognition in her smile. She beckoned for him to approach.

Hannah was in the rear of the booth, engaged in a lively conversation. It was an uncanny moment – gratifying and mystifying in equal measure. Her silver-blonde hair was tied beneath a length of red muslin. She was thinner than Clem remembered, but in a way that suggested vitality and energy rather than privation. And how like them she was! He'd never paid it much mind before, but there in that booth he saw his mother's oval face and clever grey eyes; the gentle point to the chin that he'd never cared for on himself, but on Hannah was nothing short of beautiful. There was his

37

sister, his twin, for many years his closest friend. He'd found her.

This relief was tempered with disquiet. She was surrounded by men, all of them wearing simple, faded clothes. They looked more like a band of revolutionaries than artists. Han had never been one for gangs, being an impatient, solitary type; yet here she was holding court, telling these moustachioed fellows what was what in French that sounded even better than Elizabeth's. She didn't need rescuing, by Clem or anyone else. The letter was a lie. His sister was neither friendless nor destitute; she wouldn't be leaving Paris, no matter what danger the city might be in. They'd been misled.

The copper-haired woman reached out to Hannah, attracting her attention and jerking a thumb towards Clem. His sister's astonishment seemed to smack against her, knocking her back in her seat.

'Dear God!' she cried. 'What – what the devil are you doing here?'

The booth went quiet.

'Well, Han,' Clem began, 'with everything that's going on, it was felt—'

Hannah got to her feet. 'Please, Clem,' she said, 'just tell me she isn't with you.'

II

Hannah took hold of Clement's lapel and pulled him away from the booth, into a doorway beside the bar. The material was well worn; it was the same coat he'd been using when she went, and it hadn't been new then. The fortunes of the Pardy household had plainly not improved. He'd started talking in his old manner, rambling on about how very well she looked and how much this place seemed to suit her; hearing and speaking English again after so long felt strange, a little wrong, like walking in someone else's boots.

'Shut up, Clem,' she said, 'for pity's sake.'

She considered him for a second: a guileless boy still, largely unchanged by the two years that had passed. His face, freckled by another idle summer, lacked the pinched quality Hannah had grown used to in Montmartre. Poor he might be, but he had food; he had a good bed and an easy mind. A flicker of contempt gave way immediately to guilt. Clement had been her sole regret when she'd fled from London. She'd abandoned her brother to Elizabeth. This could not be ducked or denied. He had every right to resent her – to demand that she explain herself and listen to the suffering he'd endured in her absence – but he was grinning, saying how pleased he was that they'd been reunited, whatever the circumstances. She released his coat.

'Is she here with you? Answer me.'

Clem's grin fell. He scratched at his blond whiskers and glanced along the bar. 'Over there somewhere, I'm afraid. Her blood's up something awful, Han. You'd better get ready.'

Hannah was glad of the anger that gripped her; it at least dictated a clear course of action. 'Why have you come? Why now?'

A letter was produced from his coat pocket, written in an official-looking hand. She read it with gathering dismay.

'But this is quite untrue. It's nonsense.'

'Who could've sent it, do you reckon?'

Hannah thought hard. This letter was obviously intended to humiliate. The arrival of her family from London at this pivotal time would make her seem like a hopeless ingénue – no different from the hundreds of hare-brained English girls who ran away to Paris every year, only to be retrieved by their relatives. It labelled her a tourist, an outsider, someone not to be taken seriously. The list of suspects was long. She'd learned that camaraderie between artists was a fragile thing, in constant danger of tipping into rivalry. They might share a philosophy of painting, but each one of these professed comrades, in some private chamber of his heart, desired the ruination of the rest. There were others as well; impatient creditors, a handful of rebuffed suitors, and the likes of Laure Fleurot, who'd pointed Clement in her direction with such malevolent delight. Any of them could be responsible.

Ingenuity had been required, of course, both to discover the St John's Wood address and compose a letter in English. Nobody of Hannah's acquaintance had ever admitted familiarity with her mother tongue. Translators and draughtsmen could be found throughout the city, though; and besides, who could say what knowledge people chose to keep hidden?

'I've no idea,' she said.

'Things are getting bad here though, aren't they? It's like the city has been given over entirely to soldiers. I've heard that there's to be a siege, Han – a bloody *siege*.'

Clem's experience of Paris had plainly unnerved him. Her brother led a sheltered life, seldom straying from long-established paths; he was singularly ill-equipped to cope with the upheaval that had come to define the city. The past few months had seen wild jubilation at the outbreak of war, the misery of subsequent defeat and then a blood-less revolution, swift and uproarious, unseating an empire in a single day. And now, almost impossibly, events were escalating yet further. The end of Napoleon III had not brought the end of the war he'd started. The Prussians were coming for Paris – set on razing her to the ground, it was rumoured, and then remaking her in their own forbidding image.

Hannah shook her head, remembering Jean-Jacques's words. 'These invaders do not see what Paris is,' she said. 'They think we've been cowed by the fall of the Empire and the destruction of the Imperial armies, but the opposite is true. Our city has been liberated.'

'*Our* city? Quite the loyal Parisian these days, Han, ain't you?' Clem's laugh was tense. 'I mean to say, that's all well and good, but these Prussian blighters are approaching in their *hundreds of thousands*. They have guns like you wouldn't believe. I read in *The Times* that at the battle of Sedan they—'

Hannah wasn't listening. She looked at the letter – at her address on the rue Garreau. 'How did you find me? Here in the Danton, I mean?'

Clem stopped; he grinned again, pride in his detective powers displacing his apprehension. 'Why, from your

41

paintings. This fine establishment features in a good few of them. I asked your landlady about it and she was kind enough to provide directions. Then I recognised that girl, the one in blue, from your portrait of her. Simple stuff, really.'

'You *went into my home?* What were you thinking, Clem?'

He became defensive. 'We were worried, Han. We thought you might be poorly, or starving, or—'

A murmur of excitement spread through the Danton, rippling out from the doors to its furthest corners. Many turned to stare; Hannah overheard a nearby labourer say '*l'Alsatian*' to his companions. Jean-Jacques had arrived. Two inches taller than the next tallest man, black hat still on his head, he was moving slowly towards the bar, shaking hands and giving nods of acknowledgement. A squad of National Guard pulled him among them, hailing him as a brother as they poured him a glass from their wine jug.

'I say,' Clem remarked, craning his neck, 'isn't that the black-suited fellow from your paintings – the orator? Is he going to speak?'

Hannah didn't answer. Exactly how much had her brother deduced? She tried to remember what had been left in the shed – and suddenly realised that if Clem could recognise Jean-Jacques, Elizabeth might be able to as well. A situation too awful ever to be anticipated was unfolding around her. She stepped from the doorway, hurriedly plotting the best path through the crowd whilst trying to think of an excuse that would get Jean-Jacques back outside.

'What news, Alsatian?' someone shouted. 'Where are the pigs now?'

Jean-Jacques addressed the room. His voice, accented slightly by his home province, was not loud, but it blew away the bar's chatter like a March wind. 'The latest sightings are of Crown Prince Frederick, crossing the Seine to the south.

42

The Orléans line has certainly been severed.' The Danton let out a groan. 'Do not lose heart, friends, it is but a minor loss. The Prussians will be driven back across the Rhine before a single week has passed. We will beat them.'

Those around him managed an embattled cheer, the National Guard raising their glasses to the coming victory; and between the uniformed arms was Elizabeth Pardy, poised to introduce herself to this noteworthy gentleman and ask him about her daughter. Like Clement, she seemed eerily the same – a figure from Hannah's past transposed awkwardly onto the present. Her hair was tucked up beneath a fawn travelling hat; her expression amiable yet glassy, concealing a deeper purpose. And now Jean-Jacques was turning towards her, listening as she leaned in to speak.

The next Hannah knew she was before them, quite breathless, grasping his left hand in both of hers. There were exclamations of surprise. Elizabeth planted a kiss on Hannah's cheek; her face was cold and heavily powdered, and the most extravagant praise, in French, was pouring from her lips. It took Hannah a moment to understand that the subject of this laudation was her paintings. She'd expected some overwhelming line, delivered with chilly calmness – a statement of disappointment and distress, perhaps, intended to floor her with shame. She hesitated, completely wrong-footed.

'Wonderful,' Elizabeth was saying. 'Extraordinary, beyond anything I had hoped for. I see what you are doing, Hannah, I see it so clearly. It is close to genius. You are on the verge of something great, my girl. I predict a—'

Hannah recovered her wits. She cut her mother short. 'You've made a mistake,' she said, in English. 'That letter is false. I don't need your help, Elizabeth. Go back to London. Go before it's too late.'

*　　*　　*

43

The alleyway smelled of pears and neat alcohol. It led downhill, away from the rue Saint-André; a stream of inky liquid was crawling through a central gutter. This was Hannah's short-cut to the rue Garreau, skirting the place Saint-Pierre to the south. She'd covered a dozen yards before she realised that home was useless. Elizabeth knew where she lived. She'd been to the shed and seen what was inside. She could return there at any time.

Hannah stopped beneath a lamp set in a rusted wall bracket. She'd released Jean-Jacques as soon as they'd left the Danton, running off to the right and into her alley. He'd followed, keeping up easily; he was only a couple of yards behind her now. She crossed her arms and glowered at him. His instinct for people was strong; he should have seen through Elizabeth at once, yet they'd been talking quite happily when Hannah had snatched him back. It felt almost as if he'd been an accessory to her mother's ambush – to that contemptible attempt to disarm her with flattery. He was watching her, waiting for her to speak. Their abrupt exit from the Danton hadn't perturbed him. Jean-Jacques Allix was a man beyond alarm. Throughout the summer, as France had been shaken to the brink of collapse, Hannah had found this absolute steadiness reassuring. Right then it made her want to knock off his hat.

'What did she say, Jean-Jacques? What was under discussion?'

He was quiet for a few more seconds. 'Only you, Hannah,' he said. 'Only you.'

His voice was tender; Hannah remembered the day she'd just passed, sitting at her easel on the place de l'Europe with her brushes in her lap, longing for the moment when they would be together again. But she steeled herself. She would not be lulled.

'I can't believe she's here in Montmartre. I can't believe it.'

'She told me that she'd come to ensure that you were safe. A mission of mercy.'

'Elizabeth came to *fetch me*,' Hannah snapped, 'to reclaim her wayward child and return her to London.' She covered her brow. 'I fled my family, Jean-Jacques. I climbed from my bedroom window in the dead of night and travelled alone to Paris. There it is. That's what I am. A runaway.'

Jean-Jacques nodded; up until now, Hannah had let him infer that she was an orphan, without any surviving relatives in England, but he didn't seem surprised or affronted by the truth. 'We all must adapt ourselves,' he said. 'It is part of life. The timing of this visit is strange, though. Surely any person of sense can see that there's a good chance of becoming trapped – that our foe is nearly upon us?'

Hannah sighed; she calmed a little. 'An anonymous letter was sent to London. It informed her that I was in urgent trouble and needed to be collected before the Prussians arrived.'

Jean-Jacques considered this. 'A low trick,' he said. 'The act of a coward. Do you know who was responsible?'

'I have my suspicions.'

'Your mother has been cruelly deceived – fooled into coming to Paris at a most hazardous time. You must be worried for her.'

Hannah glanced at him; his humour could be difficult to detect. 'That woman is why I am in France. It was her manipulations, her interferences and lies, that drove me from my home. And she is more than capable of looking after herself. Why on earth should I worry for her?'

Jean-Jacques looked away; a line appeared at the side of his mouth. 'You're right,' he said. 'She'll be well. Bourgeois like her always are. A haven will be found. She'll wait out the assault in perfect safety.'

A barrier ran through the population of Paris, according to Jean-Jacques and his comrades, separating the bourgeoisie from the workers. It rather pleased Hannah to hear Elizabeth placed on the wrong side of their great boundary; it gave her a sense that she had allies, not least Jean-Jacques himself. Directly next to this, however, sat the uncomfortable knowledge that but for a change of clothes and lodgings she was certainly as bourgeois as her mother.

'Such a simple path would never do for Elizabeth. She isn't one to hide away.' Hannah paused. 'It doesn't matter, at any rate. She'll have to leave Paris. She hasn't any money. A stay in a hotel, even for a single night, is completely beyond her means. To be quite honest, I'm surprised that she managed to find enough for her and Clem's passage.'

Jean-Jacques had been gazing at the surrounding rooftops, his hands in his pockets; now his dark eyes flicked back to her. 'Clem?'

Hannah cursed under her breath; she was being careless. 'Clement,' she admitted, 'my twin brother. He lives with Elizabeth still, back in London. And has come to Paris today.'

'You have a *twin brother*.' Jean-Jacques said this with gentle wonderment. The line at the side of his mouth deepened again. 'Another of Hannah's secrets is revealed.'

'It is not what you might think. He and I, we are too different to—'

Hannah gave up. It was no use. Everything was overturned. In the space of ten minutes the life she'd crafted in Paris had been irreversibly altered. Jean-Jacques had found out that she'd misled him and had glimpsed the troubles of her past. The Danton regulars, her supposed

46

friends, would be extracting all they could from poor Clem; they'd probably discover even more than Jean-Jacques had. She'd been exposed. Whatever chance she'd had of being taken on her own merits was gone. She might as well walk back to the Danton and surrender herself to Elizabeth. Her mother had won. She leaned against a wall, pressing her damp palms against her forehead. She was finished in Paris.

'Hannah,' said Jean-Jacques. 'Look there.'

Lucien and Benoît, two of the painters she'd been talking with when Clem had appeared, were strolling past the alley mouth: thin men smoking short cigars, sharing a drunken laugh as they headed towards the place Saint-Pierre. Octave, a sculptor, was a few feet behind. Hannah straightened up. Clem might be with them. She strode past Jean-Jacques, back out onto the rue Saint-André. There was no sign of her brother; the painters, however, gave a ragged roar of salutation.

'Why, Mademoiselle Pardy,' Lucien proclaimed, twisting his moustaches, 'what the *devil* is going on? You leap from the middle of a really quite stirring account of Courbet's decline to converse with a young gentleman who, from the brilliant yellow of his hair . . .'

'The delicacy of his nose and brow,' inserted Benoît, who fancied himself a portraitist, 'the fullness of his lips . . .'

'. . . can only be your brother. And then, even though this fellow has come all the way from the soot and smoke of London, you run from him after a few seconds, grabbing the fine Monsieur Allix for a – a *turn beneath the stars*, I suppose I should call it, for the sake of decency . . .'

'. . . leaving your brother entirely alone: a whiskery *Anglais* in an old suit, adrift in the Danton, too scared even to bleat for help.'

Lucien's cackle would have curdled milk. 'So we wave him

47

over. What else could we do for the brother of such a dear friend? I have a little English,' he confessed with a modest shrug, 'sufficient, at any rate, to learn that he is not the only member of the Pardy family in Montmartre tonight. There is a mother also, standing at the bar. A woman who, although undoubtedly *mature*, is still worthy of the attentions of any man who—'

'Enough.'

Jean-Jacques didn't speak with any force or volume. His tone was that of an equable schoolmaster who'd let his pupils run loose for a while, but had reached the limit of what he would allow. The half-cut painters were halted – stopped dead. Lucien looked off down the street; Benoît, frowning slightly, fiddled with his cigar.

A smile crossed Hannah's face. It had been six weeks now since Jean-Jacques had first walked into the Danton, but these Montmartre artists had yet to accept that their blonde *Anglaise* was theirs no longer. Although Jean-Jacques was always cordial, he made them both jealous and nervous; when quite sure that he wasn't around, Lucien would sometimes refer to him as 'the killer'.

'What has drawn you gentlemen from the Danton?' Jean-Jacques asked them now. 'Surely you still have wine to attend to?'

Octave, the least waspish and inebriated of the three, spoke up. 'Everyone is coming outside, Monsieur Allix. They say that the forest of Saint-Germain is burning – put to the torch by the Prussians.'

Jean-Jacques was starting for the place Saint-Pierre before Octave had finished his sentence. Hannah and the artists fell in behind. Her immediate impression as they reached the square was that Paris had somehow circled the Buttes Montmartre – that the central boulevards, normally seen glowing in the south, had been rearranged to the north-west. This light was different, though, a shimmering, acidic orange rather than the flat hue of gas; it was alive, expanding, slowly draining the darkness from the night sky.

The once-distant war had reached them. Hannah's pace slackened; her hands hung at her sides. She was not afraid. Jean-Jacques had prepared her for this. A magnificent resistance lay ahead. There would have to be sacrifices, of course, but the result would be a better Paris – the beginnings of a better world. It brought her relief, in fact, to see these fires. Over the past few days, as the city's anticipation and dread had mounted, a part of her had grown impatient for it all to begin.

A restless crowd filled the place Saint-Pierre. People squabbled and brawled, and shook their fists at the tinted horizon; scattered individuals raved and railed, predicting doom; mothers gathered up their children and hurried off in search of shelter. It felt like the moments before a riot. Jean-Jacques was a good distance away from Hannah now, pressing onto the merry-go-round in the square's centre – which was little more than a gaudy shell, its horses stowed away somewhere and its brass poles bound in sackcloth. Around him the appeals had already started.

'How bad is it, Monsieur Allix? Tell us what you've heard!'

'My saints, will the city really be next?'

A lantern was hoisted up onto the merry-go-round. Jean-Jacques climbed into its light and faced the place Saint-Pierre. Word went around; dozens turned, then hundreds more. The Alsatian was assured, unflappable, with a speech at the ready that needed only to be unfurled on the sharp evening air. He lifted his hands and the multitude fell quiet.

Jean-Jacques Allix had been speaking in bars and cafés since his return from the fighting in the east. That he was a veteran of some renown had all but guaranteed him an appreciative audience. Across the northern arrondissements, his persuasive, uncomplicated eloquence had soon resulted in him being adopted as a spokesman and leader – roles he seemed to relish. Paris was glutted with paper tigers; its halls resounded with bold claims and pledges that were wholly without substance. Jean-Jacques Allix, however, had *acted*. He had struck at the invader and bore the scars of conflict. He knew of what he spoke. He would not disappoint them.

'It is true,' he began. 'We have the evidence of our eyes, do we not? The Prussians are burning our ancient forests. Trees that have withstood the passage of many centuries – that are as much a part of our brave city as the buildings around us now – will tomorrow be but smouldering stumps. It is another shameful crime to add to the Kaiser's tally.'

'They mean to do the same to Paris!' someone shouted. 'Reduce her to ashes!'

'A fiery death!' wailed another. 'Oh Lord, a fiery death!'

'Do not be *afraid*, citizens,' Jean-Jacques instructed. 'Be *angry*. The reason for this burning, for this obscene devastation, is to deny us an escape route through the woods. They want to keep us here, every man, woman and child, to weather their assault. That is the nature of our enemy.'

There was a surge of profanity, every conceivable curse crashing and foaming between the bar-fronts.

Jean-Jacques raised his voice. 'But what they do not understand – what they do not understand and what we will demonstrate to them very clearly in the days to come – is that we have no wish to escape them. That we welcome their arrival and the great chance it gives us for revenge. Our bloodthirsty foe is blundering into a trap. Kaiser Wilhelm and his soldiers have travelled hundreds of miles to be destroyed at the gates of Paris. They will face the wrath of the workers – a million French souls – a mighty citizen army hardened by labour and united by a single righteous purpose!'

The crowd's fearfulness had departed. *'Vive la France!'* they cried, lifting their flags once again; and the *Marseillaise*, banned under the Empire, swelled up powerfully from the back of the square.

Hannah, stuck on the fringes, was quite light-headed with pride and love; she struggled to keep Jean-Jacques in sight as he dropped from the merry-go-round into the throng. He was making for a nearby hut, built to stow Nadar's spotting balloon – the contraption itself, a common spectacle during the last week, had been deflated and packed away at sunset. Before this crude, windowless cabin Hannah could see a group of Jean-Jacques's political associates. Dressed largely in black, these ultras ranged in appearance from thuggish to almost professorial. Another orator, meanwhile, had taken to the merry-go-round, a National Guard captain who set about urging every able-bodied man who had not already done so to enlist for service in the militia. In seconds, an entire division's worth of would-be recruits was pushing forward across the place Saint-Pierre, rendering it impassable.

At the balloon hut, Jean-Jacques was shaking hands and sharing embraces. His comrades were proposing that they all leave the square, no doubt to attend some red club or debating hall. He looked around, running his gaze over the crowds. Hannah waved and he saw her at once. His eyes could have held yearning, an apology, a promise; she was too far from him to tell. The next moment he was gone.

Hannah was not upset. Their partings were often like this. True ultras frowned upon romantic attachment; they were supposed to give themselves completely to the revolution. That Jean-Jacques chose to stay with her regardless,

51

despite his deepest convictions, brought her a shiver of delight whenever she thought of it.

The balmy late-summer afternoon had cooled to an autumnal night. Hannah hugged herself, wishing for the coat and cap she'd left behind in the Danton. She couldn't think of returning for them now, though – not while her mother might still be inside. The despairing fatalism of earlier had passed. She was not going to surrender to Elizabeth. She would find a way to continue. Uprooting again, finding a room over in Les Batignolles perhaps, might be the answer.

Lucien and Benoît were talking across Hannah with exaggerated nonchalance, as if unimpressed, knowing that they had been rendered yet more minuscule by Jean-Jacques's address. She wouldn't be any the worse, frankly, for leaving these fools behind. Both were members of the same radical naturalist school as Hannah – committed to an art founded entirely in their experience of the modern world. Benoît, however, was more notable for his May-queen prettiness and estranged millionaire father than any picture he'd produced; while the stooped, liquor-soaked Lucien, although possessing a touch more intelligence than his friend, was scarcely more capable with the brush. Octave had talent, at least, but the cost of stone had prevented him from ever properly expressing it. Of late, in fact, the taciturn sculptor had been reduced to making plaster angels to sell to tourists.

Recalling Lucien's claim to be able to speak English, which he'd definitely never mentioned before, Hannah wondered if he could be responsible for the letter Clem had shown her. Straightforward envy would be the motivation, complimented by a desire to punish her for neglecting them and becoming involved with Jean-Jacques. She quickly dismissed this theory. Lucien was not genuinely spiteful, for all his caustic posturing; and in any case, he had struggles enough of his own – high-minded ones against the artistic establishment, more basic ones with bodily need – to embark upon such a painstaking prank.

Consideration of the letter led Hannah back guiltily to Clem. She asked the artists if they knew what had become of him. They looked at each other.

'As we were stepping out of our booth,' said Benoît, 'Mademoiselle Laure was stepping in. Pretty smartly, I have to say.'

'Heart the size of a houseboat, that girl,' Lucien declared. 'Handsome lad like your brother – he couldn't be in better hands. I watched them, actually, for a short while. Neither has much knowledge of the other's language, but some kind of communication was being achieved. If you catch my meaning.'

Hannah swore. Laure Fleurot was a cocotte, a dancer and gentleman's companion, exiled to Montmartre from the central boulevards – not a whore, not exactly, although she was said to have accepted money for her favours in certain situations. Hannah knew to her cost that she wasn't to be trusted for an instant. What could such a woman possibly want with Clement?

Interest in the Pardy family dwindled, thankfully, the well-oiled artists moving onto discussion of their own siblings. Benoît had four sisters, it emerged, who insisted that he dine with them every week; whereas Lucien had a brother in Lille who he had not seen for more than a decade. Octave declined to contribute.

It proved a rather sobering topic. Lucien, seeking to reverse the tide, suggested another drink. Hannah glanced over at the mouth of the rue Saint-André, aware that she should extricate her brother from the Danton – and that she wasn't going to. The risk of encountering Elizabeth was too great. It wasn't as if Clement was actually in *danger*, after all; he was a grown man now, surely capable of fending off a hard-bitten Parisian tart. Like many ashamed by their selfishness, Hannah sought solace in swearing later action: I will write to him in London, she vowed, the letter I never wrote him when I first fled – a long letter that will explain everything. I will write to him as soon as this war is done with and our new lives have begun.

'Somewhere downhill,' she said, starting to walk. 'On the boulevards.'

The knocks shook the shed, rattling the paintbrushes in their jars and sending the Japanese screen toppling to the floorboards. Hannah woke; she was curled up on an old wicker chair, fully clothed, off in a shadowy corner. The morning was full-blown, lines of sunlight slicing between the slats of the warped window-shutter. Gingerly, she eased her stiff legs around and set about untangling her boots from the hem of her dress. Down in the city a bugle sounded, distant and mechanical, playing out its call and running through an immaculate repetition.

The second round of knocks, even louder than the first, dragged Hannah from the chair into the middle of the room. Staring at the door, she imagined the person who was surely on the other side: head cocked, hair and hat just so, listening intently for any movement within. The moment had arrived. Elizabeth Pardy had come back to the rue Garreau.

Returning home in the blue gloom of two o'clock, filled with cheap wine and belligerence, Hannah had actually been disappointed to find the shed empty. She'd decided to stay awake and wait. Elizabeth had journeyed all the way from St John's Wood; she would never admit defeat so easily. Hannah had lit her lamp and scoured the shed for any sign of her mother's earlier inspection. None could be found, not even a whiff of face powder, yet everything had seemed altered somehow – diminished by her scrutiny. The shed had looked smaller, dirtier, more wretched; the paintings inadequate, dull, lacking a critical element. Hannah had barely managed to prevent herself from taking up her canvas knife and scraping them clean.

Instead, she'd attempted to amend a scene of the midday crowds promenading on the Quai de la Conférence, to put in what was missing. Luckily, next to nothing had actually been done; but she'd been drunk enough to forget her smock, and as a result there was paint smeared on her sleeves and front. In the pocket of her dress, also, was a flat-headed brush, one of her best, its bristles encased in a hard clot of yellow pigment. She'd plainly sat down to assess what she was going to do and stumbled immediately into sleep. There wasn't any money to replace this brush. Cursing her stupidity, she started to pick at the dried paint with her thumbnail.

The third salvo was impatient, with emphatic pauses left between each knock. Hannah consigned the ruined brush to a jug of soft-soap. Her will to fight was utterly gone; her eyes were raw, and her head ached a little more with each movement she made. She wondered if she could hide, pretend to be elsewhere – or perhaps slip out of the window.

'It's me,' said Jean-Jacques. 'Open the door.'

Hannah snapped back the bolt and he rushed in on a gust of fresh, cold air; his kiss was hungry and tasted of strong coffee and aniseed. A hot, unthinking joy flooded through her, washing away her tiredness and her pain, fizzing in her toes and fingertips. She kissed him again, more passionately, trying to unbutton his jacket; but he moved around her and carried on into the room.

It was obvious that Jean-Jacques hadn't been to bed and didn't intend to now. Some of his usual self-possession was absent, lost in exhilaration. A lock of black hair had escaped his hat, curving across his brow – connecting, almost, with the line of the scar on the cheek below. He went towards the mattress and reached for the black coat he'd left hanging on the wall.

Hannah watched him search through its pockets – and realised that her mother and brother were sure to have seen this coat when Madame Lantier showed them the shed the night before. She recalled the speed and certainty with which Clem had identified Jean-Jacques in the Danton. They'd worked it out. They knew everything. She shut the door; so let them know, she thought. Let them form whatever conclusions they please. How can it possibly matter now?

Jean-Jacques had taken a small notebook from the coat and was attempting to make an entry inside. Writing posed a steep physical challenge for him. The hand within his right glove was a mottled, broken thing, missing both the index and middle fingers, torn to pieces several years ago and clumsily reassembled. He'd told Hannah that this terrible injury had been inflicted at the same time as the slash to his cheek, while he'd been fighting in America against the Southern Confederacy. Assisted by the wooden digits sewn into his glove, he'd managed to develop a scrawl that was just about legible. That morning, however, his distraction proved too much; he'd dropped his pencil before a single word was complete. Kneading the crippled hand, he asked for her assistance.

Hannah gave it gladly. Jean-Jacques dictated a list of names, dates and directives, rapidly covering three pages. It felt unexpectedly intimate. He was trusting her with the ultras' secrets, their plans, the lifeblood of their campaign; whereas she hadn't even been able to reveal the most basic facts of her life before Paris, leaving him to discover them by accident the previous evening. Hannah longed to explain how badly she'd needed to flee from London – to shake off

56

her tired role as the oppressed daughter and begin again – but she knew that this would have to wait. She closed the notebook and handed it back.

'What's happening?'

Jean-Jacques put it in his jacket. 'The army is marching from their camps in the centre of the city. They're going beyond the wall – to engage Prussian advance forces to the south.' His attempt at a businesslike bearing failed; he hugged her, another tight, three-second clasp, and then held her out at arm's length. A thin ribbon of light wound over his face, striping his irises with crimson. 'It is starting, Hannah, at long last. The fight is finally starting.'

Hannah swallowed; when she spoke, her voice sounded hoarse and heavy, as if it belonged to someone far older. 'What – what are we to do?'

Jean-Jacques let her go. 'We must gather everyone,' he said. '*Everyone*. We must march on the boulevards and show our numbers – our willingness to meet our enemies in battle. We must show that we are ready.'

He walked to the shed door and pulled it open. Dazed by what he proposed, by what he was already putting into action, Hannah didn't move; several seconds passed and she heard him ask, '*Are* you ready, Hannah?'

She grabbed a cloth from an easel and tried to wipe the paint from her fingers. 'I am,' she lied. 'I was about to leave myself, actually, for the place Saint-Pierre. I only took so long to open the door because I thought you might be my wretched mother, come to deliver the lecture I denied her last night.' She smiled at her own foolishness. 'But she'll be on a train by now, halfway to Calais – a hundred miles from here.'

Jean-Jacques turned in the doorway; behind him, a bank of sunlit cauliflower leaves dipped in the breeze. 'What do you mean?'

Hannah's headache twitched back to life. 'If we are engaging the Prussians,' she said carefully, 'then Elizabeth will have taken flight. The final trains will have gone.'

'Forgive me, Hannah,' Jean-Jacques replied, 'I thought you'd already know. The last railway lines were cut long before dawn. No one made it out this morning.' He paused. 'Your mother is caught.'

III

'What sort of a fellow is he, though?' Clem asked, lighting another cigarette. 'What exactly are we talking about here?'

Elizabeth brushed at her slate-grey gown. She had an impatient look to her that morning; in more ordinary circumstances Clem would have stayed out of her way for at least another eight hours. 'He is venerated as a hero,' she replied, 'and a champion of working Paris. I barely spoke to him, of course – Hannah has retained that possessive streak of hers – but his story is common knowledge in the northern arrondissements.'

'You asked after him in that place, did you – the Damson, or whatever it was called?'

His mother glanced at him testily across the cab. 'The *Danton*, Clement. And yes, I did. Jean-Jacques Allix appears to be a man of rare principle. He travelled to America to side with the Union in the late war, set on ridding that nation of the evil of slavery. It was on an American battle-field that he received the wound on his cheek. Half of his right hand is said to be missing as well.'

Clem blew out smoke. 'Hell's bells.'

'In the present conflict he has served as a free-roaming

irregular,' Elizabeth continued, 'a *franc-tireur*, the French call them. He fought in Alsace, his home territory, before falling back to Paris in August to assist with the defence. There's a good deal of chatter about his valiant deeds in the Vosges mountains: enemies slain, outposts destroyed and so forth.'

This confirmed what Clem himself had learned – the expressive faces and gestures that had met any mention of Monsieur Allix's name. He nodded; it actually reassured him a little to know that a man like Allix would be watching over Hannah during the horrors that were sure to befall Paris in the coming weeks. Leaving without her felt disgracefully negligent. Upstanding brothers did not do such things, but Clem honestly couldn't see what further action he might take. He'd heard of certain Englishmen – aristocrats for the most part – having their stray females returned forcibly to the family home, carted away in the manner of lunatics or escaped convicts. Clem's soul recoiled from the very notion; he was ashamed even to have thought of it.

Elizabeth was acting as if impressed by Monsieur Allix – as if she was intrigued and amused to be uncovering the exploits of her remarkable daughter. There was something darker in her too, however, that she could not fully conceal: the umbrage and injury of a rejected parent, made to see the extent to which their child has cast off their influence. Clem recalled the suitors Hannah had endured back in London – a procession of fey artistic types, selected by their mother, as different from this scarred Frenchman as could readily be imagined. He tapped his cigarette into one of the brass ashtrays fitted to the cab door.

'It isn't just a question of soldiering with this chap, though, is it? He's one of that crew we saw swaggering in the lanes. He's a red.'

For a couple of seconds Elizabeth said nothing, staring

straight ahead at the empty seat before her; then she drew in a breath and brushed again at her now spotless gown. 'Yes,' she said, 'it would seem so. But "red" is a designation that encompasses nearly all of those who dwell away from the grand boulevards. There is much discontent after the perversions of the Empire – much desire for change, for a fair society. Monsieur Allix will certainly be among those demanding to be heard once the war is over and a permanent mode of government needs to be put in place.'

Clem turned to the window. They were moving at speed along the rue Lafayette. All of the soldiers they'd seen there the afternoon before were gone; out at the wall, he assumed, or off parading somewhere. 'So you're quite . . . *happy* with Han's situation in Paris?'

'Lord above, Clement, is this really how I raised you? To be passing judgement like a table-thumping paterfamilias? This is not London, my boy. Such matters are viewed very differently here – more sensibly, in a manner that accords with the workings of the human heart.'

'That wasn't my meaning,' Clem said hastily, 'not at all. I was merely checking that you'd reached the same conclusion as me about that deuced letter – that it was nothing but a mean trick, a hoax. Han thinks that it was the work of her rivals, trying to embarrass her. She said that there were many possible suspects, and that—'

Elizabeth was no longer interested in the letter. 'You must tell me how you fared last night. Why, I hardly saw you after we arrived at Danton.' There was a pointed pause. 'You seemed to be getting on rather well with those people.'

'Against all expectation, I have to say. It—'

'I took the liberty of looking in your room before I left the Grand. The bed hadn't been slept in.'

Clem was growing uncomfortably warm, as if he sat before a roaring grate on a midsummer afternoon. 'Yes, well, my attempts to converse with Han's friends proved rather more—'

'Then,' Elizabeth went on mercilessly, 'you meet me in the lobby, barely able to contain your glee. And I recall that in fact I *did* catch sight of you somewhere in the back of the café-concert, just as I was leaving with Mr Inglis. You were in the company of a flash young thing in the most revealing dress, who—'

'We're there.' Clem ground out his cigarette and struggled to his feet. 'Come on, we've no time to lose.'

He hauled their bags down to the pavement, handed a coin to the driver and went on ahead. Elizabeth had seen through him at once, of course she had, and would now be making allusions to his Parisian adventure for months to come. It was hard to be annoyed by this; indeed, as Clem strode through the station doors a grin broke across his flushed face. A night with a Parisian cocotte was a seamy enough experience, he supposed, but he felt transformed by it – as if Mademoiselle Laure and her perfumed lair on the boulevard de Clichy had left a sizeable dent in his being.

And a dent it most certainly was. Clem's body was etched with fresh scratches; there was a bite-mark on his shoulder that he was pretty sure was bleeding beneath his shirt. His left elbow, too, was burning with the weight of Elizabeth's bag. At one point Laure had rolled them over with such force that they'd tumbled off the side of her bed, wrapped up together in her fine cotton sheets. They'd landed heavily, bashing joints and bruising muscles, but her lips didn't leave his for an instant. He'd never been kissed with such determined ferocity; it was almost like being attacked, but with an end so sweet it made him quite breathless to remember it.

The concourse was deathly quiet. Clem's grin disappeared.

The only people to be seen were a scattering of worried-looking civilians and some army officers gathered around a map. Overhead was clean air, free from all trace of smoke and steam. Every rivet along the iron girders could be picked out; the morning sun laid a chain of bright rectangles across the limestone floor. The ticket-gates were locked, the booths closed up; and past them, at the platforms, was a long row of dormant locomotives. Clem heard a distant creak and some shouting. Teams of labourers were derailing carriages, turning them sideways to block the station's mouth.

Elizabeth had stopped by the entrance.

'We're too late,' he said.

'I can see that.'

Perspiration prickled across Clem's skin, stinging in his various Laure-inflicted lesions. He set down their bags. In no time at all they had gone from a position of reasonable hope and security to one of total, unsalvageable disaster. He was not going home to his attic study to hide himself away among his designs and models; he was staying in Paris to be shelled and shot at by the Prussian army. It was a bizarre sensation, something like the bottom falling from a pail.

'So what the devil do we do now? There's no other way out. We're trapped, Elizabeth – we're bloody well *trapped*.'

Cool as a country church, Elizabeth Pardy swivelled on her heel and started back to the cab stand. 'The Embassy,' she said over her shoulder. 'They will be able to advise us.'

The British Embassy was located in a large mansion-house behind the Champs Elysées. There was no flag above the door; a number of windows had been smashed and a detachment of French soldiers stood at the gate.

'Your nocturnal antics aside,' Elizabeth told Clem, 'we British are not popular in Paris. I've been hearing about it

63

all night. The Queen is known to be on confidential terms with the Prussian royal family – Kaiser Wilhelm is her daughter's father-in-law, for God's sake – yet she has done nothing whatsoever to rein them in as they rampage through France and menace the capital.' She asked directions from a soldier before heading inside. 'I really can't blame them for hating us, can you?'

Clem, lugging their bags, had no reply.

The embassy was extremely busy. Several dozen anxious Britons, mostly shop-keepers from the look of them, had collected in the ambassadorial courtyard, talking loudly of the Prussians and their famous guns. Elizabeth led Clem through a set of double doors, up a staircase and into a crowded reception room. Everyone was yelling and fuming and throwing their arms about. They demanded action, threatening all manner of repercussions; they called for their ambassador as one might for an insubordinate servant; they offered bribes, money, jewels, even houses, in exchange for safe passage out of Paris. Elizabeth was attempting to discover if any form of queue was being observed when a man climbed onto a chair on the other side of the room and asked for quiet. Straw-thin with a very English pair of mutton chops, he looked both harried and rather bored.

'My name is Wodehouse,' he announced in a flat voice. 'I am in charge here in the absence of—'

'Where's that wretched ambassador?' someone shouted.

'Lord Lyons left for London yesterday.'

This provoked an explosion of discontent. 'Treason!' they cried. 'Cowardice!'

'And he advised you, ladies and gentlemen, he advised you in the strongest terms to do the same. You were given plenty of notice to leave. You have chosen to remain at your own risk.'

'Well then, sir,' a stout lady declared, 'I shall go! I am an

Englishwoman, and I shan't be shut up like a beast in a pen! I shall just walk out of the nearest blessed gate, and let's see our Fritz try to stop me!'

This met with a cheer. In moments a company of twenty or so had assembled, readying itself for a march through the Prussian lines.

'Madam, before you take such a step,' interjected Mr Wodehouse, 'I must advise you that the provisional government has implemented a strict system of checkpoints, to be observed by all regular soldiery and militia of the French army. If you are apprehended outside the enceinte – either by them or by the Prussians – you might or might not be shot, depending on the circumstances.'

The bold company dissolved; the clamour around Mr Wodehouse resumed. Clem and Elizabeth looked at each other. This was useless. Without an ambassador to helm negotiations or petition the French authorities, none of them was going anywhere – via the official channels at least.

'The Grand,' Clem said. 'We'll keep our rooms on credit. Perhaps a scheme will be established for this very purpose. It's worth a try. We can lie low and maybe in a few days they'll—'

'Credit that will be repaid how, Clement, exactly? A place like that will want some kind of guarantee.'

'Surely your Mr Inglis would vouch for us. He's well known there, isn't he? Couldn't we call on him and—'

His mother shook her head. 'Out of the question.'

'Why not? I mean, the fellow's an absolute arse, that's manifestly obvious, but we're running rather short on options, wouldn't you agree?'

Elizabeth made for the stairs, not speaking again until they had passed back through the embassy gate. The Champs Elysées lay across some litter-strewn gardens. It had the appearance of a drab, dusty fairground, its broad avenue jammed with stalls and carts, all draped in discoloured bunting. Many hundreds were milling about, mostly women and children from the workers' districts, playing games and swapping gossip. Elizabeth came to a halt on the pavement. Eyes fixed on the crowds, she explained her refusal.

'Last night, after we left Montmartre, my intercourse with Mr Inglis became a little difficult. A little heated. You may have gathered that there is a modicum of ill feeling between us; buried, perhaps, but very much present. He imagines that I once did him an injury, you see, decades ago now. It is complete claptrap – I was far more sinned against, Clement, than sinning – yet he insists on regarding me with a degree of bitterness, and welcomes any chance to disparage me.'

Clem was gaping at her, on the verge of revelation. Could *Inglis* be responsible for the letter – for their current peril? Had the *Sentinel*'s correspondent come across Hannah up in Montmartre, and then lured them there so that he might address this unfinished business with Elizabeth? More peculiar things had been done by men seeking to gain Mrs Pardy's attention.

'What – what did he say?'

Elizabeth sighed. 'Mont made it clear that he thought I meant to remain in Paris – that our talk of departure was entirely false. He knows that I still have my contacts among the Parisian press, even after all these years. He believes that I came here to claim this siege as my next subject, and that this might draw notice from his own work.' She pinched the wrist of her right glove, pulling it tight. 'Apparently he has plans to publish a diary.'

Clem's excitement ebbed; he put their cases on the pavement and wiped his brow with a handkerchief. Inglis didn't want Elizabeth in Paris – quite the opposite. He would hardly pen an anonymous letter urging her to visit.

'An open exchange of views ensued, I take it?'

66

His mother's expression grew positively icy. 'You might say that. The scapegrace told me that I intended to take what was rightfully his in order to *buff my faded star*, as he put it. He informed me that all right-thinking people considered me to be—'

From over the treetops came the thud of a heavy impact. The crowds went quiet. Several seconds passed, everything held in a strange suspension; then there was another, then three more, the sounds shaking through the bed of the city.

'That's cannon-fire,' said Clem quickly. 'That's where all the bloody soldiers had gone, back on the rue Lafayette. Dear God, Elizabeth, the battle has begun.'

The Champs Elysées was defiant. The people gathered there were not fragile bourgeois worried about their personal safety or the preservation of their property. Liberated from factories and workshops and stoked with patriotic fervour, they were eager for a confrontation with the enemy. Bonnets emblazoned with tricolour cockades were launched into the air; young boys scaled trees in their dozens, barking like baboons.

'*À bas les Prussiens!*' everyone cried. '*Vive la France!*'

Clem took hold of his mother's arm. 'We need to find somewhere to stay. This is the best course open to us. Forget your rivalries for the moment. We need to talk with Mr Inglis.'

Elizabeth was gazing skyward, anger and pride wrestling with her common sense. Common sense prevailed; she removed her arm from Clem's grasp and set off towards the boulevards.

Montague Inglis lived in a splendid apartment building barely a hundred yards from the boulevard des Capucines. He would not see them there, however; a note was sent down to the concierge's desk saying that he would be in the lobby of the Grand Hotel at ten, where he was due to meet with a friend.

'See how he tries to put me in my place,' Elizabeth said. 'Pathetic man.'

They passed an hour in a large café opposite the hotel. It was an elegant establishment, all polished brass, potted ferns and mosaic table-tops, and it was devoid of both waiters and customers. Their order was served by a woman in a brown velvet dress who Clem guessed was the proprietor's wife; she quivered at each distant rumble of artillery, spilling his coffee into the saucer as she poured.

Little was said. Elizabeth wrote in her notebook, filling several pages. Clem sat staring out at the boulevard, paralysed by imaginings of the café's wide windows shattering; the ornamental stonework being blown to powder; the great block of the Grand cracking and crumbling apart. His coffee went cold in its cup, a pastry lying untouched on a plate beside it.

Inglis was twenty minutes late for his meeting. They cornered him at the reception desk, at almost exactly the same spot where he'd greeted them the afternoon before.

'Still in Paris then, Mrs P,' he observed. 'Can't say I'm much surprised.'

The journalist's clothes were smarter today, his coal-black coat cut long in the Imperial style. Clem, in his faded travelling suit, felt humble indeed beside him – as was surely Inglis's intention. Elizabeth was not cowed in the least, though, stating without preamble that they had little money, nowhere to stay and required his assistance. Inglis's eyes held a hint of scorn, but he seemed to find it amusing to play the charitable gentleman. Clem looked from one to the other, wondering what had happened between them. Could it have been some form of writers' quarrel, back at the height of Elizabeth's renown – or a romantic entanglement, after she'd been widowed? Inglis hardly struck Clem as his mother's choice of paramour. Perhaps this had been the problem.

A manager was summoned with whom the *Sentinel* correspondent was particularly friendly. The two men reached an agreement and the Pardy luggage once more vanished behind the desk of the Grand.

Elizabeth's gratitude was restricted to a brief nod. 'You will lose nothing, Mont,' she said. 'I promise you that. I have funds enough in London to cover any bill that might be run up.'

This was patently untrue. Clem had been forced to pawn a pair of his late father's silver ink pots just to pay for their travel and a single night's accommodation. He began a silent inventory of their remaining possessions. By his reckoning, a stay in the Grand of anything over a fortnight would have them down to bedsteads and door handles.

The thump of faraway cannon sent a vibration through the hotel's glass doors. Without speaking, the manager gathered up half a dozen ledgers and a cash-box and retreated to a back room.

'Mrs P,' said Inglis, 'since you are to remain with us, I must absolutely insist that you come on this morning's jaunt. My friend and I are heading south, outside the wall. Word is that there's quite a skirmish being fought up on the Châtillon plateau. What d'you say?'

Clem nearly grinned; this was an obvious ploy, designed to draw Elizabeth out into the open. By accepting Inglis's invitation she would be effectively admitting a professional interest in the siege, confirming the suspicions he'd voiced the evening before. Clem thought of the notebook, of the many pages that had already been covered, and knew what her answer would be.

'What else do I have to occupy me, Mont, now that you have been so kind as to help us secure our rooms?' Elizabeth's tone was good-humoured and utterly unapologetic. 'I find that I have a keen desire to see something of these Prussians who are causing so much blessed inconvenience.'

Inglis laughed, a little too loudly; a contest had begun. 'How wonderful,' he said.

'Shouldn't we unpack first?' Clem asked Elizabeth. 'Take stock of the situation – get word to Han, maybe?'

His mother didn't think so. 'This may be a deciding moment, Clement. We must leave this minute. You can return to your new friend in Montmartre later on.'

Clem looked off into the hotel, a blush creeping up his neck. She'd seen through him yet again. He had indeed been aiming to slip away to the boulevard de Clichy at some point, just to let Mademoiselle Laure know that he was still in town. If Elizabeth was going on this expedition, though, he would stick with her instead. Spectating at a battle sounded perfectly insane to him; he vowed to keep them within dashing distance of the French fortifications.

A man was watching them from the far side of the lobby, almost hidden behind a column. He wore a modern grey suit with a short jacket and a round-topped hat. At his feet were several bags and cases – more than one person could reasonably hope to carry. He appeared to be waiting.

'Mr Inglis,' Clem asked, 'is that the fellow you're here to meet, by any chance? Your friend?'

Inglis turned. 'Why yes, so it is. Dear Lord, what's he doing over there, lurking in the shadows?'

The journalist took a step in the man's direction and launched into a stream of imperious French, his voice amplified by the lobby's marble-clad emptiness. Clem could understand little of it, but Inglis sounded more like a displeased employer than any kind of friend. The man emerged from behind his column and went about picking up his baggage. He did this quickly and methodically, as if following a system. Across his back went a canvas sack containing what appeared to be tent poles; under his arm was tucked a black leather doctor's bag; in each of his hands was a sturdy wooden box.

Clem suddenly realised what all this gear was. 'A photographer,' he said.

'Indeed.' Inglis moved closer to Elizabeth. 'This is the chap from Montmartre I mentioned to you yesterday, Mrs P, the associate of the great Nadar. I have it in mind to commission him to capture certain scenes from the siege – views, key personages and so forth.'

Elizabeth responded with a taut smile. Photographs meant illustration; prints could be sent back to London, engraved and then reproduced in this diary Inglis was planning to publish. The inclusion of pictures brought a strong commercial advantage. Elizabeth, if she did put together a book of her own, couldn't hope to do anything similar. She'd just been obliged to beg for Inglis's help in securing her accommodation; she certainly wasn't in a position to pay for original photographs. Inglis was well aware of this, of course. He was revelling in it.

The photographer drew near. Around thirty years old, he had the compact build of an athlete and bore his weighty equipment easily. His features were sharp and dark; his moustache long but neat, bleached a dusty brown by the sun. Inglis introduced him, in English, as Monsieur Émile Besson.

'This fine lady here, Besson, is Mrs Elizabeth Pardy, the famous adventurer and authoress. You may recall her *Notes and Reflections on the French Nation* – caused quite a stir it did, back in the late forties.' The journalist's beard twitched. 'And this is Clement, her son.'

Monsieur Besson's small blue eyes went from Elizabeth to Clement. It was plain that he'd never heard the Pardy name before in his life. *'Enchanté, Madame,'* he said. *'Monsieur.'*

Inglis ushered them towards the boulevard. Clem attempted to help Monsieur Besson with his camera – a solid Dallmeyer Sliding Box that looked like it had seen a lot of service – but was politely refused. Taking care to speak clearly, he revealed that he'd dabbled in photography himself and mentioned his regard for the portraits of Nadar. The Frenchman made a noncommittal reply. Photographers tended to come on a scale and Clem perceived that Inglis's man fell very much at the scientific end. This Monsieur Besson's interest was in chemical formulas and the specifics of lighting rather than aesthetical or theoretical matters. Clem could appreciate this; it was his inclination as well.

They ended up in opposite corners of the cab, one facing his mother and the other his prospective patron. Elizabeth and Inglis began a lively dialogue, discussing tactics and probable outcomes with an assurance that belied their obvious lack of knowledge. Any further communication with the photographer was impossible. Clem watched his mother for a minute as she talked, so ardent and so engaged with it all – and suspicion snapped open inside him like a spring lock. Had there been some truth to Inglis's accusations? Had Elizabeth been intending to stay from the beginning and deliberately allowed them to become shut in? At that moment it seemed horribly likely. This warranted a reaction – a barbed comment if nothing else. Clem shifted on the cab's thin cushions; he had no aptitude whatsoever for that sort of thing. He took out a cigarette and opened the window.

The sandbagged Louvre passed to the right; and then they were on a bridge, cutting across the nose of the Ile de la Cité. Clem smoked nervously, glancing at the barges and dredgers moored along the stone channel of the Seine. When he looked around again Besson was sketching in a pad of squared technical paper. The cab turned left, rocking on its suspension; Besson paused in his work and Clem glimpsed of some kind of valve, drawn with extraordinary exactness. What this might have to do with photography he hadn't the faintest idea.

They wound through the lanes of the Latin Quarter, skirted the deserted gardens of the Luxembourg Palace and rolled over a series of broad starburst intersections. The streets grew busier as they got closer to the cannon-fire; it was as if Paris was being tilted gently southwards, its inhabitants rattling down through the boulevards like ball bearings in a child's wooden maze. The cab slowed, taking its place in a long queue. By the time they were in sight of the enceinte they were hardly moving at all, caught in a jam to rival anything on Ludgate Hill. Farm carts loaded with forage were failing to get into the city; tumbrels loaded with cartridges were failing to get out. National Guard were everywhere. They stood about the streets like striking workers, drinking cups of wine in their spotless uniforms. Amid the general restlessness and impatience some were making strident declarations of their desire to die for their country, beating their chests as they demanded to be sent into battle.

'Look at these fellows,' sneered Inglis, 'bright and clean in all the bravery of just-served-out clothing.'

Leaning from his window, he hailed a group of militia and asked a question. They answered him with vehement energy; even Clem could tell that things were not going well for France.

Elizabeth held out her hand for the notebook. 'Clement, if you please.'

'What's happening?'

'It would seem that a French division attacked a column of Prussians, but then broke apart when their fire was returned,' his mother told him. 'They are now fighting simply to retain their original position.'

She began to write and was soon absorbed. The cannons picked up beyond the wall, eliciting an anxious murmur from the crowds outside and a whinny from the cab's horse, yet she barely reacted. What have you *done*, Clem wanted to shout at her; what have you let us in for, merely to boost your damned career? Last night had been a marvellous adventure, one to cherish, but this – the artillery, the bawling militia, the hordes of rampaging Prussians – this was really getting to be too much. The carriage had grown intolerably hot and cramped. He noticed that he was trembling; disposing of his cigarette, he placed his palms firmly on his kneecaps and splayed his fingers as wide as they would go. This brought no steadiness.

Inglis sat back from the window. 'Dear me,' he chortled, 'not a very promising start! This'll put a crack in the Parisians' rather exalted sense of themselves.' He nodded at his photographer. 'No offence, Monsieur Besson.'

Besson wasn't listening. 'Mr Inglis,' he said in accented English, putting away his sketch, 'I have a notion. I shall head up to the circular railway. I can get a good view from there – of Montrouge, of the plateau. A fine picture could be taken in this light.'

Spying Elizabeth's industry, Inglis had dug out a pencil of his own and was scribbling in the corner of an old theatre programme. 'Capital, capital,' he said. 'Just be sure that you're at that church on the rue du Château within the hour, d'you hear? I know what you're like, Besson, wandering off wherever your fancy takes you.'

Dislike flickered across the photographer's face as he slid a case from the luggage rack. He said nothing.

Clem saw a chance for escape. 'I'll come along to assist you, Monsieur Besson. I've put up a few photography tents in my time. I – I could use the air, to be quite honest.'

Elizabeth made no comment; she turned a page, touching the tip of her pencil against her tongue.

Besson eyed him with a marked lack of enthusiasm, but couldn't think of a reason to refuse. 'Very well,' he said.

The Paris circular railway ran along a steep-sided embankment a short distance from the city wall. Besson's pace didn't change as he went from the street to the slope; Clem, despite having only been given the doctor's bag to carry, soon fell far behind. When he reached the top Besson had already assembled his tent poles and was shaking free the canvas cover. Clem panted across the train tracks towards him.

'So there it is,' he gasped, setting the doctor's bag down next to the camera, 'a deuced *battle*.'

They were up above the rooftops, perched on the very edge of Paris. Directly in front of them were the fortifications, heavy ramparts of earth and stone crowded with National Guard. Just outside the city gates lay a village, Montrouge Clem assumed, its lanes blocked by stationary carts. Beyond, perhaps a mile away, was the chain of forts on which the defence of the capital depended. He could see three of them, brownish mounds heaped upon the smooth farmland like shovelfuls of clay. Past this everything grew indistinct, enveloped in a haze of sunlight and vapour; but off to the west a low plateau was boiling with dust, threads of black smoke trailing from the village atop it. Around the buildings was the shifting grey-blue stain of a large body of men, moving at speed as they obeyed some unknown command. Rifles crackled; artillery hammered out a lopsided beat. It was easier to take than Clem had anticipated. The alarm he'd felt in the carriage was allayed, more or less; he even felt an odd invigoration. He lit a cigarette and watched.

Beside him, Besson was hard at work. The Frenchman's suit rustled as he moved. It was made from some kind of fire-retardant material, with scorch-marks on the jacket cuffs and waistcoat – curious garb for a photographer.

'Tell me, Monsieur,' Clem asked, 'what particular composition do you have in mind? The action seems a touch too distant to me.'

Besson just waved vaguely at the landscape before taking a mallet and tent pegs from his canvas sack. There was something hurried about his actions; this was a man eager to dispense with a chore.

'How many images is Mr Inglis planning to include?'

The photographer crouched to knock in a peg. 'Who can say what that fool might want?'

Clem smiled. 'He's an old acquaintance of my mother's, you know.'

'They are opponents. It is plain. He plans to keep her close to make sure she does not get ahead of him.'

The smile faded. 'Yes, well, you may be onto something there . . .'

'Both are here to feast on our defeat, our misery.' Besson moved from one corner of the tent to another. He sounded more sad than angry. 'Vultures on the carcass of France.'

'I suppose that I am a vulture too then, Monsieur Besson?'

'I don't know what you are,' Besson said. He drove the final peg all the way into the ground with a single blow from his mallet. 'What are you?'

Clem raised his hands, indicating his harmlessness. 'Merely a brother, Monsieur, motivated by concern for his sister. She lives in Montmartre – that's why we came. Why *I* came, at least. And I thought I'd be long gone by now, believe me.' A shell sparked in the distance, the sound of the blast reaching them a second later. 'I certainly never imagined that I'd be seeing anything like this.'

The photographer walked around his tent: basic enough, but it would serve. He took in the view for a few moments, then he set up a tripod, attached his Dallmeyer and slotted in a focusing screen.

'She is not with you, though, this sister,' he said, ducking under the hood to operate the sliding-box mechanism. 'Could you not find her?'

'Oh, we found her all right, tucked in the seediest corner of the seediest dive – and having a bloody whale of a time.' Clem's laugh rang hollow. 'We thought that she might have need of us, Monsieur, but it swiftly transpired that she very much did *not*. There's a man involved, you understand. Some red from the provinces named Jean-Jacques Allix.'

The hood was whipped back. Besson looked at him with new interest. 'I know of him. I have heard him speak.' He made a connection. 'Your sister is his *Anglaise*. The painter.'

'That she is.' Clem drew on his cigarette. 'I suppose she must cut a pretty distinctive figure.'

'*Plein-air* painters are becoming common in Montmartre. It is a cheap place to live.' Besson worked a leather cap over the camera lens and picked up the doctor's bag. The faintest patch of colour had appeared on his cheek. 'But a woman, and a foreigner as well – this is not so common.'

'Have you actually met Hannah, Monsieur Besson? Are you two acquainted?'

'Yes – no.' The photographer started for the tent, avoiding Clem's eye as he passed. 'We have spoken on a couple of occasions. Only pleasantries. I see her, though, in the lanes and gardens. At her easel.'

Besson was talking quickly, as if attempting to deny something. Clem hid his amusement. It could safely be asserted that this photographer numbered among his sister's Parisian admirers; the poor cove couldn't even begin to disguise it. He turned to the tent. Besson was kneeling within, frowning slightly as he mixed his solutions. Keen to advance the conversation, sensing that he'd given himself away, he asked about Clem and Elizabeth's original plan.

'You meant to leave today, did you not, but have been trapped in with us.' The Frenchman slid a glass negative plate from its case. 'Why did you arrive in Paris so late, Mr Pardy? Surely you could have come for your sister a week ago. Why take such a risk?'

'We wouldn't have come at all had we not been summoned. Han is not overly fond of surprise visits.'

Clem paused; he tapped off a half-inch of ash and gave Besson the whole sad story, from the arrival of the letter in St John's Wood to their restitution in the Grand Hotel that morning. He'd never been one for holding things back; and besides, he'd gained a definite impression that this fellow might be able to help. The photographer was pretty astute, that much was clear, despite his curtness. His perspective, as a resident of Montmartre who knew a little of Hannah's life, could be exactly what was required.

If any original observations occurred to Monsieur Besson, however, he kept them to himself. While Clem rambled on he set about preparing his negative plate, coating it with treacle-like collodion, dipping it in silver nitrate and transporting it carefully to the camera.

'It is good that you are still here, Monsieur,' he said when Clem had finished, as he pushed in the plate. 'Your sister may have need of you yet.'

Clem remembered his minute-long exchange with Hannah the previous evening. 'She would disagree with you there, old man,' he replied with a rueful chuckle. 'She would most certainly disagree.'

Besson said no more. Taking off the lens cap, he wordlessly counted down the five seconds needed for an exposure; then he replaced the cap, slid out the plate and retreated again to his tent.

A cry rose from the gates, down in front of their position. Between the houses and the fortifications, Clem could see a dozen or so French infantrymen being led back into the city. They were young, as was every regular soldier in Paris it seemed, and they were plainly under arrest, their hands bound and their faces raw and bloody. Some had placards around their necks; they were deserters, those who'd fled under fire, being returned for punishment. The crowd jeered and spat, throwing whatever bits of rubbish they could find. Clem dropped his cigarette into the dirt and scraped over it with his boot. The battle had been brought disconcertingly close.

Besson emerged from the tent with the dripping negative in his hand. The image captured on the glass was visible against the pale canvas of the tent-flap. It was a failure, the contrast too strong: black rooftops and fortifications in the foreground with little else but whiteness beyond. Besson flexed his wrist and spun the plate towards the railway line, where it shattered against an iron track. He unbuttoned his jacket and sat down heavily on the grass.

'It is no use. I am no photographer.'

'Come now,' said Clem, trying to be consolatory, 'you know the process well enough. And you have this fine camera.'

'It is not mine. I borrowed it. I needed the money.' Besson winced. 'Foolish.'

'But you're an associate of the great Nadar, are you not? Surely that counts for something?'

'Not with photographs. I let the idiot Inglis think this so that he would employ me. My association with Nadar is in a very different sphere.' Besson pushed back his hat and with some pride said, 'I am an *aérostier*, Monsieur. A member of the *Société d'Aviation*.'

Clem was dumbstruck. Why the devil hadn't he realised this sooner? It was virtually bloody *signposted*. The brittle Monsieur Besson had a clear scientific leaning, yet was also practical in manner and rather weather-beaten: the exact type drawn to ballooning. That strange suit had obviously been made to withstand the mishaps commonly endured by the aeronautical gentleman. The sketch he'd been working on in the cab had been of a gas valve for a balloon.

And then there was his link with Nadar, who had once been quite a name in ballooning circles, almost as prominent as he was among photographers. An exhibition of his innovations at the Crystal Palace a few years ago had inspired in Clem a brief mania for all things air-bound; a bundle of designs for winged dirigibles was still stowed under his bed in St John's Wood. At the peak of his accomplishments, however, Nadar had been forcibly and very publicly removed from the heavens. There had been an accident on the North Sea coast, with serious injuries – Madame Nadar had only just escaped with her life. Many had chosen to regard it as divine punishment for hubris; Nadar had gone back to his photographs like a man chastened.

'I thought he'd given it up. You know, after the crash.'

'He has recovered his nerve,' Besson said. 'Nadar considers the balloon, the French mastery of free ballooning, to be a valuable weapon against our enemy. More so, certainly, than the photograph.' The *aérostier* turned towards the city. 'He is airborne now. Right there, above the Buttes Montmartre.'

Clem followed Besson's pointing finger. Suspended over Paris, over the golden domes and ancient spires and grand boulevards, was a single white sphere, so tiny that it hurt the eyes to pick it out. The basket beneath, the men inside, could not be seen. It looked like a moon that had been fished from the firmament and roped to the earth. Clem stared; he took off his hat. Merely thinking of what it might be like up there, floating alone in that boundless sky, left him dazzled with terror and elation.

'That one is fixed, of course – for observation only,' Besson told him, 'but we have our plans.'

'Such as what?' Clem demanded. His mind teemed with visions of bombs being tossed from baskets into the depths of the Prussian positions; of crack troops being delivered straight into the enemy's headquarters; of cavalry detachments strapped beneath balloons, their hooves dangling in the air. 'Do tell, Monsieur Besson!'

The Frenchman's mouth curved downwards, forming a sort of reluctant smile – the first indication that anything resembling a sense of humour might exist within him. 'We will fly out letters, dispatches, orders to the armies in the provinces. We will bring France together. The Prussians will not silence us, Mr Pardy. We will get word to the world of what they are doing.'

Clem nodded, a little disappointed by this answer. 'And will you pilot one of these craft yourself?'

'I will not. We are going to launch a great many balloons, more than the Prussians can count – or chase. Several shops are being set up to make them. There is to be one close to the place Saint-Pierre, in fact, in an abandoned dancing school. That is why I am living there. I shall oversee the work. Train the men who are to fly.'

A balloon workshop in a Montmartre dancing school! It was like one of Clem's own schemes brought to life. He held out a hand to help the *aérostier* back to his feet.

'Monsieur Besson,' he said, 'this I really have to see.'

IV

The Café Géricault was on the rue des Acacias, a hundred yards from the place Saint-Pierre. Time was short – the march would be leaving for the boulevards at any moment – but Hannah could not ignore this. It was Lucien who'd directed her there. She'd encountered him in a bustling passage, quite by chance; clothing in disarray, missing his hat and one of his boots, he'd been so battered by drink that he appeared close to expiration. Having rejected her proposal that he join the march in the bluntest terms, he'd informed her that her twin brother had popped up again, not two streets away.

'He's with somebody, over in the Géricault,' the painter had croaked. 'One of Nadar's men, I believe. Now please, Hannah dearest, could you possibly lend me five sous?'

The long room was so full that the bar itself was hidden from sight. Between the café's peeling walls the noise of the lanes was concentrated, amplified fourfold; the mostly male clientele were drinking wine, coffee and spirits, and smoking as if the city's tobacco reserves faced imminent confiscation. Clement wasn't difficult to locate. Off to the left, against one of the frosted front windows, he stood out from the locals like a dusty brown beagle in a pack of whippets. There it was – Hannah's mother and brother were still in Paris. They had been caught in the Prussian encirclement, as Jean-Jacques had said back in the shed. The sense of overpowering calamity she'd been expecting did not come. Given everything that was happening, in fact, their presence seemed almost inconsequential. Even Elizabeth Pardy would surely be dwarfed by the siege of Paris.

Clem was talking earnestly with a grey-suited man who had the look of a railway engineer or the humbler class of physician. This person was familiar – Hannah felt that she'd seen him about Montmartre – but he didn't really belong in the Géricault either. Clem and he were a pair of misfits together. Hannah started pushing towards them. They noticed her when she was about halfway over – and to her surprise the man in grey promptly took his leave. Their eyes met as he crossed to the door. He lifted his hat; his expression was hard to read, somehow both evasive and enquiring.

Clem arrived before her. 'Don't be cross, Han. Promise you won't. We missed the train, that's all. Well – to be honest, I'm not wholly sure that there was a train to miss. Stupid, I know, damned stupid. And now we're in for it, along with the rest of you.'

'What are you doing in Montmartre?' Hannah was calm – very slightly apprehensive, but nothing more. 'Shouldn't you be trying to find shelter in the centre of town?'

'All sorted out.' Clem laughed. 'Two good rooms at the Grand Hotel on an indefinite lease. Conjured, I might add, from thin bloody air.'

Hannah recalled Jean-Jacques's prediction in that alleyway across from the Danton: *She'll be well. Bourgeois like her always are.*

'I've just had the most extraordinary morning, as a matter

of fact,' Clem continued. 'I saw a battle, Han. I saw it unfold right there in front of me.' He peered after his departed companion. 'And I made the acquaintance of a truly fascinating fellow. He's an *aérostier*, would you believe, an honest-to-God balloonist. Émile Besson is his name. He lives here in Montmartre – says he's talked to you before, actually, while you've been out painting.'

This was feasible. Many on the Buttes assumed that an artist at an easel must be lonely and would insist upon supplying conversation. Hannah thought of the letter. She'd been abrupt with a couple of these people in the past, and may well have caused offence. Had she acquired a foe in Clem's Monsieur Besson without realising it – without knowing who he was?

'I remember those plans you used to draw,' she said, 'the bat-wings and screw propellers and so on. It was a fixation, Clem, even for you.'

'Yes, well, Elizabeth wasn't keen on that one. Not at all. Far too much cash involved.'

Hannah crossed her arms. 'Where is she?'

'Back at the Grand, writing away busily I expect. She sees a book in this little episode – one that will prise her from the doldrums at last.' Clem hesitated. 'D'you know, Han, I can't help but think that she might have anticipated our present predicament and not done . . . *overmuch* to prevent it.'

Hannah agreed. 'She'll have had this outcome in mind from the very beginning. From the moment she decided to make the trip.'

There was a roar in the street, and a discordant blast from a trumpet. Heads turned; the patrons of the Géricault raised their fists and shouted their support.

'What about you?' Clem asked over the noise. 'Where's that man of yours – the revolutionary?'

Hannah could tell from his voice that Jean-Jacques had been discussed in some detail. 'He's outside, gathering our friends – the people of Montmartre. We're going to the place de la Concorde. To the Strasbourg.'

Clem's face was blank. 'Another bar?'

'A statue,' corrected Hannah with a smile, 'representing the city. It's the capital of Alsace, a province occupied by the Prussians. Strasbourg has been under a heavy siege for the past four weeks yet is holding fast. She is an example – a noble example for Paris to follow.'

A party of guardsmen, overhearing the Alsatian city's sacred name, began to bellow it up at the ceiling, along with extravagant boasts about their fortitude and the pain that awaited their enemy. This served as a signal; customers began to flow from the Géricault, adding themselves to the current that coursed along the rue des Acacias.

'I shall come,' said Clem impulsively. 'I shall come with you, Han, and see what all this is about. You can introduce me to your Monsieur Allix.'

Hannah's smile grew uneasy. Seeing Clem like this, talking with him after such a long absence, had reminded her that she loved her brother, but what he was suggesting would cost her dearly. She'd strived to disguise her background, modulating her accent and every aspect of her behaviour, smoothing herself into this community as best she could. The sight of Clement Pardy parading at her side, so genial and curious and so very English, would undo these labours at once. She didn't have it in her to send him back to Elizabeth, however; heart like a lump of pig iron, she nodded towards the door.

Raoul Rigault was passing on the rue des Acacias – a stocky, full-bearded man of twenty-five in a discoloured black suit, loudly promising the crowds all manner of unlikely things. Rigault was a radical agitator from Montparnasse, a political ally of Jean-Jacques's, renowned both for his dedication to their cause and his casual mistreatment of women. He always paid Hannah a little too much attention – standing too close when they spoke, holding onto her hand for a few seconds too long, touching his tongue against his upper lip as she answered his questions. Spotting her now he sidled over, flanked by a mixed gang of black suits and militia uniforms, and tried to snake an arm around her waist. She squirmed away with a curse, tearing off his kepi and casting it on the cobbles.

Rigault bent down to retrieve it. 'Citizen Pardy,' he grinned, slapping the cap into shape and fitting it over his shaggy, unwashed head, 'are you ready for what needs to be done?'

Hannah had lost count of the number of times she'd been asked this. 'I am, Rigault. I'm as ready as I'll ever be.'

The agitator regarded her with mock admiration. 'If only the rest of Paris could partake of your bravery. Why, this very morning French soldiers fled from the enemy – Imperial Zoaves no less, flinging aside their rifles and running like chastened children. The curs should be bound to posts atop the enceinte, should they not, and made to weather the Prussian artillery.' He turned to Clem, who was trying in vain to follow their conversation. 'This must be your brother. I'd heard he was in the city. Quite the *rosbif*, isn't he – *rosbif* to the damned bone!' A bushy eyebrow arched. 'Makes one wonder how you yourself must have been, before Paris sank her teeth into you.'

As Hannah was considering her response, a young woman shoved her way through Rigault's gang and leaped onto Clem. They collided heavily with the window of the Géricault; she began to kiss him with an abandon that anywhere else would have been thought nakedly indecent, but here was met with claps and whistles. It was Laure

Fleurot, dressed in an approximation of National Guard uniform: a kepi, double-breasted tunic and pantaloons, all in dark blue. One of Clem's hands remained outstretched, the fingers slowly contracting, as if half hoping that someone would seize hold and drag him to safety.

Hannah's guilt returned. She'd left Clem at Laure's mercy and this was the result. She'd been quite wrong: of course her feckless brother had been unable to repel such a woman. The cocotte had worked her devices – bound Clem up in grubby silken cord. It felt deliberate, as if he'd been singled out. It felt suspicious.

There was a coldness between Hannah and Laure, growing slowly closer to open enmity. The origins of it were in that portrait, now more than two months old. Laure had come to the rue Garreau to sit, and it had gone well indeed. The cocotte had talked about her time in the ballet schools; how she'd been expelled after one of the masters had seduced her, forcing her to adapt both her style and her expectations to the dancing halls. There'd been no self-pity to this tale. Laure had seemed largely satisfied with her lot. Hannah had respected her resilience and enjoyed her coarse humour – only discovering after she'd gone that fifteen francs had been taken from her drawer, along with several pairs of stockings and an ivory comb. Laure had denied this theft vehemently when they'd met by accident in the Moulin de la Galette a few days later. There had been a brand new hat perched on her head, though, and paste diamonds glinting in her ears.

Hannah caught her breath: Laure Fleurot sent the letter that had summoned her family to Paris. It was obvious. The cocotte was certainly capable of such a step. Numerous morsels of Montmartre gossip attested to her malicious, unforgiving nature. She'd have hired someone to pen the letter itself, naturally; she no doubt pulled tricks like this all the time and would know the best people in the city for such work. The purpose would have been the mortal embarrassment of Hannah – the humbling of one who'd besmirched her name, albeit with complete justification. Upon Clem and Elizabeth's appearance, Laure had plainly decided to seduce the brother to cement the scheme. What better way to ensure that a gauche English brother would be hanging around Montmartre throughout these critical days, making Hannah look ridiculous? Like most of her kind, the cocotte was also an out-and-out mercenary; she'd be watching for a chance to wring whatever she could from the Pardy family. While investigating Hannah's past she'd have learned that Elizabeth had once been rich and famous, and had probably assumed that there'd be gold for the taking. In that, at least, she was in for a disappointment.

Hannah resolved to haul Laure off her brother and demand a confession. Before she could act, however, a company of drunken National Guard burst from the Géricault. They hailed Rigault with great enthusiasm, sweeping the agitator and his gang back into the main body of the march. Hannah was carried along with them; there were three bodies between her and Clem, then three dozen. She could see him still, just about – the kiss had finished, but he was utterly upended, protesting his innocence as the cocotte accused him of something, stabbing her forefinger against his chest.

Rigault was eyeing Laure approvingly. 'Conquered,' he declared, 'by a warrior princess. By an angel in uniform.'

Hannah turned away, pulling her canvas jacket tightly around her and buttoning it to the neck. 'Why *is* she in uniform? Are the National Guard taking women now?'

'She's a *vivandière*. They're attached to Guard companies to supply food, wine, bandages . . . and various other services. Their recruitment is a priority, I understand.

Someone of Mademoiselle Laure's indisputable abilities was not about to go to waste.'

'You know her well, then?'

Rigault chuckled. 'Citizen, Laure Fleurot is a celebrated lady in Montparnasse – a celebrated lady indeed. Circumstances may have compelled her to move on, but the mere mention of her name is still enough to make grown men weep with longing.' He looked around again. 'I suppose it's the turn of Montmartre now. Or rather your brother, the lucky dog.'

'She's using him,' Hannah said.

The agitator straightened his necktie. 'I was once used in that fashion,' he confided. 'It was *divine*.'

From the outset this march was different. The sky had clouded over, bleeding what light and colour was left from the lanes. Beneath the pounding of the marchers' drums was the dull boom of cannon-fire; no longer confined to the south, it now came from every direction, gathering in both pace and volume. As Hannah left the Buttes Montmartre, moving onto broader, straighter streets, she saw teams of military engineers felling trees to widen the thoroughfares for the passage of heavy guns. She heard the rasp of long saws, along with shouts and sudden cracks; a shudder ran through a mature beech and it toppled over, its globe of golden leaves collapsing as it crashed into the mud.

The people were unbowed, but in place of their usual jubilation and patriotic fervour was an angry unrest. There was just one topic of conversation among them: the crushing defeat dealt to the French forces at Châtillon. Details of the action were sketchy. Hannah heard it said that the French regiments had fired on each other in their panic; that they'd bolted at the first peal of the Prussian artillery, as Raoul Rigault had claimed. All sorts of retributions were being promised, against Prussian and cowardly Frenchman alike.

Hannah had marched more times than she could recall; it was one of the experiences barely known to her before Jean-Jacques that was now among the better parts of her life. She found an intense joy in surrendering herself to the multitude, blurring into an entity that was huge and ancient and unstoppable. That afternoon, however, she was distracted, beset with fears for Clement. Her twin had become doubly ensnared. He was caught in besieged Paris, a city in which he really didn't belong; and he was caught between the thighs of a deceitful cocotte who sought only to bend him to her wicked ends. She expected them to be at the front of the procession – Laure displaying her prize, inviting him to wave at his sister and show everyone what Hannah Pardy really was. They weren't there, though; no one she asked had seen them. It was as if they'd been lost, left back on the Buttes. This would surely run against Laure's plan. It defied understanding.

Jean-Jacques appeared through a screen of banners, about halfway down the rue des Martyrs. They'd missed their rendezvous in Montmartre; the crowds had simply been too dense, too determined in their progress down to the centre. He was in conference with some well-known radicals – ageing veterans of the 1848 uprising, peripatetic speakers from the provinces, the proprietors of red newspapers banned under Louis Napoleon – a ragtag group of extremists and eccentrics over whom he towered in every sense. Noticing Hannah, he made an excuse and came to walk alongside her. They met as comrades but stood very close, his arm brushing gently across her back. There was a new pin in his lapel, enamelled with the number 197 – a battalion number.

'I have accepted a commission,' he said. 'I am a major in the National Guard.'

Hannah looked up at his face – at the scar carved so deeply into his jaw that it had nicked the bone beneath. She found herself imagining what fresh injuries might await him outside the city wall, but buried these thoughts immediately: she would not play the hysterical lover, screaming and begging and tearing at her hair. Jean-Jacques was a soldier and the battle for Paris had begun. He had to fight.

The march cut across the rue Lafayette, merging messily with another coming down from the north-east. They'd reached the boulevard des Italiens – the grandest part of town. The workers' chants echoed off the massive buildings; their boots rumbled over acres of smooth asphalt. Off to their left was the premises of a picture dealer Hannah had petitioned for several months soon after her arrival in Paris, trying without success to get the man to take on a single small canvas. The once-sumptuous shop now had a barren aspect, its wide window iron-clad and blank. Across the door, in red letters a foot high, someone had daubed the old revolutionary slogan: *Liberté, Egalité, Fraternité*.

Jean-Jacques was up on a bench. 'The Imperial army may have failed today,' he proclaimed, 'but the *people* have not failed. We will save this luxury and bourgeois wealth from the Prussians. We will save it, my friends, and then we will see it apportioned *fairly*, for the benefit of all!' He pointed along the boulevard, in the direction of the place de la Concorde. 'To the Strasbourg! City of my forefathers – a steadfast people, inspiring us with their resistance! Showing us what can be done – that these Prussians can be held back! To the Strasbourg!'

Those around echoed his call: *To the Strasbourg!* Their black-clad leader returned to the street, unruffled by his impromptu address; Hannah felt his hand rest briefly on her hip.

'We should hurry,' he said.

Ahead of them now, on the western corner of the place de l'Opéra, was the Paris Grand. The hotel looked deserted, a majestic hulk adrift among the crowds. They pushed on past the long row of plate-glass doors, already opaque with grime; and then a voice scythed through the shouts and the singing, calling Hannah's name with commanding clarity. Elizabeth.

Hannah hadn't been worried. She'd assumed that her mother would still be somewhere in the outer regions of the city, seeking adventure and noteworthy sights – that the chances of them seeing her were simply too remote to bother about. This had obviously been a mistake. A neat blue-grey hat was moving around a Morris column covered with tattered theatre bills; Elizabeth had been lying in wait outside her hotel and must have seen Jean-Jacques make his pronouncement from the bench. Behind her was a lean, bearded man, smartly dressed, wearing a jet topper and an aloof air. They closed in fast, preventing escape. Elizabeth kissed Hannah's cheek and shook Jean-Jacques's hand – appearing to note the feel of his artificial fingers as she did so.

'Your scheme worked,' Hannah said, scarcely keeping her temper in check. 'You are here with us after all.'

Elizabeth gave her a cool smile before addressing Jean-Jacques. 'Monsieur Allix, I must ask – are the workers marching against the Prussians today, or the men who have set themselves up in the Hôtel de Ville?'

To Hannah's surprise, Jean-Jacques answered in serviceable English. 'We wish to beat our enemy, Madame. We wish for revenge. It can be done.'

His accent was strange, a mix of Alsatian and American; Hannah guessed that he must have learned something of the language while fighting for the Union. Elizabeth tried to revert to French – which she clearly spoke better than he did English – but he insisted with a politeness that was faintly confrontational.

Hannah could only watch helplessly. The conversation that she'd managed to foil in the Danton was coming to pass. The two great figures of her life were meeting on a Paris pavement. They made for a peculiar pair. The authoress and lady traveller, polished and poised despite her poverty, seemed as always to have some other goal in mind, some hidden purpose; whereas the political visionary was being courteous but distinctly guarded, his hands crossed before him like a stone knight in a crypt. Hannah honestly couldn't foresee how their exchange might unfold.

'Our government, however,' Jean-Jacques continued, 'this provisional cabinet who have taken over from the emperor – they are not so determined.'

Elizabeth had assumed an absorbed expression, ignoring the jostling of passing workers. 'Do you think they will attempt to make peace with the Prussians, Monsieur?'

'They are rich men. Rich men never wish to fight. They care only for gold – for their business.'

This was said briskly, as if Elizabeth was a part of the problem he described, but she was nodding along in agreement. 'What action will you take if the provisional government does move towards surrender?'

Jean-Jacques inclined his head, as if to say: *there would be consequences*. '"The goddess of revolt",' he recited, '"is the mother of all liberty."'

As Elizabeth tried to place this quote, dropping a sheaf of eminent socialistic names in the process, a vigorous new chant started up around them, telling Prussia to prepare coffins for her sons. The march gathered speed.

'We must get to the Strasbourg,' said Jean-Jacques. 'Excuse me, Madame Pardy.'

And so their discussion ended. Jean-Jacques was away,

catching Hannah's eye for an instant as he stepped from the kerb; he'd been civil but dismissive, as if Elizabeth Pardy was not in the least bit interesting or important. Hannah made to bid her mother farewell and follow him – but as she opened her mouth to speak Elizabeth's grey-gloved fingers locked around her arm.

'Lead on, girl,' she said. 'You must show me the best place to stand.'

Hannah stiffened, cursing inwardly; she should have anticipated this. Elizabeth had attended many popular demonstrations during her career, in France, Italy, Hungary and elsewhere – her published accounts of them, of her intrepid exploits at the heart of them, had been one of the pillars of her fame. If Jean-Jacques's manner had offended her she gave no sign of it; she had the firm satisfaction of somebody for whom everything was going to plan. Her top-hatted companion positioned himself to their rear. He was markedly less pleased to be joining the procession. Hannah knew his kind – he was one of Elizabeth's journalists. Men like him had once dandled her on their knees; quizzed her constantly on topics of general knowledge; and then, from her early adolescence, subjected her to a barrage of lechery, often before her mother's unconcerned gaze.

'Montague Inglis of the *Sentinel*,' Elizabeth informed her. 'He's proving a little more useful than he looks.'

Mr Inglis touched his hat-brim. 'Charmed, Miss Pardy,' he said. 'Truly.'

Hannah didn't react. She was stuck with her mother once again: pinioned to her side as they marched down the boulevard des Capucines. It was almost too ghastly to be real. The hopes she'd entertained in the Café Géricault now seemed quite absurd. Elizabeth Pardy would not be *dwarfed* by the siege of Paris. She'd strut about the beleaguered city as if it was a private pleasure park.

94

National Guard were everywhere, uniformed men saluting, hugging, making the usual pledges of brotherhood until death. Jean-Jacques was soon off among them. Left behind with Elizabeth and Mr Inglis, these bourgeois foreigners, Hannah weathered more slurs and hostile stares than she'd done for some months.

'Heavens, Hannah,' Elizabeth said, oblivious to this antipathy, 'I do believe that you have fallen in with an authentic socialist revolutionary!'

'Told you, Mrs P, didn't I,' chipped in Mr Inglis, 'there's a red plague in Paris, a regular contagion. Just look at this rabble.'

'They want change,' Hannah told him tersely. 'A purging of the old evils. Fairness after the Empire.'

Inglis snorted. 'A *purging* indeed!'

Elizabeth squeezed her arm. 'I appreciate that, my girl. I applaud it, most enthusiastically.' She glanced at the inflammatory phrases scrawled on the buildings; the shuttered windows and barred doors; the multitude of red flags. 'But this is beginning to look rather serious. It might proceed in all manner of grave directions.'

'Are you trying to scare me, Elizabeth? Was that to be your strategy to convince me to return to London?'

A tiny line bisected Elizabeth's brow. 'I made my journey because I believed you were in trouble. Any mother would have done the same.'

'You are not *any mother*. You are not—' Hannah took a breath. This wouldn't help. 'You must see that I'd never have gone with you. Paris is my home now.'

'I can see, certainly, that there is much to keep you here.' Elizabeth looked at Jean-Jacques. 'He's a fine one, I must say. Quite extraordinary. Mars in a plain black suit.' Her lip curled. 'Your virtue, I suppose, is but a fading recollection?'

Hannah flinched; she'd grown unused to such questions.

Elizabeth's attitude towards intimate matters had always been stark in its pragmatism – and far more direct than anyone who believed themselves respectable would accept. There had been a couple of uncomfortable incidents in Hannah's youth, errors made while conversing in general society, before she'd fully understood how irregular her upbringing had been. Her mother plainly remained beyond shock or embarrassment and was expecting a full disclosure. She decided that she would not provide it.

Elizabeth was studying her with shrewd fondness. 'I thought as much,' she said, as if an answer had been supplied. 'This is Paris, after all. Was Monsieur Allix actually the one to—' She stopped, seeming to rebuke herself. 'It is not my place to ask. I only hope you have obtained the correct preparations.'

'You've been to my house, Elizabeth. You've poked through my things. What do you think?'

'By Jupiter,' murmured Mr Inglis, 'what kind of a family *is* this?'

'*I* think,' Elizabeth said, 'that your bond with this man is still recent, and perhaps a little cautious. He doesn't actually live in the shed with you, does he? No, of course he doesn't – a noble specimen like that would hardly consent to dwell among Madame Lantier's courgettes.' She took Hannah's hand in hers; the palm of her old suede glove was rubbed smooth. 'You are grown at last. It is so marvellous to see. Returning to Paris has brought back such memories of my own residence here . . . dear Lord, more than twenty years ago now. We weren't in Montmartre, but somewhere very like it. A band of us occupied the same apartment. It was a heady time – the country was changing fast, as it is today, despotism giving way to freedom, and we gave everything we had to it.'

Hannah snatched back her hand. 'Are you honestly saying

that I remind you of *yourself?* I came here to *work*, Elizabeth, not be passed around by long-haired poets!'

Her mother's smile didn't waver. 'And what work you have done. You are thriving in Paris, my girl. The liberty of the place has nourished you.' She surveyed the march. 'There are real benefits to be derived, you know, from situations such as these. Sieges tend to break down the barriers of ordinary acquaintance. I don't suppose that you have considered this.'

And there it was, exactly as Hannah would have forecast: they'd been together for less than five minutes and Elizabeth was attempting to reclaim control. The procession had slowed to a halt before the columns of the Madeleine, too swollen to fit down the rue Royale. As they waited for this jam to clear Elizabeth imparted her advice. It took a predictable path. For one who hadn't set foot in France for almost twenty years she knew a great deal about the Paris art world, the naturalist style Hannah had adopted and the whereabouts of its most prominent practitioners.

'The grand prize, naturally, is Monsieur Manet. He is the head of your school, is he not? Creator of the *Olympia*? I gather that he does much to promote women artists – even ensuring that his female protégés are shown alongside him in the Salon.' Elizabeth's tone grew reproving. 'To be frank, Hannah, you should really be on friendly terms with him already.'

Hannah kicked at a fresh crack in the asphalt. She'd vowed that the only way she'd ever encounter Edouard Manet and his set would be if they sought her out after noticing her pictures at the Salon exhibition – for which her submissions had now been rejected two years in a row. There was no chance at all of her mother being able to understand this. She said nothing.

Elizabeth let it pass. 'I'm told that he used to be commonly found in the Café Guerbois in Les Batignolles.

It has closed, however, and its regular patrons taken flight, a fair number of Manet's friends among them. They say that he has enlisted in the National Guard, in the artillery – I'm sure we can discover where he is stationed. He'll no doubt be feeling isolated and starved of artistic conversation. Obtain a pretty gown, Hannah, and perhaps the services of a hairdresser. Take along one or two of those canvases I saw in that shed. It could transform your fortunes entirely.'

This speech was unpleasantly familiar. Hannah shrugged off her mother's arm. 'Do you mean that I should offer myself to him, like you offered me to that painter-poet of yours in Chelsea? Do you think Manet might fancy having Mrs Pardy pen a book about him as well?'

Elizabeth frowned, feigning forgetfulness. 'What on earth are you—'

Hannah pointed at the red banners cramming into the rue Royale. 'A war is being fought here – a *war* – and you are plotting my next strategic seduction. Monsieur Manet has set aside his brushes, Elizabeth. He has joined the militia. And I intend to do the same.'

She said this in anger, simply to oppose her mother, but knew immediately that she meant it. Here was the answer. She thought of Jean-Jacques's lapel pin; of Laure Fleurot in her *vivandière*'s uniform. It was so simple, so absolute and perfect, that she wanted to jump in the air.

'You aren't in earnest,' Elizabeth pronounced, the smallest hint of uncertainty in her eyes. 'You can't be. I don't for a second presume to tell you what to do, Hannah, but you are quite unquestionably English. This is an affair for the French. You might feel very close to this dashing demagogue of yours, but in the end we can only hope to be spectators.'

'Too bloody right,' said Mr Inglis, biting the tip off a cigar.

Hannah faced her mother. 'What, then, of your time in

Paris twenty years ago? What of giving the cause of liberty everything you had?'

'I meant marching and writing – making speeches and singing songs. Excuse me if I didn't take up the flag of a citizen army! Goodness, girl, how can you be so perverse? And what in heaven's name makes you think they'll have you?'

The crowd began to move again.

'They'll have me,' Hannah said, 'I'm sure of it. I'm going to enlist the next chance I get. Look at these people, Elizabeth. Listen to the *guns*, for pity's sake.' She walked forward. 'Paris no longer has any need for painters.'

The workers' march emerged onto the place de la Concorde. Dusk was approaching, grey and flat after the overcast afternoon. Someone beside Hannah sang the first words of the 'Marseillaise', and the next instant the whole parade was belting it out as loudly as possible. Elizabeth and Mr Inglis were lost behind a wall of bellowing militia. Hannah was caught in a rush of bodies; she couldn't see her mother or anyone else she knew. She was alone, suddenly vulnerable, hemmed in by National Guard. Fingers were soon pinching at her thighs and waist; drunken propositions were barked in her ear. A lamppost passed and she grabbed for it, hooking an arm around its iron stem and climbing up to safety.

The Strasbourg statue occupied a plinth on the Concorde's eastern side. It depicted a seated woman in a toga, rendered in pale stone; the statue's lap was heaped with flowers, a victory garland had been placed on its head and around its feet glittered hundreds of candles. A huge congregation had assembled before it, enclosing the gold-tipped obelisk in the centre of the square, reaching all the way back to the Seine. There were chants – *Vive la France! À bas les Prussiens!* – and the impassioned cries of a dozen competing speakers. Hannah was amazed. She'd visited the Strasbourg statue on many occasions, but never before had there been such numbers, such an armada of banners and flags. All Paris had turned out in defiance of the Prussian guns. Automatically, she began to arrange a composition – the bloated sea of hats and bare heads; the first few torches held aloft; the white statue, lit from beneath, luminous against the heavy sky.

This remarkable solidarity was short-lived. The working people from the north of the city, conditioned by lifetimes of antagonism and oppression, were soon harassing those around them. As evening came they roared out songs that exalted the poor and damned their masters; shoved and spat at the frock-coated bourgeois who'd gathered at the mouth of the Champs Elysées; hissed the arrival of ministers from the Hôtel de Ville. Hannah looked for Jean-Jacques, expecting him to be raised above the crowds, working as hard as he could to bring focus to the aggression and ill-will – to correct the pervasive feeling of anticlimax. He was nowhere to be seen.

Across the square, a detachment of mounted soldiers appeared on the Quai des Tuileries, heading for the Strasbourg. To the workers they represented the regular army, the men who'd routed in the face of the enemy that morning; the hoots and jeers reached an incredible level, obscuring even the Prussian artillery. Word spread that among these soldiers was General Louis Trochu, president of the provisional republic and governor of Paris, the man who was leading them against the Kaiser. Hannah craned her neck, leaning out from her lamppost; and there he was, a tiny uniformed shop dummy atop a skittish bay, trotting behind a torch-bearer with his right arm lifted in salute. Some sections of the Concorde applauded, but the workers, who'd welcomed Trochu's appointment a fortnight earlier, now judged him a coward and a fraud. As his party drew closer to the statue it was pelted with litter, rotten vegetables and balls of manure, obliging the general to curtail his observances and withdraw from the square.

The satisfaction of having vanquished Trochu did not last long. The men and women beneath the red banners had lost interest in paying tribute to the Strasbourg. Many were spoiling for further confrontation – and Raoul Rigault was on hand to offer it to them. From another lamppost back towards the rue Royale, he announced that a column of the morning's deserters was being brought up from 14th arrondissement for interrogation in the Louvre – and that it was their patriotic duty to ensure the worthless pigs never got there.

'Enough of Imperial justice,' the agitator cried, his full cheeks scarlet, 'that miserable sham, where cowards prospered and traitors were given generals' epaulettes! It is time, my fellow citizens, for *revolutionary justice!* It is time for the enemies of the people to get what they truly deserve!'

This met with a frenzied yell: *Death to the enemy!* The most rabid and reckless of the reds thronged to Rigault, who threw out a few dramatic gesticulations before leaping among them. They circled the Strasbourg statue, plainly intending to cut across the Jardin des Tuileries – the shortest route to the bridges that connected the Louvre with the Left Bank. These gardens, until recently the outdoor lounge of fashionable Paris, were being converted into a barracks-ground and artillery park. Army-issue lanterns glowed along the promenades; teams of soldiers were at work among the parterres and fountains, putting up dormitory sheds and hacking back the fragrant shrubs.

Rigault barrelled by Hannah's lamppost, continuing with his overheated oratory as he went. Among his followers, hanging to the rear, was a familiar black hat – Jean-Jacques. Why, after his earlier absence, had he joined this vengeful mob? It made no sense. Hannah called to him, but he didn't hear; she dropped from the lamppost and gave chase, shouldering her way through the baying crowds.

The reds ran forward through the main entrance of the Tuileries, flowing around an ornamental pond and starting down the bright central avenue. Ahead was the emperor's palace; site of a thousand luxurious debauches, it now stood empty and unlit, its broken windows gaping blackly, another husk of Louis Napoleon's Paris. The soldiers stationed in the gardens watched these intruders with a mixture of amusement and circumspection. They'd heard the songs in the Concorde; they'd witnessed the dismissal of Trochu and his escort. Hannah saw a number reach for weapons, mallets and tent pegs, and turn to a sergeant for instructions. They were ready to box ears.

'You are slaves!' Rigault called to them. 'Slaves of the state, paid killers! Cast off your shackles and be free! Reclaim your citizenship – your brotherhood!'

This of course provoked the opposite response; a loose company formed and advanced with menaces. The reds scattered, reversing or scrambling for cover. A woman screamed, twisting out of her jacket as a gunner gripped the sleeve. Everywhere people were ducking and cursing as they tried to escape. Hannah broke into a run, a blind dash that took her off into an area of the gardens still awaiting military renovation. It was dark here; she fell to a crouch by a stand of slight, well-pruned trees. For several minutes she stayed very still, her heart beating thick and raw in her throat, trying to remain as quiet as possible.

Searching soldiers pushed through foliage; shadows slid across the tree trunks at Hannah's side. She placed a hand on the gravel beneath her, sinking her fingers among the stones. This could be ended at any time. She could stand up and tell these men that she was English; that she'd entered the Jardin des Tuileries by mistake, and then fled from them in a fit of feminine distress. She could even reveal that her mother was a guest at the Grand Hotel. More than likely, they'd assume that she was what she'd been taken for by so many – an indulged daughter playing at artistic life in Paris – and escort her back to the gate.

No. It was too late. Jean-Jacques was nearby; he wouldn't have fled the soldiers, that much was certain. Hannah had made her choice. Among the noises of the gardens she heard Raoul Rigault, delivering his tirade with more vehemence than ever. He was behind her, towards the river. Several pieces of gravel had stuck to her palm; she brushed them off, gathered her breath and ran.

They were on the quay, at the corner of the vandalised palace: a couple of dozen militia and male civilians standing in a dense ring, lit from within by a lantern stolen from the camp. Rigault himself had stopped talking. He'd been challenged by one of his comrades – who was telling them all something they didn't want to hear, to judge by their shifting and scowling. Hannah came closer. It was Jean-Jacques.

'We *cannot do this*,' he was saying. 'We cannot kick men to death in the street, or string them up from lampposts. We cannot take our revenge in this way.'

Striking and severe, he projected an authority that made Rigault seem like a clownish parody. Hannah wanted to laugh with relief. Jean-Jacques was not lending himself to the agitator's violence. He was halting it.

'You all know me. You know what I've done. Nothing disgusts me more than a coward. But Frenchmen should not be killing Frenchmen, not when there are Prussian divisions massed at our doorstep. That is madness.'

Hannah left the gardens. She saw that they were

encircling three or four kneeling soldiers. These prisoners had been beaten; their faces, glimpsed between the reds' legs, were smeared with fresh blood.

'They fled when they should have fought,' a guardsman said.

'They are dogs,' stated another.

'I don't dispute that,' Jean-Jacques replied, 'but we must not become distracted by punishing the weak in our own ranks. This is not the right time. There are too many of them – too many tainted by the Empire and its corruptions.'

There was a murmur of agreement.

'We, though, we are not tainted. We are *working people*, my friends, pure of heart and pure of soul. The Imperial army has shown today how it got us to this miserable point – where we stand by the Seine, by the damned *Seine*, and can hear the guns of the enemy. It has shown very clearly that the salvation of France will fall to us. We need a sortie.'

'Yes,' said the reds. '*Yes*.'

'We need to fight. Every one of us. A mighty counter-attack. Paris in all her ferocity. *This* is where our energies should be directed.' Jean-Jacques gestured contemptuously at the soldiers. 'Not here. Not at these poor fools.'

The point was conceded; the mob deterred. Rigault, off to the side, had lit a cigarette and was affecting nonchalance. The battered prisoners were dragged to their feet. Hannah noticed that they weren't even from Zoave regiments; actual guilt was plainly irrelevant when administering Rigault's revolutionary justice. Before they could be released, however, a curt command sounded from the darkness of the gardens.

'Stay where you are. If you've harmed those men, by God you'll hang for it.'

Soldiers charged onto the quay – at least fifty of them in open order, dressed for battle with rifle-butts raised. They reached Hannah first, engulfing her. She tripped and landed badly, slapping hard against the stones. As she tried to move a knee was planted between her shoulder blades. Someone started to rummage in her skirts; she felt hairy knuckles rubbing at her thigh.

'See this, lads,' growled a voice above her, in a thick southern accent. 'See what I got myself here!'

Hannah managed to look up. There wasn't a single red among the infantry tunics. Discouraged from acting against the regular army, and outnumbered two to one, they'd clearly opted to flee. Her fright turned to terror. They hadn't seen her approaching from the gardens. They wouldn't know she'd been caught. She could barely move or breathe and she was *alone*, the sole captive, at the mercy of the regular army. These fighting men – this wiry, foul-smelling man crouched atop her now, running his callused palms up her legs – were said to be little more than beasts, brutalised by their experiences on the battlefields of the east and brimming with resentment towards the ungrateful city they were being forced to defend. Laid out on the quay, there was no limit to the punishment Hannah could imagine them inflicting upon her. She bucked and writhed, screaming through her gritted teeth.

'Quiet now,' ordered her captor. 'It's over.'

And then he was off her, wrenched off it seemed; she scrabbled onto her elbows and gulped in a desperate breath. The soldier was on his back, covering his face, moving with the slowness of someone who'd just been hit immensely hard. A black-gloved hand extended towards her.

'Hannah,' said Jean-Jacques, 'quickly.'

They ran. Another soldier attempted to block their path; Jean-Jacques felled him without interrupting his stride, his arm whipping around in a tight arc. Beside them was the endless flank of the Louvre, its upper windows illuminating

105

the quay. Hannah was steered to the right, onto the Port Saint-Nicholas, and down a shadowy flight of steps. A row of shuttered laundry boats were roped to the moorings; beyond, dim fragments of lamplight blinked across the surface of the Seine. They pressed themselves against a damp stretch of wall. This was a risk. If they'd been spotted their only option now would be to submit to capture or plunge into the water.

No one appeared. There were shouts from the Tuileries, soldiers calling to each other to report a lack of success; a faint 'Marseillaise' from those who'd remained at the Strasbourg; the stuttering thuds of the Prussian guns. After a few minutes they sat, their boots only two steps from the lapping river. Hannah was panting, trembling; Jean-Jacques drew her close. She couldn't help smiling as her head dipped towards him. This man had conversed with Elizabeth, in English, and ceded no advantage; he'd calmed a vicious gang; he'd knocked down soldiers with rapid ease. There were parts of him she was only just beginning to see.

'You – you came for me.'

'Of course. Always.'

The kiss was urgent, like one of reunion after many perilous months apart. Hannah felt dizzy, as if she was slipping – tilting from a ledge into empty space. She pulled back very slightly and opened her eyes.

'Where were you before? I thought I'd see you at the Strasbourg.'

Jean-Jacques hesitated, reluctant to answer. 'I was searching for your mother,' he admitted, 'over on the rue Royale. I didn't find her.'

'For my *mother*? For Elizabeth?' All happiness vanished. Their embrace went cold; Hannah struggled from it and edged a few inches along the step. 'Why would you do that? Isn't she a bourgeois, Jean-Jacques? Isn't that what you said?'

'Please, Hannah – listen. I was with Félix Pyat, an important man for our cause, recently returned from exile.' He was speaking carefully, as if still trying to comprehend it himself. 'I mentioned that I had met Mrs Pardy and he urged me to introduce him. He claimed that she was a great opponent of the Empire in the English press, and in her books – that she was calling for justice in France while your Queen was showering the tyrant Napoleon with gifts of friendship.'

Hannah knew all this. Although her primary motive for settling in Paris had been artistic, she'd been well aware of Elizabeth's public pledges – as a true friend of the French people – to stay away in protest for as long as Napoleon III was their ruler. Consequently, Mrs Pardy's works had been banned from sale or public loan by the Imperial censors, and her presence declared officially unwelcome; liable, even, to result in deportation. Paris under the Empire had not been somewhere she could come to look.

'That was merely a pose,' Hannah said, 'designed to foster ties in the literary circles of London. That is how Elizabeth operates, Jean-Jacques. Her postures are hollow. The end is always the same.'

Jean-Jacques nodded; he didn't quite believe her. 'Pyat said that she could help us. He was sure of it. He said that she still has an international audience, and is known at several of the main newspapers here. Apparently they'll print anything she chooses to write.'

Hannah looked out at the river. Something terrible had been set in motion. 'Monsieur Pyat exaggerates,' she said angrily. 'And besides, Elizabeth is not interested in helping anyone. She wants only to resurrect her career.'

'But she's here for you. That letter is the reason she travelled to Paris.'

'*She wrote it.* She wrote the letter. Or had it written.' This notion had been forming in Hannah's mind since the march; voicing it now made her certain. 'I had thought it was Laure Fleurot, but that doesn't fit. She'd be wanting to embarrass me as publicly as possible, not just turn my brother into her latest pet. No – it was Elizabeth.'

Jean-Jacques remained sceptical. 'How did she do this?'

'Her friends in Paris would have sent the letter itself. These newspaper contacts your Monsieur Pyat mentioned, perhaps; or Mr Inglis, the Englishman who was with her earlier. They found me in Montmartre. They chose the moment for her. It's all a *trick*, Jean-Jacques, a plan for a damned book.'

'You really think her so devious?'

'She knows too much.' Hannah was becoming exasperated. 'About you, about my painting. She wanted me to go to Edouard Manet, would you believe, and flash my petticoats. This is the sort of thing she proposes. This is why I had to leave London. Don't you understand?'

Jean-Jacques glanced over his shoulder, towards the quay; he'd talked about Elizabeth Pardy enough. 'You mustn't be upset by Pyat's interest, Hannah. It is nothing. Before very long we will have our sortie. The Prussians will be driven off. Your mother will return to London. France will be free again – *we* will be free. Everything will change.'

Hannah hugged her knees, suddenly spent, too tired to argue or think. 'Yes,' she said. 'It will.'

PART TWO

The Goddess of Revolt

I

'Six hours, Clement.'

Elizabeth was in front of him. He moved his hand, peering between his fingers. She'd opened the velvet curtains, her back to the window; she seemed almost to dissolve in the late afternoon sunlight.

'Six hours confined to a prison cell with only Montague Inglis for company. Can you imagine how aggravating he became?'

Clem swallowed. His tongue was an alien object, something dead and dry lying in his mouth. 'What happened?'

His mother paused, considering how to begin. 'We were outside the wall, on the west of the city, taking a morning drive through the Bois de Boulogne. It is in an awful, awful state – a plain of shattered stumps and shredded grass, utterly demolished. The generals intend for it to serve as a buffer against the Prussians, should they attack from that direction. Many of the ancient trees are down. Soldiers are billeted in the restaurants and camped upon the racecourse. Now, I have fond memories of the Bois, of summer evenings when I was younger; and that Imperialist rake Inglis plainly regards it as his personal property. I suppose we both grew quite animated, which won us the attention of a detachment of National Guard. They took a single look at our notebooks, at Mr Inglis's binoculars, and demanded the right to conduct a full search. Naturally we refused, and made it clear that we resented the impertinence.'

The scene was easily pictured, even in Clem's present condition. 'So they arrested you.'

'It was preposterous, Clement – spiteful. Motivated by hatred towards the English, nothing more. Would real spies be so stupid as to actually look foreign? Would they behave in a way that might attract notice? Of course they wouldn't.'

'I really don't know.'

Elizabeth became magnanimous. 'I cannot blame the Guard. They are under siege, for goodness' sake. Their regular army, what remains of it, has shown itself to be worse than useless. They are bound to be sensitive. Over-cautious.' The storm clouds returned; she began to talk very quickly, caught up in her narration, reliving her fury. 'What is harder for me to excuse is Montague Inglis keeping me in a cell with him for six hours when all the while he had papers in his coat from none other than the Prefect of Police. Six hours of him droning on about the damned emperor. Sniping at the labours of my pen. Making ham-fisted attempts to revisit the love affairs of the past – matters involving a number of departed souls that are best left alone.

'And when the dolt finally deigned to produce his papers we were released *at once*, with all sorts of bowing and scraping. The militia over at the Bois are certainly of a less radical complexion than those in Montmartre, I have to say. When I requested that he explain himself he told me that he wanted to see if they'd try to shoot us.' She let out a short, high laugh. 'He was awaiting our *execution*! There are stories going around about Prussian spies being put to death, you see, and the brilliant Mr Inglis thought that this was a good way to find out if there was any truth to them. The man really is the most insufferable idiot I have ever known.'

Clem's forehead touched the side of his armchair; he hadn't been aware that he'd even been leaning towards it. He made a noncommittal noise. Elizabeth stepped left, intentionally exposing him to the full blast of the sun. He covered his face with his hands, but the mere fall of light upon his skin caused him pain.

'Dear God, Clement, what happened to you yesterday? Where exactly did you go off to with that odd photographer?'

'Montmartre,' he replied, his voice a hoarse whisper. 'A – a balloon factory.'

'I see.' Elizabeth was doubtful. 'Yes, I've heard about this endeavour – the aerial post that's being set up by Nadar and the rest. It can't hope to be much more than a sideshow, I'm afraid.' She launched into a fresh discourse, distracted briefly from her son's wretchedness. 'France needs precise and careful coordination if she is to save herself. The armies trapped at Strasbourg and Metz need to break free and march west. The scattered forces around the Loire must be gathered and brought north. And of course this has to be tied in with whatever actions are mounted out of Paris. Balloons, though – it's like casting message-bottles into the sea.'

'That may be so,' was all Clem could manage.

His mother sat on his unmade bed, perching elegantly on the edge of the mattress. She was wearing the other dress she'd brought to Paris; coral silk with a bustle and cream bows, it would have done for a top-drawer supper party. Clem guessed that she'd been reserving it for a time like this. Elizabeth's aim was to recreate the Mrs Pardy of her heyday: a lady of matchless poise and intelligence, as

113

comfortable in the luxury of the Grand as in the salons of the bohemian elite, ready to astound the world with her observations.

Slumped opposite, Clem was in his nightshirt, socks, and a quilted dressing gown he'd found in his bathroom. In a corner was his only suit, screwed up in a heap. He couldn't see his boots anywhere. His head was wrapped in a damp Grand Hotel towel. It felt as if it was the only thing holding his throbbing skull together. His eyeballs seemed to have been taken out, boiled in vinegar and reinserted; his lungs ached; his fingertips and ears were tingling, the poisoned blood crawling through his veins. He hadn't had one this bad for a while.

His mother was considering him with that familiar combination of pity and dissatisfaction. 'And you were in this balloon factory all evening, were you?'

'No, I – we—'

Clem drew a breath. The previous night was a raw, mysterious thing. Thinking back to it was like removing a bandage from a wound you couldn't recall being inflicted. His towelled head rang with shouts and delighted moans, screams and snatches of speech; his memories were little more than a lurid mess of sights and sensations.

This much he knew. After Han's disappearance into the crowds, Mademoiselle Laure had led him from the rue des Acacias, through the lanes to a cellar bar. He'd gone gladly, all thoughts of marching forgotten – quite entranced by her uniform and the view it afforded of her lissom limbs. Tucked away in a corner, he'd watched as she mixed them absinthe with casual expertise. This ritual had fascinated him – the slotted silver spoon, the tiny blue flame melting the sugar cube, the pearly hue of the end result – and he'd reached eagerly for his glass.

'*La fée*,' she'd said, lifting hers up with mock solemnity. '*Vive la fée verte.*'

114

The taste was so disagreeable that Clem nearly spat it out: cloying like sweetened liquorice, floral somehow, but with the rabbit-punch aftertaste of deadly strong liquor. He forced himself to stick with it, assuming that they'd have a couple more and then retreat to her rooms on the boulevard de Clichy. Sure enough, they had a second, and a third, Laure drinking the stuff down like watered wine, smiling evilly as she urged him to do the same. Clem's mouth went numb and he could taste almost nothing. He was happy to be with her again, though, and excited at the prospect of what must lie ahead. They moved closer; she threw her leg over both of his and started to kiss him.

Then her friends began to arrive. Clem did his best not to be cross, chuckling along with the collection of tarts and thieves as if he understood what they were talking about. Slowly, however, he came to realise that they were in fact talking about *him*, and not in an entirely flattering way. Laure said a few lackadaisical words in his defence, elbowing him in the ribs with what he supposed must be affection. He swallowed a great gulp of absinthe to cover his discomfort.

At some point the venue changed. They were in an attic, with two huge windows, looking out over the rooftops of the newly encircled city. Most of it was dark and quiet as a graveyard; there were some dregs of light lingering in the main squares, but nothing else. Fear of the Prussian artillery, of the legendary range of their guns, had fastened the Parisians' shutters, blown out their candles and switched off their lamps. This view had a sobering effect, reminding them of what the coming days and weeks would hold. The revellers soon turned away from it.

More people crowded into the attic and the night altered, accelerated, began to grow strange. Among the newcomers was the thickset chap from outside the Café Géricault, the one who'd seemed to know Hannah. Clem had found him rather appealing – a true Parisian character, he'd thought. A lot of fuss was being made of him; he'd been involved in some sort of righteous fracas after the march into the centre, from which he'd apparently emerged the victor. Seeing Clem, the fellow swept aside his admirers, came over to the fireplace where he was standing and introduced himself, in English, as Raoul Rigault. There was a shade of the secret policeman about him, combined with a roué's dissipation and the menace of a seasoned thug. He'd put on spectacles since the afternoon, presumably to make himself appear more intellectual; instead, it just looked as if he'd stolen them from someone.

'Your sister and I are good friends, Mr Pardy,' he said, his voice heavy with innuendo. 'She is a fine woman.'

Christ, Clem thought, this cove's completely roasted. 'Is that so?'

Rigault narrowed his eyes. 'You are fortunate,' he declared. 'You will be here when we destroy.'

'The Prussians, you mean?'

The Frenchman made a sweeping gesture. 'Everything, Monsieur. France is rotten. You see it everywhere you look – and so all of it must be destroyed.' He said this with careless pride, as if it was both terribly impressive and nothing very significant. 'The workers must be given their freedom. And this is how it will be done.'

Clem grinned, reckoning that a French joke was being played on him. 'By heaven, Monsieur Rigault,' he said, 'I do believe that you are some kind of radical. A socialist, I dare say!'

Rigault stepped back and gave him a shallow bow. 'As is every man with a brain, with a heart, with a stomach that needs his share of food. Your sister's lover, Jean-Jacques

Allix – he is the greatest *socialist*, as you call it. Blood, Mr Pardy, is nothing to him – not the blood of his enemies, the enemies of his cause. He is born for the revolution.'

There was no joke here. 'Well, yes,' Clem murmured, looking around for Laure, 'I'm sure you're right.'

'But enough of this serious talk,' Rigault said. 'The revolutionary must be well rested, no? His passion is fuelled by the pleasures he tastes, so I always say.'

The orator took out an object, a bar of something wrapped in grease-proof paper, and slapped it down on the mantelpiece beside them. This was done with a flourish, attracting attention throughout the room. Several clapped their hands in anticipation and came over; Laure, nowhere to be seen a second earlier, floated to Rigault's elbow. He undid his little parcel, sliding a knife from his sleeve. Within the paper was a dark green block, set from a liquid from the look of it. He began carving off chunks and distributing them freely.

'Hashish,' he explained, presenting one to Clem. '*Les richesses du monde.*'

Clem held this slimy sliver between thumb and forefinger. All around him people were gobbling it up, Laure included. He considered the situation. Rigault was a weasel, certainly, with an alarming philosophy – but this was an extraordinary moment. Paris was facing its end. God only knew what ordeals lay ahead. If there was a chance for some fun he'd better bloody take it. He put the hashish in his mouth. The texture was soft, like pork fat, the flavour acrid and herbal. He got it down as quickly as he could.

For a while there was nothing; and then, quite suddenly, the night unbuttoned itself, its contents falling out in a gaudy jumble. A lot more absinthe was drunk, the party abandoning the preparation ritual to swig the jewel-green spirit straight from the bottle. Clem's hands pulled at doors;

117

his feet tripped down staircases. The night air splashed across his face. There were horses close by, their hooves clopping on cobblestones. He was lying in the street, Rigault pulling playfully on his whiskers; an instant later he was propped up on a pile of cushions, laughing hard, feeling as if he was drifting down a warm river. The light was low and orange-red. Laure was on him, her National Guard tunic opened to show a purple bodice beneath. She wriggled inside his jacket, biting his lower lip, purring like a cat. Two of the girls, Laure's friends, were stretched out on a divan, kissing and undressing each other, sharing an intimate caress to the appreciative hoots of the company. Laure had left Clem's side to join them; he remembered seeing her running her tongue along another girl's naked shoulder as she popped the laces of her corset.

'The sight of women making love,' he'd heard Rigault proclaim, 'is the one good argument I know of for the existence of God.'

The next afternoon, in the plush surroundings of the Grand Hotel, Clem could almost convince himself that it hadn't happened – that it had been the product of his intoxicated imagination. He stared at the carpet pattern between his socks. After this was only blackness. He'd come to with a cheek pressed against the Grand's cotton sheets. How he'd got back from wherever he'd been he hadn't the foggiest idea.

'I saw Han yesterday,' he said, dodging his mother's question.

Elizabeth turned to the window. 'So did I. The girl is as impossible as ever. Her petulance will pass, though. I am confident that she will prove an asset to our investigations.'

'I – I beg your pardon?'

'I have commenced a new work. I expect you have deduced this already. As we are detained here it would be foolish of me not to take the opportunity. There will be such interest in the plight of Paris – in England, in America, across the civilised world. It could be exactly what we need.'

Clem wiped a tepid drip from his brow. He waited for her to continue.

'But there will be competition. Montague Inglis. Labouchêre from the *Daily News*. Whitehurst from the *Chronicle*. A horde of gentlemen correspondents writing siege diaries in their clubs, planning to get them on the sales racks the same week the blockade lifts. In short, an edge is required. A quality to distinguish my volume from the others.' Elizabeth checked her hair – which was worn up that day, in a more Parisian fashion. 'Something is stirring among the ordinary working people of the city, those neglected and exploited by the Empire. You've seen it – their spirit, their desire to resist. Not only to defend their homes and families against the enemy, but rebuild their country as a better, fairer place.'

Clem heard Rigault's voice, vowing destruction and bloodshed. 'It might not be quite so noble as you make out.'

Elizabeth ignored him. 'I require your help, Clement. So much is happening. Your youth conveys advantages, not least of which is stamina – that dreadful parade yesterday, and the prison this morning, are experiences I have little desire to repeat. You have no real grasp of the language, it is true, but you are making friends regardless. Your sociability has always been your great gift; you are very like me in that respect. You could be there, in the lanes and the debating halls and the *assommoirs*. At the marches. It would give my account an immediacy – a *realism* that Mr Inglis and his kind can't hope to match.'

There was a silence; soldiers' boots tramped along the boulevard outside. Elizabeth had never asked for assistance before, from Clem, Hannah or anyone else. Those Mrs Pardy books – towering triumphs, moderate successes, unmentioned failures – had always been hers alone. Was this a genuine admission of *frailty*, of encroaching old age? Clem glanced up. Elizabeth was studying him, divining his thoughts, everything about her businesslike and utterly formidable.

'I will pay you, of course,' she added, 'and ensure that your contribution is known. A mention in the text, perhaps – or even a note on the title page.'

Clem shifted in his armchair. A joint clicked; a belch bubbled somewhere inside him, bringing the taste of liquorice to the back of his mouth. He held it in, fighting down a strong surge of nausea. 'Hell's bells, Elizabeth,' he replied eventually, 'I'm no deuced writer.'

His mother's expression said *I'm well aware of that*. 'You wouldn't actually need to put pen to paper in any considered way,' she said. 'Simply tell me everything about what you see, where you go and who you speak to. Hannah's sweetheart, our Monsieur Allix, would be a good place to begin. He speaks some English.' She smiled, her lips compressing into a narrow line. 'I have a sense that he doesn't much like me – thanks to Hannah, no doubt. But with you it might be a different story entirely.'

'I'm not sure if he and I—'

'Consider what I am proposing. Such an endeavour could lead to any number of other things. It will be a *proper accomplishment* for you, Clement, at long last, after all your tomfoolery. It will show the world that you are a person of substance.'

Clem nodded. He was a regular victim of his mother's honesty – those succinct, devastating assessments that came disguised as advice or support. Lacking the energy to make a response, or even to think through her offer, he shut his stinging eyes and leaned back into his armchair.

Elizabeth rose from the bed. She placed a hand upon her son's shoulder. 'You may let me know your decision in the morning.'

*   *   *

The main hall of the Elysées-Montmartre was rather run down – cracked plaster, signs of rodents, warping floorboards – but its mirrored walls were reflecting some truly astonishing activity. When Émile Besson had brought Clem up there two days before, the hall had been empty; you could almost still see the tutus lined along the practice bar. Now, though, it was every inch a balloon workshop. The heady smell of varnish hit you as soon as you opened the doors; the rattle of sewing machines made it impossible to converse in much less than a shout. Patterns had been laid out across the floor, to which vast white sheets of treated calico were being cut. The finished pieces went over to the sewing benches, where a hundred seamstresses were stitching the balloon envelopes together under the direction of a patrolling supervisor. Ahead, in the dancing school's modest courtyard, Clem could see a few dozen sailors, part of the contingent sent to Paris from the northern ports, fighting to inflate a completed balloon with a hand-driven metal fan; the thing rose and collapsed, wheezing like an expiring sea monster, while naval officers strolled around it on the lookout for holes.

Besson stood with his arms crossed, in the same grey suit, radiating quiet pride. Clem couldn't tell if the *aérostier* was glad to see him again, but he was certainly relishing the chance to show off the transformation of the dancing school. No word of explanation or apology had yet been given for his departure from the café on the day of Châtillon. He'd made his exit the very second that Hannah had appeared. If the fellow was infatuated with her he had a decidedly unusual way of expressing it.

The *aérostier* glanced towards the hall's entrance. 'I must watch for Monsieur Yon. He had to attend a meeting with Colonel Usquin of the Balloon Commission, but he will soon be back. We are not supposed to allow anyone inside. Especially not foreigners.'

Clem smiled. So this spiky customer is taking a risk having me here, he thought; he must value my company a little. 'A superior, Besson? Why, I thought this was to be your place.'

'Gabriel Yon is an experienced balloonist and an old friend of Nadar. It is an honour to work with him. I am learning much.'

'Of course you are. Of course.'

Clem put his hands in his pockets. The brown flannel suit was creased and dirty, with a new tear in its jacket lining, but nothing he couldn't live with. The after-effects of the absinthe and the hashish had almost lifted; all that remained was fatigue and an odd hollow feeling. He put this from his mind. It was time to begin.

He'd agreed to Elizabeth's plan over breakfast, in the echoing splendour of the Grand's dining room. He wasn't one to hold out through either pique or principle; that was more Hannah's style. What else, anyway, was he to do with himself? He was stuck in Paris – for how long was anyone's guess. The days had to be filled somehow. And besides, if Elizabeth was correct, if there was really a chance for her to resurrect her career with a bravura account of the siege of Paris, then why the devil shouldn't he partake of the spoils? Clem found that he was sick of poverty. Elizabeth might be right: this could be the start of something good. It could be that he had a knack for investigation – that he, like his mother, was an observer. After all those experiments, all those failures, had the solution been directly under his nose?

Elizabeth had been unsurprised. She'd produced some cash, a loan from Inglis she'd said, and had issued him with ten francs for his expenses; hardly a fortune, but it gave him a few more options. Clem had quickly decided that he wouldn't seek out Jean-Jacques Allix that morning, as she'd suggested. Hannah's battle-scarred beau was far too daunting for a first foray. A return to Besson's balloon factory was more manageable; he'd walked from the Grand full of purpose.

'So this is where it happens, eh?' he asked. 'This is where the balloons are made?'

'Well, the rope-work is done upstairs. The netting, the tackle – the baskets and ballast also. The sailors' skills are proving most useful.' Besson led Clem towards the courtyard. 'But this room is inadequate. We need more height to hang the calico properly. A second factory has been founded in the Gare d'Orléans – there they can hang it from the roof, from the iron girders. Far better to see imperfections in the material.'

They stopped in the courtyard's open doorway. Clem took out a cigarette, offering one to Besson. 'When will the first siege balloon actually be ready?'

'Our first launch is scheduled for the day after tomorrow, in the place Saint-Pierre,' the Frenchman replied, refusing it. 'The *Neptune* – the old spotter balloon Nadar has been running up for the past fortnight. They have made some repairs and say it is good enough for the flight. A few others have been located as well, around the city, and are being inspected.'

'How about these, though?' Clem nodded at the balloon outside, which billowed briefly only to catch a breeze and be flattened against the façade opposite. 'The ones you're making here?'

'Two weeks, perhaps. They must be thoroughly tested, you understand.'

'My dear chap,' Clem said with a grin, 'the war might well be over and done with in two weeks, if your newspapers are to be believed. They're full to bursting with reports of French heroism. Two hundred Prussians captured in the Bois de Vincennes. A fourteen-year-old boy from La

Villette killing an enemy sentry with his own rifle. Letters found on dead Uhlans revealing how the poor blighters just want to pack up and head home. They are all but beaten, surely?'

Clem hadn't read any of this himself, of course; he'd sat across from Elizabeth that morning as she'd translated from the heap of papers she'd had brought in. The Parisian press was in a funny fix indeed. Censored to the quick by Napoleon III, it now flourished like weeds in springtime, new papers sprouting up daily. However, a mere forty-eight hours into the siege, this profusion of organs was already running short of real news; and as a result no piece of baseless conjecture, no ludicrous boast or lie, was too outrageous for them to print.

Besson did not rise to it. 'It is talk only,' he said. 'You know this. The Prussians have whipped us back – contained us. They are waiting to see what we will do.'

Clem adopted a thoughtful look. 'I hear that Trochu has sent Vice-President Favre through the lines to Bismarck, to discuss terms for peace.'

The *aérostier* dismissed this. 'A formality. It will come to nothing. The Prussians will demand too much, and Jules Favre is not a weak man.' He smiled grimly. 'Besides, the government is terrified of how the ordinary people might react if they surrendered. And any terms acceptable to Bismarck would definitely be seen as surrender.'

'They've been too stoked up by the reds, haven't they?' Clem flicked ash through the doorway. 'Tell me, what do you make of those types – the radicals and ultras?'

There was a pause. Clem thought he'd been being pretty slick so far, extracting information with deft delicacy; now, though, Besson was staring at him as if he was an absolute imbecile.

'They will finish us, Mr Pardy. Surely you see this. *Les Rouges* will end all hope of a fair and enduring republic, with their Marx and their Proudhon and whoever else. Freedom is what they want, so they say, but it is not a freedom that I recognise.' He looked back at the pattern cutters, guiding their shears through creamy folds of fabric. 'The old ones are veterans of the revolutions of '48 and '51. Many were exiled or put in prison, and they have their scores to settle. As for the younger ones – who knows? Every society has its madmen. And they have influence in the poor districts. Here in Montmartre, for example. The workers suffered under Napoleon. They have nothing to lose.'

'I met one of these *Rouges* the other night, you know, after we parted ways in that café. Raoul Rigault, his name was.'

Besson was growing angry; his slight, hard-won amiability disappeared. Clem remembered the spoiled photographic plate – the shattering of the glass against the track. 'Rigault is among the worst. They say he wants to set up a guillotine in every square – a *guillotine*, Monsieur. The Jacobin fool would return Paris to the darkest days of the Terror.' The *aérostier* snorted. 'That is a strange kind of freedom.'

'What about our Monsieur Allix, then?' Clem asked. 'How does he compare? Rigault couldn't praise him highly enough.'

This was a further mistake. Besson lowered his eyes; he pulled at his sandy moustache. 'Him I do not know about,' he muttered. 'You should ask your sister.'

Clem threw his half-smoked cigarette into the courtyard. He thought of their first conversation, as Besson had prepared his camera on that railway embankment. The Frenchman hadn't given an opinion on Allix then either, merely performing a subtle sidestep. The reason for this was suddenly clear.

'You'd say he was a bad lot though, wouldn't you? A source of danger? Worth removing Han from, maybe, should the opportunity arise?'

Besson did not look up. 'You are talking about that letter,' he said. 'You think that I wrote it.'

An incisive fellow indeed. 'You speak English pretty damn well, Monsieur Besson. You plainly care for my sister and know a fair bit about her sweetheart and his friends. What would you think?'

The picture was compellingly complete. This intelligent, awkward man had watched from the wings as Jean-Jacques and Hannah paraded around Montmartre. He'd seen the situation get more fraught, and the rhetoric more heated – with Hannah caught right at the heart of it. Delving into her past, he'd found out about Elizabeth and penned the letter. Perhaps he'd even discovered the connection with Montague Inglis, contriving a professional link in order to monitor Mrs Pardy's movements. Perhaps their acquaintance had been no accident.

'If I cared for her as you claim,' Besson asked, 'why would I want her gone? Why would I want her back in London?'

'To know she was safe,' Clem replied, 'well away from Allix and Rigault and their revolution. It was selfless, I'll give you that. You're a decent man, Monsieur Besson.'

'If *you* were a decent man,' the *aérostier* snapped, 'a decent brother, you would take action. You would separate them. You would do it today.'

Clem chuckled uneasily. 'Lord Almighty, what the deuce d'you think is going to happen here? What do you—'

Besson shook his head; he walked off, back into the busy hall. 'I have duties to attend to,' he said. 'You must leave, Mr Pardy. At once.'

*　　*　　*

Clem stepped into the street outside the dancing school, imagining Hannah on the barricades, waving an enormous tricolour; sitting on a revolutionary committee, at Allix's right hand, sending scores to their deaths. Comrades, inevitably, would turn on each other. He saw Han climbing the scaffold; saw the great angled blade rising in its frame, catching the light; heard the flat *thunk* as its lever was released.

No, Clem told himself sternly – none of this would occur. He'd become infected by Besson's melodrama. Han was a sensible girl, for the most part; she'd run a mile from such lunacy. Still, it might be wise to pay her a brotherly visit, just to get the lie of the land. He stood for a few seconds, trying to remember the way to the rue Garreau, then fastened his jacket and started uphill. It was a glorious day of blue skies and sharp shadows. Cannon-fire sounded in all directions, but it was no longer causing much alarm among the few who milled on the pavements around him. Give people twenty-four hours, he supposed, and they'll get used to more or less anything.

As he approached a corner someone rushed up behind him, grabbed his buttock and squeezed hard. He spun around; Laure was giggling, chewing, lunging in for another pinch. She was in her *vivandière*'s uniform, but bare-headed, her orange hair loud in the sunshine. In her left hand was a roll, missing a couple of bites; a thin cigarillo smouldered between her fingers. Her eyes shone with delight at having caught him unawares. She certainly isn't angry with me, Clem thought as he hopped to the side; I can't have disgraced myself too badly.

Laure said something in her deep, tarnished-sounding voice. Clem understood none of it. He stopped weaving about, his mind brimming with questions. What exactly had happened that night? What did he do? What did *she*

127

do? How in God's name did he get back to his room in the Grand? He hadn't a hope of putting these in comprehensible French, though, or of following her replies.

Seeing that he'd lost interest in their game, Laure halted her attacks and offered him her roll. He declined it so she took another bite herself. Around her mouthful she said something else, nodding back towards the school; she'd spotted him going in, it seemed, and had waited in the street for him to emerge. From her gesticulations Clem gathered that she'd once been a pupil of the Elysées-Montmartre, until an unknown circumstance had obliged her leave. To prove this she threw the remains of her roll into the gutter and performed a pirouette in the middle of the pavement, the cigarillo still poking from her fingers; and although hampered by her ankle-boots, she pulled the move off with remarkable grace.

Clem smiled and clapped, but his mystification was growing. What was going on here? What could she possibly want from him? They were long past the point where she might ask for money; besides, he'd never felt that what was happening between them was any sort of transaction. He'd assumed that they had simply ended – that it had gone as far as it could. He wasn't at all sure of his experiences in the later stages of that night, but he suspected that he'd drifted a good few feet out of his depth. Watching Laure now, in fact, triumphant after her pirouette, caused a memory to resurface: her lying in the arms of her friends, her blouse open, laughing like a docker as one of them licked her nipple. Could a girl really share the embraces of other women and then return to her lover afterwards without a care? Was it just how things worked in Montmartre – the habit of a certain class of *Parisienne*? Clem considered himself a thoroughly liberal-minded chap, but this made him pause for thought.

Laure had no time for his confused deliberations. She sucked a last drag from her cigarillo before reaching out to take his hand. *'Viens.'*

Her skin was cool and slightly damp; its touch negated every question, every other concern. The events of that night were plainly nothing to her, so they were nothing to him. It was as simple as that. Clem looked at her again, the mischievous, voracious smile, the perfect line of her nose, the fine china complexion, and knew that he'd do pretty much anything she wanted him to. She tugged him downhill, towards the boulevard de Clichy. A few more steps and she'd moved to his side, her breast pressed against his upper arm. Before very long her hand settled on his midriff, soon finding its way through both his waistcoat and shirt; and then Laure changed her mind, altering their course, steering them to the nearest alley-mouth.

'Mademoiselle Laure,' said Clem as they stumbled inside, her lips seeking his, 'you are completely bloody *amazing.*'

The *Neptune* could be seen from several blocks away, huge and dirty white between the buildings, bulging like a sack of flour. Laure squealed, removing the cigarette from her mouth to plant a smacking kiss on Clem's cheek. It was only a few minutes after seven, the sun just breaking over the rooftops, but many hundreds had already arrived in the place Saint-Pierre. A good number had come up from other districts, filling Montmartre to capacity; balloons were common enough in Paris, but this first expedition of an aerial post, in a city still reeling after its encirclement, was being exalted as a grand act of defiance.

Clem and Laure hadn't slept. They'd stayed in bed all of the previous day, emerging at last in the early evening. The cafés had been starting to close, operating on an austere siege timetable. Laure had convinced the owner of a small place on the rue Pigalle to serve them an entrecôte, which they ate as he mopped the floor around them. The main streets were soon dark and dull so they'd returned to the *assommoirs*, embarking on a second tour of backrooms, attics and basements. There had been demonstrations against the government that afternoon, they'd learned, down in the square before the Hôtel de Ville. National Guard battalions from the northern arrondissements – the red battalions – had come out to demand that none other than Victor Hugo be given a seat in Trochu's cabinet, to serve as their voice. Clem had felt a vague guilt at having missed this – that instead of fulfilling his role as Elizabeth's eyes and ears he'd been engaged in vigorous and ever more inventive fornications – but he couldn't honestly say that he regretted it. There'd be another protest soon enough.

They approached the southern side of the place Saint-Pierre. The *Neptune* seemed almost to block out the sky. Recent repairs marked the side of the old balloon – sections that had been patched up like the elbows of an old coat. Clem took Laure's cigarette and puffed on it happily. He'd avoided absinthe, hashish, and any other strange pipes or powders – he was just drunk, and proudly so. Laure was still in uniform, trading flirtatious salutes with passing guardsmen, although he had yet to gain any idea of what her actual duties were or when she might be required to perform them.

In Clem's hands was a bottle of champagne, bought in the last bar they'd visited. It was for Émile Besson; Clem envisaged them toasting the balloon post as the *Neptune* rose into the air. He was determined to make amends for that unfortunate conversation in the balloon factory – and to show that if the *aérostier* had sent the letter, he admired him for it more than anything else. The bottle had been out of ice for over an hour and was starting to lose its chill.

130

For the fourth or fifth time Laure indicated that he should just open it, turning away with an exaggerated sigh when he refused.

A detachment of National Guard – not from the Montmartre battalion – had cordoned off an area beside the merry-go-round. Arrayed around the *Neptune* were several ranks of dignitaries, many in uniform, lending the launch a ceremonial atmosphere. To his excitement, Clem spied the great Nadar among them, a corpulent, pale-suited impresario with an impressive waxed moustache, beaming at everyone as if savouring a moment of vindication. And there was Besson, one of a small team carrying out the final operations – winding back the coal-gas pipe that had been used to inflate the envelope, checking the valve at the base of the balloon, loading on the ballast. He was doing all this with the same precise, measured manner he'd gone about his photography.

Clem pointed him out to Laure. '*Mon ami*,' he said.

She nodded absently, kissing him again before joining in the inevitable 'Marseillaise' that was building around them. A tent had been pitched nearby, behind the dignitaries; the crowd cheered as several large canvas mail-sacks were carried from it and secured in the *Neptune*'s basket. Besson was now standing to one side, his work done. Clem tried to lead Laure towards him, within earshot at least, but with no success. There was much he wanted to ask. Could the Prussians try to shoot the *Neptune* down? Could they send their own aerial contraptions after the balloons of Paris – mount an airborne pursuit? Would the Parisian *aérostiers* be able to outmanoeuvre them?

The *Neptune*'s pilot appeared from the tent, causing a surge towards the cordon. Clem felt a sudden impact, liquid gushing across his thighs and stomach – the champagne cork had popped out. He swore, searching about for it, thinking that

131

he could maybe work the damned thing back into the bottle neck. When he gave up a minute later the pilot was in the basket. The fellow was young, no more than twenty-five, and looked undaunted by the voyage ahead of him; his jacket was made of heavy brown leather and the letters 'AER' had been stitched in gold on his flying helmet. Raising a gloved fist, he shouted *'Vive la République!'*

As the crowd roared it back the tethers were released; and very slowly the balloon left the ground, like an ocean-going steamer easing from its berth. The pilot let down two of his ballast sacks, then two more. This accelerated his ascent dramatically; in two seconds flat the balloon had cleared the rooftops of Montmartre and was breaking out into open sky, the morning sun blazing against the envelope. Clem watched it get smaller and smaller, gaping with tipsy exhilaration. Standing on the stones of the square, it seemed to him that gravity had been reversed – that the balloon was actually falling upwards, away from the earth, a bright white ball plummeting into the heavens with some brave fool roped to its underside.

A breeze caught the *Neptune* and it was carried off to the west – prompting massive movement in the place Saint-Pierre as many made to follow. Across the square, among the blues, greys and browns of the remaining crowd, Clem noticed a spot of coral. It was Elizabeth, up from the centre of the city to witness the launch. In her hands were her notebook and a pair of binoculars. Inglis was next to her, feigning boredom with the whole business. Clem got an uncomfortable sense of how he must appear: pink-cheeked, clothes dishevelled, clutching a bottle to his chest. He wanted to look away, to pretend he hadn't seen her, but he couldn't.

Elizabeth had seen him too, of course, and Laure; she knew very well that he'd been neglecting his task – taken on barely a day before – to romp about with his cocotte. A cold nod directed her son's attention to the opposite side of the square. Jean-Jacques Allix and some others were at the mouth of the rue Saint-André, surrounded by a company or two of the Montmartre National Guard; Clem recognised a couple of faces from the evening after Châtillon. They were standing apart from the rest of the crowd – watching the event rather than participating in it.

Hannah stood on the edge of this group, dressed in a uniform similar to Laure's. This was worrying; Clem recalled an intention to call on her, smothered by recent distractions. It was clear, anyway, what Elizabeth expected of him now. He assessed his wine-drenched trousers: nothing could be done about it. Laure was still staring after the *Neptune*, a hand over her eyes, squinting as she tried to keep the minuscule sphere in sight. He touched her shoulder.

'*Ma soeur,*' he said.

His lover turned neatly on her heel. She glanced at Hannah with magnificent disdain before plucking the champagne bottle from his grasp, firing out a half-dozen words as she lifted it to her lips. Clem didn't understand them, but her meaning was plain enough: *Off you go then.*

II

Hannah sat in a corner of the Club Rue Rébeval, a gas jet hissing at her ear, sketching the left-hand section of the stage with a piece of charcoal. She worked fast, the brittle black stick scratching into the paper, attempting to cast off her intellect, her artistic training – to make the act of drawing as instinctive and unthinking as she possibly could. The *effect* of the hall was what she sought: the effect of being in the hall at that precise moment, rather than a mere record of its appearance. A rapid touch was vital. She drew an elbow, the back of a hat and the hair poking beneath it, hatching in shadows, not labouring the lines or dwelling on details. All of it would pass – the knot of kepis and cheap bonnets by the stage, the fall of the light – shifting about then breaking apart for ever. She had to be quick.

The Club Rue Rébeval was in the north-east of Paris, amongst the serried tenements of Belleville. The hall had been used for dancing before the war – decorative tin stars were still nailed around the gas fittings – but like hundreds across the city it was now given over to political debate. It was full, the air close with the heat and stink of several hundred clustered, unwashed bodies. Most were red National

Guard or their wives, many of whom had infants on their hips and children clinging to their skirts. These women participated in the evening's discussions with even more energy than their husbands, cheering riotously when the government or the clergy were denounced – which was often.

Hannah grinned with every shriek. She wore the uniform of the 197th – Jean-Jacques's battalion, and as red as ripe tomatoes. They'd taken her almost without question, not even commenting on her nationality. She'd told her recruiting officer that she'd lived in Paris for a decade, considered France her mother country and would willingly die for the cause of French honour; he'd murmured *bravo*, made an entry on her form and waved her through to collect her uniform. She hadn't expected to be so affected by the sensation of belonging. Strangers who might have sneered a week earlier now smiled and saluted as they hailed her as a brave citizen – a sister-in-arms.

The day after she joined had been the 22nd September: New Year's Day by the Republican calendar of '93 and a sacred date for any French revolutionary. It had been marked by a demonstration before the Hôtel de Ville, attended by ten thousand red guardsmen and as many civilians. Their initial demand had been a seat for an ultra in Trochu's cabinet, in the hope that such a representative might be able to challenge the hesitancy that was already coming to define his administration. When they arrived before that great palace of a building, however, with its statues and grand gates, it soon became plain that this wouldn't be enough. Chants against the Prussians became chants for the resignation of the entire provisional government – and then, for the first time, for a people's commune like that established during the first revolution. The commune was a hallowed idea for Jean-Jacques and his comrades: a society turned on its head, arranged from the bottom up, with administrative power shared between large numbers of citizens drawn from all stations in life. Hannah had added her voice to the chorus. It seemed like a clear improvement to her.

Guardsmen from the Marais battalions, local to the Hôtel de Ville, had appeared along the rue de Rivoli. Their uniforms were different, a little lighter, and all of them were armed – unlike the red units, who had at best one ageing rifle for every four or five fighting men. Hannah had taunted them along with the rest of her company, telling these petit-bourgeois soldiers to put on their aprons and return to their shop-counters and stock-rooms. As the insults had sailed across the square she'd felt a crazy flutter of joy. This was progress; this, at last, was *action*.

The protest had come to a disappointing end, guttering before it had a chance to flare. Someone had lost their nerve when a few stones were thrown, issuing the order to disperse. Nothing had been accomplished; no real statements had been made or concessions won. They were left simply to begin planning the next demonstration, endlessly formulating and debating their demands.

This night in the Club Rue Rébeval was no different from a half-dozen others Hannah had been to since the march on the Hôtel de Ville. Five speakers sat up on the stage, behind a table that had been put there solely to be struck by determined fists. It was a rogue's gallery of Parisian radicals. In the chair was Auguste Blanqui, wizened and white-bearded, an elder statesman of the ultras known for his uncompromising views; he was said to advocate the shooting of some forty thousand men who'd been involved in the running of the Second Empire, for the good of the French state. To his right was Raoul Rigault, a little out of his league, blustering and boasting to compensate for his inexperience; and beside

Rigault was the veteran journalist Félix Pyat, staring into the club as if searching for someone who'd done him a great wrong. This was the man who'd made Jean-Jacques search the rue Royale for Mrs Pardy on the opening day of the siege. He hardly seemed like Elizabeth's typical reader, but Hannah had avoided him nonetheless. She had no desire to hear his laudation of her mother first hand.

On Blanqui's left were the military men. Gustave Flourens, self-appointed battle chief of the reds, cut a splendid figure in the most embellished version of the militia uniform that Hannah had ever seen; his commitment to socialist principles clearly did not preclude lavish displays of rank. Willowy, well-groomed and effeminate, with a faintly ironical expression fixed to his face, he looked like a highly improbable warrior. Jean-Jacques sat at the end of the table. He was out of uniform, his black jacket melting into the shadows, his hat in his hands as if he was about to make for the door. The tendency of Parisian radicals to plot and pontificate irritated him. He'd told Hannah that he came from a different tradition: he would argue his point when necessary, but like her he always favoured decisive deeds over this endless talk. Their eyes met for a second; they shared an unsmiling smile. The discord of the Port Saint-Nicholas hadn't lasted. They'd been reconciled, in fact, by the time they'd returned to Montmartre, and Jean-Jacques hadn't mentioned Elizabeth since. Why am I not just drawing him? Hannah asked herself. Why do I ever draw anything else?

Under discussion was the provisional government's failed attempt to negotiate peace with the Prussians. Pyat was recounting in his nasal voice how Chancellor Bismarck had reduced Vice-President Favre to tears with the harshness of his terms. The Prussian had demanded the ceding of Alsace and Lorraine, the immediate surrender of holy Strasbourg and a host of other painful concessions. Hearing this, the crowd looked across to Jean-Jacques: his home province, the land of his forefathers, was under threat. He made no reaction.

'A brave soul,' the people agreed. 'A truly brave soul.'

'The demon Bismarck wants to ruin France!' somebody shouted.

Rigault jumped at the chance to air his favourite theory. 'But citizens,' he cried, 'surely France *should* be ruined! What is she to us, as she stands? Look at this government of ours, these so-called republicans! What are they doing now, I ask you?'

'Nothing!' replied the hall obligingly. 'Nothing at all!'

Blanqui raised a hoary hand. 'They are waiting, my friends,' he said portentously. 'Trochu and Favre paste up their defiant declarations across the city, but they want to surrender. This is certain. They know, however, that if they do so now we will not stand for it – that they will have a revolt to deal with. So they are waiting. Our food is running low. Prices, already, are starting to rise. Little thought has been given to how the supplies we have will be shared out. You can be sure that it is us, the poor, who will go hungry if the siege drags on.'

'True,' said the crowd. 'It's always this way.'

'This is what Trochu wants,' Blanqui continued. 'He wants us weakened. My friends, he is counting on it. He wants us half-starved – too wretched and frail to prevent the complete re-establishment of bourgeois rule. He will set up a society much the same as the last: all power in the hands of a corrupted elite, all wealth in the pockets of the bourgeoisie. They will turn on the workers. They always do, in every revolution this country has ever seen. The bourgeoisie use us to rid themselves of the undesired leader, and then they turn us back into their slaves. We are promised liberty – and are rewarded with further tyranny!'

Flourens stirred, spurs and scabbard jangling in a fine impersonation of a noble spirit roused. 'Then we must act.' His voice was cultured, soft; not for the first time Hannah wondered at the influence he'd gained with the *ouvriers* of Belleville. 'We must make them hear us. Paris must save Paris.'

'*Paris must save Paris!*' thundered the Club Ruc Rébeval.

Rigault and Pyat leaped from their chairs, applauding this stock phrase as if it wasn't repeated at every meeting they attended. Various dramatic steps were proposed and debated. Rigault wanted bloodshed, Trochu's head on a spike; Pyat wanted rifles, a Chassepot for each red guardsman; Blanqui favoured seizing food stores so that the government could be held to ransom.

After a few minutes Jean-Jacques stood like a man who'd heard enough. *At last*, Hannah thought, finishing off her drawing. The Alsatian loomed over the table; Rigault and Pyat sank back into their seats. The hall fell quiet.

'My fellow citizens,' he began, 'this is all well and good, but we must act against the *Prussians*. If we can beat them then Paris would be ours. The government seems to think that our foes are invincible. I tell you that they are not. They are just men. The people need to be reminded of this. They need to be reminded that a sortie,' – the hall muttered at the word – 'a *sortie* would bring us certain victory. We are told that the enemy has encircled our city. I ask you: can this *really* be so? How many men can Prussia and Bavaria spew forth? Are they not also besieging the cities of Strasbourg and Metz – and occupying several other large territories as well?'

'It is ridiculous,' interjected Flourens, keen to show something of his own bravery and strategic insight. 'It can't be done.'

'A fortnight ago we were saying that cutting off Paris was impossible. Well, my friends, perhaps it is. Perhaps this mighty siege is nothing but an illusion. What do we know – I mean truly *know*? A single minor victory has been won against the scum of the Imperial army. Some woods have been put to the torch. These events prove nothing. I put it to you that large stretches of the Prussian line are all but unmanned. It would be easy for us to break out and end this siege. The 18th, 19th and 20th arrondissements alone could field a hundred thousand men. We could do it tonight!'

His audience growled its accord; the other men on the stage pounded the table and stamped their boots.

'This is what the government tries to hide from us. They *want* the siege – Citizen Blanqui is right. They want to wear us down with hunger. They want to drain the lifeblood from the revolution. And if we are not brave, citizens, if we are not determined, they will surely succeed. We must—'

A commotion at the side of the hall forced him to stop. '*Spy, spy!*' the people there yelled. 'Hold him – don't let him escape!'

This was common in the Club Rue Rébeval, a favourite bit of theatre; the reds, mistrustful by nature, were constantly rooting traitors from their midst. Hannah climbed on her stool to get a better look. The interloper was dressed in a grey suit, his arms lifted over his head to fend off the slaps that were coming in from every direction. It was Clem's new friend – Monsieur Besson, the *aérostier* from the Elysées-Montmartre who'd run out of the Café Géricault in that unaccountable manner. Since that day, Hannah had begun to notice him in the place Saint-Pierre and the lanes around it; he seemed to be slipping into a shop or café whenever she turned around. She'd actually started to suspect that he was a government agent of some sort, planted among the balloonists to observe red Montmartre. Instead of fleeing or pleading innocence, however, as those accused of spying tended to do, this Monsieur Besson shouted out a rebuttal.

'I am an honest republican,' he stated in a loud, clear voice, 'and I say that those up on that stage would be ten times more tyrannical than Louis Napoleon – him there with the scar worst of all! They are your *enemies*, can't you see? They would soak Paris in Parisian blood! They would—'

The *aérostier*'s words were buried under a landslide of taunts and curses. The Club Rue Rébeval closed in, punching him to the floor. A signal was given from the stage; a few of Gustave Flourens's personal guard, a crack militia detachment known as the *Tirailleurs*, were tasked with ejecting Monsieur Besson from the building. Hannah watched them haul him to the street, afraid that she might see her brother. She did not – but there was a chance that he'd been standing further back and was already outside. She put the drawing in her knapsack, got down from her stool and started to push her way to the exit. She had to be sure.

Clem was troubling her. The last time they'd met, at the balloon launch, he'd been wretched to behold: dirty and steaming drunk, slurring his words, his trouser-leg dark with an unmentioned dampness. Introduced to Jean-Jacques, he'd spluttered and rambled, spouting a variety of half-baked notions about socialism and the International, making a thoroughly disastrous impression. It had been obvious, also, that he'd come to an arrangement with their mother. Her twin was the least cunning creature alive; his attempts at leading questions were so clumsy they'd made her wince. Hannah had got rid of him as quickly as she could, revealing nothing, but it had pained her to see him so reduced. She felt that he was losing his way in Paris, surrendering to his basest appetites, taking up with the likes of Laure Fleurot whilst the city around him grew more hazardous by the day. How it might end, though, or what she might do to help him, she really didn't know.

Four large guardsmen were beating Monsieur Besson in

the gutter, by the grimy yellow light that spilled from the club's windows. He was lashing out at his attackers whenever he could, but it was futile; he fell to his knees, then onto his side. The militiamen showed no sign of relenting.

Hannah rushed over. 'Stop, stop! Christ above, what's wrong with you?'

The guardsmen backed away, glancing into the shadows; Rigault stood there, down from the stage, smoking a cigarette. Their victim rolled over, panting as he checked himself for injury. Hannah crouched before him and laid a hand on his forearm. He flinched at her touch.

'Are you all right, Monsieur?'

The *aérostier* nodded, keeping his head bowed; he seemed ashamed and would not meet her eye. He pressed the cuff of his grey jacket to his lip, a black blood-spot spreading across the fabric.

'Mademoiselle Pardy, please,' he whispered, 'you must get *away*.'

Hannah blinked, startled by the feeling in his voice. She recognised it; they'd definitely spoken before, a couple of cordial exchanges as she'd painted around Montmartre. She glared at Rigault, covering her perplexity with anger. 'What is this?' she demanded. 'What were you going to do – kill him?'

Rigault shrugged.

'The man makes *balloons*, Rigault! What possible threat does he pose?'

'Those balloons could connect Trochu with the rest of the French army,' the agitator replied, 'with the machinery of national government. And anyway, citizen, surely you know that there is more to our Monsieur Besson than that. He is an enemy of the revolution. I hear that he's been asking about Jean-Jacques all over the city. We can't permit this. The revolution requires—'

'You are *insane*,' Hannah broke in, rising from the gutter. 'You are a murderous *pig*, a—'

The doors of the hall banged open and Jean-Jacques strode across the street towards them. 'Damn it, Rigault,' he said, 'must I always be on hand to halt your cruelties?'

Hannah let out an exclamation of relief: reason was restored. Without looking at her, Jean-Jacques ordered the *Tirailleurs* to set Monsieur Besson free. Rigault protested, but to no avail. The *aérostier* was pulled to his feet; the hat that had been dislodged during the fight was handed back to him and he was shoved away down the unlit avenue. Despite the punishment he'd suffered, and the further damage that would doubtless have been inflicted had he stayed, Monsieur Besson limped off with distinct reluctance.

'Bravo, Jean-Jacques,' said Rigault, 'you've just turned loose a government spy. And one, furthermore, with a particular interest in you.'

Jean-Jacques's expression was suitably contemptuous. 'That man is no *spy*. Would one of Trochu's men really make such a spectacle of himself in a red club?' He turned to Hannah. 'No, there is a different explanation here. I believe that Monsieur Besson is taken with Citizen Pardy.'

Hannah saw at once that this was true. 'How can that be so?' she said. 'I – I don't know him at all.'

The slightest touch of amusement entered Jean-Jacques's voice. 'Yet somehow you have won his devotion. This *aérostier* is an old-fashioned sort, I think. He no doubt imagines that he must rescue you from my clutches. From the clutches of the socialist cause.'

Rigault chuckled. 'Tragic.'

'It's harmless enough,' Jean-Jacques added, 'but he must be discouraged. We cannot look vulnerable, not to anyone. Not now.'

Hannah supposed that she understood, but this incident

143

had left her confused – almost as if she and Jean-Jacques were a party to Rigault's violent excesses. Suddenly she remembered Clem, anxiety surging up and then subsiding just as quickly. He plainly hadn't come to Belleville with Monsieur Besson. Of course he hadn't; he'd be drunk somewhere, wrapped around his cocotte.

The meeting in the Club Rue Rébeval was still in full flight, Blanqui's voice booming out through the doorway. Hannah, though, had heard enough. She told Jean-Jacques that she was going back to Montmartre. He didn't object, smiling gently as he bade her goodnight.

'I wouldn't really have let them *kill him*, citizen,' Rigault called after her. 'Not here in the street. How stupid do you think I am?'

Puffing out his chest, thumbs hooked in his braces, the militia sergeant launched into his song. Before the siege he'd been a professional, working on the *café-concert* circuit, and his strong tenor filled the room. He'd chosen a recent success called 'The Walrus and the Langoustine'.

Laure Fleurot emerged from the kitchens. Uniform gone, she was down to her corset and petticoats. To the fast rhythm being clapped by the guardsmen, she put her hands on her slender hips and shimmied across the floor, poking out her rear twice to the left, then twice to the right. One patent boot was planted on a chair, the other onto the top of the long table, and she was up before them all, throwing herself into an energetic dance. She raised her knees as high as they would go, flashing naked thighs and lacy undergarments; she made snipping movements with her hands, mimicking the claws of the poor little langoustine; she screamed along with the song's refrain, giving it a breathless lift.

'He'll gobble me *up*! He'll gobble me *up*!'

Hannah watched from a bench set against the far wall.

She was in good spirits; even learning that Laure was the other *vivandière* on duty that night had done little to spoil them. Some hours earlier, in an inevitable contradiction of the claims she'd made to Elizabeth, she'd gone back to her easel to start a canvas based on her study of the Club Rue Rébeval. Although wary of self-praise, Hannah couldn't deny that it was turning out brilliantly well, far beyond her hopes. She was improving. It excited her just to think that this painting *existed* – that it would be standing there when she next opened the door of Madame Lantier's shed. That she had done this, created this picture, infused her with energy and purpose; the urge was building now, in fact, as she looked at Laure whirling and bobbing with a dozen guardsmen slavering around her ankles. She took out her sketchbook and charcoal.

'The Walrus and the Langoustine' ended to hearty cheers. Laure fell backwards from the tabletop into the arms of the militiamen, who held her aloft, carrying her on a lap of the room. This guardhouse had been a private residence before the siege, that of a wealthy merchant; he'd fled several weeks previously, leaving the city to claim his property for the billeting of her troops. It had been ransacked, stripped of everything of value. The walls were covered with slogans and crude cartoons. Hannah's contributions – a forlorn Louis Napoleon being led to captivity on a donkey, a globular Bismarck eating a baby on a spit – were rather more expert than the rest and had won her some grins, but she could hardly compete with Laure for popularity. She did her duties, which revolved around collecting rations from the *mairie* and then distributing them in the guardhouse kitchen, and stayed on the margins. Her well-known connection with Jean-Jacques spared her the harassments endured by the other girls. No one wanted to cross Major Allix. They simply left her alone.

145

Laure was deposited in a large armchair. 'Which of you dogs,' she demanded, still panting with exertion, 'was feeling my arse? Whoever it was owes me ten sous!'

'Is that the rate?' asked a guardsman. 'Why, I've got it right here!'

'So have I!'

A second later Laure was standing on the chair, her elbows on its back, presenting herself to the room. The men formed a line, but she lost interest just as the first one was about to lay his hands upon her. She turned, pushing him back a few steps; she'd noticed Hannah.

'Mademoiselle Pardy,' she called out, 'are you a *spy*? Only you certainly look like one with that there drawing in your lap.'

Hannah worked on, shading the cocotte's stockinged calf. She'd resolved to be distant, contained – to get through the shift and hope that this situation didn't recur. It wasn't likely to; Laure's record of attendance was something of a joke in the 197th. This was actually the first time Hannah had seen her in the ten days since she'd enrolled.

'Why would a spy be here?' she said. 'What is going on that could possibly be of any interest to anyone?'

Laure tossed her head; some of her hair had come loose and was clinging to her sweaty neck. 'Your brother is a lot more fun than you are, I have to say. He knows how to take his pleasure – and give it too.'

Hannah sighed. This is provocation, she thought; this is not my fault. She put down her charcoal. 'What are you doing with him, Laure? What do you want?'

The cocotte perched on the back of her armchair, crossing her legs, dismissing the still-hopeful queue with a single flick of her boot. 'Just to fuck. He ain't afraid of a little spice, your brother. Big cock as well.' The guardsmen sniggered like schoolboys. 'You understand this, Hannah, I know you

146

do, somewhere in that frosty English heart of yours. It's what you get from your Jean-Jacques, after all.'

'How do you have any idea what I—'

'Now *there's* one I'd like to try out. Me and every other girl in Montmartre, eh? Tell us, what's our Major Allix like, you know, in the act? I've had my share of soldiers. They're always a bit strange, aren't they? Rough, sometimes?'

'You are unbelievable.'

'So I'm told – by your brother, among others. *Ay-may-sing.*' Laure's pronunciation of the English word was deliberately laboured. 'That's what he calls me, over and over.'

The last glimmer of Hannah's good mood disappeared. 'God above,' she said, louder than she'd intended, 'do you even know his damned *name*?'

The guardsmen were silent, totally agog. This was a rare show indeed and they weren't going to miss a second of it.

Laure buffed her fingernails against the frilled strap of her corset, acting as if she hadn't heard the question. 'Have you ever thought why he likes you?' she asked. 'Jean-Jacques, I mean? Why you, rather than anyone else? You're pretty enough, I suppose, but that can't be it. This man could have *anyone*, so why choose a bony *Anglaise* who lives in a shed, putting out these ugly damn pictures that don't even look properly finished? It don't make sense to me. Perhaps you can explain.'

Hannah was on her feet now, thinking how easily she could tip that armchair over and send the dirty slut rolling into the fireplace, when their singer-sergeant came forward to propose another number: 'The Cockerel's Lament'. He did this as a diversion, to avoid further upset to an important man's girl, and had started the opening line before his squad properly realised what was going on.

'*No one heeds my cry, in Paris this fair morning . . .*'

There were disappointed groans; the guardsmen wanted

147

to see a fight and at first the clapping was reluctant. When Laure hopped back onto the table, however, hoisting up her petticoats, they forgot about her confrontation with Hannah completely.

Hannah sat down and stared hard at her drawing. Something was there, a dash of Laure's lithe vigour, but she couldn't continue with it now. She was thinking of Clem – wondering where he was at that precise moment. If he and Laure could speak the same language it would never even have got close to this. She folded the page in two, and then again, sliding the quartered sketch behind the bench.

'The Cockerel's Lament' concluded with the unfortunate fowl going into the cooking pot, put there by Parisians sick of being disturbed during their amours. Laure dropped a deep curtsey and shouted for wine. It was all gone, the guardsmen told her; and what was worse it was past twelve. The liquor seller over on the rue Oudot would have packed up for the night. Someone would have to go down to the place Saint-Pierre.

Hannah went to the table. 'Give me the money,' she said. 'I'll do it.'

The squad reached gladly into its pockets, counting out coins and placing orders.

Laure, unimpressed, broke into an impromptu jig. 'See how the mouse tries to make you her friends!' she gasped as she kicked up her heels. 'Oh, see the dreadful burdens she'll carry!'

There was more laughter; the guardsmen looked to Hannah, thinking they'd been granted a second bout.

'No, Laure, honestly,' Hannah replied, collecting the money, 'I just want to get away from you.'

The cocotte stopped her dance, crossing her bare arms, abandoning her jibes for a full-on assault. 'What are you even *doing* here, you English bitch? This is *Paris*. We are all Parisians here. Go back to London, back to your coal and fog, your—'

Hannah slammed the door behind her. The guardhouse yard was dark; the lane beyond little better. Above, the stars were brighter and more numerous than she could ever remember seeing in Paris, swirls and fronds spreading deep into the heavens. She walked through the streets, concentrating her thoughts on the painting of the Club Rue Rébeval. She recalled how she'd captured the play of gaslight upon the coarse fabric of National Guard uniforms; the blending and jumbling of forms, exactly as a common audience might appear; the charged feeling of the whole, the sense of urgency that ran through it. Her earlier enthusiasm began to return.

There was a screech ahead – a cry of grief and horror. Hannah rounded a corner expecting an accident, an overturned cart or someone flung from a horse, yet all she saw was a group of people before the *mairie* of Montmartre – the offices of the Mayor. Above the doorway, a large red flag almost concealed the hole in the architrave where there had until recently been an Imperial eagle. A bulletin from the Hôtel de Ville had obviously just been read; a fresh bill was pasted to the noticeboard. Hannah hurried towards it.

'It's over!' an old woman wailed, slumping onto the kerb. 'We're finished now – undone!'

'Cowards!' spat a National Guard corporal. 'How could they let this happen? Did they not think of *Paris*, of what was at stake here?'

The bill was in the standard official format. One word was struck across the top in the largest type, legible even in the murky street: *Strasbourg*.

There it was. Hannah looked up again at the night sky. Holy Strasbourg had fallen.

*   *   *

149

Relieved at seven the next morning, Hannah went straight to the central boulevards to see what more she could discover. Huge numbers were out, but to mourn rather than demonstrate; the prevailing mood was one of dazed disbelief. She followed the old current onto the place de la Concorde. So many flowers had been piled upon the Strasbourg statue that the figure itself was almost lost to sight.

Nestled amidst this sorrow and sympathy was a canker of selfish fear. An entire division of Prussians, emboldened by victory, would be on their way to Paris, to bolster the besieging forces. They would be there in a couple of weeks at most. There would be no glorious fight – no heroic triumph. All the Parisians' patriotic vows and brave words would count for nothing. The few details that had reached them about Strasbourg's end fuelled dire predictions of the fate that awaited their own city. Many ancient buildings, including a library famous throughout learned Europe, had been destroyed by Prussian bombardment. This is what they are prepared to do, people were telling each other – what they will surely do to us. Soon Notre Dame will be in flames, the Pantheon in ruins!

It had also been reported that the defenders of Strasbourg had been starved into submission rather than defeated in battle, emerging from their confinement in a condition of wretched emaciation. Everyone was now certain that this would be the course of the siege of Paris as well. Hannah overheard much intense discussion of how long they could hold out; of how many sheep and oxen were grazing in the city's parks, and how much grain there was in the government's stores; of what foodstuffs were already becoming scarce. She thought of Auguste Blanqui in the Club Rue Rébeval, predicting that Trochu would use the hunger of a lengthy siege to suppress the reforming poor, and headed for Montmartre to find Jean-Jacques.

No one had seen him. He'd been with some other officers from the 197th when the news about Strasbourg had broken, but had disappeared shortly after. This wasn't uncommon; Hannah gave up and went to the rue Garreau. Her painting was there in the shed, propped on its easel. It was now unsatisfactory in a host of different ways. A whole section close to the bottom – part of the audience, the passage she'd thought so successful – would have to be redone. She snatched her palette from the wicker chair and set to work without even taking off her National Guard jacket.

The arrival of dusk finally forced her to stop. She stepped back and squinted at the canvas: she'd knocked it off balance, labouring some aspects and effacing its best qualities in the process. She swore and threw down her brushes, standing for a moment with her face in her hands; then she went to bed, too tired to do much more than remove her boots. She was asleep in seconds.

A creak woke her; she stared at the rafters, her body rigid. Someone, a man, had crept in through the door, over on the other side of her Japanese screen. She'd forgotten to fasten the bolt again. Dawn was close, a soft light filling the shed; the shutters must be open as well. Her eyes went to the shelf where she kept her canvas knife. Could she reach it before he reached her?

The intruder shut the door behind him. He put something on the floor, several metal objects; a chain rattled into a bowl.

'Hannah.'

She let out her breath. 'Here.'

Jean-Jacques came straight to her and lay down heavily, on top of the blankets. She put an arm around his shoulders. Something had happened; his clothes were damp and carried the fresh odour of the countryside, of leaves and dewy grass, underlaid with the tang of sweat. They stayed like this for almost a minute.

'Where have you been?' Hannah asked.

He didn't answer, burying his face in her neck instead. His nose was cold against her skin; she could feel the scar and the bristles of a three-day beard. She sat up, folded back the Japanese screen and looked over at the objects he'd dropped by the door. Three metal helmets shone dully in the early dawn. The six-inch spikes set in their crowns caused them to lean to the side, resting on the floorboards like spinning tops. She recognised them from countless cartoons published in Paris since the start of the war: they were *Pickelhauben*, the helmets of the Prussian infantry.

'I killed them.' His voice was quiet – grim yet unashamed. 'I went out alone, yesterday evening. Slit their throats at a watch post near Le Bourget.'

Everything shifted. Hannah made an involuntary sound, close to a laugh. She put a hand over her mouth. Her head went light, red spots fanning across her vision; her limbs began to tremble. He rose beside her and she found herself wondering if he still had the blade on him – if there was any blood on his jacket or trousers, soaked into the black material. All she could see of his face was part of the split cheekbone. She felt like a child, petrified before something obscure and monstrous.

'You killed them,' she said at last. It sounded absurd. It couldn't be true.

'I've killed many, Hannah. Thirty-six over in America. Seventeen in the Vosges Mountains.' He turned away. 'Such is war.'

Hannah tried her hardest to push the abhorrence from her mind – to recover her perspective. She *knew this*: not the facts, perhaps, but she knew what he must have done. She'd talked about it with her friends even, on at least one inebriated night in the Danton. It was thrilling, she'd told them, to be held by a man who'd fought in battles; who'd done great and serious things. *Thrilling* – that was the very word she'd used.

But this was different. They weren't talking about another continent or a distant province of France: this was *Le Bourget*, for Christ's sake. Hannah had visited the village only that spring, to paint with Benoît and Lucien; they'd eaten sheep's feet in a café before catching the train back into Paris. And now Jean-Jacques, the lover she adored and had given herself to completely, had killed three men there. He'd cut throats in the corner of one of those pretty meadows. This deed wasn't somewhere in the past. It was *hours old*. The bodies might still be warm, their blood still flowing. She squirmed from under the blankets and stood up, looking around for a basin. She was going to be sick.

Jean-Jacques stood as well; his elbow struck against the Japanese screen, sending it clattering against the bookcase. 'This has to happen, Hannah,' he said, taking hold of her wrists. 'The people need to be shown that the fight is not lost – that these men, these Prussians, will die like anyone else. It has to be done. You saw the city yesterday, how shaken it was.'

Hannah squeezed her eyes shut, shivering as she gulped down her nausea. She nodded; he was right. They were at war and this had to happen. Jean-Jacques lowered them back onto the bed, relaxing his hold on her a little but not letting go. Hannah was weak; her head ached and her mouth was sour. She realised that she hadn't eaten since the guardhouse. She longed to lay her head on his shoulder, but she couldn't. Something was sticking her in place – keeping her sitting stiff and upright on the edge of the mattress.

'Everyone says we are doomed,' she murmured.

'This will show them that there is still hope. It is terrible, I know it is, but it will *work*.' Jean-Jacques's manner became more practical. 'It must go into the papers, into as many papers as possible. I'll talk to Pyat and Blanqui; they'll put it in theirs, that's certain. But this is only the red press. We need to speak to *all Paris*. The northern arrondissements can't prevail alone, not any longer. We'll need the National Guard of the whole city, and the regulars and marines as well, if the circle is to be broken. There must be a massive sortie, a single overwhelming attack. Everybody out at once.'

Hannah guessed what he was about to ask. 'No,' she said. '*No*. You cannot expect that. Please, Jean-Jacques.'

'We need your mother, Hannah. We need the famous Mrs Pardy. She is already writing for the French papers – for ones we can't get even remotely close to. The *Figaro*. The *Gaulois*. You must take me to speak with her.'

'You don't understand, you or your friend Monsieur Pyat. She will use you for her own ends. She will—'

'I know that this is difficult. I've seen how things are between you. But we have one final chance to strike at the Prussians before they become unbeatable – before our government can starve the strength from the ordinary people. We must act quickly or we will be lost.'

Jean-Jacques tightened his grip again, fixing her with an unwavering stare. Hannah glanced at him and was caught. She could feel herself beginning to yield – literally giving in like crumbling mortar. *This*, she thought, *is the price*.

'Very well,' she said, 'I'll do what I can.'

III

They were walking side by side up the main staircase of the Grand, from floor five to six: Hannah and the black-clad Monsieur Allix, on their way to Elizabeth's rooms. A prisoner and her guard, thought Clem, ducking behind a column. He didn't want to encounter them any earlier than he had to. Raindrops tapped against the glass dome overhead; Paris's Indian summer, all that radiant sunshine and infinite blue sky, had come to an end. The bad weather was beginning.

There were shouts somewhere below, and a piteous scream. Clem peered over the balustrade, down into the lobby. Doctors in surgical gowns were rushing through the grid of iron bedsteads that had been set out across the marble floor, receiving a wounded soldier from the fortifications – the victim of a sniper, most likely. Clem leaned back. He'd witnessed several operations in the week since the lower floors of the Grand had been turned into a hospital, and had concluded that he was most definitely not of a medical inclination.

The rain grew harder. Clem didn't know what to make of this visit. His attempt to question Hannah about red activity had been a bit of a debacle. It still made him blush to think of those wet trousers. She'd sent him packing, clearly indicating that there was no place for him or their mother in this Montmartre life of hers. And yet here they were, in the heart of the Opéra district, calling on Elizabeth at Hannah's own request. The previous morning a few of the ultra newspapers had trumpeted a deadly raid that Major Allix of the National Guard had made against the Prussian encampments at Le Bourget – apparently he'd slain several men single-handed and claimed their helmets as trophies. Later that day, a Montmartre guardsman had delivered a note to Elizabeth from her daughter, asking for an audience. The two things were certainly connected, any blockhead could see that; quite how, though, Clem wasn't sure. He smoked a quick, apprehensive cigarette and followed them in.

Elizabeth's suite was larger and finer than his. The central sitting room, lit against the rainy gloom by half a dozen bronze gas fittings, was richly papered and carpeted, and filled with heavy furniture. There was a warm smell of sandalwood; in the grate rippled a jolly little fire. Two tall windows offered a commanding view of Garnier's opera house. That gilded heap of Imperial extravagance was now being used as a military depot, its stone eagles shrouded in sackcloth. Inscribed in gold across its façade was the legend *Académie Nationale de Musique* – the *Nationale* somewhat fresher than the rest, having only recently been painted over the original *Imperiale*.

Hannah, Allix and Elizabeth sat in a triangle, his sister and her lover forming the base with his mother at the apex. Only one chair was left, in a far corner. Clem picked his way to it like a latecomer at the theatre. Rather unexpectedly, the Frenchman was talking in English, and acquitting himself well. An effective radical must speak many languages, Clem reasoned, the better to disseminate his incendiary creed. Right then, however, he was querying the necessity of Clem's presence; the fellow plainly thought him a liability, a drunken joke. Clem could understand this. He hovered by the chair, awaiting judgement.

'Clement is in partnership with me,' Elizabeth replied; Clem saw a sneer dart across Hannah's face. 'Anything that concerns my work concerns him as well. Don't worry yourself, Monsieur Allix, he can be trusted completely.'

Allix wasn't pleased, but he accepted it. 'If you say so, Madame.'

Clem took his seat. That was one mystery solved, at any rate: it was the services of Elizabeth's pen that they were after. The partnership she'd mentioned was actually in doubt due to his rather woeful performance up to that point, but this was his mother's way: a unified front before outsiders. Settling down, unbuttoning his jacket, he looked over at her guests.

Jean-Jacques Allix had a near-invisible hint of supplication about him, but otherwise remained as impressive as ever – if anything, lent a dark gravitas by his lethal actions in the field. Hannah, meanwhile, sat with her legs and arms crossed, making it very clear that she was there against her will. Clem had been told by Laure – through disconnected, emphatic words and a range of scornful gestures – that his twin had been the cause of much annoyance at their guardhouse. Her militia uniform, creased and baggy with paint stains on the cuffs, was worn with none of Laure's insolent panache. She'd lost yet more weight, gaining a skinny, unapproachable look, and her blonde hair was tied up in a greasy knot. He remembered the moment he first saw her in the Café-Concert Danton, little more than a fortnight earlier, and how enormously happy she'd seemed. That, he supposed, was the real change. Hannah was no longer happy.

157

'And to answer your question,' Elizabeth said to Allix, 'I certainly saw them. Every one of this city's journalistic efforts finds its way into this room. I have an example here, in fact.' She plucked something from the small table beside her chair: two sheets of folded, membrane-thin paper swarming with words. It was *La Patrie en Danger*, a red rag printed up in Belleville, the entirety both written and edited by the same barmy old fanatic. She put on her spectacles and began a bone-dry translation.

'*We, the working people of Paris, unite in praise of the brave efforts of Major Jean-Jacques Allix of the 197th Battalion. Alone he slashes into the Imperial oppressors, a humble man bringing down the servants of a king with the fire of righteous patriotic anger. In him we witness the power of an honest soul, and are reminded yet again that the emancipation of the workers is the task of the workers themselves.*' Elizabeth stopped. 'He goes on in a similar vein for another nine paragraphs.'

Allix sat up, placing those black-gloved hands – the right one a touch rigid – on the arms of his chair. His embarrassment did not suit him. 'Citizen Blanqui means well,' he said, 'but we want this to *awaken Paris* – not to speak only to those in Belleville and Montmartre who are already eager to act. I did not undertake it lightly, Mrs Pardy. I want it to have meaning.'

Elizabeth removed her glasses, listening closely, a tiny seed of flirtation in her manner. The ultra held her gaze, as serious as can be; Hannah stared at the opera house, ignoring them both.

'We will demonstrate, of course,' Allix continued. 'Further marches are planned. But time is running out. They have taken Strasbourg. Metz, our one surviving fortress in the east, could fall at any moment – the commander, Marshal Bazaine, is an old Imperialist and will not give his best fight. Food prices are rising, and we—'

'Indeed they are,' Clem interrupted, searching his pockets for cigarettes. 'Why, a pat of butter already costs more than a lawyer's letter.'

There was a pause. Why the devil did I say that? Clem wondered. Why can't I stop myself confirming their low opinion of me?

Elizabeth lifted a thoughtful finger to her lips. She was loving every damned second of this. Here, in the handsome and enigmatic Major Allix, was an alternative to her unreliable son – a source of information far more compelling and authentic than anything Clem could hope to provide. And beside him, of course, was Hannah, the prodigal returned. It didn't matter how unwilling she was, or ungracious: she had returned. She'd run away to Paris, and now she was sitting in the Grand. For her mother it was quite the result.

'I have some sympathy for your cause, Major. I am no radical myself, you understand; well,' she qualified, 'not an *active* one at least, not any longer. But I respect what you are doing, you and your comrades. I see the lassitude, the empty bombast of the central arrondissements – and I see the workers of Belleville and Montmartre, trying to hold your timorous politicians to account and demanding the chance actually to fight against your invaders.' She tossed *La Patrie en Danger* back onto the table. 'I realise, also, that the deed reported so impressively by Monsieur Blanqui and his peers is a part of this . . . programme of action. What is it, though, that you could possibly require of me?'

Clem lit a cigarette, looking from his mother to the Frenchman opposite her. Elizabeth had worked it out, probably before they'd even arrived, but she was going to make him say it. Clem recalled her mentioning that Allix didn't like her, that he'd been set against her by Hannah. Something had happened when they'd met on the day of

159

that march – a slight, perhaps, or a show of indifference. This was Elizabeth settling the score.

Allix met it head on, delineating his proposal with direct clarity. The famous Mrs Pardy would become his champion in the moderate press – the papers that catered to the broad middle class of Paris. With each day of isolation the city's news hunger grew more acute. Both of them knew that a Parisian hero, a man seen to be striking against the Prussians, would be seized upon and lauded to the heavens. Major Allix of the 197th battalion could be fashioned into a powerful example of French courage – a tool to be used against the hesitant Trochu.

Elizabeth adjusted the fall of the coral gown, acting as if she was preparing to grant Allix a grand favour; although in truth this had come to her like an answered prayer. She'd managed to get a couple of pieces in the major papers, trading on those connections of hers, but it had been far from easy. There was too much competition, she'd complained to Clem, boredom having swollen the ranks of the Parisian press to an almost unsupportable degree, and her once-renowned name had counted for very little. Privileged access to a tale like this, however – backed up with hard proof, unusual indeed in besieged Paris – would surely lead to her being sought out rather than obliged to seek. And then there was the book. Even Clem could see that this might serve as its backbone, and distinguish it at once from the other siege diaries crowding the bookstalls.

'I could do this, certainly,' she said. 'Remove the social-istic rhetoric, if that is what you want – give the whole a bit of dash. I'd need regular reports, though, on your activities and everything that frames them. And some details about your background, Major; your noble actions, love of your country, and so forth. The part you played in the American war.'

'Naturally, Madame,' Allix replied. 'Shall we begin now? There is not a minute to be lost.'

Elizabeth had one more request to add. 'I will need a portrait,' she said, without looking at Hannah, 'for the illustrated papers both here and abroad. A more considered version of the one in that shed, perhaps.'

Oh God, thought Clem, just about suppressing an urge to hide behind a cushion, here we bloody go.

Hannah turned from the windows. Her expression served as an unwelcome reminder of those last months before her departure from London – of epic clashes that had run on for hours, with much slamming of doors and shattering of china; of a red hall in Chelsea, filled with parakeets, gentlemen in evening dress chortling in the background.

'I brought Jean-Jacques here at his request,' she said in a hoarse voice, 'but so help me, Elizabeth, if you think that I'm going to—'

Allix spoke over her, covering her hand with his. 'This can be discussed later. What is important now is that we reach as many as possible. We need to act.'

Hannah whipped away her hand and sprang from her chair. She made for the door but seemed to hit the end of a tether, swinging back around until she stood fuming silently by the fireplace. Elizabeth wore a detestable little smile. Her notebook was at the ready; she'd just finished writing a heading when the gas lights flickered out, dropping the room into shadow.

'It must be nine o'clock,' she said. 'They started doing that yesterday. Everything, I suppose, must soon be rationed.' She laid down her pen. 'Clement, be so good as to fetch us a candle.'

Two squads of militia met at a narrow junction, one red and the other bourgeois; after swapping a few insults the

161

former went for the latter as if confronted by a mortal foe. Clem was walking past, thinking about Laure in his usual state of intermingled confusion and desire, when one of the reds, a typically lean, shabby specimen, spotted him and seized his arm. An awkward dance began, Clem lunging across the pavement whilst the scrawny guardsman held onto him, boots scrabbling for purchase, shouting at the top of his voice. Clem's jacket began to slip from his shoulder. He was wondering how long this tug-of-war could reasonably go on when Émile Besson appeared, detached the red from his sleeve and sent him tumbling to the ground, followed by a few harsh-sounding words.

'Come, Mr Pardy,' he said, turning to Clem, 'this way.'

They walked off quickly.

'What – what was he saying?'

'That you were a dirty foreigner, eating food meant for Frenchmen.' Besson glanced behind him. 'That you should be shot.'

As if on cue a pistol was raised in the air and discharged. Clem started, almost breaking into a run; the red guardsmen scattered with a flurry of oaths. The bourgeois officer who had fired, a sleek grocer type in a lieutenant's uniform, lowered his smoking gun and began yelling at the men sprawled around his feet.

'Lucky for me you came along, then,' Clem remarked, straightening his jacket.

Besson didn't respond. He looked down the street; having untangled Clem from the brawl he plainly wanted to be away.

'Join me for a brandy, Monsieur Besson. I owe you that at least.'

'I regret that I cannot. I have an urgent appointment.'

'Come on, old man, it'll take a minute only. I've been looking for you, as a matter of fact – I've something to show you. This is a fine coincidence.'

It was anything but, of course; Clem had taken to patrolling this street at lunchtime, knowing that Besson ate his meals in a restaurant halfway down. Through sheer persistence, he'd managed to get himself and the *aérostier* back on a broadly amiable footing after their misunderstanding over the letter; Besson remained Clem's prime suspect, but it no longer seemed of any great consequence. He was determined to develop their acquaintance into a proper friendship. After nearly a month in Paris he was beginning to feel seriously lonely, Laure's attentions notwithstanding.

Seeing that it was easier to consent than resist, Besson indicated a small restaurant with a laurel green front – his establishment of choice. Several joints of ageing meat were arranged on plates in the window. The *aérostier* was welcomed by name; he selected a table close to the door, ordering coffee, and a brandy for his companion. Clem grinned, but felt a little crestfallen; this conversation was sure to be a brief one.

Besson took off his round-topped hat and set it on the table, exposing a head of dark, close-cropped hair. The crescent-shaped bruise on his face was almost gone. Over the past fortnight, at intermittent meetings in and around the balloon factory, Clem had watched it change from black through dark blue to purple; now it was a greenish yellow, the colour of herbal soap, a ghost of what it had once been. Clem had made a couple of attempts to extract an explanation for this lurid wound, but had come to realise that none would ever be given. 'They attacked me near the Elysées,' was all Besson would say. 'I don't know why.'

The *aérostier*'s restaurant was a pleasant enough place, clean and unpretentious; a single room kept quite dim, it had a low ceiling, polished floorboards and plain white tablecloths, and was infused with the smell of fried mushrooms. As unobtrusively as he could, Clem examined the

163

diners' plates. Only one dish was on offer that lunchtime, an oblong of greyish flesh served with some withered beans: the municipal meat ration. Introduced a week or so before, it had already been cut to a hundred grams per person per day. Clem had partaken of this stuff at the Grand. Beef was the official description, but it had a gamey sweetness unlike any cow he'd ever tasted; and it could hardly escape one's notice that the boulevards were being increasingly left to pedestrians, the horses of Paris disappearing in order of palatability.

Poking from the inside pocket of Clem's jacket was a sheaf of designs for aerial contraptions. He'd felt positively inspired of late, his old imaginings reanimated by what he'd been seeing in the Elysées-Montmartre. His particular obsession at the moment, having heard of the difficulties in guaranteeing both the direction and duration of flight when free ballooning, was with the notion of actually powering a balloon – of making a kind of aerial steamship with an engine and propellers. He was desperate to discuss this idea with Besson. As soon as the drinks arrive, he told himself; that is when I shall produce my drawings.

The *aérostier* took out a copy of that morning's *Figaro*, pushed aside their cutlery and spread it on the tablecloth in front of him. Clem's face fell. He'd been hoping that this development might have passed Monsieur Besson by. But no – the *aérostier*'s sharp features were angled towards an article in the bottom right corner. It was large, six or seven inches long, and was headed *Encore Saute le Léopard*.

'You know about this?' he asked. 'The exploits of this so-called "Leopard"?'

Clem nodded; he had in fact been given a complete English rendition of this particular piece – Elizabeth's third on Jean-Jacques Allix – a few hours earlier, before he'd even risen from his bed. She'd come in, prodded him awake and started to read. It told of an excursion made the night before last into the Prussian-held village of Pierrefitte. A field gun had been spiked, two Prussians killed by Allix's blade and two more injured by an explosion of powder. All exciting stuff, to be sure, and Elizabeth's triumph knew no bounds; she was especially pleased with this character she'd created.

'I thought of *Le Loup* first,' she'd confided, 'but they are pack creatures; it is the Prussians who are the wolves here, wouldn't you say, circling us as they do? No, I wanted a beast that creeps, that stalks, that pounces with deadly force – that has a beauty to its actions, even as it kills. In short: *Le Léopard!'*

Clem had tried to talk to her about Hannah and her obvious despondency, how she seemed trapped by the whole business, but Elizabeth had been without mercy.

'I will not try to rescue the girl for a second time, Clement,' she'd said. 'This is what she wanted. Don't you recall how angry she was to see us here? Besides, that sweetheart of hers is about to become a hero. She'll soon be the most envied woman in Paris.'

Besson smoothed his *Figaro* and translated a few sentences aloud. *'The great gun stood useless, so much dead metal, robbed forever of its fire. Its operators, coming to investigate, met their ends without ever seeing their assailant. Major Allix, our Leopard, having primed a powder keg to burst, slid back soundlessly over the emplacement wall; and by the time it blew, knocking down two more of the foe, he had vanished. A relief party arrived, searching this way and that for the saboteur; but all they could do was curse the night – curse fate and the greedy Kaiser who had led them on this needless, ignoble invasion.'* The *aérostier* was impassive. 'Quite an adventure, no?'

'Somewhat over-dramatised, perhaps . . .'

'It is signed only "a friend of free Paris", but everyone knows it is your mother. She is famous once again. And this creation of hers, this Leopard, is being talked of in every arrondissement.'

The coffee and brandy were brought. Clem frowned; there was accusation in Besson's voice. 'What can I tell you? It has absolutely nothing to do with me. He sneaks up to talk with her while I'm out in the city. I know literally as much as you do – as any reader of the *Figaro* does.'

Clem had been consigned to the sidelines, required only to admire. Elizabeth, having Allix at her disposal, no longer troubled herself very much to learn what he'd seen. 'If I ever pen a report on harlots' boudoirs or low drinking dens, Clement,' she'd told him, 'I'll be sure to consult you.'

Besson was eyeing him steadily; he had more to say, but was holding his tongue. Sipping his coffee, he allowed Clem to switch the subject to ballooning – even to get out his designs and lay them over *Encore Saute le Léopard*.

'Changes are coming to the balloon post,' he said, picking up the topmost. 'Nadar has decided to move all operations from the Elysées-Montmartre to the Gare du Nord.'

Clem was impressed; this would be a significant undertaking. 'A question of space? I recall you bemoaning the height of the ceilings in the dancing school.'

'In part. There is a feeling, also, that Montmartre is turning against us. Our position has become fragile since the evacuation of Monsieur Gambetta. *Les Rouges* now believe that we are merely an arm of the government.'

Just over a week earlier Léon Gambetta, Trochu's Minister of the Interior, had flown out from the place Saint-Pierre, with instructions to head for Tours and assemble an army that could come to the aid of Paris. Clem had been in the crowd that gathered to cheer Gambetta's departure. The brave statesman had looked distinctly sick as he climbed into the tiny wicker basket – and close to fainting as he was carried up and off, away into the dreary October sky.

The reds hadn't liked this development at all. It was said that they wanted Paris to be left entirely alone and unaided, their leaders convinced that they could vanquish the Prussians with their ragtag militia battalions and then establish their socialistic commune before anyone from outside had a chance to stop them. The radical agitations were becoming more violent and determined by the day; the brawl in the street just then had been the smallest taste of the discontent that seethed across the city, boiling down from the north. Clem thought it pretty obvious that these rampaging ultras would single out the Elysées-Montmartre as a target. Perhaps this was the story behind the *aérostier*'s beating.

Besson was studying Clem's design: the best one in its author's opinion, detailing a two-tier steam propeller mechanism. He didn't reel with amazement or anything like that, but his half-smile held genuine approval.

'There is work here,' he said, 'serious work. I take it you are not so committed to your cocotte as previously?'

The *aérostier* had seen Clem and Laure together at the launch of the *Neptune*. He derived some mysterious amusement from the thought of their liaison.

'Don't, old man.' Clem knocked back his brandy. 'Things in that quarter, to be quite frank with you, have grown somewhat strange. I've been trying to stay away a bit, in fact, as much as she lets me, in the hope that this might cool it all down a fraction. I don't know if it's the boredom of the siege or just the normal course of things for a woman such as her, but . . .'

Besson returned the propeller design to the pile, looking over as if inviting him to go on. Clem put his glass on the table and sighed. There really was no one else he could tell about this.

'God knows, I am no prude,' he began. 'Oral pleasures I

can deliver, enjoy even. Her apparently quite pressing need to insert her finger into my . . . well, you know . . . may not be something I've encountered before, but I can submit to it.' He cleared his throat. Besson was sitting very still. 'Her wish to bring others into the room, however, of both sexes, and involve them in the proceedings – or to introduce these . . . *objects* of hers . . . These things I find more difficult to accept. Why, only the other day she commanded me to push a hen's egg up her—'

Besson rose suddenly from his chair. 'I must go,' he said. 'Really I must. My appointment – time has run on. I apologise, Mr Pardy. I will see you before long, I am sure.'

The *aérostier* pressed a coin into the hand of the nearest waiter and put on his hat. Clem, left sitting alone, had to laugh; he tried to make an affable protest, to plead a few more minutes, but found himself addressing the inside of the restaurant's door. He stared at his designs; at Besson's forgotten newspaper; at the starched tablecloth beneath them both. His confessions had been too graphic. He should catch the fellow up and apologise for his thoughtless crudity. The *aérostier*'s meeting was sure to be at the offices of the Balloon Commission, near the Gare d'Orléans. It occurred to Clem that he could tag along – ask for an audience with whichever official was available and present his designs to them. He smiled, his belly warm with brandy; this was a *brilliant* idea. He gathered the balloon drawings and hurried into the street.

The grey-suited *aérostier* was heading in altogether the wrong direction for the Balloon Commission. Clem gave chase anyway, and was soon walking along the boulevard de Clichy – passing Laure's apartment and looping westwards into Les Batignolles. Besson led him down avenues of looted townhouses; around a park packed with tents; over intersections barricaded with prised-up paving stones. Whilst turning a corner the *aérostier* looked back – and without thinking Clem ducked behind a cast-iron water fountain. Nose to nose with an oxidised angel, he admitted to himself that he was now tailing Besson rather than pursuing him.

The walk continued. Clem's thoughts went to his luncheon, which was getting later by the yard; even the prospect of his horsemeat ration became appealing. The mystery of it spurred him on, though – the thrill of detection. This siege had focused people. No one strayed from the path dictated by their duty; yet here was Émile Besson advancing into a quarter uninvolved in the balloon post, miles from his designated place. Clem resolved to know why.

They arrived in a long street of mansion houses. One of the grandest was festooned with flags, half a dozen Old Glorys, and had a queue of civilians stretching from its doors: the American Embassy. Besson approached a man standing outside and engaged him in conversation. Dressed in a porter's uniform, this person was grey-bearded and bandy, with a leathery, well-smoked look. His coat and cap were smart but there was something of the stray about him, as if he was no stranger to sleeping under bridges and carts. After a few seconds they crossed the road, going down a side street and into a café.

Clem took up a position opposite, beside a green barouche that seemed to have been parked there for several weeks. The lane was dark, its buildings tall and close. He peered into the café's front window; each occupied table was picked out by a candle. Those he sought were over in a corner. Besson had obtained this porter a plate of meat – his own ration, it had to be – and a carafe of wine. Ignoring his cutlery, the man drew a clasp-knife from his pocket and hewed the unappetising lump apart; he then speared a large piece and worked it into his mouth, chewing industriously, inserting a second chunk before the first had been swallowed.

Clem watched with some fascination. Christ, he thought, is the fellow actually *starving*?

Besson was asking questions, jotting down the porter's monosyllabic answers in a notebook. The *aérostier* appeared to be verifying things he already knew, checking facts rather than discovering them. This interview did not last long. Once he'd reached the bottom of his page Besson prepared to leave, laying a banknote on the table. The porter barely glanced up from his plate. The café door opened; Clem pulled back behind the barouche. Besson didn't see him. He strode towards the embassy and went north.

Clem thought for a moment. In all likelihood, Besson was the one who'd sent that anonymous letter – the one who'd brought Clem and Elizabeth to Paris. He plainly had a new project underway, a secret scheme that might very well involve the Pardy family again. Clem straightened his hat; he collected his wits. He had to find out what it was.

The porter was devouring the last of his meat, wiping up gravy with a tendril of fat. Clem stopped at his shoulder; he decided not to sit.

'Excuse me, sir, could you—'

'A John Bull, by God.' The man gulped down the fat and turned without interest. Clem had taken him for about sixty; he now saw that he was rather younger. 'What the devil d'you want?'

'Are you an employee of the American Embassy, might I ask?'

'I am. Sergeant George Peabody is my name.'

Sergeant. He certainly had the manner of a veteran – an uneasy, faintly angry quality. 'You were once a military man, I take it?'

Peabody cleaned his knife on the tablecloth, folded it away and returned it to his jacket. 'What goddamn business is that of yours?'

Clem produced a silver ten-sou piece and placed it beside the prongs of the American's unused fork. 'Did you fight in the late war, by any chance?'

Peabody took the coin; he shook his head. 'I ain't going through all that again. Not in one goddamn meal. Not unless you got a huge stack more o' these.'

There could be no doubt: Émile Besson had been questioning a veteran of the American Civil War. It was true that balloons had been used widely in that conflict, for artillery spotting mostly, and a number of sieges had been fought. The *aérostier*'s interest could be wholly professional. But if this was the case, why had he been so damned secretive – so abrupt in his departure? Clem couldn't explain it. Then he thought of that rainy morning a week or so before; the black-gloved hand lying inert on the arm of one of Elizabeth's parlour chairs. Jean-Jacques Allix had been in America. He'd fought heroically for the Union – endured horrible injuries for the cause of liberty. Elizabeth referred to this often in her Leopard articles. Could it be that Besson, so convinced of the danger Allix posed to Han and others, had started an investigation into his past? What on earth, though, could he be hoping to discover? And had he found anything?

Clem searched through his empty pockets. 'Would you accept a note of credit, sergeant? I can guarantee—'

'You got nothing, John Bull.' Peabody stood, studying Clem scornfully; he swiped the wine carafe from the table and started for the door. 'I believe I'll bid you good afternoon.'

Three days later a soft ruby light spread out across the evening sky, hiding the stars; it was as if Paris had been transported to the bed of a claret sea, a tinted sun shimmering down through the waters. The various residents of the Grand Hotel – guests, nurses and walking wounded

– clustered in the middle of the boulevard des Capucines to gaze up in wonderment.

Elizabeth identified the phenomenon immediately. '*Aurora borealis*,' she said, wrapping herself in a shawl. 'I saw one in Norway, back in fifty-nine. That, though, was aquamarine; I suppose red is more appropriate for our current circumstances.'

Those around them were chattering excitedly in French.

'Our friends here think that the Prussians must be responsible – that they must be testing a new weapon of some kind, or setting the whole of the French countryside on fire.' Elizabeth listened again and made an impatient sound. 'Now they are claiming that it is a sign from God, warning of some imminent disaster. Honestly, the popular imagination is so shockingly confined.'

'It's the result of natural electrical activity on the surface of the earth,' Clem volunteered. 'Or so I've read, at any rate.'

His mother regarded him with condescending pride – *see, Clement*, said her eyes, *you are not a total loss* – before addressing the other spectators. Clem understood enough to know that a forceful appeal was being made on behalf of science and rationality.

It was a chilly night; realising that nothing was going to happen beyond the spectacle itself, most of the hotel's inhabitants went back inside. Elizabeth soon followed, declaring that she had deadlines to meet. Clem sat on a bench, staying out in the street long after the aurora had faded away. He stared along the boulevard; once the world capital of luxury, Paris was now as barren and dirty as a failing port-town. The sense of imprisonment had grown unexpectedly profound. Many people lived through their entire lives without leaving their home city; Clem himself had seldom wandered far from London. To have the option of departure removed, however, to be forcibly confined to the six square

172

miles of Paris, was beginning to feel intolerable – and the glorious French capital cramped beyond belief.

Worry didn't help. Clem had tried repeatedly to meet with Besson, to see if he could learn any more about the *aérostier*'s clandestine conversation with Sergeant Peabody. He'd remained out of reach, though, occupied day and night with the relocation of his workshop to the Gare du Nord. Serious thoughts about Jean-Jacques Allix, about what his ultimate goal might be, had started to gnaw at Clem; it seemed pretty clear to him that the black-clad radical and his friends were building towards something that would count more than Prussian sentries among its victims. He'd considered arguing for a little bit of distance, but knew that neither his sister nor his mother would heed him.

Elizabeth's siege was going very well indeed. For the first time in many years her words were reaching a large and enthusiastic audience; the people of Paris all but tore papers from the stands when they carried a new Leopard article. Major Allix was fast becoming a legend, celebrated in scrawled slogans across the city. Since Clem's exchange with Peabody, Allix had killed his first officer, a captain, returning with his sword. The Leopard's grim tally was now well into the twenties; the Café-Concert Danton, his personal strong-hold, had a small armoury of enemy equipment on display. And he spoke only to Mrs Elizabeth Pardy, the 'friend of free Paris'. Any volume assembled at the siege's conclusion would make her rich – as famous and admired as she'd ever been. She would hardly agree to break off midway and leave the story unfinished.

Hannah was a rather different matter. She'd been a sobering sight back there in the Grand, so bloody miserable – appalled both by the course her lover was taking with this Leopard business and the part she was being made to play in it. The memory weighed on Clem's conscience; once or twice he almost reached the point of going up to find her on the rue Garreau. He'd stop though, as he reached for his hat and coat. He was certain that she'd be unreceptive, perhaps actually hostile, to anything he might say. *These are my decisions to make*, she'd shout; *it has nothing whatever to do with you*. So Clem stayed around the Grand, biting his nails and smoking endless cigarettes, forever on the verge of meaningful steps.

In the week after the red aurora the siege went through several swift, lurching turns. The first was an advance, a victory so surprising that at first Paris scarcely dared believe it: the French army, the regulars camped outside the walls, retook Le Bourget from the Prussians. News of the conquest was announced from the door of every *mairie* and emblazoned across the top of that evening's *Gazette Officielle*. Elizabeth was quick to remind her readers that Le Bourget had been the site of Allix's first raid. She stated that the French government had been obliged to act by her Leopard's gathering fame – ignoring a rumour that the village had in fact been attacked impulsively by the commander of Saint-Denis, against General Trochu's instructions.

Mere hours after this article was published, Le Bourget was claimed again by the invaders. Word went around that the French soldiers had got blind drunk on wine found in the village's cellars, fallen asleep at their posts, and been caught unawares by a Prussian force more than twenty thousand strong. Their resistance was accordingly brief; the 14th battalion of the Seine and a legion of *francs-tireurs* were annihilated. Le Bourget had been held for just under two days. Elizabeth went back to her desk. The Prussians had planned the whole misadventure, she asserted, as punishment for the Leopard's stunning depredations; he very obviously had the enemy scared, and would keep striking at them as long as there was breath in his body.

On the same day as the rout at Le Bourget came confirmation that Metz, the final point of French resistance in the east, had surrendered the week before, along with one hundred and eighty thousand troops. Allix's prediction had been correct. Marshal Bazaine, the commander of the town, had made no attempt to break out, simply sitting behind the walls until his supplies had dwindled away. The battle-hardened Prussian Second Army was at liberty to join the siege of Paris.

'That's it,' said Elizabeth when the news reached the Grand. 'Something is bound to happen now.'

'Have you noticed, Mrs P,' asked Montague Inglis, 'the change that has come over the dogs of this city? No longer will the happy stray sniff around your boots as you wait to cross the road. The pets of acquaintances recoil from a once-welcomed hand, scampering beneath the nearest piece of furniture. They have become *wary*. They have seen the first pick of horses vanish from the streets and stables, and somehow they know that they'll be next – that the stranger approaching with an open palm and a kind smile could very easily have a kitchen knife concealed behind his back.'

Clem tried in vain to move his knees into a comfortable position. The cab was too small, the seats too narrow and close together; it was all they'd been able to find, though, even on the grand boulevards. 'I'm not sure I could eat a dog,' he said. 'It doesn't seem decent.'

Inglis sighed, vexed as usual by Clem's presence. 'Yes, well, the rawness of *want*, Master Pardy, is rapidly banishing the qualms of habit. Only last night, for instance, I dined on ragout of cat. It was so delicious that it made me wonder why the creatures aren't consumed more generally. I mean, they're common enough, easy to rear – and a dashed nuisance, for the most part . . .'

'Gustave Flourens,' said Elizabeth. 'The Belleville swashbuckler.'

Inglis peered out of the window. 'Ah yes, with those men of his: the *Tirailleurs*, they call themselves. What a confounded booby.'

They were parked at the base of the Tour Saint-Jacques, the single surviving section of an ancient cathedral destroyed in some previous expression of French revolutionary wrath. This disembodied bell tower, rendered in the stark angles of the Gothic age, rose up eerily from the middle of a trampled, denuded garden. Past it filed a crowd of thousands, heading east along the rue de Rivoli towards the Hôtel de Ville. Their driver had advised them not to get any closer to the demonstration, intimating that his vehicle, modest though it was, could serve as a magnet for the mob.

'He's quite right, Mrs P,' Inglis had opined. 'Wouldn't be the first time that a carriage was flipped over by frenzied socialists.'

It was raining, the cab windows misting almost as fast as they could be rubbed clear. Elizabeth and Inglis were trading observations like a pair of cagey poker players, taking care to keep their best cards hidden. The *Sentinel* correspondent looked positively scruffy that morning, his beard even having been allowed to overgrow; some pains had been taken, he'd said, to create 'a toilette sufficiently *canaille* for the communists'. Clem, too, had invested some of the meagre allowance still granted to him in some second-hand clothes. He was dressed in a simple woollen coat, a worker's blouse and linen trousers, bought from a stand on the Quai Voltaire and carrying a faint redolence of onions. On his head was the obligatory kepi.

The three of them studied Flourens as he marched by: a tall, pale man, girlishly slender, kitted out as if he was the grandest field marshal in Europe. A force of several hundred militia, distinguished by a special crimson sash, were arrayed behind him in close order.

'These red guardsmen are having the time of their lives, aren't they?' said Inglis. 'They play at soldiers, doing no work, all the while plotting to overthrow the very government that is paying and feeding them. Amazing behaviour.'

Elizabeth refused the bait. She opened her notebook and started to write.

'How about your Leopard then, Mrs P, the legendary *pantera pardus*?' Inglis spoke lightly, but there was strain around his eyes – something very like a wince. 'Is he due to make an appearance today? He must be, surely, man of action that he is. Why, after reading that last piece of yours in the *Figaro* I wouldn't be surprised if the blighter leaped down from the rooftops and ousted Trochu's men with a flourish of his bayonet.'

Inglis's jealousy at Elizabeth's recent success was too enormous and too agonising to be hidden. This was sweeter to her than either the restoration of her name or the riches to come. She was envied by her rivals, by Montague Inglis of the *Sentinel*: her satisfaction was complete.

'Major Allix will be here,' she said, 'supporting the people of Paris as always.'

'The people of Paris!' Inglis exclaimed, seeking solace in angry bluster. 'What is it that they want, these *people of Paris*? What is this damned commune that they shout for at every opportunity?' He began counting items off on his fingers. 'They would do away with all worship and appropriate church property; stop all the theatres, gag the press, and dismiss the army; repudiate all engagements entered into by previous governments; and, in a word, do everything to prove once more to the civilised world that there is no such tyranny as absolute liberty – the motto of which is *"if you do not do as you like, I'll make you."'*

Elizabeth wouldn't hear this. 'You seem to imply that I am taking their side, Mont,' she said, snapping her notebook closed, 'that I am calling for a commune through my sponsorship of Major Allix. This is simply untrue. Do you think for a second that *Le Figaro* would publish me if I was? No, I merely sympathise with the plight of those who your beloved emperor overlooked entirely and allowed to languish in the most terrible deprivation. It is high time that Paris listened to her workers and permitted them their proper freedoms.' She lifted her chin with unimpeachable, queenly authority. 'Besides, you foolish man, in order to have tyranny there must be a tyrant. These people marching today want *democracy*, a body of elected officials who represent their views, with power shared among ordinary men – rather than that puffed-up libertine you so adore, who appointed himself ruler and then used soldiers and secret policemen to silence any opposition!'

Clem had heard several versions of this argument already that morning. He moved closer to the window, ignoring it as best he could, scouring the passing multitudes. If Allix was there, Hannah would be as well. Sight of his sister, he hoped, would show him what he should do.

Suddenly he was pitched forward into the rain. The door he'd been leaning against had been opened from the outside. He just managed to grip the frame, halting his fall; but then his collar was seized and twisted, someone pulling him the rest of the way down. Stumbling to an ungainly crouch, he looked up to see Laure in her *vivandière* uniform, framed by one of the Tour Saint-Jacques's pointed archways. Her arms were crossed, two fingers drumming on an elbow. It was more than a week since they'd last seen each other; she was waiting for an explanation. Clem got to his feet. Now, standing before her, he couldn't begin to account for all this time. Absence had only sharpened her appeal – refreshed that misleadingly delicate beauty of hers. What, precisely, had he been thinking? The reservations he'd tried to communicate to Besson were lost to him completely. Her unimpressed expression, even, was beguiling: very slightly ironic, as if on some level this lovers' confrontation amused her.

'I am sorry,' he said, 'truly sorry. Um – *désolé*. It was not my intention to—' He stopped. 'I simply needed to be by myself for a while. You understand, don't you? I needed to clear my thoughts, to—'

Laure rolled her eyes, miming a yapping mouth with her hand; then she moved in, step by step, putting on a mock-innocent smile as she fitted her body against his. Clem's mind emptied. She kissed his neck, pressing their hips together. He was being reclaimed.

Something caught her attention, past his shoulder. She shifted to one side, drew in her breath and blew the most enormous raspberry Clem had ever heard. He looked around to see Elizabeth and Inglis watching them through the cab's open door; and when he turned again Laure had gone, making for the rue de Rivoli. It was plain that she wanted him to follow her. He told his mother that he was going to get a better look at the demonstration. She sat back in her seat, shaking her head.

All along the avenue were signs that trouble was brewing. Concierges were at their gates; shutters were going on shop windows; demagogues were doing their level best to whip those who passed them into a state of violent dissatisfaction. The narrow square in front of the Hôtel de Ville was crammed with workers and red militia. Many held umbrellas; their flags and banners hung limp, heavy with rainwater. The Hôtel itself, a vast baroque manor house, sat solid and splendid before their chants.

'*Vive la France!*' they cried. '*Vive la commune!*'

There was an authentic revolutionary crackle in the air:

the peasants were about to storm the castle. This is a tale for the memoirs, thought Clem – how I once pursued a girl into the heart of a genuine French revolt. Laure was worming further away from him, though, showing no actual desire to be caught. Keeping her in sight wasn't too difficult; the plait of hair that poked from under her kepi stood out like orange-peel on asphalt. Her kiss lingered on Clem's neck, tingling against the skin. He pushed after her as politely as he could manage, *'pardon'* constantly on his lips. The sheer density of people was astonishing, a warm, breathy crush, rich with human smells. Along with the umbrellas were a good number of rifles, worn with their stocks upward: a gesture with its origins in the first revolution, Elizabeth had informed him earlier, to display support for the people. Frock-coated speakers, ministers of the provisional government Clem guessed, appeared at first-floor windows to appeal to the crowds. They could barely be heard over the calls for their downfall.

A battalion's worth of regular soldiers was guarding the Hôtel's grand double-doors, arrayed on the steps with guns ready in their hands. Clem heard singing in Italian; a man in militia uniform was up on a stone bollard, treating them to a solo in a professional-sounding tenor. A senior army officer slid out through the double-doors and attempted to make a speech from the top step. It was none other than General Trochu, Governor of Paris and acting President of France, coming before them without ceremony or escort – without even a cap to keep off the rain. Bald, with a pristine little moustache, Trochu spoke like a man who imagines that he is popular, easily capable of winning over a mob with his oratory. Those massed before the Hôtel de Ville disabused him of this notion at once.

'À bas Trochu!' they screamed, surging forwards. *'Vive la commune!'*

The governor promptly disappeared back into the building. Clem tried to remain calm, to preserve a sense of detachment. This is not your fight, he told himself; you are here for Mademoiselle Laure and that's all. But Trochu had distracted him at a critical moment – he'd lost sight of her. She'd been ducking beneath an umbrella over to the left, and now she was gone. His beacon was put out. What the devil was he to do now?

The pushing got stronger, more determined, the red militia snarling and sloganising as if girding themselves for a great collective effort. Clem abandoned the chase, deciding to return to the neutral ground of the rue de Rivoli; he could track Laure down later. Upon turning, however, he discovered an impassable barrier of kepis and dirty blue jackets, hemming him in on every side. Pleas and protestations yielded no results. He wasn't going anywhere.

A shot sounded up ahead, then two more; there were fearful cries and yells of *baissez-vous, baissez-vous!* The crowds heaved away from the Hôtel like a wave thick with flotsam retreating messily from the rocks. Clem struggled to stay on his feet, grabbing at arms and shoulders. As he lifted his head to gasp in a lungful of air he spotted Laure. She was off safely to the side, under a large black umbrella with three or four others; they were laughing at something, passing around a cigarette. He wiped the rain from his eyes. She'd done this on purpose.

They were moving forward again, breaking the line of soldiers and bashing apart the double-doors, funnelling into the Hôtel de Ville. Clem was caught in the mob, unable to do anything to alter his course. One moment he was out in the driving rain; the next he was in a high stone corridor, deafened by a thousand echoing shouts, charging into darkness.

IV

The cordon around the Hôtel de Ville opened immediately to admit Jean-Jacques. Hannah stayed directly behind him, barely resisting the urge to hold onto his coat. Something white flapped past her face; stacks of government papers were being thrown from the windows of the Hôtel, scattering onto the National Guard below and being tramped to mush beneath their boots. They advanced through several layers of armed men into the covered central courtyard. The first of the occupiers had already been inside for a couple of hours. Everyone was talking very loudly. Militia were present in large numbers, of course, but Hannah also saw workers in blouses and a handful of better-dressed gentlemen she took to be newspaper correspondents. Women were a distinct yet vocal minority; hard-eyed, dressed in rough peasant clothes, they were trying to outdo each other in their declarations of revolutionary zeal. Lists were being drawn up of those who might serve in a new socialist administration. The courtyard resounded with names both familiar and unfamiliar – Pyat, Delescluze, Rollin – whilst off in a corner a lone trumpeter was sounding a flat reveille.

Jean-Jacques was given an enthusiastic welcome. He was

saluted, slapped on the back, offered weapons; there were cries of *'Vive le Léopard!'* The general assumption was that he was there to cut down Trochu and his ministers – to serve as their executioner. He went to the grand staircase in the middle of the courtyard, stopping on the landing to address the crowd.

'We will shed no blood today,' he announced. 'We are here to negotiate.'

A few booed or groaned, but someone said 'he's right'; another 'it's necessary'.

'We will get fairness, however. I promise you that. We will secure the freedom of the people. And we will get action against the invader. We will get our sortie.'

This word was gaining in power; mere mention of it was enough to prompt a cheer and a spirited rendition of the 'Marseillaise'. Jean-Jacques carried on up the staircase as they sang, covering three steps with each stride. As Hannah went to follow, someone grasped the leg of her pantaloon through the balustrade and would not let go. It was Clem, wearing the panicked expression of someone who'd accidentally boarded the wrong ship. Rather less surprised than she might have anticipated, she ran back down the steps and punched him on the arm.

'You really are an *idiot*, Clem,' she hissed. 'You are too thick-headed to live. You are like an exceptionally stupid child.'

'Please, Han,' he begged, 'please listen to me. I've been stuck in here for an absolute *age*. The rogues on the door won't let me out. All they'll tell me is that I need to see somebody called Blankey – *Blankey*, for Christ's sake!'

A grin nudged through Hannah's exasperation. '*Blanqui*, you dolt. Auguste Blanqui. He's one of the red leaders.' She glanced around. Nearby, two guardsmen were bashing in some ornamental stonework with their rifle-butts, apparently just to pass the time. There was no Elizabeth, though, or anyone else she recognised. Her brother was alone. 'Did she send you in here?'

Clem had always blushed easily; a deep beetroot colour was now spreading out from beneath his blond whiskers. 'No, I – I actually came in after Laure. Well, I followed her to the gate. She gave me the slip, though, and I was swept inside. It's all been a terrible mistake.'

'Laure Fleurot still. Honestly, you *goose*.' Hannah sighed. 'I should leave you here. That's what Elizabeth would do. Let you learn your lesson.'

He clutched at her sleeve. 'Oh dear God, Han, please don't. I need to get out. This place isn't for me, it really isn't.'

The sound of English was beginning to draw unfriendly attention. Hannah affected confidence, as if this was her element and she was in complete control – as if she was not almost as apprehensive as Clem was.

'Very well,' she said, lowering her voice. 'Stay close – keep quiet. We'll go to Jean-Jacques. He'll be able to help you.'

Clem scratched his head. There was a reluctance about him; Hannah saw that her twin would never be comfortable with Jean-Jacques. Perhaps he'd developed a misguided sense of brotherly protectiveness, as everything started to gather pace – or was simply aware of how insufficient he seemed by comparison. It passed, at any rate; Clem recognised that he was in no position to be particular.

'I'd be most grateful,' he said.

They set off up the staircase. At its top was a shadowy labyrinth of tiled landings and marble-clad corridors. Hannah couldn't tell which way Jean-Jacques had gone. Red militia were everywhere; whichever loyalist force had been guarding the Hôtel had long since departed. On these upper floors the disorder of the courtyard was turning into something darker. Looting had begun, any objects of value vanishing into National Guard knapsacks. Furniture was being over-turned and stamped to bits. The few remaining symbols of older regimes, imperial, royal or otherwise, were meeting violent ends – stone torn down, portraits shredded, wood scored and scratched.

'We have to *get out*, Han,' Clem whispered. 'We have to get out before they burn the bloody place to the ground.'

Gustave Flourens went by with a company of his *Tirailleurs*, all flashing brass buttons and brightly coloured sashes. Although he'd met Hannah on numerous occasions he showed no sign of recognising her. He'd certainly be heading towards the centre of things – towards Jean-Jacques.

'This way,' she said, starting after them.

Flourens and his men burst into a large oak-panelled room, poorly lit and packed with people. The provisional government, caught by surprise, had been trapped in their seats; twenty or so ministers and their aides were still in place around a baize-topped conference table. Only Vice-President Jules Favre was on his feet, dapper in a grey frock coat, arguing fiercely with the intruders. In front of him were the socialist leaders; Blanqui was foremost, a tricolour cockade pinned to his kepi, shouting at Favre with as much strength as he could muster. Jean-Jacques had taken up a position nearby, applauding Blanqui, watching everything.

Flourens didn't speak or wait for a moment to introduce himself to the debate. Instead he pulled out a chair, using it as a step to climb onto the table. This won him the atten-tion of the room; he paced back and forth, kicking over inkwells, crunching pencils and pens beneath his boot-heels, all the while reeling off his demands with aristocratic care-lessness. There was nothing surprising in what he said – dismissal of the current cabinet, immediate municipal elections, expedited planning for a massed sortie against the Prussians – but his swaggering delivery served as an additional provocation. Favre went scarlet; several other ministers rose from their chairs. Many among the reds were also displeased by Flourens's performance, Blanqui looking as if he'd gladly shove the dandy guardsman from the table and bloody his nose. The only person to remain calm and quiet was General Trochu, the target of so much of his fellow citizens' wrath, who smoked a cigar as if he sat by his parlour fire.

Hannah and Clement squeezed into the chamber. Moving towards the table was impossible; they had to settle for a place beside a window. Hannah's thoughts went to her drawing materials, stowed as always in her *vivandière*'s bag. This frantic scene was worthy of a study, but there wasn't enough room even to raise a piece of paper before your face; and the National Guard were continuing to jam themselves in, clambering up on bookcases and sideboards. Hannah could no longer see the conference table, catching only occasional glimpses of Flourens's wagging, oversized head as he sauntered around firing out more orders and ultimatums. She turned to the window; the day's light was fading.

'He's arrested them,' reported a tall man in front of her. 'Colonel Flourens has arrested the provisional government for failing to resign. Blanqui's accepting it. The mayors are to be summoned. We have a commune. By the devil, citizens, it's done!'

The red guardsmen congratulated one another, making themselves believe it. Hannah was unconvinced; it couldn't be this easy. More would be asked of them than a few bold words. Sure enough, before the celebrations had properly begun there was a new commotion over by one of the other windows. A battalion of loyalist militia had been sighted:

they were cutting across the square towards the Hôtel, forcing the red guards back to the very steps of the building.

'Les Batignolles!' someone cried. 'It's the men of Les Batignolles, damn them, come to the aid of their false president!'

The shouting grew louder. A dozen men joined Flourens on the conference table, insisting that they be heard. It was proposed that Trochu be taken to the entrance of the Hôtel and held at rifle-point – prompting a fresh storm of disagreement and dispute.

'Heavens, Han,' muttered Clem, 'will you just call your man over? It ain't right, us being shut in here with these fanatics. We need to leave.'

'You're assuming that I'm here against my will.'

'Come off it, you're a bloody painter – an *English* painter, not some blasted French revolutionary. This is all absolutely ridiculous.'

Hannah began to bristle. 'That doesn't matter a jot. I believe in what's being done here, Clem. The people of Paris were promised elections when the Empire fell. These have been denied – postponed indefinitely. They were promised decisive action against the enemy, and this has failed to happen too. It's becoming plain that this provisional government, these so-called republicans, are going to betray the people and instate another dictator like Louis Napoleon. Paris needs this change. She needs these brave men.'

This little speech left Clem mystified. 'What the deuce are you on about? Another *Napoleon?* Do you really think that's likely?'

Hannah considered her brother in his fake *ouvrier*'s outfit and felt a stab of disdain. 'Look at yourself, Clem, will you? Stuck in Paris because you followed Elizabeth on a whim. Tangled up in this action because you were panting after that slut Laure and got lost. Everything in your life is a

187

damned *accident*. You believe in nothing – you commit to nothing. Why exactly should I heed your opinion?'

Clem met her denunciation with infuriating good humour. 'You may be onto something there,' he agreed, taking out a cigarette, 'but don't try to pretend that you're a proper part of all this. I saw you in Elizabeth's suite in the Grand – your reaction to this Leopard business. Your face when she instructed you to make his portrait.' He lit up, adding his smoke to the dense cloud overhead. 'It took me back to those times in London where she'd have you paint some old lecher of her acquaintance to further the cause of Mrs Pardy. Or that evening in Chelsea just before you left – the one with the wallaby.'

Hannah frowned; this, she thought, is the true meaning of family. Your relations can instantly revive your most dismal, humiliating moments, the moments you long to forget. Like no one else, they can remind you what a wretched creature you really are.

'We only went to her because we had to,' she replied. 'Some use may as well be made of her presence in Paris. It's Elizabeth you have to thank, you know, for all of this. She was responsible for that letter. I'm sure of it. It's been her doing from the start – one of her stratagems.'

Clem coughed on his cigarette; he shook his head. 'Impossible. No Han, you're wrong there. I saw it arrive. I saw her open it. Elizabeth is no actress. We were at breakfast – she was so startled she dropped the bloody teapot. Leaves everywhere.' He took another drag, the ember glowing in the murky chamber. 'You've no proof, I suppose?'

Hannah admitted that she did not. 'She knows a great deal about my life, Clem. Things she shouldn't. As if she's been studying me.'

'Yes, well, that's just Elizabeth, isn't it? It pains me to say so, Han, but you're being unfair. That letter came from someone in Paris. In Montmartre, like you originally thought.'

Hannah saw that he was right; this intensified her annoyance. 'Do you know *who*, by any chance?'

Before Clem could answer those around them began to step aside. Jean-Jacques had noticed the twins from the conference table and come over, that famous black coat quickly clearing a path through the militia. Hannah's irritation lifted, dispersing in the smoke. He embraced her and laid his forehead briefly against hers. Never had he done such a thing in public; our situation, she thought, must be serious indeed. His skin was cool despite the room's choking heat, a single bead of sweat rolling down the channel of his scar. He gave Clem a fleeting look of distaste – the kind you might direct towards a drunk who'd strayed into a library.

'This is no place for you,' he said. 'Either of you.'

'What's happening?' Hannah asked. 'Is there really to be a commune?'

'There has been some overstatement. We are negotiating. We want municipal elections, which will surely lead to a commune.' Jean-Jacques glanced at the window and the ranks of loyalist militia outside; they'd come to a halt and were standing ready, waiting for an order. 'I don't like this, though. They're trying to hold us here. Something is wrong.'

Hannah straightened her tunic, squeezing the material to stop herself trembling. 'They're going to retake the building.'

'You must leave. There will be arrests. If you are caught, as a foreigner, you'll be accused of spying.'

'I want to stay,' Hannah protested. 'I'll fight them if I must. I want—' *I want to stay with you.*

'They'll put you before a firing squad.' Jean-Jacques touched her cheek with his good hand; his eyes were black in the gloom. 'I could not forgive myself if you were to be hurt because of this.'

'I don't—'

'I can take you as far as the square outside. Go somewhere they would not think to look. Stay hidden for a few days.'

Hannah managed a nod. 'Very well. A few days.'

'What now?' asked Clem; his dalliance with Laure Fleurot had plainly not improved his French. 'What are we to do?'

'Your wish has been granted,' Hannah told him curtly. 'We're leaving.'

Jean-Jacques led them back to the summit of the grand staircase. The revolutionary clamour of earlier had subsided, the central courtyard taking on the character of a rowdy tavern, with laughter, songs and drinking. They were halfway down, crossing the landing, when the jollity around them was suddenly disturbed. There were shouts of alarm; the sound of doors being flung open; the thunder of boots somewhere below, in the base of the building. Jean-Jacques increased his pace, moving onto the courtyard floor.

'This is it,' he declared to everyone around him. 'They are coming for us. It is time for us to show these bourgeois that we are the true men of Paris.'

Regular infantry began to appear from behind the staircase, red and white stripes emblazoned upon their dark blue tunics, beating people back with their rifles. The crowd dissolved at once, civilian and militiaman alike flying in every direction.

Jean-Jacques did his best to rally them, pointing at the staircase. 'To the top of the stairs!' he cried. 'Form a line, like you've been taught! Ready yourselves!'

Some of the red guardsmen obeyed, loping past Hannah and Clement, fumbling with their guns. 'They're coming in through a damned tunnel,' one of them yelled, 'a tunnel in the cellars! There's hundreds of the bastards!'

More and more soldiers were entering the courtyard, like

a torrent of seawater flooding the hold of a sinking ship. Jean-Jacques got the Pardy twins to the double doors and then leaned in to kiss Hannah farewell; it was quick, three seconds only, but she felt it throughout her body, in every pore and strand of hair, down to the soles of her feet. By the time she'd opened her eyes again he was already striding back towards the stairs. The two sides were mounting up, the reds and the regulars, massing in formless gangs at either end of the grand staircase. Insults filled the air. Cartridges were loaded into rifles; stocks fitted into shoulders. In the middle stood Jean-Jacques and a civic official of some kind, both of them unflinching and stern, commencing a heated altercation. Hannah watched from the doors, faint with dread. You are about to see him die, she thought, and there is nothing you can do to prevent it. For ten seconds nothing happened, besides more shouting; then twenty; then a full half-minute.

'Time to go, Han,' said Clem at her elbow, his voice quavering. 'Now or bloody never.'

Hannah turned away sharply and hastened from the Hôtel. Out in the evening she waited to hear the fusillade – the cascade of gunshots that would signal her lover's demise. Still nothing came. The loyalist National Guard had received their order and were slowly closing in. She went left, towards the river, her brother close behind.

A squad peeled off to apprehend them. 'Stop!' cried their sergeant. 'Stop there!'

'They think I'm one of you,' said Clem. 'They think I'm a bloody red!'

'That's a risk you run, Clement,' Hannah snapped, 'when you attend a socialist demonstration in working man's clothes.'

Their hurried walk became a sprint, across the quay and onto the Pont d'Arcole. Hannah heard a huff and a scraping thud: Clem had stumbled, falling sprawled out across the pavement. She shouted his name with a mixture of dismay and frustration. Three loyalist guardsmen were on him, kicking eagerly. Dashing back, she pushed one of his attackers into the gutter and took a determined swing at another, her fist connecting with the man's ear.

'Red bitch!' he grunted, his arm flailing. 'You'll get yours!'

A second squad arrived from the square, joining the man she'd struck as he advanced on her. The ultras liked to say that the militia from other districts were nothing but soft bourgeois – fat, cowardly shopkeepers waiting out the war, full of brave utterances but secretly very pleased with the provisional government's passive stance. These men, however, were not at all soft or fat: they looked more like railway workers or market-porters, definitely not to be trifled with. Poor Clem was lying there like an empty coal sack. If Hannah stayed she'd be beaten or worse. They'd arrest her; they'd try to execute her. Her nerve failed. She started running again.

The life of a *plein-air* painter – carrying easels up hills and across large sections of the city – had made Hannah strong and fast. The guardsmen couldn't catch her; she was even extending her lead as she reached the Ile de la Cité. This island, Jean-Jacques had once said, was the oldest part of Paris, the bud from which the rest had flowered. In recent years Louis Napoleon's planners had razed its winding medieval streets, setting down an ordered grid in their place, as they had done to so much of the city; the cathedral of Notre-Dame, its jagged profile jutting up ahead, was almost all that remained. Hannah headed for the nearest building – the Hôtel Dieu. Four storeys high and plain, there was a bright light on its river-facing side that threw a deep shadow over the rest. She slipped around a corner into absolute darkness. Her pursuers, losing sight of her, soon turned back.

She leaned against a wall and put her face in her hands. Everything was in ruins. The red coup had been a disaster. What was going to happen to Jean-Jacques now – to her brother? Where could she possibly go where the provisional government's men wouldn't find her?

What was she going to do?

The door opened inwards, pressing Hannah against a framed print of a famous locomotive. Monsieur Besson walked through, reading that morning's copy of the *Gazette Officielle*. The *aérostier* noticed her at once; the room, tucked beneath a girder at the top of the Gare du Nord, was so tiny that he could hardly do otherwise. He stood still for a few moments, the folded newspaper lowering slowly in his hand. Like many men in Paris he had put away his razor, allowing a thin dark beard to form around his moustache. He tossed the *Gazette* onto his cluttered desk and removed his hat. Hannah noticed that he was only an inch or two taller than she was.

'The riot,' he said. 'The occupation of the Hôtel de Ville. You were involved. They're after you.'

'It was not a *riot*, Monsieur. We had to act before the new Prussian army arrives from Metz. We—' Hannah stopped herself. This was not the way to secure the *aérostier*'s help. 'I apologise for creeping in like this.'

'How did you do it, exactly?'

'I forced the window of the lost property office and found my way up.' She paused. 'Your name is chalked on the door.'

'You're quite the housebreaker, Mademoiselle Pardy, I must say.'

'I need to hide. I can't go home, or to my mother. I thought of you – of this place. Nobody knows that we are acquainted.'

Monsieur Besson closed the door behind him, hanging his hat on a peg. 'We are acquainted, Mademoiselle?'

'We've spoken a couple of times. In the lanes, back in Montmartre. And I've seen you at the launches of your balloons.'

He didn't react. The devotion to Hannah identified by Jean-Jacques was nowhere to be seen. Right then, in fact, it seemed entirely possible that he might eject her – even alert the authorities.

'You came to the Club Rue Rébeval that night.'

'I remember. I still have bruises.'

Hannah's cautious smile disappeared. 'I halted it as soon as I could. Please believe me, Monsieur. If I—'

'Do you imagine that I went to that meeting for you?'

This question was a touch too abrupt. There is Monsieur Besson's love for me, Hannah thought: an awkward, burdensome thing that keeps starting into view despite his best efforts to hide it. He'd obviously been worrying that he'd revealed himself with his foolhardy behaviour in Belleville. A pained look crossed his face; he knew that he'd just made it worse.

'The notion never entered my mind,' she said.

The *aérostier* went to the office's single, rounded window, staring out at the early morning sky. 'I was there, Mademoiselle, to hear what the radicals were debating. To get an idea of their intentions. I was curious.'

'Yet you did not simply listen, Monsieur Besson, did you? You made a rather prominent contribution.'

He bowed his head, bringing it close to the glass. 'I didn't plan to do that. My anger got the better of me. I couldn't stand in that hall and be accused of spying. Those people speak of Paris as if everyone within the wall was a socialist. As if—'

Monsieur Besson was growing angry again now. Hannah

had wanted to ask him about what had happened afterwards, what he'd said to her in that alley, but decided to return the conversation to more immediate matters. 'They arrested my brother last night,' she interrupted. 'He was caught on the Pont d'Arcole, just outside the Hôtel de Ville.'

The *aérostier* was taken aback; some sort of attachment had plainly formed between him and Clement over the past six weeks. 'But he is no *radical*. He has no political sense at all that I have seen. How on earth could this have happened?'

'An accident, of course – a mistake. Typical of Clem. Something to do with that damned cocotte.' Hannah drew in a breath. 'It's being said that any foreigners apprehended by the government are to be shot.'

'Dear God.' Monsieur Besson ran a hand through his thick, short hair. 'You must not worry about this,' he said, trying to be reassuring. 'There is much talk of shooting, of summary executions for minor crimes. It is heavily exaggerated. When this war finally ends we will no doubt discover that very few were actually put to death – that hardly any of the grand, bloody deeds laid claim to by the men of Paris were actually performed.'

There was a veiled reference here; Hannah regarded Monsieur Besson tentatively as he gestured for her to sit at his desk. He turned to his small fireplace, crouching down to scrabble beneath the grate, picking out crumbs of unburned coal and arranging them in a pyramid. This modest pile was supplemented with just two fresh lumps from the scuttle. The *aérostier* was rationing himself. Fuel was set to become scarce – which could lead to a terrible crisis indeed if the coming winter was as harsh as predicted. He twisted a piece of blotting paper, pushed it into the pyramid and lit it with a match. The glow of the fire spread over him, over the green rug beneath his knees, colouring the chilly, monochrome office.

Monsieur Besson rose from the hearth, edged around to the other side of the desk and opened a large entry book. 'Are you quite sure that no one saw you come in?'

Hannah nodded; he was going to let her stay, for Clem's sake if nothing else. 'The street was quiet.'

'Then tell me, Mademoiselle Pardy,' he asked next, sliding a pen from between two piles of papers, 'can you work a sewing machine?'

Monsieur Besson, it turned out, had his contacts; by the end of the day he'd learned that Clement was being held in the infamous Mazas prison in the 12th arrondissement, a short distance upriver from the Hôtel de Ville. Reliable information was hard to come by, but it didn't seem that he was in any immediate danger of execution. Furthermore, the stand-off on the grand staircase had somehow been resolved without bloodshed. The subsequent negotiations between the provisional government and the rebels had carried on until the early hours of the morning. All hostages had been released, and Flourens's declaration of a commune retracted, on the understanding that elections would be held within a week – and no reprisals would be made. After the pandemonium of the day everyone simply went their separate ways.

This news left Hannah dazed with relief. 'I can go, then,' she said. 'I don't need to hide.'

Monsieur Besson begged to differ. 'There are men in the government who won't accept these terms, and the lack of arrests in particular. Edmond Adam, who brokered the truce with Blanqui and Delescluze, resigned this afternoon as the chief of police. Nobody knows why. His replacement, though, is a Monsieur Cresson, who is said to lack Adam's conciliatory attitude. I would advise you to stay out of sight a while longer.'

Reluctantly, Hannah admitted the sense of this and agreed to remain for a few more days. They established a routine, fitted around that of the balloon factory. A bed was made beneath his desk from coats brought up from the lost property office that had first granted her access to the station. Besson would come in with a lantern at around half-past five, bringing her food for the day – rice, cabbage, coarse brown bread, sometimes a few scraps of boiled meat. She'd change into the work gown he'd found her while he waited outside; he'd unlock the station bathrooms for her to use; then they'd go down together through the empty tiled stairwells to the concourse.

The lampposts were dark, the ticket barriers gone and the tracks beyond obscured by swathes of calico that hung from the rafters like waterfalls of hardened wax. The two of them would head across the weaving area, between rolls of netting and the wild stalks of half-spun baskets, to the sewing benches that lined the far wall. Hannah would take her place at one of these, Besson walking off to begin his endless round of checks and inspections. It was carefully timed; within five minutes the other workers would start to arrive, the seamstresses, sailors and other *aérostiers*, complaining about the cold and swapping the latest rumours. For the next twelve hours or so – with a half-hour for lunch – she would do her part in fashioning the balloon envelopes, stitching and double-stitching under the direction of Madame Vuillard, the overseer.

There was an unexpected peace in this noisy, repetitive labour. Hannah's thoughts would wander far into the past, to places and people she hadn't seen for a decade or more. In particular, she found herself returning to a train journey she'd once made with her father – to Guildford or Reading or somewhere like that, where he was due to give a lecture on his poems – when she'd been eight years old. As she worked her machine's foot-pedal, running cloth beneath the stuttering needle, she recalled the way the countryside had unfolded around them; and the great wash of contentment she'd felt as he'd taken hold of her hand.

The other women on the sewing benches were told that Hannah's name was Jane Ashford and that she was the daughter of a coachman employed at the British embassy, but they clearly had their suspicions. It was not lost on them that this *Anglaise* had appeared the morning after that business at the Hôtel de Ville. Wages in the balloon factory were good, though, and had never been needed more; Émile Besson's standing there was strong; and Nadar, who wielded ultimate authority, was said to be a communist sympathiser who'd once had Félix Pyat over for supper. The seamstresses decided that he must be in on it, whatever it was, and that they'd better stay quiet. They kept Hannah at a distance, eyeing her warily, making their excuses if she ever tried to strike up a conversation – leaving her well alone.

Monsieur Besson himself behaved with perfect honour. Hannah hadn't known quite what to expect from the *aérostier*, but he never so much as hinted at the precariousness of her situation, or her dependence upon his goodwill. There were no lunges for a kiss; no lingering sadly in doorways; no excruciating attempts to enquire whether romance between them was truly beyond hope. His conduct was so restrained, in fact, that it made her wonder if she'd been mistaken. Perhaps this man was not so smitten by her after all.

Each morning, along with her food, her host would hand her a small sheaf of newspapers. It was in his office, therefore, only two days after the occupation of the Hôtel de Ville, that she learned of the arrest of several dozen prominent reds and the dismissal of sixteen battalion commanders of the National Guard for their radical activities.

Monsieur Besson had been right. This was a barefaced betrayal, showing total contempt for those betrayed. Hannah's sole consolation was that Jean-Jacques hadn't been among those taken. Along with Flourens, he'd escaped Cresson's policemen, disappearing, the moderate papers claimed, into the lawless ultra underground that spread across the northern arrondissements.

Then came the miserable sham of the elections. Rather than a proper municipal vote that could deliver a commune, the city was granted a plebiscite. They were asked merely to answer the question: *Do you support the continuance of the authority of the provisional government?* A 'yes' was widely viewed as a vote against unrest and disorder, against the red insurgency – and a vote for peace, as a story was going around that negotiations were again underway with the Prussians. Hungry bourgeois longing for normality turned up at the ballots in droves, whilst left-leaning Paris stayed away in protest. Trochu's government won by a staggering majority; Jules Favre made a public declaration that this meant the negation of the commune.

After reading this Hannah stood up at Besson's desk and threw her newspaper at the wall. In the Gare du Nord, however, her fury could not be bolstered or magnified by that of like-minded comrades; it felt disconnected, uprooted somehow, and soon subsided into brooding. No one here cared. They were concerned instead with the confirmation that armistice talks had indeed been conducted with Chancellor Bismarck – and had already collapsed for a second time. The siege was to grind on. This brought dejection to the sewing benches; the women employed there, like so many in the central districts of Paris, were ready to give up.

Hannah grew convinced that Jean-Jacques must be trying to find her – to get word to her about what was to happen next. She took to sitting at the office window long into the night, watching for a signal or a figure on the tracks below. There was a store of candles and matches in the desk, meaning she could read or draw after dark. She'd get out her sketching materials, thinking to ease her tormenting sense of impotence with work, but more often than not she'd just stare at the studies she'd made of her lover in the last days before the march on the Hôtel de Ville, in preparation for Elizabeth's portrait. There was Jean-Jacques seated with his arms crossed; leaning forward, reading a pamphlet; standing with his head lifted, as if about to speak.

Having had the task forced upon her, Hannah was now determined to make this portrait the best thing she'd ever done. She wanted to shame Elizabeth – to have her admit how wrong she'd been to treat her daughter like a ten-a-penny illustrator. She could picture the end result very clearly: a half-length likeness on a five-foot canvas, an interior in natural light that would present Jean-Jacques in such a way that no one who saw it could possibly doubt his conviction or his visionary intelligence. This was rather more ambitious than any of her previous portraits. The prospect was daunting, and a part of her was relieved that circumstances had denied her the means to begin.

Hannah usually had no difficulty with solitude; before Jean-Jacques, she'd painted alone in Madame Lantier's shed for days on end. Here in the balloon factory, however, she found that she had a keen desire for company. She began to look forward to the short conversations she had with Monsieur Besson as they paced through the station corridors or tried to warm themselves by his meagre fire. At first he simply updated her about Clement – who was well, as far as he could ascertain; safe from firing squads, at any rate.

'Elizabeth will be attending to this,' Hannah said, to convince herself as much as Besson. 'She won't let them keep him locked up in there.'

200

Gradually, though, they moved onto other topics. Hannah discovered that the *aérostier* possessed a sceptical wit; she came to enjoy dispelling his habitual terseness and drawing it out. Judging her work to be an uncontroversial area, she showed him the couple of sketches she'd managed to set down since her arrival – views from the office window, depicting the twelve sets of empty rails running into the station and the tall weeds growing around them.

'I depict what I see, Monsieur,' Hannah explained, 'what is before me, shorn of contrivance. We naturalist painters want to bring about an age of *freedom*, in which a sincere art can be nourished – a true art. No more nonsense from the Bible, or Ovid, or French history, or anywhere else. Nature without invention or manipulation is the goal – thrown raw upon the canvas.'

'So it is a scientific approach, in essence,' Besson said. 'You make yourself like a photographic plate, devoid of preconception, merely setting yourself before your image – awaiting the impression the light will make upon you.'

Hannah conceded that there might be something in this, but her brow was furrowed; she'd always considered photographs to be dull, mechanical things, lacking any real creative power. She decided to steer them away from artistic theory from then on.

They spoke of their lives. Besson made his revelations in plain, compact sentences; this was not a man comfortable with talking about himself. Hannah learned that he'd been born in the Marais, the son of a cabinet-maker, and had trained as an engineer in the Imperial schools before devoting himself to aeronautics. During the Exposition Universelle of 1867 he'd worked as a pilot for the gigantic balloon *Captive*, taking visitors up fifteen times the height of the exhibition hall, over the green and golden sprawl of Napoleon III's Paris. Strangely enough, on one ascent he had stood but four feet from Crown-Prince Frederick of Prussia – who now directed the besieging armies from a state room at Versailles.

'Several among his party were terrified, but the Crown prince surveyed the city without a tremor.' Besson shook his head. 'Many times since have I wondered what he was thinking.'

In return, Hannah told him about her last years in London – about her mother's attempts to direct her life, to interfere at every stage and in every area. Hannah wanted to paint; so Elizabeth immediately produced these artist friends of hers, stolid old Royal Academicians stuck firmly in the thirties and forties, to whom she could be apprenticed. She'd barely turned fourteen when various eccentric gentlemen – poets, musicians, radical philosophers – began to call at the Pardy home for no obvious reason. She came to realise that these were suitors, of a sort, candidates for the first of her public affairs; a vital component, apparently, of a Pardy woman's renown.

Besson gave her his uneven smile. 'So instead you choose to live in Montmartre – in a shed, your brother tells me.'

'I do,' Hannah answered proudly. 'Every year I submit my work to the Salon, and every year I am rejected. I live on vermicelli and day-old bread. I fail, Monsieur Besson, but on my own terms. I wouldn't go back to England for anything.'

Their connection could only ever be a fragile one, though, no matter how many private recollections they shared. Both of them felt it: a great subject sat unmentioned between them. Hannah was careful to conceal her sketches of Jean-Jacques when Besson was in the office, but she knew that he couldn't stay hidden for long.

*　　*　　*

202

One painfully cold morning, almost three weeks after Hannah first sought refuge at the station, Besson strode straight into the office without his customary knock. He dumped the day's newspapers on the desk and went to the window. At the top of the pile was the *Figaro*. Emblazoned across its front page was the headline *Le Léopard Est En Retour*. Hannah sat down; she glanced at Besson's back and read on.

'This true hero of Paris is once again spilling the blood of the enemy that so cruelly confines her. This newspaper can reveal that only last night he was out stalking his prey in the forest of Bondy – snaking between the trees, eyes fixed on the lights of a Prussian outpost glimmering up ahead. Gunpowder is tipped from a cartridge at the base of an oak; a match is touched to it and it fizzes furiously, sending a white flash across the canopy of branches above. The sentries are sent out to investigate. Our Leopard strikes with all the grace and savagery that Paris has come to expect. It is knife-work, requiring an expert hand; and the second man dies before the first has fully collapsed among the fallen leaves. The unlucky third has seen nothing, but he senses that danger is near; the trees around him seem to be moving, closing in around him. He offers a last prayer to his German God, firming up his grip on his rifle, and he advances to his end. Later, the Leopard slinks back to Aubervilliers, and then to the wall, seen by no one, three brass helmets stowed in his haversack.'

There was more, several paragraphs in fact. The only reference to the recent red ructions and the role the Leopard might have played in them was Jean-Jacques's drop from 'Major Allix' to a mere 'Monsieur'; he'd evidently been stripped of his rank along with so many of his Montmartre comrades. Numerous allusions were made to a sortie, Elizabeth stressing that it was the patriotic duty of all Frenchmen to follow the Leopard's bold example. Prussian morale, she claimed, was desperately low due to the coming winter and their fear of Parisian might. There was no better time to strike.

'*The invaders are like beaters standing fearfully around a thicket heaving with wild beasts,*' the article concluded, '*of which our Leopard is just one. They know that at any second thousands of ferocious fighters could pour out through those gates, their bloodlust sharpened by their deep and abiding love for their land. They know, in short, that they would be massacred – lashed back to Prussia with their brave Kaiser leading the retreat!*'

'It's going to happen,' said Besson. 'There will be a sortie now. You reds made Trochu look weak, holding him hostage for half a day in his own inner chamber. Our hesitant general has been embarrassed into action. Gambetta has managed to assemble an army, out in the countryside somewhere to the south-east, and is reputed to be doing great things. Trochu imagines that a coordinated action is possible – that the forces of Paris will be able to break through the Prussian line and link up with this other army.'

'You *know this*, Monsieur?'

'Men close to the cabinet have all but confirmed it.'

The *Figaro* was shivering in Hannah's hands. One of their aims, at least, would be met. 'It will turn the war,' she said. 'It will give us our chance.'

'You cannot think that.' Besson looked over at her. 'Mademoiselle Pardy, you are a clever woman. You cannot honestly think that a sortie is the best course.'

Hannah put down the newspaper, stung by the trace of condescension in his manner. 'What would *you* do, then?'

'Surrender,' the *aérostier* replied, 'at once, on any terms. They have won. We are beaten. Can you really not see it? All a sortie will achieve is more dead men. If the government and the generals honestly think that the Prussians won't work out this plan of theirs – won't see it coming a hundred miles away – then they are fools who deserve their doom. The tragedy is that so many will be made to follow them.'

Disagreement surged through Hannah so strongly that it propelled her from her chair. 'A sortie can succeed, of course it can!' she cried. 'There are millions of us, far more than there are of the Prussians. How can it possibly fail?'

'It is *too late*. Our enemy is dug in. They have been adding to their forces for two months now. Perfecting their strategies. How many sieges have they won so far, in this poisonous, pointless war? Three, four? And they have the men from Metz, don't forget – two hundred thousand experienced troops.'

They faced each other over the desk. Hannah knew then that it would be bad – a collision between immoveable objects.

'You talk like a bourgeois defeatist,' she told him. 'A man who just wants to get back to his damned shop.'

'Perhaps I am. What is so wrong with that? And why do you care so much, anyway? You are *English*. Why have you adopted the cause of France with such passion?'

'Christ Almighty, I am so very tired of hearing that! The question, Monsieur Besson, is why *you* have abandoned it!'

Besson stopped for a second; this had struck home. 'Life would be hard for a while if we surrendered,' he admitted, 'and our pride would suffer a grave blow. But we would go on. We would rebuild.' He nodded at her drawing folder. 'You could resume your work – properly, I mean, without all this distraction.'

Hannah glared at him. He doesn't believe that I mean any of it, she thought; he thinks that my politics are an affectation that I will shrug off, as one might an obsessive interest in Italian opera or the modern novel. 'You underestimate the people of Paris. You don't realise what they are capable of.'

'I am a *Parisian*, Mademoiselle Pardy, and I realise it very well. It is one thing to proclaim a wish to die for your country – and quite another to actually risk doing it. Your Leopard should know all about that.'

Silence filled the tiny office, like that which follows the smashing of something valuable. Hannah blinked. 'What – what do you mean?'

The *aérostier* appeared momentarily regretful, as if impatience had led him to speak out of turn; then he pressed on. 'These heroics – this prodigious murder of Prussians. Does it not seem improbable to you?'

Hannah controlled her anger; she wanted to hear what he had to say. 'Elizabeth dramatises,' she replied. 'She exaggerates. That is her style. The Prussians are definitely dying, though, if that's what you are implying. Jean-Jacques brings back the helmets of the men he has killed – and their weapons, letters, anything he can carry. I've seen them.'

This did not persuade him. He crossed to the mantelpiece; then he was at the desk again, trying to frame a difficult question, unable to phrase it to his satisfaction. Hannah remembered the alley outside the Club Rue Rébeval – what he'd whispered when she went to assist him.

'Do you still think I should leave Paris?'

Besson misunderstood her; he paled a little. 'You have been talking to your brother,' he said. 'I did not write that letter. I would never do such a thing.'

So this was Clem's Montmartre suspect. It certainly made sense. The *aérostier* was resourceful enough, and headstrong as well – utterly set on doing what he thought was right. Five minutes previously Hannah would have been convinced by his denial. Now she wasn't so sure.

'What on earth do you think Jean-Jacques is up to, Monsieur Besson?'

The only reply he'd give her was another question. 'Have you ever wondered exactly how well you know him – this man on whom you have staked your entire existence?'

206

'How well I *know* him?'

'I am an *aérostier*, Mademoiselle Pardy. I design and fly balloons. You draw and paint – your work, even the quickest sketch, shows a lifetime's training. These are facts about us. What facts are there about your Monsieur Allix?'

'He is from Alsace,' Hannah answered, as if talking to an idiot, 'a village near Strasbourg. He fought in America, and was injured there. He killed many Prussians in the Vosges Mountains and now he has come to defend Paris – to help lead her people to freedom.'

Besson's expression hardened. 'That is his account, Mademoiselle. There's no evidence to support it. I grant you that he seems to be a soldier of some kind, but have you ever met anyone who served with him? Any old friends from before the war – any family?'

Hannah could think of no one. 'Many revolutionaries are like this,' she said. 'They move constantly from place to place. It is how they must live in order to spread their ideas and avoid imprisonment. They deliberately sever their attachments to the ordinary world.'

The *aérostier* leaned forward, his blue eyes looking intently into hers. 'Then why,' he asked, 'has Allix attached himself to you?'

Hannah balked; she felt sick, hollowed out, giddy with rage. She edged around the desk, knocking against a stack of ledgers. 'Now we get to it, Monsieur Besson, don't we!' she shouted. 'You are *jealous*, here in your cupboard of an office, surrounded by your plans, with seamstresses who laugh at you behind your back and call you names, and balloons that vanish into the clouds never to be heard from again!'

Besson stepped from her path. There was resignation on his face; he'd known it would come to this. 'That is not true. I wanted to—'

'I thought you were a friend. I was wrong. A friend would

207

never say these things – would never even *think* them.'
Hannah set about gathering her things. It didn't take long.
'What am I even doing here?' she asked herself, snatching
up her *vivandière*'s uniform from beneath the desk. 'They'll
hardly be looking for me now, after all this time. You've
kept me with you, haven't you Monsieur Besson, on false
pretences. You've been biding your time, weaselling your
way into my confidence, waiting to deliver this speech about
Jean-Jacques – a more decent and brave and principled man
than you could ever hope to be!'

Besson's voice was quiet. 'Mademoiselle—'

Hannah threw open the office door. 'I have to find him,'
she said. 'I have work to do.'

PART THREE

Wolf Steak at the Paris Grand

I

Clem studied his hands, rotating them slowly. They were trembling so much that they seemed almost to blur. Half an hour's scrubbing with the Grand's carbolic soap had failed to shift the dirt; it was ingrained in the skin. There was an ugly line between the thumb and forefinger of the left one that he could swear hadn't been there a month earlier. The nails were all gnawed down to raw stubs. He plucked the linen napkin from his shirt, brought it below the level of the table and twisted it as tightly as he could.

Montague Inglis sat next to him, chewing thoughtfully, his head angled towards the gilded ceiling of the hotel dining room. Clem had been surprised to find Inglis at the Grand when he returned; and more so when he stayed to dine with them. There was something different about both the conduct and the demeanour of the *Sentinel*'s Paris correspondent. His beard had been left wild, never recovering its courtier's precision, and he was thinner too, of course – everyone was thinner – but it ran deeper than this. The rivalry had receded; that ancient row with Elizabeth, whatever it was, had been laid to rest. He was more a familiar now than a competitor. Then, as they'd taken their seats in the empty room and Elizabeth had asked about the day's special dish, Clem had spotted a complacent look passing between them. Oh Christ, he'd thought, not that. Anything but that.

'So this is *canis lupus*,' declared the newspaperman. 'Mother of Rome, slavering nemesis of countless bedtime stories, reduced to the status of luncheon.' He regarded his plate without enthusiasm. 'Rather horrible, ain't it?'

Clem studied his own portion: a steak the colour of damp rosewood, withered coins of carrot, nubs of potato in a thin white sauce. It wasn't very enticing, even for a man just out of prison.

'There is not much to be said, certainly,' Elizabeth observed, 'for the tenderness of wolf.'

His mother was opposite him in a new dress, a practical but fetching chocolate-coloured gown. She looked poised, redoubtable – honed by the siege and the role she'd taken in it. A notebook was open on the table beside her; she was writing as she ate. Along with her unsparing exposure of frippery, corruption and cant, and her unconventional mode of living, Mrs Elizabeth Pardy had been famous for her iron constitution. It was like that of a wild boar, they'd said, a hippopotamus made from stone; the reading public had delighted in the contrast with her elegant appearance. When on her adventures of yore, she'd been able to digest the most dubious of local delicacies – to thrive on them, even. Details of her gastronomic experiences had been a much-loved element of her books. It was obvious that siege cuisine was to have its place in the current one.

'A step too far down the carnivorous path, perhaps,' Inglis continued. 'It is no accident, Lizzie, that the more appetizing beasts are those whose natural diet most resembles that of standard livestock.'

Clem winced at that *Lizzie*. Its meaning was unmistakable.

'We covered the equines long ago, Clement,' Elizabeth explained, without looking up from her notebook, 'and the domestic pets. We have had our share, also, of rat and mouse.'

'Oh, one must try rat,' interjected Inglis. 'One cannot say one has truly been besieged otherwise. And it ain't nearly so bad as you'd think, once chef has chopped it into a nice *salmis*.'

'Within the past fortnight, however, the Jardin des Plantes has opened up its zoological department to the butchers of the Faubourg Saint-Honoré. Many intriguing morsels have become available. What have we had so far, Mont? Bear, reindeer, dromedary . . .'

'All of which were superior to the poor wolf – vastly so. And everything I've tasted pales beside kangaroo. I dined on a length of tail, don't y'know, at Brebant's the other night. Dashed expensive – something like eight shillings a pound – but I have to say that it was the very best game I've ever eaten.' Inglis paused, a smirk tugging somewhere beneath his beard. 'Strange, though we ate a good deal of it, none of us felt at all – ahem! – *jumpy* afterwards.'

The newspaperman laughed loudly, glancing at Elizabeth; this joke had plainly been one of the evening's gems. She granted him a measured smile.

'I've been among National Guard for the past several weeks,' Clem said. 'I didn't see any of them sampling such exotic fare.'

'Well no, boy,' chuckled Inglis. 'Highly unlikely that the blighters can afford it. They'll be sticking to their horse, I should think.'

Elizabeth caught the meaning behind her son's comment. They had yet to speak of what had befallen him on the day of the red revolt, and his ensuing absence. Meeting upstairs in the corridor outside her suite, she'd merely asked if he

213

was well – and then instructed him to bathe and shave before luncheon.

'You blame me for your incarceration,' she said matter-of-factly, setting down both fork and pencil; Mrs Pardy did not beat around the bush. 'Need I remind you that we were deliberately waiting by the Tour Saint-Jacques. We were maintaining what my military friends refer to as a *safe distance*. It was entirely your choice to scamper off after your harlot.'

Inglis tilted in towards him. 'I might well have done the same, in your shoes,' he murmured. 'A true nymph of the *pavé*, that one. Why, before I—'

Elizabeth silenced the journalist without moving, speaking or even looking in his direction. 'You knew that a riot was possible, Clement, and you went on regardless. You cannot hold me responsible for the loyalist militia placing you under arrest.'

Clem had rehearsed many cutting lines in the Mazas, enough for an entire stage-play of recrimination and wrath, but right then he couldn't remember any of them. Setting down his twisted napkin, he readied himself to speak as best he could. 'Elizabeth, I was in there for nearly four weeks. You didn't visit. You didn't enquire after me.' A fat tear popped into his eye, wobbling at the edge of his sight. 'You didn't try to – to get me out.'

They'd put him in a cell on his own, a deathly cold box with an unglazed window that showed only a square foot of sky. He'd been fed weak broth and bread that appeared to have been made from straw. Twice in the first few days a pair of National Guard officers had come in and told him he was to die – forcing him to kneel and pointing revolvers at his head, laughing as he begged for mercy. Everyone he'd encountered claimed not to understand English, refusing to listen to his explanations for his presence in the Hôtel de

214

Ville that day, or his pleas for word to be sent to his mother. Eventually he'd just been released, turned loose carelessly, nobody bothering to tell him why.

Elizabeth's one chance had been that she didn't know where he was – that she'd been hunting for him across the city, her book and her Leopard forgotten. This clearly hadn't been the case. It was futile to try to make her feel guilt or shame, however, or to extract any form of apology. There was a silence. Clem wiped his eyes on his cuff. He picked up his knife and fork; his hands were behaving themselves, so he sliced off some of his steak and put it in his mouth.

'I knew that they would not dare to shoot you, Clement,' Elizabeth told him, a single atom of conciliation in her tone, 'and that they could not reasonably hold you for more than a few weeks.' She looked at her notebook, rereading the last few lines, reaching for her pencil to cross out a word and write its replacement in the margin. 'To be quite honest, I felt that a spell in gaol might be just punishment for your idiocy.'

Clem almost choked on his wolf. Inglis was right; it was revolting, pungent and stringy. He spat it into his napkin. *'Just punishment?'*

'You are back now, though,' Elizabeth went on, ignoring him, 'in the shelter of the Grand, and I suggest you stay here. Things are about to heat up. Our lily-livered General Trochu finally appears to be steeling himself for serious action. The Leopard's example is being heeded at last. My reports are having their intended effect.'

Sheer astonishment overwhelmed Clem's anger. 'How the devil did he get away? It's – that's—' He struggled to imagine it. 'The last time I saw him he was before the government's soldiers. Between two great mobs of armed men. How did he escape arrest – or injury, for that matter?'

Elizabeth raised her eyebrows, as if to say *well, that's just the kind of fellow he is*. 'Monsieur Allix slipped the clutches of the government and went into hiding. He continues his raids on the Prussian positions, providing invaluable scouting information as well as eroding enemy morale. And then he comes to see me, in my sitting room upstairs, to give me what I need for the *Figaro*.'

Clem felt as if he'd been pummelled about the head. 'What happened to Han?' he asked faintly. 'We got split up when I was—' He glimpsed the stamping boots and grimacing faces, and tasted the blood in his mouth. 'When I was detained.'

'She's quite safe,' said Elizabeth. 'In hiding. Not with Monsieur Allix, but he knows where she is. The reds went too far that night. He acknowledges this. They allowed themselves to be carried forward by their less rational members. I am assured that the politicking will be played down for a while. There will be no more revolts, but the ultras cannot recognise the plebiscite. Their view is that there can be no fair elections in a city under attack by a ruthless foreign enemy. They are focused upon the sortie – which was one of their central demands, after all. They intend to show bourgeois Paris what her working people can do. What they are owed by their fellow citizens.'

Inglis restricted himself to a single cynical grunt.

'Troops are being moved around the city,' Elizabeth enlarged, 'from north to south. The National Guard is being asked for active volunteers – men who will serve outside the wall, who will fight rather than merely stand upon a rampart.'

'Needless to say,' Inglis added, 'very few of those noble warriors have availed themselves of the opportunity as yet.'

Elizabeth pretended not to hear him. 'But you mustn't concern yourself with any of this, Clement. You're not suited to it – that has been demonstrated conclusively. You'll be safe enough here in the Grand, helping the orderlies or something similar, provided the blood doesn't prove too much for you. There shouldn't be more than a week left in this siege now.'

'Good heavens, old chap,' grinned Inglis, leaning in again, 'I do believe that she's confining you to quarters.'

Clem knocked over his chair as he stood. He decided that he would shout; it came out like the yelp of a petulant adolescent. 'You can stuff the Grand, *Mother*. You can stuff my room. You can stuff your wolf steaks. And you can stuff your bloody Leopard.'

Inglis failed to smother his laugh. 'Stuff your leopard! Oh my word!'

Elizabeth stared at her son. She was not visibly cross, but her voice was at its very firmest. 'Sit down.'

'No. Not this time. I will not.'

Clem strode from the table, his fury driving him through the makeshift hospital in the lobby and onto the boulevard des Italiens. Elizabeth didn't believe he was serious; she seldom did. She considered him utterly ineffectual. He began recounting everything he should have said to her in a low mutter, resentment prickling against his skin like new tweed. The stone of the barren boulevard glowed coldly in the late November sunshine; there was a smell of burning leaves. A circuit of the arrondissement was required, to clear his head – to rid him of this corrosive bitterness.

Swerving to the right, Clem entered the Passage des Panoramas, a narrow, famously garish arcade that led away from the grand boulevards. That afternoon it was grey with shadow, dirty and deserted. Shattered glass crunched underfoot; several of its fine shops had been broken open and ransacked. Laure had brought him here one night in the early days of the siege. The Passage had still been partially lit then, multicoloured transparencies projecting images of clocks, hats, fans and other goods across the shop-fronts. Chains of white and red lamps had hung from the glass roof, lending the air itself a luminous haze. They'd been drunk on absinthe, so much so that they could hardly stand. She'd insisted that he take her right there in the doorway of a closed-up confectioner's. Clem could just about remember the bunched folds of her satin dress; the pale flash of the legs beneath as they wrapped around him; the nudge of a passer-by's elbow against his.

Approaching that doorway now, he felt the smart of betrayal, painfully enough to send him weaving across to the other side of the passage. It was Laure Fleurot who'd landed him in that trouble at the Hôtel de Ville – whose absurdly disproportionate prank had led straight to his stretch in the Mazas. He'd cursed her name with each drop of frozen dew he'd picked from his whiskers; each mouthful of that foul straw bread; each precarious bowel movement over the drain in the corner of his cell. It was impossible for him now not to view the whole liaison through a lens of regret. What the hell had he been thinking, gadding around with a scarlet woman – copulating in the street like a dog? Had he actually been insane, his mind upset by the drinking, the lovemaking, the hashish and everything else?

Clem emerged gratefully from the arcade's other end and began to walk south-east down the rue Montmartre. Amidst the various declarations painted on walls – mostly communistic and anti-Trochu in tone – was a *Vive le Léopard!* in a toxic shade of yellow. The watery sun had disappeared; it was barely two o'clock, yet night was already on its way. The jacket of his trusty brown travelling suit flapped baggily around him. It had been waiting in a Grand Hotel ward-robe, some kind soul having even attempted to give it a clean. It seemed to have doubled in size since he'd last worn it, though, so much of him had dropped away in the

Mazas. He put his hands in the pockets, trying vainly to gather it in.

The rue Montmartre brought him to the great market of Les Halles, the so-called belly of Paris, its wide iron-and-glass aisles busy with a drab siege crowd. Old people – why was everyone in Paris suddenly so old? – haggled like cawing crows. All pretence that the meat on offer had come from anything but beasts of burden had been abandoned. Stall after stall was decorated with the heads of horses, asses and donkeys, tongues lolling from their blackened lips. It was truly nauseating; Clem tapped a cigarette from a pack bought with one of his last French coins, thinking to block the stench with tobacco smoke. This is ridiculous, he told himself, directing his gaze towards the grimy skylights. You know what to do; you made your decision in the Mazas. Why delay it any longer?

Clem lit his cigarette and went on through the market to the boulevard de Sébastopol. He paused to get his bearings; then he turned up his jacket collar and headed north.

The Gare du Nord was filled with sounds that had no natural place in a railway terminus – the constant rainstorm of pedal-driven sewing machines; hammer-blows and saw-rasps; the lilting shanties of the sailors as they toiled over their ropes, nets and baskets. As Clem walked in there was a sudden swell of cooing and the cramped half-beat of confined wings: a dozen cages of carrier pigeons were stacked against the station's far wall, before a hand-painted advertisement for a boot-maker in the Passage de l'Opéra. The gloomy hall ahead of him was dominated by a row of balloons, laid out where the locomotives had once idled. Some were being inflated, others let down, the bulging white envelopes rising and falling like the bellies of snoring giants.

In the centre of it all was Émile Besson, dressed in his grey suit, standing on a train-rail with his arms crossed. He was overseeing the installation of a gas-valve on a completed envelope – an especially large one with a blue stripe painted around its base. The tin funnel was being fitted onto the balloon's mouth, being made airtight with a thick rubber band; Besson shouted a direction, repeated it, and then stepped from his rail to take over.

Clem stopped by one of the station's iron lampposts, watching them work. After a few minutes someone noticed him and alerted Besson. Their last parting, Clem remembered, had not been the friendliest, the *aérostier* cutting him off mid-sentence to go to his meeting with Sergeant Peabody. There was no guarantee that he'd be greeted with any warmth at all – but Besson actually broke into a smile as he walked across the concourse. Clem smiled back, despite feeling very far indeed from any kind of contentment. He put the remainder of his strength into their handshake: Besson had to think him fit and able.

'By Jove, old man,' he said, 'what an astounding operation! Why, it must be three times the size of the dancing school. Whole balloons, from start to finish, fashioned before one's very eyes! Books will be written, my friend. Songs will be sung.'

'Mr Pardy,' said the Frenchman, 'you do not have a coat or hat.'

'Oh . . .' Clem glanced at his suit, as if noticing this for the first time. 'I left the Grand a little impulsively. A disagreement with my mother.'

Besson seemed to understand. 'You look well, I must say. All things considered.'

So much for the display of robust good health. 'You know, then? Where I've been?'

'More than that. I tried to see you – to find out why you

were being held. The Marais militia would not allow me past the gate. They saw that there had been a mistake, I think, but would not admit to it. I am sorry.'

'That is—' Clem's chest tightened; he began to tremble again. He looked at the station's cracked marble floor. 'That is dashed decent of you. Dashed decent.' He could feel Besson's concerned expression on the top of his head. 'I am tired, I must say . . . I thought I'd catch pneumonia in that place, at the very least. I suppose I'm fortunate.'

'Many are finished by a stay in the Mazas. You are a resilient man, Mr Pardy.'

Enough wallowing, Clem thought. It was time to get to the point. 'Listen, Besson, I need your help. I wish to enrol. I want to pilot one of your balloons – to become a . . . what d'you call it?'

'*Aérostier.*' Besson had been expecting this. 'That is the term favoured by the *Société d'Aviation.*'

'You need volunteers, do you not?'

'Indeed we do. They are usually men with some ballooning experience, though, or sailors. You have only ever flown in a fixed balloon, is that correct?'

Clem nodded. They'd discussed this before his incarceration. He'd exaggerated wildly about both the number of ascents he'd made and the role he'd performed during them. Besson was under the impression that there had been over a dozen, and that he'd manned the valve for at least half of these, expertly controlling the return to earth. In reality he'd gone up just once, on a foggy summer morning over the Crystal Palace. He'd been a mere passenger, kept well away from the valve-cord and everything else. They hadn't gone very high, scarcely a hundred yards by Clem's estimation. Views had been restricted by the weather conditions: a silhouetted steeple, a few dull lanes, the glint of glass from the palace roof. Clem had found it rather disappointing.

'Free flight is different. It is *dangerous*. The balloons can go in any direction, any direction at all. We talk much of winds, of pressure, but once you are up there . . .' Besson shrugged. 'You must be ready to improvise.'

'I don't mind the risk.'

The *aérostier* studied him. 'You think you have something to prove.'

'I just have to get out of this city. I've had enough, old man – far more than enough.'

'Your mother?'

'Well, yes, she is pretty central to it all.' Clem's bitterness returned. 'She could have freed me from that damned cell any time she chose, but she left me to bloody well rot – to freeze and starve. I swear, Besson, she was on the verge of forgetting me altogether. She only cares about this accursed Leopard business. The *Figaro*, her damned career, the stupid books she's going to write.' Railing against Elizabeth felt good – a relief, like tearing off a stifling collar on a hot afternoon. 'She's taken Montague Inglis as a lover, too. I'm certain of it. I have to get away from *that*. Her affairs are always an absolute ordeal, believe me – epic bloody dramas in which everyone in the vicinity is impelled to play a part.'

'I thought they were lovers already,' Besson said, 'or had been, perhaps, in the past. Such shows of contempt suggest great intimacy.'

'I really have no idea.' Clem reached for a cigarette but the pack was empty. 'Something is up, though, and I don't want to see any bloody more of it.'

Besson hesitated. 'What of your sister?'

Clem pushed the pack to the bottom of his pocket. 'Han has no need of me. I am nothing but a nuisance to her. We had words in the Hôtel de Ville during the uprising. She made it pretty clear that she judged my presence in Paris to be a comical mishap.'

222

'She was worried for you when you were in the Mazas. She would have come to you had she been able.'

'You've seen her, then? Since my arrest?'

The unthinkable occurred: Émile Besson became distracted. 'Mademoiselle Pardy came to me that night,' he admitted, 'looking for somewhere to hide. We'd spoken, you understood, when I—' He stopped. 'I found you for her. She was afraid that they might shoot you. She stayed a good while, in the end, in case the police were searching for her. More than three weeks.'

'Good Lord.'

Surely this episode would have been a great gift for Besson – his beloved at his mercy, requiring his help and left for ever in his debt – but something told Clem that it hadn't gone well. Before he could work out how best to extract the details Besson moved their conversation into another area completely.

'A massed sortie is coming in the next few days,' he said. 'We have received word from General Trochu. The attack was to be mounted in the north-west, near Neuilly, where the Prussian line is known to be weakest. There has been an upset, though – a change in strategy.'

'Elizabeth mentioned this. A troop movement.'

'Reports from the provinces claim that Minister Gambetta has been distinguishing himself as a field commander. His army is apparently winning victory after victory and will soon be in a position to relieve us.' Besson looked back at his balloons. 'I do not trust it myself, but our leaders are desperate for a French triumph. The main force for the sortie is in the process of being relocated to the south-east. They are going to push through the woods at Vincennes and then loop around to meet Gambetta as he advances from Orléans.'

Clem was doubtful. 'I'm no soldier, Besson, God knows,' he said, 'but that sounds pretty damned ambitious to me.'

Besson agreed. Clem had heard him criticise Trochu before; the provisional government, in his view, had yet to make a single right step. 'Nonetheless,' he said, 'several highly important flights have to be made, to convey details of our intended actions, and coordinate the two armies as closely as possible. They have us working night and day, dispatching our creations as fast as we can make them.'

Clem saw a chance – saw Besson dangling it purposefully in front of him. 'So you'll be needing all the pilots you can get.'

Besson was shaking his head. 'It would never be allowed – not an amateur, and an Englishman as well.' He became conspiratorial. 'But I have a suggestion. They have ordered me to make one of these flights myself. I am the most experienced balloonist left in the city, you see, excepting Nadar and Monsieur Yon. A package of the most vital communiqués has been prepared, and another manager trained to replace me here in the Gare du Nord.' The *aérostier* moved a step closer. 'Nadar knows that I have a basic knowledge of the camera. He wants photographs of the Prussian positions, taken from the air as I leave Paris. He insists that this is possible. There are men in Orléans, he says, who will miniaturise the results so they can be sent back in by pigeon. Should the siege run on they could prove invaluable.'

This scheme had an immediate appeal. Clem gave his whiskers a ruminative stroke, his excitement building; he could tell what was coming. 'Fascinating notion.'

'If you truly wish to leave, Mr Pardy,' Besson said, meeting his eye, 'you could join me.'

Clem grinned. 'I do,' he replied. 'Christ Besson, I do and I will. I accept!'

The *aérostier*'s lip curled the tiniest fraction. 'We need not train you. There is no time, anyway. You know balloons, in theory at least, and you know cameras – so you can assist me with both. It is good luck, in fact, you emerging from the Mazas when you did. For the pair of us.'

Besson's enthusiasm was slightly overdone; Clem perceived that he was concealing something, leaving an aspect of their proposed expedition unmentioned. He made no attempt to discover it. This was a friend, despite his secrets – someone who'd been trying to help him while his own mother sat eating cats and camels in the Grand. It would be nothing sinister. Clem wanted to cheer. He'd just secured a route out of Paris, and one that promised a thrilling exploit to boot. This could be a book, he thought suddenly: 'An Airborne Escape from the Siege of Paris', by Clement R. R. Pardy. *This could be a bloody book*. That would show her, and no mistake!

'When are we scheduled to leave?'

'Tomorrow – the day after at the latest.' Besson pointed out the balloon he'd been working on earlier, the large envelope with the single blue stripe. 'That is our craft there. *Aphrodite*, Nadar has called her. Come, I will show you the car.'

The two men started to walk back over the concourse. Besson looked at his new comrade, a curious, almost amiable expression on his face.

'Are you really ready to abandon everything here in Paris, Mr Pardy?' he asked. 'What of your cocotte?'

Clem saw Laure Fleurot outside the Hôtel de Ville on that tumultuous afternoon, laughing and smoking under a black umbrella, indifferent to his fate. 'We are done, old man. Played out. Dead and bloody well buried.'

'It is often the way with such women,' said the *aérostier*.

'An affair that intense,' Clem mused, 'can't hope to endure for very long.'

Besson put a commiserative hand on his shoulder. 'Or perhaps she realised that you have no money.'

II

The commanders of the 197th had provided wine for the four hundred or so who'd volunteered for the battle-group – but from the liberality with which Laure Fleurot was distributing it you'd be forgiven for thinking that she'd laid it on herself. She whirled through the Moulin de la Galette with a bottle in each hand, overfilling cups, splashing wine on the dulled parquet, instructing everyone to drink and be happy. In return, the tipsy militiamen promised her dozens of kills; a land cleansed of Fritz; France liberated before the week was out. It would be five minutes at most, Hannah guessed, before Laure made it to where she was sitting. She wondered what she was going to say.

The Galette had been shut since late summer and was going the way of all Paris's amusements, from the grandest to the most humble. Hannah had visited it from time to time, in her life before the war – before Jean-Jacques Allix. It had been the kind of place you might drop into on a Sunday afternoon for a glass of vermouth and a few gentle waltzes. Now, though, it was dark and slightly dank, the fading furnishings creating a disheartening atmosphere.

Hannah was up on the bar, sitting in a line with Benoît,

Lucien and Octave. The three artists had joined the National Guard shortly after her, driven by a sense of duty she'd scarcely imagined that they possessed. A few days had passed since her return from the balloon factory. The 197th had welcomed her back without a word of rebuke; the Leopard's girl, it appeared, could absent herself indefinitely and suffer no penalty. The circumstances of her life had been oddly unchanged. Rather more of the shed's damp-warped exterior was visible due to the seasonal ebb of the vegetables planted around it, but everything inside was exactly as it had been left. Someone had paid her rent for the month, sliding the money under Madame Lantier's door; as a result, the land-lady hadn't even realised that her tenant had been away. Nobody had come looking for her, no soldiers or bourgeois militia or secret policemen. All that caution had been for nothing. Her stay in the Gare du Nord with Monsieur Besson had just been so much wasted time.

Everyone out in the cafés and bars had been talking of the sortie. The National Guard would lead it, they'd declared, and it would be a massive victory, ushering in a new age for Paris and for France as a whole; the working man would become the hero of the nation and would finally be given his due. There'd been no trace of Jean-Jacques. It seemed that Elizabeth now had truly exclusive access to the Leopard of Montmartre, in order to produce those articles of hers. The thought made Hannah want to bite her hand until it bled.

Once word had got around that she was back, Hannah had assumed that Jean-Jacques would come to her, or at least make contact somehow. Nothing had happened. The only explanation she'd been able to entertain was that he was still in hiding – still under some kind of threat from the provisional government. Lying on her mattress in the shed, she'd found herself imagining his reappearance so keenly that she could almost bring him into being: walk him in through the door, shed his coat and boots and shirt, slide him under the blanket and arrange him around her.

Hannah was not the sort, however, to become lost in longing sighs. Growing impatient, she'd risen, cleared a space in the middle of the shed and set the ruined picture of the Club Rue Rébeval on an easel. She'd stared at it for a moment, fixing its failures in her memory; then she'd scraped off the paint with her canvas knife, using a pumice stone afterwards to rub the surface clean. Taking up a length of charcoal, pinning her preparatory studies to the wall, she'd begun her portrait of Jean-Jacques. It was against her method to work without a model, but she'd pressed on regardless. Strange times called for adaptability.

It hadn't been right. This much had been plain within an hour of starting. Something hadn't been flowing through properly. Errors were frequent and clumsiness rife; it had been like trying to play the piano in thick winter gloves. The fundamental problem, she'd decided, was the absence of Jean-Jacques. How could she strive for naturalism without the living man here before her? How could she hope to show him as he was, honest and whole? She'd dropped her brushes back into their jars. Elizabeth's commission would have to wait.

No one in the Moulin de la Galette that afternoon knew why they'd been called there. The battle-group had already been given its orders for the following day: they were assembling two hours before dawn at the Pont de Charenton to march out alongside General Ducrot's regulars and break through the Prussian defences to the south-east. Lucien, Benoît and Octave smelled trouble. Set apart from the rest of the hall, gripped by a black recklessness, they were trying to outdo each other in their predictions of defeat.

'When men in uniform are given free drink by their

commanders,' said Lucien, 'you can bet that things are bad.'

'The gates have been shut, did you see?' muttered Octave. 'Every blasted one of them. There was a stampede to get back in – people out foraging beyond the wall and so forth. I heard some old fellow was trampled to death.'

'Surely the Prussians will guess that an attack is coming?' asked Benoît nervously. 'Surely the shutting of the gates is an obvious sign – as good as sending up a damned signal rocket?'

Lucien threw out a bony arm towards their comrades. 'These idiots don't care either way. Nothing but socialist fanatics, drunks and simpletons – many all three at once.' He sucked hard on his cigarette, the spark creeping between his paint-stained fingers. 'And the attack plans are already widely known. Paris a very leaky vessel. You'd be foolish indeed to believe that Marshal von Moltke doesn't have them on his desk at Versailles, with a crushing retaliation prepared.'

There was a tense silence; they'd postured themselves into a corner. Octave lowered his head, linking his hands. Across the hall some of the other guardsmen started to sing the 'Marseillaise'.

'Why the devil did you volunteer, then?' Hannah asked them, failing to keep the exasperation from her voice. 'If you're so sure that we're doomed, that this sortie will fail, that these brave men whom you hold in such contempt are wasting themselves, then why are you here? Plenty aren't! You could leave now, if you so wished!'

'Our country is under attack,' Octave replied. 'We must defend France.'

The painters nodded, smoking and scowling as if they thought their position – this noble campaign to which they had pledged their lives – utterly ridiculous.

Hannah banged her heel against the panels of the bar. 'But how can you expect to be beaten? Haven't you been listening to all that's been said? We outnumber them. And we are defending our home. This gives us a natural advantage. This gives us a motivation that—'

They weren't listening. Hannah realised that Laure was weaving her way towards them. There was sash of plum silk around the waist of her National Guard tunic, and a pair of patent-leather bottines on her feet – dainty ankle-boots several leagues above the scratched workhorses Hannah was wearing. She'd slept with Benoît, this was common knowledge, and very probably Lucien as well; she hailed the men with a languid tilt of the head, ignoring Hannah completely.

'Mademoiselle Laure!' Benoît cried, grasping at this distraction. 'How strange to see you in the Galette. I always think of you as a lady of the Mabille. For you to be *here*, well, it's rather like putting a shark into a duck pond.'

Laure set down one of her wine bottles and slapped his arm. 'Quiet, you beast. I come to the Galette on occasion. I rather like it.'

'We were talking about the sortie,' Lucien told her, 'and why we've joined up. Hannah here thinks that only the most devoted reds are qualified to fight.'

Laure snorted as she filled Benoît's cup, emptying the bottle. 'Not a surprise. There are ultras who wear it lightly, aren't there, and then there are those who become the most *incredible* bores . . .'

'That's not what I said, Lucien, and I don't like—'

'Why did *you* join up, Mademoiselle Laure?' Benoît interrupted.

The cocotte shrugged, tossing the bottle behind the bar. 'My boys love me. I can't let them down, now can I?' She met Benoît's stare. 'You got a cigarette for me, black-eyes?'

The young painter took one from his jacket, lighting it between his own lips and then passing it over with a flourish. 'For ever your slave.'

Laure winked at him as she inhaled. 'There's a rumour,' she said, quite pointedly not to Hannah, 'that a certain spotted cat has been sighted around here – this afternoon, in broad daylight and everything.'

Hannah sprang down from the bar. 'Where did you hear that?' She barely stopped herself from seizing the cocotte by the shoulders and shaking her. 'Answer me!'

Laure's right eyebrow rose a cruel inch, her red mouth parting at the corner to release a coil of smoke. 'Sounds to me as if someone's feeling a little neglected.'

Hannah stepped back, regaining her composure – cursing herself for having handed Laure an advantage. 'He needs to stay hidden,' she said, 'to keep striking at the Prussians and supplying stories to the *Figaro*. You know this.'

'To your mother, you mean,' corrected Laure, acting as if she was trying to get the situation straight in her head. 'To keep supplying stories to your mother. You don't see him for weeks but he can go to the centre of the city, into the Grand Hotel no less, meet with that famous old mother of yours and gab away quite happily about all the Prussians he's killed. Isn't that right?'

Hannah looked to her artists for support. None was forthcoming. Benoît and Lucien were grinning; Octave didn't seem to be enjoying himself, but he wasn't about to intervene. 'He has his reasons,' she said. 'He does what is best for our cause. For this city and everyone in it.'

'And he is a hero. A *hero*! Don't be coy about it, Mademoiselle Pardy! The slogans are everywhere. And the paw-prints. Have you seen that? Red paw-prints on the side of buildings? So *sweet*.' Laure flicked ash onto the floor. 'Nobody knows where he is. Nobody knows what he'll do next. All very exciting. For everyone, that is, but you,' she took a drag before adding, 'the forgotten lover.'

The anger felt physical, like a blow to the stomach; Hannah blinked, slightly winded. She clenched her fists. The blood surged beneath her skin, pressing around her fingernails. '*Enough*. I won't hear this. You are an enemy of my family. You led my brother into the heart of a riot and then you abandoned him to his fate. Did you know that he was arrested – thrown in the Mazas? That he rots there still?'

Laure rolled her eyes. Hannah couldn't tell if she'd already known Clement was in prison; she obviously didn't care much anyway. 'Your brother,' she replied, 'is a hopeless horse-prick who deserves whatever happened to him. He dropped me, Mademoiselle Pardy, like men spit into the gutter. Like I was nothing.' She gave Hannah a meaningful look as she picked tobacco from her teeth: *Like your lover has dropped you*.

Hannah was consumed by the desire to fight. She was aware that Laure would be by far the more experienced brawler, but this didn't check her. She wanted to act, to *hurt* – to punch this callous bitch on the chin.

A murmur rose from the back of the hall, gathering quickly to a cheer. The commanding officer of the 197th, a local apothecary turned colonel named Chomet, had climbed up onto the bandstand to address the company. Benoît and Lucien hopped off the bar, blocking Hannah's path to Laure. It was useless to protest. Hannah crossed her arms, biting hard on her lower lip. She resolved to leave the second Chomet had made his proclamation.

The colonel, a stocky, moustachioed man with a ponderous manner, began by announcing a twenty-four-hour delay to the sortie. This elicited a disappointed groan from his militiamen. He told them that the recent rainfall had swollen the River Marne, making General Ducrot's planned pontoon

232

crossing to the Villiers Plateau impossible. All arrangements were to be put off by a day.

'One good thing, however, has come from this,' Chomet continued, starting to smile. 'It means that we have an opportunity to salute the very best among us – a champion of the common man, of the worker, who has evaded the policemen of our weak and compromised government for well over a month . . .'

The battle-group shifted; Hannah forgot Laure Fleurot immediately. She looked over to the edges of the bandstand – to the doors of the hall. He was here.

'. . . who returns to lead us in this crucial hour. Our wretched government may have stripped him of his rank, of his official post in our battalion, but they cannot stop him from taking up arms beside his fellow citizens. They cannot stop us from following his noble example.' Chomet paused, beaming now, savouring the moment. 'I present to you: Monsieur Jean-Jacques Allix.'

The militiamen lost themselves in cheering. A fast chant shook the hall: *Vive le Léopard! Vive le Léopard!* Hannah stood up on a chair to get a proper view and there was Jean-Jacques, thanking Colonel Chomet and wrapping him in a brotherly embrace. The sight untethered Hannah from the earth. Her breath felt shallow; her vision seemed to drift. Octave planted a broad palm on the middle of her back, steadying her as she teetered atop her chair.

Jean-Jacques was the same. His clothes were plain but immaculate; his hair was swept from his brow, as always; his broken jaw-line was freshly shaved. Paris was slowly coming apart, weathering, fraying, crumbling; yet amongst all this Jean-Jacques Allix was like a polished black stone, perfect and immutable, proof against any hardship. He faced the hall, his posture opening, drawing everyone to him as he prepared to speak. If he saw Hannah, he gave no sign of it. The speech was typical of him: it appeared spontaneous yet appealed powerfully to his audience in terms they understood at once. After extolling their bravery, he told them of the pitiful numbers who'd volunteered to fight from the bourgeois militia divisions. So keen to gun down their fellow Parisians at the Hôtel de Ville, they would not now take this great chance to turn their weapons on the Prussians!

'And I'll tell you this,' Jean-Jacques went on, 'if the saviours of Paris are her ordinary working people then Paris will afterwards be obliged to give us a proper hearing. To give us the fair, free society that we deserve.'

'They'll give us fairness!' someone cried. 'They'll have to!'

'Prepare yourselves, my fellow citizens, for what lies ahead of you. Our foe is ruthless. His stranglehold upon our city is strong. But we will break it – we will inflict a defeat that will be remembered for centuries. This coming day is your last as untried militia. By the end of the next you will be *soldiers*, heroes of France!'

'That,' muttered Lucien, 'or cadavers.'

Hannah did her best to disregard him, to applaud and cheer, but something felt wrong. The exhilaration that usually came when she heard Jean-Jacques speak was missing. Had she been infected by the artists' cynicism – by Émile Besson's senseless doubts? Was her commitment weakening? She'd always taken these speeches as the earnest avowals of a man of deep conviction. Now, though, she saw a clear end to the oratory – a manipulation, almost. It was a performance as expert as that of any professional stage-actor, intended to stoke up his audience: to get them running out gladly before the Prussian guns.

Few others in the Moulin de la Galette shared her uncertainty. Jean-Jacques's words met with a roaring affirmation, the battle-group declaring that it would follow him to death. He was mobbed as he left the bandstand, dragged into a lengthy round of embraces, toasts and congratulations. They were asking him about this Leopard mission or that, so he began to retell a story from the *Figaro* with understated verve; soon there was laughter and exclamations of praise.

It was growing dark. Candles were lit – there had been no gas in the Galette for several weeks – and more wine poured. Hannah got down from her chair and waited by the bar. The others talked on, Laure needling her again; and then their conversation stilled. Jean-Jacques was approaching. Laure slid herself before him – hip and head cocked at opposing angles, fingers splayed along her collarbone – and attempted to launch into a flirtatious exchange. His response, although friendly enough, presented her with an unmistakable dead end.

Hannah could tell from his face that he'd known where she was from the start. The artists greeted him, offering vague words of admiration. Jean-Jacques had caused them enough disquiet before the siege, when they all used to gather in the Danton; now he was the far-famed Leopard of Montmartre they hardly dared to look his way.

He nodded at them. 'Will you come outside with me, Hannah?'

The courtyard of the Moulin de la Galette had been its great attraction before the war, the outdoor dances attracting revellers from across the arrondissement. That evening, however, jackdaws flapped through the splintered remains of its acacia groves, and dun-green mould striped the glass globes of its lampposts. It was bitterly cold. Hannah hugged herself, saying nothing. There was an unfamiliar smell about him, sharp and floral. She didn't know what she was going to do or what he expected from her. *Why*, she nearly shouted, *did you abandon me?*

After a minute or so Jean-Jacques said, 'I have been here, Hannah, since that night in the Hôtel de Ville. Up there, to

235

be exact.' He turned, looking beyond the dance hall to a tall shape behind, rising from the roof of an adjoining building: the windmill from which the Galette took its name. 'Would you like to see?'

Hannah followed him into the lane, through a small door and up a tight, musty stairwell. The windmill was about ten foot square and twenty-five tall. In the darkness she could just make out the cluster of gears behind the sails and the central column of the driving shaft. It was filled with the same raw, flowery smell that clung to Jean-Jacques's suit. He lit an oil lamp, shuttering the flame to prevent light escaping through the many cracks in the walls. The wood of the mill was old, the bleached beams full of knots and fissures; what metal parts there were had rusted over entirely. He'd bedded down by one of the circular millstones. There was a blanket-roll, a small sack of clothes, two spare pairs of boots and an assortment of military equipment, both Prussian and French from the look of it, including a shining revolving pistol. It was neat, Spartan: a soldier's bolt-hole. Hannah wondered how he stayed so clean. She couldn't even see a mirror. Opposite where he slept was a bale of dried plants – the source, she realised, of that odour.

'Iris root,' Jean-Jacques said. 'The owners grind it for a perfumer in Les Batignolles. Everything I possess reeks of it.'

Hannah sat on the millstone. She was going to get an explanation. 'Where have you been, Jean-Jacques? Why didn't you try to find me?'

'I knew you'd be well.'

'But why didn't you *look*? Didn't you care what had happened to me?'

'The provisional government was at my heels, Hannah. They would have imprisoned me, or worse. I've not been in a position to wander the city. I'm not now.'

'You've been going to my mother, though,' Hannah countered, thinking of Laure's sneers. 'You've been managing to get to her.'

Jean-Jacques moved closer, taking three slow steps through the creaking mill. The cramped surroundings made him seem astonishingly tall, his shadow stretching up among the sail-gears. His hands were crossed in front of him, the left holding the damaged right at the wrist. He wore a slight, patient smile.

'I've been sending her written accounts. Chomet has them taken down into the city for me. I can't risk the Opéra quarter, Hannah. I only go north – past the wall, out of the city.'

Hannah glanced at his crippled hand, motionless within its glove. 'That must be difficult. The writing, I mean.'

His smile slipped; there was a faint contraction of the skin around the scar. 'I have a guardsman to whom I dictate. One of Chomet's adjutants – a lawyer's scrivener.' Jean-Jacques stopped for a moment; he plainly felt that he'd revealed enough. 'But you must tell me where you went after you left the Hôtel de Ville. Everyone said it was as if you'd dived into the Seine and swum out to the ocean.'

Hannah told him about the Gare du Nord and Émile Besson – omitting to mention their argument on the day she'd left.

Jean-Jacques understood; he showed no surprise or jealousy. 'You did what was necessary. It is the same for us all.'

'My brother was arrested as we fled, though, by some bourgeois guardsmen. He's been in the Mazas ever since. Can anything be done for him?'

'He's out,' said Jean-Jacques simply. 'He was released at the same time as several of our comrades.'

Hannah stared; a laugh burst from her lips. 'Thank Christ,'

she exclaimed. 'Thank *Christ*. I – I was afraid that he'd die in there. That they'd let him starve.'

'I hear that he is with your *aérostier* now, as a matter of fact, in the Gare du Nord. The odd fellow appears to have swapped one Pardy twin for the other. They'll soon be leaving Paris – flying out in a post balloon.'

Hannah's happiness was marred by confusion; Jean-Jacques seemed well informed about her brother's movements. 'Are you having Clem followed?'

'No. No, of course not.' He was beside her now, blocking the lamp's light. 'Rigault told me. The fool wants us to bring down the balloon post. He has people watching both the Gare du Nord and the Gare d'Orléans. I tell him that it's a waste of effort, but you know how he can be.' He sat beside her. Their legs pressed together; his thigh felt hard and warm against hers. There was deep tenderness in his eyes, along with the first stirring of desire. 'It's the truth.'

Hannah felt a spike of guilt so abrupt and painful that she almost looked away. How could she ever have doubted this man – this remarkable man who'd shared so much of himself with her? It was Besson's fault, Besson and her stupid, detracting friends. Their utterances had sent her scouring through Jean-Jacques's words and deeds, hunting for duplicity where there was none – whipping up needless conflict in the one calm part of her soul. Well, no more. All this noxious suspicion would be cast aside. The siege might force them down strange and onerous paths, but they would endure. Hannah was sure of that now.

'I know,' she said.

Their foreheads touched; her shoulders sagged with relief at his kiss. He lifted her from the millstone to his place on the floor, settling over her, enveloping the two of them in his black coat. The shape and weight of his body, so familiar yet absent for so long, made Hannah squirm with bliss. She opened his jacket, tugging his shirt free from his belt and coiling her arms around his naked waist; then she slid a hand up, over his flank and ribs until she could feel his heart, beating quickly against her fingers.

'Jean-Jacques,' she murmured, 'I love you.'

He pulled back; his hair fell onto his face, hiding it. 'Please, Hannah,' he said. 'Don't.'

They rose at dawn the following day and went together to the rue Garreau. Jean-Jacques gave Hannah three hours; he was an excellent model, sitting completely still, barely seeming even to breathe. She concentrated on the face and especially those fine dark eyes, knowing as she worked that she was capturing a clear likeness. The setting she'd chosen – a spot beneath the window, well lit by the morning sun – was being painted as it was, and her sitter precisely as he appeared in it. She didn't break off to make a considered assessment until after he'd gone, off to a last meeting with some senior ultras. Putting down her palette, she walked over to the shed door; she folded her arms, the rounded end of her paintbrush poking into her ribs; then she took a breath and turned.

Still it was no good. The best naturalist portraits Hannah had seen – Edouard Manet's of his journalist friend Monsieur Zola, Edgar Degas's of his sister and her husband – had immediacy, and realism purged of affectation or contrivance, but they had something else as well; a suggestion of private meditations, of human complexities; an inner light that revealed a *life* rather than just a form. Nothing lay beneath the surface of Hannah's portrait of Jean-Jacques. This subtle illumination was absent. Her image was a shadow, a shell, as empty as a photograph.

I could go to them, Hannah thought suddenly. Monsieur Manet and Monsieur Degas have remained in Paris – they are in the artillery division of the National Guard. I could go to them and ask for guidance. Their whereabouts are common knowledge. Manet was up in the north, past Montmartre, in Bastion 40; Degas to the east in Bastion 12. I could cast off my objection to such fawning and use this damned siege to get ahead. Why on earth shouldn't I? Degas was a renowned misanthrope with an especial hatred for women and foreigners; speaking with him would most probably be futile. Monsieur Manet's reputation, though, was quite the reverse. Much was said about his fashionable attire, debonair manners and sophisticated conversation – and his notable fondness for assisting young female painters. All it would take was a walk out to the fortifications. The scene was easily imagined. Hannah could see the parapet, with its row of cannon; the artist at work in a quiet corner, sketching men stacking sandbags perhaps; herself approaching under some pretext or other, and making a comment; the instant affinity between them.

The paintbrush clattered against the floorboards; Hannah swore, jerked from her daydream. This was the exact strategy her mother had proposed on the day of that march to the Strasbourg. Taking on this commission had evidently tainted her with Elizabeth's reasoning. She stooped with a grimace, retrieved the thin, foot-long brush and snapped it in half, throwing the pieces across the room. She was not that desperate; she would never be that desperate. She wasn't going to offer herself to Edouard Manet or anyone else.

Hannah wiped the paint from her hands and looked again at the painting. More work was needed; whether it was a few small corrections or another task for the canvas knife she couldn't tell. It felt as if she'd been driving in a nail that had gone fractionally off-centre with the hammer's first stroke, every subsequent blow making things worse until

240

all she'd got was a chipped wall, a bruised thumb and a bent, useless nail.

It would have to wait. Hannah was due at her guardhouse in less than ten minutes. She located her *vivandière's* satchel and ran for the door, leaving the portrait gazing out from its easel.

III

Clem was shaken awake, none too gently. He rolled over. It was still dark. There was snoring around him and the distant sound of cannon-fire. His throat was dry, his head swimming; he picked a speck of sleep from his eye with the tip of his forefinger.

'Pardy,' said Émile Besson, close to his ear. *'Nous allons.'*

After a second's blankness Clem remembered what they were to do that day. He bounded from his pallet, all thoughts of bed banished, wobbling only slightly as he pulled on his trousers and worked his feet into the heavy boots supplied by the Balloon Commission. A minute later he was fully dressed, his long navy-style coat buttoned and belted, striding from the sailors' dormitory four paces behind Besson. He felt alert, immensely capable, powerful almost. For the first time in his life he was part of something righteous and important. The gold 'AER' embroidered on the front of his leather flying helmet seemed to glow like a miner's lamp, guiding him across the cold tiles of the Gare du Nord. Thirty yards into the concourse they peeled apart, Besson heading straight to the balloon, while Clem went to where they'd stowed the borrowed Dallmeyer. Slinging a large canvas sack over his shoulder, he heaved up the camera, the plate-box and the doctor's bag of photographic solutions, and edged out backwards through the main doors.

The *Aphrodite* stood in the square before the station façade. Fully inflated and upright, it looked far larger than it had inside, easily five storeys tall. In the low light of early dawn the envelope was a flat grey; like a whale, Clem thought, or an outsized elephant. A breeze crept in from an intersecting boulevard, and the *Aphrodite* quivered and veered, straining against its cables. This was a rather different proposition to that fixed balloon he'd ridden in at the Crystal Palace: bigger, certainly, but also somehow *fiercer*. He'd always conceived of balloons, even free balloons, as essentially tranquil: soap bubbles, dandelion seeds, that sort of thing. The *Aphrodite*, however, verged on the monstrous. That bulging envelope had a pent-up energy that was completely its own, beyond all control, easily enough to tear down a house or capsize a boat – or dash the hapless idiots attached to it against a remote, airless mountaintop.

'What the devil am I doing?' he muttered under his breath, equally amused and apprehensive. 'This is *madness*.'

There were no lamps lit in the square, due to the danger of igniting the coal-gas. Everyone there was relying on their eyes and their extensive experience with the procedures underway. Sailors laboured in the murk around the basket, winding in the gas-pipe, attaching the ballast sacks and fighting to keep the whole contraption secured to the ground. No one paid Clem any notice; the arrival of the crew was routine, without interest. A handful of officials were huddled a few feet from the car, conferring with Besson as they partook of some light refreshments. The *aérostier*, standing there in his flying garb, was a reassuring sight. Their impending escapade did not appear to be bothering him in the least. His lean, precise face was composed; he

243

actually seemed in significantly better spirits than usual. Anticipation, Clem supposed. He went over, set down the camera equipment and accepted a glass of what turned out to be brandy-and-water.

One of the officials, still tending to fat despite the siege's privations, was dressed in an unlikely mauve greatcoat and a broad-brimmed hat. It was the great Nadar himself, come to see off his protégé. Spotting the Dallmeyer, he swivelled his bulk towards Clem, took hold of his hand and pumped it up and down as if he was working an uncooperative machine.

'My friend,' he said in an extravagant French accent. 'My friend, so very good to meet you.' He released the hand as suddenly as he'd seized it and turned to Besson. 'Émile tells me that you are a genius with the camera – among the best of your nation. An apprentice of Mr Fenton, no less?'

Clem turned to Besson as well; the *aérostier* was smiling thinly. 'Ah, indeed. Mr Fenton, yes,' he said. 'A capital fellow. Taught me everything I know.'

'Well, I certainly look forward to seeing what you can capture with that device there. You have not been in a free balloon before, I understand?' Nadar tutted at Clem's reply. 'Then you have not flown, Monsieur. That is all I can say. It is like comparing a horse at a circus, on a—' he made a circular motion, describing the path of a merry-go-round, 'with being on a living animal, charging over the fields. And a lively animal at that!' He let out a classic fat man's laugh, throwing back his head with a fist on his hip. 'C'est vrai, Émile, oui?'

Besson agreed. 'Speaking of which,' he added, peering past the *Aphrodite* to the surrounding rooftops, 'we must soon be off. The sun will be up in minutes, and we have a favourable wind.'

Clem's palms began to sweat inside his heavy gloves.

He longed to request a brief postponement – a little more time to talk with the great Nadar (an encounter he could make much of in his book, he reckoned) and study their balloon. Instead he downed his drink, nodded in what he imagined was a suitably manly, no-nonsense manner and started to load up the Dallmeyer. A pigeon cage was strapped to the outside of the basket, the fifteen or so birds inside staying still and silent. This was surely an ill omen. Didn't pigeons have some kind of instinct for disaster? Hadn't he heard that somewhere?

Besson exchanged a few final words with the assembled officials. A packet of documents was handed over and secured inside the *aérostier*'s coat – the orders and plans for Gambetta. As Clem tried to slot the plate-box beside the bulky mailbags that had already been piled into the basket, he noticed that the Frenchmen were saying 'daguerre' rather a lot: it seemed that they were presenting a concern to Besson that he was brushing off. Clem knew that a balloon of that name had been launched earlier in the month from the Gare d'Orléans. When Besson came to the car he asked what had been under discussion.

'Nothing of importance,' was the *aérostier*'s reply. 'Come, let us get inside. It will be easier to pack if we are in our places.'

They both climbed in, squeezing between the ropes. There was barely enough room; the valve-cord dangled in Clem's face, through the reinforced wooden hoop that anchored the netting. The basket itself seemed appallingly flimsy, making a really quite loud noise every time he or Besson moved.

'It can't be done, old man,' Clem said – hoping ashamedly that this would lead to the mission being cancelled, or at least delayed by a day or two whilst a larger car was weaved. 'We're not going to be able to do it.'

245

Besson wasn't deterred. 'Move that bag there,' he instructed, 'the one in the corner. I will lift in the tripod.'

Clem bent down; the bag was immoveable. 'I'll try, but—'

'*Vive la France*,' said the *aérostier*, out into the square.

Many voices, Nadar's among them, repeated the slogan back to him. '*Bonne chance*, Monsieur Besson,' someone called.

The weight in the basket increased – a rapid doubling of gravity. Clem lurched forward; beneath him the wickerwork squeaked and shifted. He stood with difficulty, his legs straining. A half-sized Nadar, standing at the front of a similarly diminished crowd of sailors and officials, was kissing his hands and throwing them open in an operatic gesture of farewell. The square around them was contracting, shrinking in on itself. The *Aphrodite* was off and climbing fast.

'You *demon*, Besson!' Clem cried, clutching for the basket's rim – and realising for the first time how bloody *low* it was – just over waist height, for Christ's sake. 'You – you damned villain! You pulled the old dentist's trick on me! We were to go on three – but you yanked the bloody tooth on *two*, didn't you!'

Besson was unrepentant. 'You were losing your nerve, I think,' he said. 'It was for the best.'

They were six storeys up, seven – catching the wind, clearing the rooftops, moving out over Paris. The sound of the guns, of the eastward forts firing ahead of the morning's sortie, grew louder as they rose from among the buildings. Clem closed his eyes and tightened his grip. He had an acute, sickening sense of the space yawning above them, its absolute endlessness, and the yards of empty air opening up beneath.

'The *Daguerre*,' he said. 'What happened to it?'

'The Prussians shot it down near Ferrières,' Besson replied, prepared to talk now that they were away. He made a contemptuous sound. 'You know how they adore their heavy guns. The Balloon Commission has heard that Herr Krupp, the German cannon-maker, has made a gun especially for shooting at our balloons. A compliment of a kind, no? It pivots, you see, like a telescope, so it can track a balloon, and is mounted on its own special cart.'

Clem swallowed hard. 'And you aren't at all concerned by this?'

'I know the risks of what I am doing, but I do not think we need to fear Herr Krupp. Not today.' Besson breathed a sigh of liberation – of a man returned to his element. 'You should open your eyes, Pardy. It is an unbeatable sight.'

Gingerly, Clem lifted his eyelids and came very close to a dead faint. His knees buckled; he stumbled to his haunches. Outside the *Aphrodite*, beneath a glassy, silver-blue sky, was Paris in miniature – a model rendered in squares of slate, copper and sandstone, glimmering points of gaslight edging the main thoroughfares. The effect was stately, supremely ordered, the grand blocks, boulevards and starburst inter-sections like symbols in some monumental formula. As Clem watched, the Seine caught the first of the day's sun; the whole length of the river exploded with light, engulfing its islands and reducing its bridges to a series of thin black lines.

Besson glanced at the valve. 'We are not high enough.'

Clem was incredulous. 'Look over there! Look!' About sixty yards to their left was a woolly, golden shape. 'That, Besson, is a bloody *cloud*. If I had a cricket ball I could hit the damned thing from here. How can you possibly say we're not bloody *high enough*?'

Besson shook his head. Any pleasure he'd been taking in their flight was gone. The fellow cannot stay satisfied, Clem thought; there is nothing he cannot spoil. The *aérostier*

247

placed a boot on the rim of the basket and hauled himself up, clasping the netting hoop as he checked the valve. Then, after wrapping a rope around his wrist, he hung over the side, leaning at a diagonal so he could examine the envelope. The basket tipped horribly: Clem grabbed at the doctor's bag; his heart expanded in his chest, squashing his lungs, hindering his breathing with its thick thuds. He stared at his companion in amazement, framed there against the winter dawn. This was no sailor, clambering on the rigging of his ship. Beneath a sailor was only the ocean, in which you could bob quite merrily until someone fished you out. If Émile Besson happened to lose his hold on the *Aphrodite* he'd be smashed to paste against the stones of Paris.

Clem turned back to the view. The solitary golden cloud had moved, drifting away to the west. It was impossible to say how fast they were travelling. He could almost believe that they were stationary, simply suspended two thousand feet above the city streets. The Gare du Nord was already remote, though, its tubular roof disappearing in the haze of distance; and now the *Aphrodite* was passing over a large cemetery, the tomb-rows rising and falling across the roll of a hill. They were drawing close to the fortifications, to the limits of the capital. From the air these appeared impregnable; the Prussian decision to stay back and not chance an all-out assault seemed a sensible one indeed. Huge numbers of people were swarming in the lanes between the embankment of the circular railway and inside the enceinte – well-wishers there to see off the troops and be the first to hear news arriving from the battlefield.

Besson slipped inside the car. 'I cannot see anything, not from here.' He plucked something from his moustache: a pellet of ice. Clem's own whiskers were similarly matted.

His nose, cheeks and even his forehead were totally numb. He rubbed his hands together, thinking to generate a bit of heat between his gloves and then put them to his face. It did nothing.

'Look.' Besson was pointing east, past the wall. 'The army of General Ducrot.'

Columns of soldiers and guns were forming up, preparing to launch their attack. For several minutes Clem watched them wheel about and march off through a bleak landscape of earthworks, swampy fields and decimated woods. It was a vast military diagram brought to life, a lesson in logistics and strategy played out before them. He honestly hadn't expected to see everything so clearly. You could tell the line regiments from the militia; the field-guns from the mitrailleuses. He looked around, towards the centre of the city. That lone cloud was some distance back – and significantly higher up.

Besson was at the valve again, standing on a mailbag this time. 'I know,' he said, guessing Clem's question. 'We are losing altitude. It should not be happening.' He murmured something to himself in French. 'We will be over the Prussians fairly soon, Pardy. You should get the camera ready.'

Clem was aware that he was being given a job to stop him worrying, but found that he didn't object to this at all. The two men worked silently on their different tasks until Besson jumped back to the floor of the basket. The wickerwork cracked loudly; Clem's stomach flipped over like a performing dog.

The *aérostier* was mystified. 'I can find nothing wrong with this valve,' he said. 'Not even the smallest leak. The wind is good. We should be twice as high – twice as far. I do not understand it.'

The two men looked at each other over the top of the

Dallmeyer. They were going down over what would shortly be a full-blown battle. The descending balloon would be a magnet for Prussian fire. They were very probably going to die.

'The ballast,' Clem blurted.' Surely we could jettison some bloody ballast.'

Besson undid the buckle of his flying helmet, running through the possible causes of their predicament. 'No,' he replied, 'not yet. Not until we are only fifty metres up. We might still rise. There may be some atmospheric explanation for this.'

The *Aphrodite* crossed the wall, and a good portion of the French army. They seemed to be gaining speed as they got closer to the ground, whipping over a fort the shape of a Christmas star. All of its south- and east-facing guns were firing, the battlements lost beneath a white mantle of gunpowder smoke.

Kneeling between two mailbags, Clem arranged a length of tarpaulin above him to create a cramped, improvised darkroom. They'd rehearsed this operation in the Gare du Nord and declared it viable. Now, though, in the sinking *Aphrodite*, it seemed positively ludicrous. At least twice the available room was required. It was too bloody cold to remove your gloves – and who could take a photograph in gloves? The silver nitrate, one of the hardiest stains there was, would spill over everything. And they were about to damn well *crash*, for God's sake! What was the point of taking a photograph if the plate was to be destroyed along with the rest of the basket's contents, the bloody photographer included?

Clem stopped himself. He rested his hands on his thighs. This was not heroic thinking. Émile Besson, his companion and partner on this mission, was certainly not surrendering to despair. He appeared to be considering a leap up onto the netting, in fact, so he could climb around the side of the envelope. Clem thought of his mother, how she'd attempted to confine him to a hotel room to wait out the siege. If he was going to go down with the *Aphrodite*, he would take the best bloody aerial photographs in human history before he perished. He put in a focusing plate and dragged the Dallmeyer onto the edge of the basket.

The photographer's hood provided Clem with a momentary illusion of warmth and sanctuary; then he removed the lens cap and was presented with a crazy, plunging view of a battalion of French infantry, waving their kepis at the balloon as it glided overhead. He angled the camera up, towards the heights to the east. General Ducrot's advance force was concentrating in a loop in the River Marne, beside an old stone bridge that linked the two halves of what had recently been a peaceful village. Three broad pontoon crossings were standing ready, a first wave of red-trousered Zoaves assembling before them.

And up on the Villiers Plateau were the Prussians. Clem had been keen to set eyes on the besiegers after all these weeks, but actual sight of them brought only blackest foreboding. The view of their defences from the basket of the *Aphrodite* was startlingly clear: a loose system of earthworks, fortified farms, churches, and houses, populated by a serious amount of men and artillery. They knew what was coming from Paris and were fully prepared to deal with it. Clem perceived a number of traps – false outposts, hidden emplacements – designed to encourage the poor eager French to push forward and overextend themselves. Untouched by the bombardment from the forts, they were firing not a single shot in response. They were waiting, biding their time until their attackers had crossed an invisible line – a point of no return.

'Christ Almighty, Besson,' he said from under the hood,

'your lot don't stand a damned chance. It'll be butchery, old man, bloody slaughter!'

Besson saw it too. 'A photograph,' he said, 'quickly.'

The *aérostier* crouched among the bags, taking out a plate and searching for the bottle of collodion; this would be a joint effort. Clem lined up a shot and made an adjustment to the Dallmeyer's lens.

The basket shivered beneath their boots. Clem assumed that it was the wickerwork shifting again; then, through the camera, he saw the puffs of rifle-smoke coming from the Prussian positions. He threw back the hood and a bullet clipped past him to the right. Another struck the car only a foot from where he was hunched, ripping through the rim.

'Damn it all!' he shouted, starting to panic. 'The fiends'll hole us for certain!'

Besson was rolling the collodion over the plate; he'd wedged himself into a corner to keep steady, and was frowning at the fluid's unpredictable path. 'They will not do any serious damage, Pardy,' he said. 'I think they are aiming for the basket.'

The *Aphrodite* was now past the Marne, above the plateau – officially in enemy territory. They were welcomed by a massive blast from somewhere below. The next instant a shell streaked past about twenty yards to the left, rocking the car on its ropes. Clem ducked, cursing; and the Dallmeyer slipped from his grasp, toppling over the side. He lunged forward, hands outstretched, but it was no use. The camera was a spinning mahogany cube, dwindling down to nothing; it landed in the courtyard of an occupied farmhouse, breaking into so many different pieces that it seemed to vanish.

Besson showed no anger at the Dallmeyer's loss. 'That should keep us airborne a while longer, at least,' he said. 'Get us well past the Prussian lines.'

'What – what was that? What fired at us?'

'The special artillery I was talking of before.' Besson answered as if this was obvious. He pointed. 'There it is.'

A huge gun was squatting on a village green, directed up at them – or at where they'd been a few seconds before. The brown-uniformed crew was working hard to rotate it, but they hadn't a hope; the low-flying *Aphrodite* was really racing along now, faster than Clem had ever travelled in his life. If it weren't for the prospect of my imminent death, he thought, this would be tremendously exciting.

With swift efficiency, Besson began to bundle the rest of the photographic equipment out of the basket, unleashing a hail of bottles, boxes and trays. The tripod rattled into a café garden, scattering some breakfasting officers. Ahead of them, past one last village, was open country: occupied France, and very peaceful it looked too. Purple-grey fields were dappled with snow; here and there smoke rose from the chimney of a sleepy farmstead. If we can make it far enough, Clem dared to speculate, Besson might be able to use the trail-rope to land us without mishap. We might stand a chance after all.

'Horsemen,' announced Besson as he jettisoned the doctor's bag. 'Uhlans, if I am not mistaken.'

There were a dozen of them, leaving that last village at full pelt, ahead of the *Aphrodite*, but going in the same direction – intending to get them the moment they hit the ground. They were only a couple of hundred feet up now, the envelope visibly flabby, weakened by the loss of gas. The balloon passed over the cavalry; sunlight glittered across their helmets and bridles and the scabbards of their sabres.

Besson's coolness was finally starting to ebb away. 'This can only be one thing,' he said, but did not reveal what. 'I believe that it is time for the ballast to go.'

The dumping was done methodically, in stages, half a sack of coarse sand at a time. Clem willed it into the eyes of their pursuers, but it dissolved into the air like salts in a glass of water. A more or less level height was sustained and the chase began. The perspective from the *Aphrodite* was a fascinating one, he had to admit: galloping horsemen seen from above, held in place it seemed, the fields and lanes flowing beneath their hooves. He wondered why more artists didn't exploit the possibilities of flight. An hour's work up here would make your name. The notion led him to Hannah, the astonishing talent she'd always had; and how she was enrolled in that army he'd just seen queuing by the Marne to meet its ruin. He sat heavily on the basket floor. This cold November day might well see the last of them both.

Besson let the final empty sack leave his fingers and twist away on the wind. He moved across the basket, stepping over Clem's legs, taking hold of the side as he surveyed the landscape ahead of them. 'Look here, Pardy,' he said. 'Get up. Come on.'

Clem struggled to his knees. 'What?'

Besson indicated a dark mass, low-lying, moving out from the mists of the horizon. 'A forest.' He reached for the rope and grappling iron fastened to the basket's exterior. 'We can land there. Lose the Prussians.'

'Surely the blighters'll still track us down. This thing we're riding in is rather conspicuous, you know.'

'It is better than a field.' The *aérostier* opened his coat, drew out a revolving pistol and handed it to Clem. 'Hold this.'

Firearms were one of the few areas of human mechanical ingenuity that had never attracted Clem's interest. He was no pacifist, but the idea of applying his powers of invention to more effective methods of killing and maiming was devoid of appeal. The device in his hands was unfamiliar, ugly, unpleasantly weighty; he almost dropped it.

'Hang on a bloody second, old man,' he said hastily, 'I'm not shooting at anyone. I'm not a damned soldier. When I volunteered I didn't—'

'I will take it back when we land.' Besson gripped Clem's shoulder. 'We are going to run, Pardy. We must. We can avoid them.'

The forest was evergreen, pines it looked like, the trees carpeting a long dip in the countryside. The Uhlans pulled up at its periphery; Clem could hear somebody shouting what sounded like orders and they split up, one party urging their mounts among the trees, the other commencing a patrol of the borders. The pine-tops were closing in, a bed of black-green spikes rising to meet them; the pigeons on the side of the basket came alive, scratching and pecking at their cage. Besson lowered the rope, the grappling iron spinning at its end. Clem rifled through his brain for something profound and meaningful to reflect upon in the last minute of his life. All that came to him was Mademoiselle Laure, crying out in French at the height of one of their embraces; the feel of her heel pressed against his cheek, slick with perspiration. Ah well, he thought with a distracted flush of arousal, that'll just have to do.

There was a snap, followed by rustling – the sound of the iron dragging through the trees. Clem saw a doe on the forest floor, looking up in alarm before taking flight. He searched about for a solid handhold.

The iron caught. The rope flew through Besson's grasp. Six loops left; five; four.

'This is it,' said the *aérostier*.

Clem shut his eyes again. *'This is madness!'*

*   *   *

255

A single bin of autumn fruit remained in the apple cellar, filling the room with its sweet, earthy smell. Clem opened his eyes. He was lying amongst an assortment of farmyard detritus: broken machinery, barrels, coils of rope and chain. His head ached something ferocious, as if his skull was slowly being tightened – a screw turned at the top of his neck. He touched the spot near his temple where he'd bashed against that low branch, shearing it clear from the tree; there was a swelling the size of a ripe plum, squashed against his skin. He was extremely lucky to be alive, Besson had told him. An inch or two to the left and it would have been curtains. Clem looked around. He had a vague memory of entering the cellar, but it had been lighter then; he must have fallen asleep.

They'd staggered around for a day and a night, attempting to lose their pursuers. Those reinforced *aérostier* boots Clem had been so proud of in Paris had become like lead ingots strapped to the feet; he'd cursed them a little more vehemently with every mile they'd covered. It had been desperately close on a couple of occasions, Uhlans passing within a few yards of where they'd been hiding. The Prussian horsemen had been a fearsome sight – *terrible*, Clem had thought, in the old-fashioned sense of the word. These were men who really knew how to use their swords and guns, and enjoyed doing so: actual, proper soldiers, a stark contrast to the green regulars and strutting militia of Paris. He'd worried anew for the sortie, for his sister – who must have been in the very act of crossing the Marne as he cowered there among the ferns, praying not to be discovered.

Besson was on the other side of the cellar, sitting against a wall. Seeing that Clem had woken, he struck a match and lit a small white candle. He was dressed in peasant clothes: a smock, a shapeless woollen cap and a canvas jacket. A similar outfit had been piled before Clem, along with a bread roll, a pitcher of water and a wedge of cheese.

'Eat something,' he said. 'Change your clothes. And hurry – we cannot risk keeping the candle burning for too long. The flame might be seen.'

Clem scrabbled over to the pitcher. He took a long, gulping drink and then turned his attention to the bread. For one accustomed to a Parisian diet, the taste was overwhelming, fresh and full, a moment of ecstatic revelation; five bites and it was gone. He noticed that Besson was nursing a bird in his lap, stroking it softly. It was one of their carrier pigeons. It looked rather dead.

In the minutes directly after the crash, while Clem had crawled among the browned pine needles thinking that his head was cracked open and its contents dripping out, the *aérostier* had been occupied completely with his fallen *Aphrodite*. He'd pulled at the envelope, bringing it down from the trees, rummaging through the deflating folds until he'd found what he was hunting for. He'd stopped, his face cold – then he'd attacked the calico, fists thrashing, disappearing in the sagging remains of the balloon.

The next Clem had known the Frenchman was over at the flattened basket, the pigeon cage open at his feet. He'd been surrounded by escaping birds, grabbing at them as they flapped past him into the air. Incredibly, he'd managed to get hold of one, arranging its wings and tucking it inside his coat. Only then had he come to Clem's aid, helping his stricken partner to his feet before looking around briefly for the pistol – which was long gone, catapulted into the undergrowth. They'd left the *Aphrodite* just as the first hoof-falls sounded among the pines.

'That poor creature isn't going anywhere.'

Besson made a hopeless gesture. He set the body beside him; you could almost believe that the bird was sleeping but for the curled claw that poked out from under its plumage. 'It must have suffocated in my pocket.' He stared at the candle. 'We have to get word back to Paris. Tell them what happened.'

Clem started on the cheese: firm, nutty, utterly delicious. He just prevented himself from cramming it all in his mouth at once. 'About the orders for Gambetta, you mean – how they haven't got through?'

Tension carved a line through Besson's brow. 'About that, certainly,' he answered, 'but also about the *Aphrodite*. She was sabotaged, Pardy. A seam in the envelope had been worked loose so that we would come down early – a seam close to the top, where it stood less chance of being noticed. They probably hoped to drop us among the Prussians.'

This was a shock; Clem nearly stopped eating. 'Who would do such a devilish thing? The reds?'

'It was not the reds. It was Jean-Jacques Allix.'

'But Allix and the reds are one and the same, ain't they? He's their Leopard, their general, their inspiration and—'

'Pardy,' said Besson wearily. 'Listen for a moment. After all this you deserve an explanation. Allix is not what you imagine. Something about this man has troubled me from the start. I have gone to the red clubs and seen him standing before them – this brave, idealistic orator, this battle-hardened soldier, prepared to do anything – and it is too perfect. Do you understand?'

'Too *perfect*,' repeated Clem around his cheese.

'Allix was exactly the man these ultras needed to rid them of their squabbling and their inaction. The only thing he lacked was people who knew him, but his natural gifts have made him plenty of friends since. They have won him Hannah Pardy, *la belle Anglaise*, who had rejected so many others.' Besson hesitated. 'And then this business with your mother in the *Figaro*, this name he has made for himself – the timing just so – as if it had been engineered somehow. Guided from on high.'

'Besson—'

'I know how I sound,' the *aérostier* said. 'Bitter. Envious. Perhaps I am both. But this is real.'

'You've been asking questions about Allix, haven't you? Around the city?'

'You mean my meetings with Sergeant Peabody.' Besson was unsurprised; a note of irony had crept into his grim expression. 'However did you learn about that?'

Clem realised he'd been spotted that afternoon. 'You led me to him on purpose. You wanted me to find out what you were doing.'

'How much did the sergeant impart?'

'Barely anything, I'm afraid. I only had a few sous on me. I don't believe the fellow's overly fond of the English, either. He fought in the American war, didn't he?'

'For the Union. He is a veteran of the Richmond–Petersburg campaign. He was with General Miles at the battle of Sutherland's Station.'

Clem saw where this was headed. Allix was supposed to have particularly distinguished himself during this engagement, as a lieutenant in one of Miles's battalions. Elizabeth had mentioned it several times in her reports; how he'd broken the Confederate line single-handed, taken more than thirty prisoners despite terrible injuries, and then stood on the station roof, waving the enemy's colours in the air.

'And the good sergeant doubts our Leopard's version of events.'

Besson nodded. 'I have questioned him closely on several occasions. He has no memory whatsoever of a Lieutenant Allix performing the great acts accredited to him in Paris – or serving in the Union forces at all. No memory *whatsoever*.' The *aérostier* was growing animated. 'Jean-Jacques Allix is no hero of the American Civil War, as everyone loves to say. He *wasn't even there*.'

'What of those injuries of his, then? The scar – his mangled hand?'

'A tavern brawl. A riding accident. There are many possible explanations.'

Clem finished off the cheese. He wasn't enjoying it quite so much now. 'This is all based on the word of one man,' he said, 'and a rather strange man at that. Your Peabody may be mistaken, you know. He may be lying himself.'

'I quite agree.' Besson sat up, preparing for a further disclosure. 'That is why, after we had made our delivery to Minister Gambetta, I was intending to call on a certain American resident of Tours.'

Here it was: the hidden aspect of Besson's mission that Clem had detected during his recruitment in the Gare du Nord. 'Another veteran?'

'A man who knows veterans – many veterans. A newspaper reporter. Peabody gave me his name. I was going to request that he telegraph his contacts in Washington, so that I could learn exactly what Jean-Jacques Allix did over there. Where he fought, if anywhere.' He glanced across at Clem. 'My hope was that you would witness any reply I received.'

Clem raised his eyebrows, unsure if he'd been lied to and manipulated or admitted into Besson's closest confidence. He decided to stick to assembling the *aérostier*'s story. 'Allix found out, though, and tried to kill you. To kill us both.'

'He has been watching the factory. I am sure of it. He knew that I was asking questions about him and he has some very serious secrets to protect. I was safe while your sister was at the Gare du Nord. As soon as she left, however, he was looking for his chance to be rid of me.'

Clem considered this; he said nothing.

'Who else could have done it, I ask you? Who else would want me dead?' Besson took the packet of orders from his

260

smock. 'Even those reds who hate the balloon post know that the fate of France could have rested on Gambetta. They might want the provisional government to fall, but they do not want defeat.'

The case was a pretty convincing one. 'What are these secrets, then?' Clem asked, laying a hand across his clammy forehead. 'What is Monsieur Allix hiding?'

'He is no ultra, that much is definite. I suspect that he is an agent for General Trochu, or a hidden faction that supports the return of Louis Napoleon – or even the House of Orléans. Some of these people do not care if France is beaten. They would prefer it, even, imagining that they can deal more successfully with a conquering king than a popular republic.'

'Are you really saying that he *opposes* the reds?'

'Jean-Jacques Allix is undermining the socialist cause, Pardy. That is his purpose in Paris. He has gained their loyalty, their adoration, in order to destroy them – to convince them to commit massed self-slaughter before the Prussian army.'

'Dear Lord.'

'You must think of your family.' Besson's voice was insistent. 'They are very close to this man. Think of your sister.'

Anxiety brought Clem's headache to a new, excruciating pitch. Something inched across his lip: blood was seeping from his nostril. He climbed awkwardly to his feet, dabbing at his face. The food he'd gobbled down sat in his belly like a heap of cold rocks. Trying vainly to blink away the pain, he managed to pick up the peasant clothes left for him, but couldn't even begin to start changing into them.

'But we're – we're . . . where the hell are we?'

'Tournan-en-Brie, they told me.'

'We're in *Prussian-controlled land*, Besson. Would they even give us a trial if they caught us – us or the folk who stowed us in here? Wouldn't they just shoot us all against the nearest bit of wall?' Clem shielded his eyes; the dim cellar had grown unbearably bright. 'And have you thought about Paris? It's *sealed tight*. There's no way in. The balloon was a one-way ticket, old man. You knew this – you of all bloody people.'

'Calm yourself.' Besson rose to his haunches and pinched out the candle. 'I have an idea.'

They were seen at forty yards. The Prussians tumbled from the low stable they'd been sitting in and formed an impromptu firing line.

'Lift your hands,' said Besson. 'Now.'

Clem obeyed, thrusting his arms up to their full length. He linked his thumbs to make a bird and let out a hoarse whistle. 'Recognise it?'

Besson ignored him; his eyes were fixed on the Prussians.

'Come on, Émile old man, it's a nightingale. A bloody *nightingale*. You have 'em, don't you, here in Frog-land? *Light winged Dryad of the trees, in some melodious plot of beechen green, and* . . . erm . . . dah-da-dum, something something *of summer in full-throated ease*.' Clem had never been very good at remembering poetry, to his mother's oft-stated disappointment. It felt uncommonly important, however, to press on now. '*Oh for a draught of vintage! that hath been—*'

'Keep quiet.' Besson was impassive. 'Remember the plan. You are English. There was field artillery. A farm girl. You need to see the front.'

They'd burned their *aérostier* uniforms the previous evening, heavy boots, embroidered flying helmets and all. Clem had been too groggy and nauseous to care. Besson had added his packet of special orders to the flames – useless now, founded as they were on an impossible French victory at the Villiers Plateau. He'd then talked their way up the hierarchy of Tournan-en-Brie until they were sitting in the parlour of the village doctor. A long, very French conversation had ensued: much impassioned gesticulation with a round of handshakes and embraces at the end. Clem's wound had been cleaned and dressed, the physician passing him a phial of clear liquid once the bandages had been pinned in place.

'For the pain,' Besson had explained.

Clem had drunk it at once. It had no real taste, but there was a redolence of peaches – or rather of an artificial, peach-like flavour. Soon afterwards his head, so leaden and agonising, had lifted clean off his shoulders. That parlour, he'd decided, was the cosiest, most comfortable little corner he'd ever been in his life; he'd snuggled down in his armchair, wishing that he could be buried for ever among its tasselled cushions.

Then he'd been in a bedroom, a matronly woman undressing him in the straightforward manner one undresses an invalid, replacing the smock and canvas jacket with a suit of dark green wool. He'd closed his eyes and found himself in the back of a cart, bumping along a chalky road through fields of blackened corn-stubble. A second later and he'd been sitting with Besson in a small, close wood, having their plan of action described to him in terms his addled brain could absorb. Everything had been bright, colourful, unaccountably amusing. He'd been warm as toast despite the dead white frost. All around them invisible birds had trilled in the trees; for a single instant he'd caught the sound of a choir, sliding somewhere beneath the wind. As soon as they'd got it all reasonably straight, Besson had led him over a grassy rise to the Prussians.

One of them – a corporal or sergeant or something, with the most shockingly yellow set of stripes on his arm – stepped to the end of the stable, shouting back towards a quaint farmhouse. An officer emerged, shaving soap on his jaw, pulling on a pair of pebble spectacles. It was the funniest damned thing Clem had seen in a while; he had to bite his cheek to stop himself from laughing. In a flash, this officer was standing in front of him, brandishing a pistol rather like the one briefly entrusted to Clem in the doomed *Aphrodite*. The shaving foam was gone, wiped away with a handkerchief; he was round-faced and ill-tempered, with the smell of fresh bacon on his greatcoat. Clem's eye was drawn to his belt-buckle: a huge silver eagle, fantastically detailed, literally every feather on the creature's breast picked out. He stared at it, dumbfounded.

The man demanded something of Clem in accented French. Besson shifted at his shoulder, waiting for him to deliver the response they'd rehearsed.

With mammoth difficulty, Clem tore his gaze away from the eagle and lowered his arms. 'English,' he managed to say. '*Ing – glish*. Reporters. From a newspaper. Here.' He took a notebook from his pocket, the pages covered with a fake narrative penned by Besson the previous night in his mechanical-looking hand. 'That's what we do. Write things. About you lot.'

The Prussian relaxed a little, but remained hostile. He asked Clem a question in German – and sighed at his friendly, uncomprehending smile. '*Namen?*'

'My name? Mr Inglis. I, my dear fellow, am the English Inglis. English the Inglisman.' Clem glanced at Besson. Be unashamed, the *aérostier* had instructed him; be assertive. That is what they will expect. 'I am Montague Inglis of the *Sentinel* and I want my bloody breakfast.'

A runner was sent off down a lane to another position. Clem looked between the farm buildings towards Paris. Smoke was trailing from unseen fires, melting into the overcast sky; and another Prussian officer was before him, a man who could speak his language. He had a quieter manner than the shaving-soap chap, along with a light beard and large, faintly amphibian eyes. His uniform, too, was different – less bellicose, lacking all the spikes and eagles that festooned the others. This, Clem reckoned, was a species of intelligence officer. He delivered the explanation drilled into him in the wood: they'd been covering the sortie until some French field artillery had fired on them, forcing a retreat into the countryside. Now, having finally found their way back, they were eager to see the results of the battle for their paper, the *Sentinel*.

The Prussian was flipping through the notebook, reading Besson's work. 'What happened to your head, Herr Inglis?'

'Farm girl,' Clem answered promptly. 'Approached this plump Juno for directions, didn't I. Some mistake that was – the prim young madam mistook my intentions and pushed me into a ditch.' He touched the bandages that wound around his crown, under one of the doctor's hats; he could feel the dampness of blood beneath them, but no pain at all. 'A deuced rocky ditch, as it turned out. If it hadn't been for Graves here I'd have been done for.'

The Prussian returned the notebook, smiling dryly. He plainly had no trouble believing the violent tendencies of French farm girls – or that Clem was a bumbling cad. I'm quite the liar, Clem reflected, when I apply myself to it; that all came out as smooth as bloody silk.

'This man is your servant, I take it?'

Besson was dressed in brown tweed. The village doctor had been closer to Clem's size; the *aérostier's* trousers bunched on top of his shoes, and his coat hung emptily around his shoulders. He'd shaved himself clean in an effort to seem more English, and the removal of his beard had altered his appearance quite profoundly. He looked younger and paler, as people always did; and the revelation of a slight fall to his lower lip lent him a studious, cerebral aspect. He resembled a professor more than any kind of servant – but damn it all, Clem thought, we must work with what we are given. We are a pair of survivors, Émile Besson and I. We are like *brothers*.

'My clerk, yes. Mr Graves – and never did a chap have a more apt moniker. Oh yes! No more words from Mr Graves than are *strictly necessary*.'

The Prussian kept on smiling. Clem decided that they could be fast friends. If only they could sit down for a proper chinwag – a bit of schnapps, perhaps, with some roast chicken or duck. It occurred to him that he was perishingly hungry.

'And you want to see the front line?'

'Indeed we do, sir, and post-haste. Got to keep the blasted editor off my back, you understand. Can't afford to dilly-dally. It has to be *current*.'

This was at the heart of their plan. Back in the wood, Besson had explained to him that the Prussians would be keen to get reports of Parisian defeats into neutral news-papers – papers that would be sure to find their way through the blockade and weaken the defenders' morale. They would surely want to help an unlucky English reporter get to his story; and Clem was so very English that no Prussian could possibly doubt that he was what he claimed to be.

'You are a good distance from the Villiers Plateau,' their officer told them, 'but the French were also crushed at Choisy-le-Roi – just over there, where I am stationed. My name is Major Hempf. I will escort you, and will endeavour to answer any questions you might have for your report.'

The major shook their hands and guided them across a field. It seemed to spring beneath Clem's feet like a fluffy sponge cake, the cracking frost a drizzle of lemon icing.

He was about to remark on this to Hempf – thinking it a rather diverting observation – when the word *crushed* suddenly registered. The French had been crushed. Han had been crushed. Struggling to keep his voice casual and his bouncing boots under control, he asked about the sortie. In short, economical sentences, Hempf told him that the French had been allowed to advance a certain distance out of the Marne valley – where they'd been halted, contained and soundly beaten, before finally being allowed to crawl back again. Something dark awoke within Clem and started trying frantically to scratch its way out. Hempf offered him a cigarette; he accepted with gratitude. Besson had prepared him for this. I can do nothing for her, he recited inwardly, sucking down smoke. We are going to Paris as swiftly as we can. We will learn everything then; we will help her then. We must stay focused on our goal.

They arrived in Choisy-le-Roi. Signs of savage fighting were everywhere. Twenty or so dead Prussians lay in a back garden, awaiting burial by a dilapidated clapboard fence. Clem coughed and looked away.

'The French lost far more,' Hempf assured him. 'Over one thousand shot down in this engagement alone – and it was merely a diversion. The main sortie was a massacre. A farce. Is that the word, in English? A stupid performance – a debacle?'

'Yes,' Clem replied, dropping his cigarette. 'Yes, that is a farce.'

'Marshal Moltke felt obliged to declare a cease-fire so they could come out to collect their dead and wounded. Although I must tell you that their orderlies were more interested in digging up cabbages and potatoes from abandoned vegetable gardens than removing their fallen comrades.' There was disgust on Hempf's face. 'I saw

267

men ignoring the injured to strip the carcass of a dead horse. No Prussian would ever behave with such dishonour.'

'Where?' said Besson, his voice lowered to disguise his accent.

'Er, yes,' Clem added. 'Where indeed. Show us, major, if you'd be so kind. We'd like to see where the Frenchies advanced, poor devils.'

Hempf led them to the northern edge of town, past bare backstreets, burned-out houses, a ruined church and some of the most gob-smacking artillery Clem had ever laid eyes on. The black guns seemed otherworldly – engines of hell transported to the outskirts of Paris. The shells alone were the size of beer barrels. He slowed, gaping; it took several sharp prods from Besson to move him on. Those Prussian soldiers not at the guns or in the trenches were sitting around fires, feeding on fried eggs and mutton cutlets. Clem watched them enviously, a loud growl rising from within the doctor's green waistcoat. There was nothing like that where they were headed.

Paris and her forts were hidden in the morning mist. The fields before the city were dotted with figures and carts, trailing around with little visible purpose. Besson tugged Clem's sleeve, offering him a pencil to remind him who and what he was supposed to be. Gamely, Clem attempted to make an entry in the notebook, but his hand was not quite his own. His letters resembled those of a small child, huge and misshapen. Hempf looked over; he quickly turned the page.

'The fabled *franc-tireurs* tried to get by us there,' the major told him, pointing eastwards, 'down by the river. Their abilities, we found, have been rather exaggerated. Come, I will show you.'

They left the main roads, starting along a mean, rutted lane. Besson was hanging back a step or two; something was about to happen. Clem felt sick behind his amiable smile. Hempf was chatting away about the progress of the siege, how it couldn't possibly go on for much longer now and the men were hoping that they would be home by the year's end – and then he was groaning on the ground, his cap knocked off, writhing in the frozen mud. Besson crouched over him, a brick in his hand, striking him again at the top of his neck. There was a wet crunch; Hempf's movements stopped abruptly.

The *aérostier* took Clem's arm and dragged him across a rubble-filled yard, out through a gate, towards the sloping bank of the Seine. Above was a raised section of railway, running parallel to the river. They passed underneath it, going to the waterside.

'What – what did you do?' Clem stammered. 'Did you kill him?'

'He was a Prussian. My enemy.'

'Yes. I know that. He just – seemed like a decent sort . . .'

'Do not waste any more thought on it. You did well,' Besson glanced around, 'given the circumstances.'

Clem was about to thank him when he slipped, flopping through leathery reeds into a bed of silt. It was soft as custard and not at all cold; its rich, rotten odour rushed up his nostrils as he floundered onto his back. He began to laugh.

Shouts came from Choisy-le-Roi; the alarm was being raised. Major Hempf had been discovered.

Besson's hands hooked under his shoulders. 'Come on, Pardy,' the *aérostier* hissed as he started to pull. 'Come *on*.'

The Grand's heavy glass doors had been replaced with canvas curtains, in order to assist the constant passage of stretchers. The lobby beyond, that luxurious lobby with its columns and glass dome and patterned marble, was a gaslit abattoir, glaringly bright after the dull boulevard; the screams, the pleading, the sound of bloody *sawing*, was past nightmares. Clem went directly to the stairs, Besson half a stride behind him.

They reached the sixth floor and crossed the landing to Elizabeth's suite. Clem paused to recover his breath. The narcotic glow imparted by the doctor's solution was almost gone. Textures had changed; that which had been smooth and shiny was now coarse as a whetstone. Greyness was seeping into everything. Pain bloomed once more in the seat of his skull, gripping the stem of his brain and buzzing in his ears. His clothes, so comfortable that morning, were like ill-fitting sackcloth, encrusted with mud that reeked of the river.

Besson was regarding him with concern. 'Are you well?' he asked. 'Do you—'

'Wait here, old man,' Clem muttered. 'I'll be out again as soon as I know what's what.'

Elizabeth's sitting room was dark. Only a single candle had been lit against the evening, standing on a round table between the two windows. His mother sat on one side of the tiny flame; and on the other was Jean-Jacques Allix, huge and still, dressed as usual in one of his spotless black suits. Their hands were linked, resting before the candle. Clem saw that Elizabeth had been weeping. He didn't know whether she'd heard he was leaving in the *Aphrodite*, but she showed no surprise at his return. She sat up straight, attending to a loose curl. Without releasing Allix's fingers, she turned a part of the way towards him, her face directed at the carpet.

'Clement,' she said in a voice three hundred years old, 'your sister is dead.'

IV

Laure had got herself a small handcart from somewhere, of the sort used by flower-girls or lemonade sellers, upon which she'd mounted a cask of brandy. In a basket underneath were a dozen loaves of indigestible municipal-issue bread; God only knew how she'd managed to get her hands on so much of the stuff. It was a symbol, this cart – a demonstration of Laure's commitment to the 197th. Hannah found it equally admirable and irritating. The wheels were a touch narrow, designed for short shunts along the Champs-Elysées rather than cross-city marches. The cart kept coming to jarring halts against even the lowest kerbstones; and then, no more than a hundred yards or so from the Porte de Charenton, it became firmly wedged in a drain grate. The battle-group, now part of a column of National Guardsmen several thousand strong, carried on into the earthworks of the Bois de Vincennes. Their *vivandières* were being left behind.

'Here,' said Hannah, going to the cart's other side, 'let me help.'

Laure didn't look at her. 'If I needed any damned *help* I'd ask someone else.'

Hannah put her hands on her hips. 'And who else is there, precisely? The battalion's marching out the damned gate!'

Laure fought with the cart for a second, but to no avail. She turned around. 'Well, how about this fine gentleman?' she cried, suddenly friendly. 'How about it, colonel? Lend a girl those strong arms of yours, will you?'

Chomet was walking towards them. He did not reply or smile. Unlike the majority of his men, the 197th's colonel was completely sober; his wide face was ashen and his voice, when he spoke, was tissue-thin. He looked exactly like a man who three months ago had stood behind the counter of an apothecary's shop – yet this morning somehow found himself going out to face the Prussian army.

'I'm very sorry,' he said, 'but you must wait for us here, inside the wall. Word has just arrived – General Ducrot's specific orders. A condition of the National Guard partici-pating in the sortie. No women on the field of battle.'

Laure slammed down the handles of her cart. 'Now they say! *Now they damned well say!* Look at this here – all this bread! Do you think it dropped from a damned cloud? Do you, Chomet, you fat worm?'

She's overdoing it, Hannah thought; in truth she's relieved. 'What about our friends, colonel? We haven't even wished them goodbye.'

'It's not my decision, Mademoiselle Pardy. There's nothing I can do.' Chomet started after his troops. 'Be thankful. Believe me, it's a real piece of luck.'

This was no comfort. What point would there be to staying safe and well if Jean-Jacques was to receive another crippling injury, or to die? He was at the head of the National Guard column, dressed in black: the deadly Leopard of Montmartre. During the march he'd walked back to see how Hannah was faring. There had been a

272

short conversation; an arrangement to meet at the shed later; the briefest touch of hands. That, she supposed, would have to serve as their farewell. She remembered the night in the windmill – the way he'd deflected her declaration of love. Jean-Jacques would hardly want an emotional leave-taking. Besides, he didn't share Chomet's apprehension about the coming battle. He'd told Hannah that the Prussian positions to the south-east were scattered, undermanned and uncoordinated; he'd patrolled around there extensively and was confident that a path could even be found *between* them, with a bit of good fortune. The fighting of which so much was being made would not be very severe.

Hannah had tried to be reassured, but the militia force now disappearing through the Porte de Charenton had made this impossible. None of them had slept the previous night; almost all were steaming drunk. The red guardsmen frequently fell out of line, laughing as they tripped over their own boots. Greatcoats hung open; cross-belts were removed and left in the road; kepis sat awry on overgrown, unwashed hair. The Montmartre *mairie* had managed to obtain the 197th's battle-group a full supply of American Remington rifles. These were dropped on toes, waved around wildly or lifted into shoulders for mock pot-shots at the sergeants. Watching from the rear, Hannah had heard Émile Besson, as clearly as if he'd been standing beside her: *All a sortie will achieve is more dead men.* The doubts she'd felt in the Moulin de la Galette had returned, had multiplied many times, but what could she do? It was too late.

Field artillery was coming up behind the National Guard column. Ignoring Laure's protestations, Hannah took hold of the cart and yanked it free. Together they wheeled it to a doorway close to the gate. The artillerymen whistled as they passed; Laure found it in her to blow them a kiss.

273

For the better part of an hour, the two *vivandières* stood silently at opposite ends of the cart, listening to the rolling crash of cannon-fire and doing their best to ignore one another. The morning sun struck the fortifications, a bright band advancing down the inside of the wall. National Guard, men from the bourgeois arrondissements who had declined to volunteer for battle, began to assemble in the surrounding streets. Several approached the cart, spying the brandy barrel; Hannah and Laure united temporarily to drive them back, telling them that their provisions were for the warriors of France, not gutless, bragging cowards.

A carnival atmosphere developed despite the cold. Hundreds of civilians joined the bourgeois guardsmen, many in their Sunday best as if to attend a grand public display. A boiler-cart selling hot *sirops* arrived and did a roaring trade; men with telescopes set up on the embankment of the circular railway, charging a sou for a peek at the Prussians. The loyalist militia smoked and drank, dancing polkas as if the ferocious cannonades that shook the city were nothing but the timpani of an enormous dance hall orchestra. There was a cheer from further along the wall as a postal balloon drifted by. Hannah hurried to catch a glimpse of it, hoping that this might be the craft Clem was flying out in, that he might be waving over the side, but could see only rooftops and empty sky. She'd wanted to go to him the morning after the Moulin de la Galette, to find out how he was and apologise for deserting him on the Pont d'Arcole. Jean-Jacques had discouraged her.

'Seeing you might convince him to stay,' he'd said. 'The situation in Paris looks set to escalate. You must be honest with yourself, Hannah: your brother is not a serious man. It is better that he leaves.'

Runners passed through on their way to the Louvre and Hôtel de Ville, bringing word that Ducrot had crossed the

Marne without significant loss. The mood around the Porte de Charenton grew positively jubilant, the crowd convinced of the sortie's impending success. Their liberation was at hand; Paris had set her disputes aside and was taking the bold steps that her destiny required. There was much talk of French nobility, their superior civilisation, and the barbarism of the German states. We are sublime, the people agreed; we are valorous. We must prevail.

Laure smoked cigarettes, scanning the street as if on the fringes of a huge party. Other *vivandières* had appeared, along with an assortment of nurses and female orderlies. A fair number were drawn from the demi-monde – cocottes who'd lived in debauched plenty during the Empire, only to be left to fend for themselves when their rich protectors fled the city. Like Laure, they'd gravitated towards the militia, finding ready accommodation caring for the guardsmen. She seemed to know most of them, in fact; boredom soon overrode her enmity and she began to talk, listing names and exploits. One arrival in particular aroused her interest.

'Cora Pearl,' she said, pointing with her cigarette. 'Lord, she's looking thin.'

This notorious courtesan hailed from Plymouth; joking comparisons with her had been the bane of Hannah's first couple of months in Paris. Small and slender, she was strolling beside a dainty ambulance drawn by two white stallions. These were the healthiest, fleshiest horses Hannah had seen in weeks; those they trotted by eyed their haunches covetously, no doubt imagining them roasting on a spit. The courtesan's outfit was like a saucy, ostentatious version of the Lady with the Lamp, all sable trim and décolletage; her hair was of an unnatural hue, a fiery auburn that could only have been the result of chemical experimentation. So much jewellery dripped from her person that she glinted and glittered with every movement.

'Princes and barons have grovelled at those feet,' Laure said. 'They say the emperor himself once sent her a vanload of orchids – which she had strewn across the floor so she could dance a can-can on them. A can-can, on the emperor's orchids!' The cocotte sighed. 'She may be an *Anglaise*, but she's definitely got style. A friend of mine once—'

'*Vive la France!*' cried the crowds. '*Vive la République!*'

The first injured were being brought in through the gate – soldiers of the line, struck by bullets in their arms and shoulders. They were given over immediately to the courtesan's ambulance. One of the bourgeois militia declared that he'd gladly shoot himself to earn a place alongside them. His comrades laughingly agreed.

'Here's a way to get in an ambulance, if that's really what you want,' Laure shouted. 'Get off your arses, go through that gate there and *fight our damned enemy!*'

The ambulance undertook a laborious turn, Cora Pearl appealing in mannered, harshly accented French for her dear friends to clear the way. As Hannah looked on she noticed Elizabeth edging along the rue de Charenton, followed by the bearded Mr Inglis. Her mother was dressed for action in a heavy black cloak and a flat-topped hat tied around with red ribbon; she'd be aiming to get outside the wall and have a perilous experience on the battlefield. This was her method, part of her mythology almost: the fearless Mrs Pardy chancing life and limb, then fashioning the experience into a heart-pounding narrative. Hannah gauged the depth of the doorway behind her, wondering if there was room enough for her to hide.

'I wouldn't bother,' Laure advised. 'The old trout's looking for you.'

It was true. Elizabeth was paying special attention to the *vivandières* as she neared the gate, checking each one.

Hannah went to the front of the cart, accepting her fate. Her mother didn't hurry over. An expression that hinted at maternal warmth flitted across her face; but then her grey eyes darkened, expecting something that could not be delivered.

'Where is my portrait, Hannah?' she asked, in English. 'I will need it, you know, within the next fortnight.'

A tearing, metallic sound came from beyond the wall, distant but very loud. Much of the street turned in its direction.

'That'll be the mitrailleuses,' said Mr Inglis, attempting a surreptitious leer at Laure – who'd lit a fresh cigarette and was considering the pair with guarded contempt. 'The French army's rapid-firing field-gun, don't y'know – in German hands as well by now, of course. Thirty-seven rifles bundled together and worked like a barrel-organ. An impressive contraption, to ordnance enthusiasts at least. They say—'

The indifference with which Elizabeth spoke over him revealed at once that an affair was underway, the poor newspaperman being led by the nose. 'After this battle,' she said, 'Jean-Jacques Allix will be a great hero of France, and the appetite for a volume will be keen. We must act. I know you don't care a fig for *my* fortunes, Hannah, but think at least of yourself. This will make you. Think straight for once.'

Hannah met Elizabeth's gaze. 'I have nothing. Nothing whatsoever.' Saying this, seeing her mother's dismay, brought her a furtive satisfaction. 'I can't seem to find him.'

'*Find him*? What in heaven's name are you talking about, girl? Did he not sit for you?'

'You know my meaning, Elizabeth. In my painting. He – there isn't anything there. It's empty.'

Elizabeth's remonstrations were halted by the arrival of

more casualties. It was not a couple of stretchers this time but a veritable train, Zoaves from the look of them; the blackened, shredded state of their uniforms made identification difficult. Hannah had seen her share of wounded around the city, at ambulances in squares and parks, or limping around on the arms of nurses and doctors. She'd never encountered anything like this, though: splashing, spurting injuries, the colours simultaneously raw and rotten, lurid and charred, revealed in all their horror as the men they'd been inflicted upon sobbed and screamed and wailed for their mothers. The crowd's cheers faltered. A few rushed forward, searching for relatives and friends or to ask questions about the fighting.

'This is the beginning of it, Lizzie,' said Mr Inglis gravely. 'This is all that can happen today. Unless those Prussian outposts are actual fakes, that is – cardboard cannon manned by tailors' dummies in *Pickelhauben*. Which doesn't strike me as very likely.'

Elizabeth pursed her lips, taking a pencil from under her cloak. She was wearing a new-looking dress, Hannah noticed: a durable garment in a deep brick-red, with a light bustle and black piping. Mrs Pardy was one of very few in Paris who was enlarging their wardrobe for the winter.

'Mont, will you please be quiet? You've trotted out these dire predictions of yours many times before. *Paris will save Paris*. These brave men here believe that – they went into battle believing that. Your beloved emperor isn't coming back, you know. The people of this city are going to show their worth. It is the noblest of causes and you are naught but a sceptical Imperialist fiend.' She requested her notebook – which he'd been carrying for her in an outside pocket of his coat – and began to write, effectively ending the discussion.

Hannah's unease grew. Elizabeth was using the same line

278

of argument that she had with Émile Besson back in the Gare du Nord. Now, though, on the day of the sortie, it struck her as markedly inadequate – a position based on faith rather than reason and evidence. It wouldn't be enough.

The wounded kept coming: fifty, sixty. Some had obviously died on their stretchers. Hannah spotted a National Guardsman, pasty and still, missing his right foot. The number on his kepi revealed that he was from the 254th, a Belleville battalion – one of those the 197th had been merged with. Jean-Jacques was fighting. Men around him were falling to Prussian shells. It was more than she could bear.

'I'm going forward,' she said to Laure. 'I can't wait here.'

Laure wasn't surprised. She looked around her queasily, as if hoping that a way out would reveal itself. 'They won't let you on the battlefield. You heard Chomet.'

'Forget Chomet! I can't just stand about doing nothing. Our friends are under fire, Laure. They're being injured. Don't you understand?'

'I don't see what we—'

Hannah picked up her *vivandière*'s bag from the doorway. 'I'm going to the Marne at least, so that I can get a better idea of what's happening. It's no use. I have to know.'

Laure muttered something, threw away her cigarette and got behind the cart. She stared at Hannah, hiding her fear behind an indignant pout.

'Help us push then, will you?'

Together the two women crossed the Bois de Vincennes, moving as fast as the handcart would permit them. They passed drained ornamental lakes laced with muddy snow; entire woods reduced to foot-high stumps; a steeplechase track being used as a camping ground. The soldiers manning the Porte de Charenton had let them through for a tot of Laure's brandy, happy enough to disregard General Ducrot's orders concerning *vivandières*. Elizabeth and Mr Inglis had not been so fortunate when they'd tried to follow. All civilians, they'd been told, had to remain within the city walls.

'Be careful, girl,' Elizabeth had shouted after Hannah. 'I'll want a *full account*, do you hear?'

A fort came into view on the right, over the Marne, spikes of red fire darting from its guns. The noise of battle was now truly horrific; Hannah felt as if she was creeping onto the floor of an infernal factory, its rasping, clanking, booming machines all working out of time. They reached a crossroads on the borders of the park, past a set of rusting iron gates. The fighting had consumed the entire landscape in sparks and smoke; ambulances were moving off in every direction, their attendants hurriedly swapping information about concentrations of casualties.

'Which way?' asked Laure, wincing a little at the pinch of her bottines.

'Straight ahead. Towards Saint-Maur.'

Jean-Jacques had spoken of this, explaining the loop and thrust of the main French attack. They would march down into a bulge of open land encircled by the river, cross via the pontoons, then sweep up through the hillside town of Champigny to the Villiers Plateau. Ducrot's regulars were going to lead the assault, but the National Guard would be there as well, in support, showing their worth – Jean-Jacques would see to it.

Saint-Maur, like most of the villages outside Paris, was now a ragged cluster of ruins, the buildings burned and blasted beyond any hope of repair. A couple of hundred French infantrymen had taken cover in the shattered houses. Every eye was fixed on Champigny, now visible across the Marne, spreading from the valley floor to the heights. A frenzied fight filled its streets, bleeding into the paddocks and gardens along its northern edge. Banks of smoke rose and drifted off, glaring white in the sunshine. Beneath them, Hannah could see soldiers swarming through gates, into outbuildings, over fences. She heard the rising crackle of a rifle fusillade; a bugle-call halting abruptly mid-bar; the nerve-rending grind of the mitrailleuses. Each instant brought a dozen more deaths. Hannah watched men stumble and disappear under the boots of those behind. She stopped walking. Something was being piled onto her, it seemed, in great shovelfuls; she was being suffocated, slowly buried alive.

'Wake *up*, Mademoiselle Pardy!' Laure yelled.

Inhaling sharply, gripping the handcart for balance, Hannah forced her attention back to the road. The pontoon crossings were close. They'd been moored beside the old stone bridge of Champigny, using it as a shield against the Prussian artillery fire. This was much needed – shells whistled down constantly from the plateau, their paths marked by arcing trails, cracking against the bridge's granite flank. Non-combatants were being held on the southern bank until word came through that the town had been captured. Hannah and Laure joined a queue of ambulances and ammunition wagons waiting in the remains of a farmyard. The drivers were discussing a diversionary attack that had been made towards Choisy-le-Roi a while earlier – an absolute disaster, apparently, hundreds upon hundreds killed with nothing whatsoever to show for it.

Half an hour later the bugles started playing a new refrain, and semaphore flags appeared amongst the rubble: Champigny was under French control. There were no cheers or patriotic exclamations at this news. All it meant out here was that the army would now have to attack Villiers. The battle would continue into the afternoon and evening. Many more would fall.

281

Cleared to advance, the ambulances and wagons formed two lines and started across the pontoon bridges. Under their weight the floating platforms sank down almost to the surface of the still-bloated Marne; the Prussian artillery picked up, sending splinters from the bridge splashing in the water. Hannah led the handcart onto the right-hand crossing, closest to the cover of the bridge. Laure was virtually dragged behind, tottering on her bottines, swearing loudly with each tremble and rock of the boards.

A number of the ambulances parked on the Marne's opposite bank, discovering an immediate supply of wounded. It was unclear whether these men had been brought back from the town or had simply fallen moments after stepping from the pontoons. The suffering was beyond comprehension. Hannah and Laure focused on negotiating the handcart over the churned ground.

Soon they reached the outskirts of the town. Officers, regular army types in smart jackets and red trousers, were striding about, searching for their men – hauling them from shelter, trying to assemble them for the next stage in the advance. The two *vivandières* attracted the odd curious glance, but no one had the time either to answer their questions or ask any back. They were moving along the broad street that formed the spine of Champigny when a small hotel not thirty yards from them took a direct artillery hit, exploding into a stretching star of powdered plaster, brick and glass. Hannah felt an unbelievable wrench, both her arms whipping away from the blast and wetness flicking across her cheek. For a petrifying split-second she thought she'd been caught by shrapnel, but no: it was the handcart. A fragment of either shell or hotel had bashed it to bits, blowing Laure's bread hoard apart, splattering them both with brandy and leaving them holding only broken lumps of wood. Laure was too stunned even to curse. She dropped the pieces in her hands, blinking; the next instant she'd scampered across the road into a deep gutter.

'I don't even *like you*,' she screamed at Hannah, curling into a ball, 'I *never have*. Why'd you make me do this? *Why*? It is *insanity*, the most ridiculous, the most stupid damned thing I have ever . . . have ever . . .'

Hannah's body seemed horribly light, made of hay, as if the breeze alone might knock her down and send her skittering along the pavement. A bullet zipped by, smashing a shop window, reflected light flashing crazily over the cobbles as the shards fell; and she was down with Laure, wrapped tightly around her, face pressed against the cocotte's greasy copper plait.

How long they lay like this Hannah couldn't say. Laure's limbs shivered next to hers, her breaths heaving and huge; she was mumbling some kind of incantation or prayer. The vinous stench of brandy filled Hannah's nostrils. She shifted her head a little. A rivulet of blood was running thickly beneath them, half an inch from their pantaloons, dripping into the drain.

Eventually Champigny grew a little quieter. The fight had moved on, further up the hill. Hannah got them both to their feet and looked around. They were the only people standing upright in the entire street. Recovered from her shrieking fit, Laure set about salvaging what bread she could, filling her pockets with dirty crusts.

The two women made their way towards the town's upper edge, climbing through lanes littered with snapped-off rifle stocks, bent blades and bits of bloody uniform. A number of houses and shops were occupied, rifles jutting from windows and holes knocked through roofs. Runners dashed past, taking reports back from the front; several Zoaves sat slumped against a wall, hands clamped hopelessly over mortal wounds. They reached a modest square set out around a dry-stone well. Beneath a row of cherry trees, a chaplain was attempting to tend to twenty or so of the badly injured, the dying men clawing at his robes as they begged him to hear their confessions. The battlefield was close; the din of heavy gunfire was shaking streams of dust from between the stones of the buildings. Bugles sounded beyond the rooftops, followed by cheers and a howl of agony.

'There's a whole damned army out there,' Laure said, her voice hoarse, '*two* damned armies, and all mixed up. We'll never find them.'

'We will. Stay with me.'

Hannah was certain that she'd be able to spot Jean-Jacques. He'd be conspicuous, even in the chaos of a battlefield. She could envisage his situation clearly: he'd be throwing himself into the worst of the fighting, trying single-handedly to turn the tide. It would only be a matter of time before he caught the attention of a Prussian sharpshooter, or happened to be standing in the wrong place when a shell landed. She had to reach him as quickly as possible; she might be the only one who could convince him that the sortie had been a dreadful error and that they had to retreat to Paris.

On the other side of the square several teams of horse artillery were preparing to move forward. The *vivandières* went over, intending to follow them onto the field. Just as they were leaving, however, this column came to a sudden halt, the drivers at the front shouting that they needed to reverse. Hannah looked around the rearmost gun-carriage. A great stampede of French infantry was cresting a rise, pouring back into Champigny. A few dozen of the fastest sprinted past, on towards the centre of town; and then there were thousands thronging across the cobbles, ramming the square full. They packed around buildings, startling horses, overturning cannon and trampling the wounded. Laure pulled Hannah to the well; by clambering onto it they managed to avoid being immediately swept away. Most of the men were reserves from the north, but Hannah saw significant numbers of militia, including some from the 197th. Every one of them was in a state of absolute panic.

'They are here, they are here!' somebody yelled. 'Oh God! Oh Christ!'

A neat line of Prussian artillery appeared on the rise, the crews rotating their firing platforms. One, a captured mitrailleuse, opened up with that grating rattle they'd been hearing all morning, a jet of flame stuttering before it like fat spitting from a griddle; down on the square a flailing, bloody corridor was struck through the routing Frenchmen. Next came the field guns, firing with a series of flat crumps, splitting a cherry tree to the base of its trunk. The chaplain, still standing nearby, was among those felled by the flying slivers of wood. An officer shouted for his men to hold their ground, to aim for the crews – to give some account of themselves. He was ignored.

Bodies were pressing hard against the well on every side. Hannah and Laure jumped off as it started to collapse, the stones leaning inwards and then coming apart, toppling into the shaft. Swallowed by the deluge of soldiers, they were carried irresistibly downhill.

'The Leopard!' Hannah cried. 'Has any of you seen the Leopard?'

The faces around her were blank, glazed with terror, staring straight ahead. Nobody answered.

*   *   *

By the time Hannah and Laure had struggled back up to the square the short winter day was over. High cloud hid the stars and it was brutally cold, frost sparkling over the debris and the heaps of dead. The French had rallied, after a fashion; they'd been repulsed from the plateau, having failed signally to punch through the blockade, but they were clinging onto Champigny. That little square was effectively the front line. Barricades had been thrown up and there were soldiers in many of the buildings, vainly scouring the heights for a lantern or campfire that might indicate the location of the Prussians. Only a single cherry tree had survived, the demolished well had been filled in and one of the larger houses on its outer edge was on fire. No one chose to stand near it, though, despite the freezing temperature. That would make a man an easy target for a sniper; and although a cease-fire had been instated for the collection of casualties, the regulars posted in the square weren't about to trust their enemy after the day they'd just endured.

The two *vivandières* hadn't eaten or slept now for twenty-four hours. Hannah felt spectral, barely there, forced onward by the sole purpose of finding Jean-Jacques. Laure was grumbling to herself about the blasted *Anglaise* and her interfering ways – about how, if it wasn't for her, she'd be back in Montmartre by now, her belly full of liquor and a nice young guardsman in her bed. Not once, however, did she talk of leaving. Duty to the 197th held her in Champigny; and it was she who spotted Octave.

The sculptor sat on a kerb next to a long row of corpses. He was weeping, one of those wide, rough hands held over his eyes. As they approached they saw that the body directly beside him was Lucien's. The painter's mouth was slightly open, as if drawing breath in the middle of one of his acerbic discourses; but there was a tiny, precise hole in his left cheek, and a second, far larger, behind his right ear. His beard was white with frost; his skin the colour of clay. The sight left Hannah numb, her mind wiped clean. She heard herself say 'no', but had no sense of having said it. The last time she'd met with her three artist friends they'd been at the rear of the National Guard column, lit up by absinthe, reciting Victor Hugo's latest siege-verses in less than reverential falsettos.

'We couldn't even *see* them,' Octave said. 'Not one Prussian soldier. The bullets were coming in from all over.'

Laure bent down, putting her arm around his shoulders and offering him a grimy hunk of bread. He acted as if she wasn't there.

'Where's Benoît?' the cocotte asked. 'Is he well?'

Octave uncovered his eyes, his brow furrowing. 'I should think so. He fled the very instant the Prussians opened fire – him and half our wretched battle-group. Back to Paris they went, and wouldn't be told otherwise.' He stared at Lucien. 'We were the committed National Guard – the brave ones. Remember us in the Galette? We were going to fight for France. We were a damned *joke*.'

Hannah fastened both hands around her satchel strap, bracing herself. 'What of Jean-Jacques?'

'Our Leopard?' The sculptor shook his head. 'He talked up a storm, I'll give him that, all the way through Champigny. Once we were at Villiers, though, trying to reach the château along with Ducrot's lot, he just vanished.'

A frozen bolt was driven straight through Hannah's chest, leaving her quivering upon it. 'He vanished,' she repeated.

Octave wouldn't look at her. He wiped his mouth and chin. 'I don't know what else to tell you, Hannah. No one saw what happened to him or where he went. We were by these bales of straw, ready to charge. There was rifle-fire. A few shells. And he was gone.'

Without another word or thought Hannah strode from

the square, past the barricades, into the sloping, undulating fields that lay between Champigny and the Villiers plateau. The orange dots of oil lamps marked out the French ambulances as they toiled to remove the dead and rescue the wounded. Hannah peered into every waxen, contorted face she came across; in almost total darkness, she searched copses, bushes and hollows for that tall, spare frame, those broad shoulders, that black coat and hat.

It was futile. Hannah's muscles were stiffening, protesting against the effort and the cold. She turned back, smothering a sob, took a step and then turned back again. She couldn't leave. A tear crept over her jaw and raced down her neck, under the collar of her tunic. He'd fallen. It was the only explanation. He'd been at the head of the militia column. The Prussians had known who he was; Elizabeth's Leopard articles were bound to have found their way into enemy hands. They'd have been hunting for him, looking out for the man who'd so humiliated them over the past months and killed so many of their sentries. He'd been shot down, rolled aside; or far worse, taken as a trophy, overpowered somehow and dragged away for a public execution at the Prussian headquarters at Versailles. Hannah saw Jean-Jacques on the scaffold, a noose being readied for his neck – standing before a firing squad like Manet's *Maximilian*. She tore off her kepi with a cry. It was too much, too much! The very worst had happened, the *unthinkable*. She'd pressed for this, shouted for it, demanded it, and here was the result: a failed attack, a minute, tenuous extension of the line and the death of her love.

No – this was not known for certain. There was still hope. Hugging herself, stamping her boots, Hannah formed a gap between her lips and exhaled hard. She tried to be scientific, to deduce the course of the doomed French advance so that she could identify the best areas left for her to search, but it was no use. The Prussians had been coming from all sides, manoeuvring the French into a killing ground, a massive trap. It had been folly, in short – folly on a calamitous scale.

Hannah began to lose her place in the landscape. The dim glimmer of Champigny was behind her, then to her left; she seemed to have been set adrift on the grey hillside. She tripped on a rock, stumbling to her hands and knees. The long grass beneath her crunched with frost yet was inexplicably inviting. She lay down, resting her head on the icy ground. Sleep crept through her, warming her, sinking her into the earth.

A tapered toecap poked against her hip, testing for life; a pair of patent bottines, scuffed and crusted with mud, completed a sauntering circuit of her body.

'You're an idiot,' said Laure. 'A sick-hearted fool. I told you this was pointless. You'll never find him. You're wasting your damned time, and mine too. Risking our lives.'

She's been following me, Hannah thought, ever since I left the town. 'I didn't ask you to come,' she replied, without moving. 'Go, go on.'

The cocotte sighed, drawing on a cigarette; she'd recovered a good deal of her Parisian poise. 'He could well be alive, I suppose – in Paris, or Champigny, or Saint-Maur. He could even have got past Fritz, knowing him, and be halfway to Tours by now. But he sure as hell isn't out here.'

'Let me be, will you?'

Laure didn't respond; she'd noticed something. Hannah pushed herself up onto an elbow. The lanterns of the ambulances were moving downhill, heading for the French line like fishing boats returning to shore. Laure had thrown away her cigarette and was holding out a hand.

'Mademoiselle Pardy,' she said, 'I do believe that we should go back. This minute.'

They were about fifty yards from Champigny when the shouting started, countless male voices joined in a mad battle roar. Hannah looked over her shoulder, into the darkness. The horizon itself was shifting, the heights rising and sliding towards them – the entire Marne valley trembling. The two women broke into a run, all tiredness forgotten. Their greatcoats flapped around them, Laure's shedding ragged chunks of siege-bread. One of the bottines suddenly gave way; Laure caught hold of Hannah's sleeve and they staggered into the square, clutching onto each other tightly.

The French soldiers stationed there were checking rifles and strengthening barricades with the grim concentration of the condemned. All were men of the line, with their Chassepots and red trousers – there was no sign of any militia, Octave included. A couple were complaining about the limited supply of ammunition; that it wasn't yet dawn, the agreed end of the cease-fire; that they hadn't been reinforced, as had been promised by General Trochu. Others were saying their prayers.

Hannah and Laure ducked into a ruined shop, a bakery that was missing half of its upper floor. Seven regulars were already inside. They managed some laughter at the appearance of women at this point, but the firing started before anyone could ask a question or make a crude remark. Bullets sliced through plaster – pinged off metal and stone. The *vivandières* hurried behind the shop counter, crouching together on the chipped floor tiles. Through an open doorway Hannah saw several hundred brown greatcoats rushing in the side of the square, charging around the sole surviving cherry tree.

'We're being overrun,' shouted one of the soldiers, his voice wavering. 'Damn it all, my friends, we're being *overrun!*'

Then there were Prussians in the bakery. The first was

shot down; those coming in behind him bayoneted the shooter and shot two more. The remaining four French regulars ran upstairs, bellowing oaths as they went. Rifles were trained on Hannah and Laure, a semicircle of alert young faces staring in at them. The cocotte screamed at the top of her voice. One of the soldiers yelled out a query, and a sergeant strode over, an older man with a long, ruddy face and drooping moustaches. He leaned across the counter and slapped Laure hard about the head, knocking off her kepi. She fell silent immediately.

More enemy troops entered the shop. Orders were given, two staying with Hannah and Laure while the rest piled up after the Frenchmen, the sergeant in the lead. There were cries; furious scuffling and four or five shots; the thud of bodies hitting floorboards. The survivors, all of them Prussian, descended the stairs.

It was finished. The firing was already subsiding, or at least shifting down the hill into Champigny's centre. The French had been driven back in moments, swept from their positions, leaving Hannah and Laure at the mercy of their enemy. Hannah had heard many times what happened to female prisoners of the Prussian army. She tried to watch every man in the bakery, to be ready for whatever move they might make; her eyes darted about so much that they started to ache with the strain. The infantrymen seemed huge, barbarian-like, menacing despite their youth; they wiped the blood from their bayonets and straightened their spiked helmets. Hannah attempted to compose an insult, something they would understand – something that might goad the soldiers into killing them then and there. Invention deserted her, however, so she simply threw out her arms, across the dazed Laure, jamming them both into the right angle between the counter and the wall and preparing to kick, gouge and bite. If this was to happen, if they were

291

to be ravished and murdered, she was going to make it as difficult for these Prussian devils as she possibly could.

The sergeant regarded Hannah for a few seconds and then lunged forward. His grip was improbably powerful; he hauled her up onto the counter in a single movement, pinning her to it and pointing in her face. His manner was one not of malice or lascivious excitement but immense boredom.

'You are prisoner of Kaiser,' he told her in careless, makeshift French. 'You fight us, you die.'

PART FOUR

Illumination

I

The atrium of the American Embassy was filled with people, as it had been on Clem's five previous visits since the sortie. All nationalities were present among this crowd, but by far the majority were Germans, the Prussians and Bavarians who'd lived in Paris under the Empire – waiters, jewellers, barbers, locksmiths, along with their wives and children – and been sealed in by their own army. As they lacked official representation, and met only with hostile unconcern from the French, no attempt had been made to secure them safe passage out of the city. They were a miserable, persecuted-looking bunch, gaunt and shabbily clothed even by the standards of besieged Paris. Sticking together in groups of a dozen or more, they murmured in their guttural language and glanced constantly towards the doors, as if expecting National Guardsmen to burst in and start making arrests.

It was around half-past three on the afternoon of Christmas Eve, and these German mendicants were gathered for a festive almsgiving. The American minister, the honourable Eli Washburne, had taken it upon himself to care for all who found themselves stranded in Paris without the means to live, sustaining several thousand from his apparently bottomless stockroom. Some Second Empire bureaucrat had thought it a great jest to assign the world's one true republic a building decorated in the most splendid, palatial fashion. Trestle tables were set out across lush red carpets; boots, blankets and tins of grits were being dispensed beneath gilded archways and pilasters; earnest exhortations not to neglect religious observance at this holy time of year were echoing from ceilings splashed with pastel-hued rococo debauches.

Clem disposed of his cigarette end in a marble urn. 'Stirs the deuced soul, don't it,' he said, scratching his beard. 'Such disinterested charity. Basic humanity and all that, asserting itself in a time of crisis.'

Besson was peering ahead into the gloomy hall, which was unlit in the late December afternoon – gas had been turned off across the city a fortnight earlier. He was attempting to catch the eye of an official standing at one end of the tables. He didn't comment.

'Puts one in mind of Richard Wallace,' Clem went on, enjoying this rare spot of positive reflection. 'The only rich Englishman left in Paris, Émile – who's now feeding all the poor ones. I've heard that he's taken recently to walking from *mairie* to *mairie*, leaving packets of banknotes for the relief of the needy. They say—'

The *aérostier* went forward without a word, snaking through the queues, honing in on his target. Clem wondered briefly if he should follow and decided that there was little point. What could he possibly add to the discussion? He lit another cigarette, slid a flask from his pocket and took a swig; and recoiled with a hard shudder, the hair standing up on his neck and forearms. He'd bought this stuff a few minutes earlier, out in the street. It was rum, he supposed, but had a suspiciously chemical whiff about it – rather like formaldehyde or some kind of preserving fluid. What was a fellow to do, though? The second sip was not so bad; the third actually quite pleasant.

Besson was walking back over – and straight past, towards the doors. Clem followed him out into the street. Thirty or forty Parisians were gathered around a government bulletin that had been pasted to the wall of a church, striking familiar attitudes of dismay and disbelief. This notice told of another decisive defeat, scarcely three and a half weeks after the hammering at Champigny. A few days earlier, the unlikely decision had been reached to attempt a second break-through, this time to the north. There had been a surprising amount of enthusiasm for this assault, both in the government chamber and on the boulevards – to cleanse the humiliation of their previous trouncing, Clem guessed, or just to alleviate the stifling ennui. The word at the Grand, however, as the casualties had started to come in, was that the French had been outclassed once more. The National Guard had again fled the field, infecting the reserves with their cowardice and insubordination. Regular troops sent to dig forward trenches had found the earth frozen hard; and had been left shivering on the battlefield, without orders and close to mutiny, until the Prussian artillery had opened up and torn them to scraps.

Clem buttoned the doctor's green wool suit – now the tone and texture of old moss after an unsuccessful attempt at laundering in the lower reaches of the hotel. The rum sloshed about in his pocket. He would have taken another gulp to rub the edge off the gruelling cold, but was obliged to adopt a sort of half-trot just to keep Besson in sight. He couldn't tell if the Frenchman was actually going some-where – or if he was walking at this speed to shake off his emotions, in the way that a man might try to rid himself of a persistent wasp.

'They haven't seen him, then?' Clem called out after they'd covered a couple of blocks. 'No sign?'

Besson stopped, waiting impatiently for Clem to catch up. There was hatred on his sharp, quick face – hatred for all mankind. He turned, extending his right hand. 'Sergeant Peabody has disappeared,' he said.

Clem tossed him the flask. Tracking down the ravenous American had been Besson's fixation since their return to Paris; Clem had joined him as soon as his headache had subsided to a manageable level. Peabody was the link, Besson was sure of it. He was the only person who'd known of the *aérostier*'s intention to speak to that American newspaperman in Tours. He must have told someone else, someone who could be traced back to Allix. They were going to find him, Besson had declared, and obtain a confession. This would be the proof they needed, the definite connection between Allix and the demise of the *Aphrodite* – and enough, surely, to merit a full investigation into the Leopard of Montmartre.

Sergeant Peabody, however, had eluded them utterly. No one had seen or spoken to the embassy night-watchman in weeks. They'd been all over the city, to every one of his haunts; a string of drinking dens and low theatres on the Left Bank; the arcades of the Palais Royal, where he'd apparently liked to linger with his pipe, staring at the shop-girls. It was as if he'd slipped out somehow, run the line, or taken refuge in a private hideaway unknown to any of his countrymen. They were at an impasse.

'What now, then? A word with Allix himself?' Clem suggested – seriously doubting as he spoke that he'd have the nerve for it.

This won him a withering look. Besson, like Clem, hadn't shaved since the doctor's house in Tournan-en-Brie; there were a couple of new silver hairs in his beard. He drank

298

down a long draught of the rum, not seeming to notice its coarseness.

'Do you honestly think I have not tried that?' he said, wiping his mouth on his glove. 'I could not even get *close* to him. The mood in Montmartre has deteriorated further since the sortie – grown yet more aggressive towards anyone seen to be bourgeois. If they thought I was attempting to blacken the name of their great chief they would hang me from a windmill sail.'

Jean-Jacques Allix had been far from quiet in the storm of fury and recrimination that had followed the Prussian recapture of Champigny. He'd not been chastened by the devastation he'd helped to bring about. His bereavement, if it had affected him at all, appeared to have only intensified his desire to fight – to lead the National Guard into battle after battle. He'd been one of the louder voices demanding this latest disastrous action, and had continued his one-man raids; several strident calls to arms had been worked into Elizabeth's accounts in the *Figaro*. Those daft little red paw-prints and sets of cat-fangs were being painted everywhere, across every arrondissement, alongside slogans that called for the destruction of the Prussians and the destruction of bourgeois Paris as if they were heads on the same monster.

The two men walked onto the place de l'Étoile. The Arc de Triomphe was encased in wooden panels and sandbags to protect its statues, making it resemble a huge gravestone – appropriately enough, Clem thought. Lengths of cord were strung across the mouths of the avenues leading into the square, from which petroleum lamps had been suspended. These were a common sight in Paris since the end of the gas, casting a thin, insubstantial light that seemed to deepen the murk rather than relieve it. At night you sometimes got the sense of no longer being in a city, surrounded by man-made structures and people; it was easy to believe yourself shut up in a system of giant caverns, far underground.

Several companies of militia milled about near the Arc, lounging on the artillery emplacements around its base. Clem couldn't tell if they'd been engaged in the recent action, but they'd responded to defeat as the National Guard responded to everything: through the consumption of heroic quantities of hard liquor. Paris had next to no food left, but was still awash with drink of every description, the populace pickling itself to forget its woes, seeking solace in the bellowed certainties of intoxicated patriotism. There was bickering among these guardsmen, though – debates and brawls and defensive declarations. Some passers-by were shouting abuse their way; a group of women in black raincoats informed them that they were *la honte de Paris* before hurrying off down the avenue de Friedland.

Clem went to a bench beneath a cluster of inert lamp-posts. 'Come on, old man,' he said, 'let's rest ourselves for a minute.'

They drank in silence, passing the flask back and forth. This taste for grog was a recent thing for the *aérostier*. Clem had been unsurprised to discover that the stuff made him a touch surly.

Neither had mentioned her name, not once. They were both united by their grief and completely divided by it. Besson, on the surface at least, was angry. In his mind was a list of the people responsible for what had happened: Jean-Jacques Allix was at the top, no doubt, and Émile Besson in the first five. He now strove to make things right, as he saw it, despite plainly knowing that this was impossible – and when he was finished and all was over she would still be gone.

300

For his part, Clem was confused, mainly; numb as well, definitely numb; and more than a little anxious. He did have a sense that he could have done more – insisted that she leave the National Guard or something like that, the way that brothers were supposed to be able to – but was also aware that she'd have just ignored him as always. The situation really was unfeasibly strange. Hannah Elizabeth Pardy, his twin sister, so vital and astounding, had been brought down by a Prussian sharpshooter. She wasn't away in another city or another country but *dead*, extinguished for ever, buried by Allix in an allotment on the fringes of Champigny – to spare her the indignity of a soldiers' mass grave, he'd said. It was beyond anything Clem could bring himself to imagine. He was familiar enough with loss, from the passing of his father and others, to realise that something else was coming, something bad: the blackness that follows the blind shock of impact. Often, as he wandered half-cut about the dreary streets of Paris, he could feel it hovering above his head, ready to drop over him. He was waiting for it.

'You'd think,' Clem said at last, indicating the National Guardsmen by the Arc, 'that our Leopard would have tired of lionising that lot by now. I mean, they're proving a bit of a bloody disappointment, aren't they?'

'He might also be inclined to hesitate,' Besson remarked, 'if he appreciated that the provisional government is delaying our surrender in order to kill off as many of his potential revolutionaries as it can in these foolish sorties.' He paused to drink. 'Unless, of course, he appreciates this all too well.'

Clem snorted. 'That scheme hasn't got much chance of working, has it? The blighters drop their guns and run the instant anybody takes a shot at them.'

Besson had nothing to add and the conversation lapsed. Clem considered broaching the topic of Christmas, now only hours away; the shrivelled turkeys on sale in Les Halles for upwards of two hundred francs apiece, for instance, or perhaps the story of the gent on the rue Lafayette who was fattening his pet cat to serve up in place of a fowl – to be garnished with grilled dormice, it was rumoured, as substitutes for sausages. Right then he found that he regarded Christmas with a certain vague fondness, largely on account of the association with crackling fires and large dinners. As he opened his mouth to speak, however, he saw Hannah, his companion at so many of those festive tables, sitting next to him in her best dress as Elizabeth lectured them on the specious wickedness of Christianity, or relieved their elderly butler of the carving knife so that she could hack at the goose herself. The memory was indescribably painful. He leaped away from it, casting about desperately for something else to say.

'Have – have you been up to the Gare du Nord, Émile, of late?'

Besson shifted uncomfortably on the bench. 'I go there, Clement,' he muttered, pronouncing the name to rhyme with *cement*, 'but there is little point to it. They are giving most of the flights to Godard's men now, over in the Gare d'Orléans. I do not know why. Nadar thinks—' The *aérostier* stopped talking and sat very still for a few moments. 'None of it is any use. We are wasting our time, every one of us. We would be better off surrendering – letting the Prussians march up our boulevards, barrack their soldiers in the Louvre, stable their horses in Les Invalides. If we do not hand Paris over to them they will see her burn. It has all been for nothing.'

He looked away suddenly, towards the Arc, as if disgusted both by his own outburst and the passions that underpinned it. Cursing in French, he rose to his feet and strode off, making for one of the north-eastern avenues.

302

This had become Besson's standard leave-taking. Clem didn't try to follow or find out where he was going. 'See you later then, old man,' he said to the pavement, giving the flask a shake to gauge how much was left. 'You know where I'll be.'

The gates of the Jardin des Plantes had been left open to admit anyone who cared to enter. Elizabeth went through first, skirting the museums of natural history and mineralogy, heading for what appeared to be a refreshment pavilion; Clem was a few steps behind, retying the voluminous scarf he'd fashioned from one of his bathroom's purple velvet curtains. It had been a long walk. There were no cabs or omnibuses in Paris any more; every horse saved from the abattoir was harnessed to a gun-carriage or an ambulance-cart. The morning was clear and not too blindingly cold, meaning that the crowds on the central boulevards were heavier than they'd been for a while. People were stamping up and down the rue de Rivoli, between the Hôtel de Ville and the place de la Concorde, damning Trochu and his wretched failure of an administration, waving their red flags and demanding all sorts of fine-sounding, unachievable things. The boulevards themselves were dirtier than ever, caked in mud as noxious as any found in the back alleys of Limehouse or St Giles. Pasted declarations and counter-declarations, torn and weather-bleached, hung from every available wall like beggars' rags.

Elizabeth had maintained a determined pace through all of this, despite her claims of increasing frailty; she'd refused even to let Clem carry the small satchel she'd acquired for her notebook and papers. Now they'd arrived at the Jardin des Plantes, though, her priority was plain. She needed to sit down.

303

No one had set foot in the iron-and-glass refreshment pavilion for weeks. The potted plants were dead; the mosaic floor was scattered with smashed crockery; the kitchens, located at the back, had long since been broken open and looted. Elizabeth selected a table close to the doors. Clem took the chair opposite her.

'When is it to happen?' he asked.

'Ten, I believe,' she replied, 'at the park's western extremity.'

Composed as ever in a blue winter bonnet, she was giving the impression of one who might be suffering but would admit no weakness, not to anyone, not for an instant. The spines were up on the Pardy porcupine. She was continuing with her life. Clem was reminded of when his father had died, very suddenly, while he and Hannah had still been children. They'd known widows – the black dresses, the sobbing, the months of seclusion – and had expected that their mother might behave in a similar way. Open expressions of sorrow, however, were few and far between. There had been a round of commemorative dinners and public recitals, staged by his poet friends and a handful of literary societies, at which she'd dazzled all and sundry; and before the season was out she was romantically linked to a rising playwright. Mrs Pardy was not one to languish in desolation.

Elizabeth had come into Clem's room the previous evening and specifically requested that he accompany her on this expedition to the Jardin des Plantes. He'd considered enquiring why she was prepared to accept him as her assistant once more, having denigrated him so roundly over their wolf steaks – and perhaps mentioning again how she'd abandoned him to the Mazas, or her lack of interest in his balloon crash and the injury he'd sustained, or the possibility that she, through her alliance with Allix and active promotion of these luckless sorties, might actually bear some measure of responsibility for Hannah's death. Energy was required for this, though, a lot more than he possessed, and an appetite for further confrontation; so he'd merely agreed and started to get ready. There was never any real reconciliation to be had with Elizabeth, just a sort of weary recognition that you'd have to accept what she'd done and carry on. It was ridiculously optimistic to expect her to admit wrongdoing – or even realise that it had taken place.

Also, in truth, Clem had little else to occupy his hours. His room at the Grand was too cold for anything but burying oneself in bed; upon rising that morning he'd had to thaw his toothbrush over a candle. He'd actually made an attempt to start his book, his *Daring Airborne Escape*, but had quickly given up. The crash had rather attenuated the narrative, and complicated it with suggestions of sabotage; the whole episode now seemed a tragicomic mess, certainly not the stuff from which great adventure stories were made. He had an odd clouded feeling as well, that he couldn't quite shake – as if his mind was a sheet of smoke-blackened glass through which only dulled outlines could be seen. He'd begun to fear that his knock to the head had permanently reduced him.

It was good to be out of the blasted Grand, though, and have the pervasive smells of blood, lint and chloroform washed away by the winter breeze. The hotel had been the setting for by far the most dismal Christmas of Clem's life. Beef replacing horse in the municipal ration had been the sole official concession to merrymaking. This repast, tooth-looseningly tough and totally without flavour, had been eaten in coat and gloves to an unalleviated accompaniment of wails from the hospital in the lobby. What yuletide wishes had passed between the remaining guests had been delivered with bitter sarcasm. Elizabeth had chosen to deal with the occasion by not emerging from her room. Drinks with Besson in the Café de la Paix, Clem's one slight hope for a spot of jollity, had been an utter failure. The *aérostier* had been hollow-eyed and silent, his vigorous spirit finally defeated by the disappearance of Sergeant Peabody. Clem had got the idea that seeing him reminded Besson of Hannah – so he'd decided to be merciful and stay away, for a while at least.

Outside the refreshment pavilion, a gang of obvious newspapermen were advancing into the gardens, loudly disputing the quickest route to the zoological department as they went. It occurred to Clem that he hadn't heard the gravelly tones of the *Sentinel*'s Paris correspondent in well over a week. His mother, for all the notice she'd brought upon herself, had been a solitary figure of late.

'Doesn't Mr Inglis want to witness this event?' he asked, taking out a cigarette. 'I'd have expected him to be here.'

Elizabeth pulled her cloak tighter around the shoulders. 'We have decided to spend less time together, Mr Inglis and I,' she replied. 'He'd been tiring me most dreadfully, Clement, with his despairing pronouncements. As his beloved Empire is gone, he is quite happy to will absolute destruction on France and her people.' She sighed. 'I don't honestly know what I was thinking. It was the result of simple boredom, I suppose, like that wretched carrot-topped cocotte of yours.'

Clem lit up, looking away; the tobacco was stale, like that of every cigarette left in Paris. Laure Fleurot was a delicate subject. Four days earlier, while at a particularly low ebb, he'd resolved to find her. Her treatment of him, he'd decided, hadn't actually been so very bad; he'd convinced himself that there might be some chance of reunion if he apologised profusely enough. All he'd wanted was to lie alongside her and feel her copper hair against his cheek.

Montmartre, however, had refused to give Mademoiselle Laure up – her or anyone else Clem knew. The atmosphere in those lanes, as Besson had warned, had been most unsettling. Quarantine notices for smallpox were everywhere, disease being the inevitable corollary of the extreme hunger that gripped the poorer arrondissements; truculent queues wound away from the shops designated as *cantines municipales*; every other door-knocker was wrapped in black crêpe. He'd gone down to that apartment on the boulevard de Clichy, of which he had so many potent, precious memories, to find it serving as a kennel to half a dozen slack-jawed Breton reserves. He'd retreated, deeply perplexed, unsure of what to do next.

'Probably for the best,' he said. 'Mr Inglis, I mean.'

Clem's own guess was that Han's art had been involved in the rift between his mother and the journalist. The contents of Madame Lantier's shed had been brought in its entirety to Elizabeth's rooms at the Grand. Clem recalled Inglis's powerful scorn for these paintings on that first night; it was easy to imagine this overcoming his lover's docility or respect for Elizabeth's loss and some disparaging comment leaking out. Such a slip would have earned him a prompt excommunication. Han's works had been made sacred by her death. Elizabeth would talk about them with the faintest justification; she was talking about them right now, in fact.

'She made several very accomplished *en plein* studies here, you know. They depict crowds, naturally, rather than beasts in their cages or anything like that. People, ordinary folk, experienced as we truly experience one another in these places. Chance encounters. A glimpse – a passing gesture. Momentary fragments of other lives. No story, Clement, no forced meaning or trite little tale, just what we observe as we move through the world.'

Clem nodded, studying the tip of his musty cigarette; any second now she'd get onto the portrait.

'Obviously they are not as considered as the large portrait. There we have the *chef d'oeuvre*. To think that she would not have embarked upon it had Jean-Jacques and I not urged her to! He is *before you*, Clement – brought directly before you.'

I should bloody hope not, Clem thought; he mumbled something that could have been interpreted as concurrence. Elizabeth had made it plain that she didn't believe he'd been anywhere near vocal enough in his praise of Han's productions. He had to admit that he was rather reluctant to admire a portrait of the Leopard – the man who'd brought down the *Aphrodite* and set his sister, his *artist sister*, on the route that had led to her death on a battlefield. The thing stood over Elizabeth's fireplace, in her sitting room. He'd glanced at it once, agreed it was excellent, and not looked its way since.

'I am sure that when my book is published,' Elizabeth continued, 'interest in her work will *soar*. That such a talent was permitted to flourish without encouragement, unacknowledged, will be seen as a monumental sin – emblematic of all that was rotten about the Second Empire. Monsieur Manet and his set at the Café Guerbois will never forgive themselves.'

Elizabeth was growing agitated. She'd been facing across the pavilion; now she turned sharply towards Clem, the legs of her iron chair scraping on the floor.

'It was true devotion, Clement. She felt the world so *keenly*. This was why she could give so much of herself to Jean-Jacques and the ultras. Theirs is the cause of the *people* – the wider world. She wasn't interested in the theoretical assertions of Herr Marx or Monsieur Blanc or any of them. For her it was simply a question of *justice*, of the poor being allowed their rightful freedoms.'

Clem kept his eyes down. 'Justice, yes,' he said. 'Freedom.'

'You don't understand, of course,' Elizabeth pronounced with some contempt. 'You were always opposite twins, were you not? You are like your father, a glib being at heart, inclined towards whimsy. Hannah was a resolute soul, a dedicated soul. We were so alike, she and I. It is why we could not be together, ultimately – why we squabbled so.'

Clem had heard this many times before. His own view was a little different. There were certain similarities between Han and their mother, but it was their father she really resembled: they'd both been artists to the marrow of their bones. Seeing something of the life she'd built here in Paris had made that abundantly clear. Where this left him and Elizabeth, as distinct from one another as ink and engine oil, he couldn't begin to say. He accepted, however, that in times of bereavement the dead have their lives and characters remoulded to meet the needs of those still living; so he nodded again, doing his best not to listen to what his mother was saying.

Elizabeth rose from her chair. 'Come now,' she said abruptly, as if it had been Clem's idea to sit in the first place. 'It is almost time.'

They went outside. The drumming of shell-fire was louder and more insistent here on the Left Bank. The Prussians were finishing off the year with a sustained bombardment of the southern forts. It seemed that they were becoming tired of swatting back these risible sorties, and were preparing to get serious.

Before Elizabeth and Clem was a network of tarmacadamed paths, winding off around clumps of trampled shrubbery. The fingerposts had been removed for firewood, but Elizabeth appeared to know where she was going. Soon they began to see the cages, as fine as miniature exhibition halls. Roofs bulged into exquisite onion domes; slender bars were painted white with red and gold capitals. Some had perches or hutches, or small ponds for swimming, while others opened onto landscaped paddocks. Every one was empty.

'I've heard that certain beasts have been spared,' Elizabeth said as she led them on, deeper into the zoo, 'notably the simians. The directors know their Darwin, I suppose, and judge it to be a shade too close to cannibalism.'

A male crowd, both military and civilian, was gathering up ahead around an outsized stable, twice as tall as normal, on the edge of a straw-strewn enclosure. Elizabeth was recognised as they approached and the men parted, making a passage to a place at the front. They were greeted by a terrible bellow, a screeching blast of distress from a very large animal: the cry of the elephant. Through the stable's open doors Clem could see two huge forms, shifting in their separate stalls. Manacles and chains were being prepared on a paved section of the enclosure. An address was underway, a grizzled fellow in a broad-brimmed hat holding forth with his hands clasped behind his back. At first, Clem couldn't catch much of what he was saying and assumed that he was a keeper – the elephants' custodian, perhaps, paying the unlucky creatures a final tribute. He came to realise, however, that this was actually the man who was to shoot them, describing in some detail the special ammunition he'd selected for the task. Theatrically, this executioner produced a bullet for their inspection: a chrome cone the size of a two-shilling cigar.

The first elephant was led out, surrounded by keepers and park officials.

'Castor,' said Elizabeth, her notebook at the ready. 'His brother Pollux is to follow – they are twins, you see. I hear the butcher Deboos on the boulevard Haussmann has bought them both for eighteen hundred pounds. He plans to have skinned trunk in his window by the end of the day.'

Clem swallowed, digging his chin into the curtain-scarf, suddenly appreciating what he was about to see. He'd never been to Regent's Park Zoo and certainly never to Africa or anywhere like that. All he'd experienced of elephants were etchings and paintings, and a skeleton, once, in the Oxford museum. He'd never set eyes on a live specimen before; and now he was to watch one be put to death.

Castor was an unlikely-looking jumble of parts – legs awkwardly long, shoulders hunched, bundled together under a loose, colourless skin. He knew that danger was close, but he evidently trusted a couple of the people around him and allowed himself to be manacled without complaint. Clem was struck by the tiny, swivelling eye in the enormous skull; the hairs and pale spots on his crown; the shrunken, wrinkled ears. The elephant's tusks were mere stubs, all but buried in the folds of his face. He was adolescent, Clem estimated, still a distance from full maturity. The famous trunk was feeling the air with gentle caution, searching for something that plainly was not there. It was positively ghoulish: a genteel crowd of natural scientists, reporters, sportsmen and soldiers congregating to end this gigantic lump of life. Clem ground his teeth, wondering what the devil he was doing. He really hadn't thought this one through properly.

The shot was startling, a flat, ringing bass note, deeper and more penetrating than a standard discharge. Castor was hit beneath his right shoulder, the bullet leaving a coin-sized hole in his hide; he barely flinched, blinking in the powder-smoke as his executioner lowered his double-barrelled sporting gun. Rooted to the spot, Clem was seized by the mad hope that the shot might have been absorbed somehow – that Castor's immense bulk might render him

311

indestructible, at least to the weapons of man. But then one leg wobbled, giving out; and the stricken creature started making this horrible gargling noise, choking from an internal haemorrhage. Butcher boys rushed forward with buckets to catch the blood that was now pumping from the bullet-hole, spurting to the slowing rhythm of the elephant's heart. Several among the crowd let out exultant exclamations, those closest to him jumping clear in case he toppled over. Castor dropped to his knees; Pollux let out another plaintive cry from inside the stable. The first bucket was taken away, filled to the brim, the blood-flecks on the butcher boys' wrists bright and rich as fresh blackberries. The elephant slumped onto his side, head lolling and trunk gesticulating weakly. The second bucket was soon full as well.

Clem's paralysis eased. He tried to breathe. For Christ's sake, he told himself, it is only a blessed animal, a beast like any other – like all the horses and dogs and God knows what else we've killed for their meat. He felt intolerably stifled, though, as if he was drowning in the open air. Turning to go, anxious to escape before the dispatching of Pollux, he noticed that Elizabeth was no longer next to him. This was strange. Why had she dragged them both halfway across Paris only to skip out just before the main event? He scanned the edges of the crowd, catching sight of her blue bonnet as it disappeared behind a screen of laurel bushes. Glad to have a decent reason for getting well away from the dying elephant and its doomed brother, he went after her.

Past the laurels was a broad courtyard. Elizabeth was at its opposite side, entering an austere neo-classical building. Three large cages were attached to its eastern wall, constructed not from bars but a sturdy grille. There wasn't a soul around; everyone was at the elephant enclosure. Clem hurried across the courtyard and followed his mother through the doors. Beyond was a wide central corridor, running between reinforced panels of the same grille as outside. It was dark and barn-like, the dusty atmosphere soured by the rancid odour of cat urine.

Elizabeth was halfway down this corridor, talking with a tall, clean-shaven man. Clem swore under his breath. It was Jean-Jacques Allix. He was leaning slightly towards her, listening carefully to what she was telling him, an expression of profound concern on his face. The Leopard of Montmartre was not in his signature black for once, but a grey overcoat and a kepi, pulled low over his eyes: the disguise of a wanted man. This was clearly a pre-arranged meeting and the real reason for their visit to the Jardin des Plantes that morning. Allix passed his mother a packet of papers. They embraced, speaking earnestly as if reaffirming a vow; then he gave a shallow bow and started for the doors.

Allix showed no surprise upon seeing Clem. Coming to a halt, the Leopard considered him calmly, his gaze lingering on the patchy beard and the purple curtain-scarf. Clem felt about four feet high.

'I am pleased to see that you have recovered from your accident,' he said.

Clem glared back, imagining what Besson would do in his place – the furious accusations he would level. He began to tremble. 'Yes, well,' he managed to reply, 'no bloody thanks to *you*.'

The Leopard's smile was pitying; he patted Clem's shoulder with his crippled hand, the wooden fingers rattling inside the glove. 'Take care, Mr Pardy,' he said as he went. 'There is much still to come.'

Elizabeth was close behind. Clem's headache was returning, welling around his eyes. He pushed up his hat, mopped his brow on the sleeve of the green wool jacket and attempted to regain his equanimity. It was pointless to try to talk to his mother about Allix. Everything had gone too far. Hannah's lover, like her paintings, was completely beyond question, as was the radical cause they'd shared. Any allegations against him were seen as a conspiracy; Émile Besson she regarded as a government man through and through, out to damage Jean-Jacques with baseless lies. She looked rather pleased that Clem had witnessed her little tête-à-tête. It served as an effective declaration of her continuing stake in Allix – of her determination that the Pardy connection with him would last beyond Hannah's death.

Staying quiet was undoubtedly the best course, but Clem couldn't help himself. 'I thought these interviews took place in your sitting room at the Grand,' he said. 'Tales of bloody mayhem by the fireside, that sort of thing.'

This earned him a warning glance. 'It is too dangerous. The link between us is too widely known. They tricked Gustave Flourens during the first sortie, Clement – arrested him when he went forward to join his *Tirailleurs* and threw him in the Mazas. A similar trap could easily be laid for Jean-Jacques.'

'But he came to you before the sortie, didn't he?' Clem insisted. 'A visit for every article, you said.'

Elizabeth harrumphed and sighed, waving this away; and Clem realised that the time Allix had come to tell her about Han had actually been the Leopard's sole appearance at the Grand Hotel. These packets were their main means of communication, and the raw material from which the *Figaro* articles were formed. Growing defensive, his mother now treated him to a dollop of her usual rhetoric, rambling on about how the government was planning to starve the people into submission; how the army was effectively colluding with the Prussians; how Allix and his guardsmen

314

were burning for action; how Paris must save Paris and restore the martial honour of France.

Clem remembered what Besson had said, in the place de l'Étoile and elsewhere. 'Surely, though, these lunatic sorties play straight into the provisional government's hands? Every red guardsman gunned down by the Prussians is a trouble-maker they don't have to worry about any longer.'

This made Elizabeth angry. 'Do you propose, then, that we sit here and do nothing?' she snapped. 'Many in Paris want *revenge*, Clement, Jean-Jacques included. The Prussians are a merciless, dishonourable foe. Did you know that they frequently surrender on the battlefield, only to open fire when the French approach them? They have raped and torched and shot their way through huge swathes of this country. Countless innocents have fallen.' She stepped towards him. 'Can you forget so easily that they killed your sister?'

This stunned them both into silence; it was harsh, even by Elizabeth's standards. Clem turned to one of the grille partitions. A shape moved behind it, against the far wall. The size of a large gun dog, the animal kept close to the ground as it passed through a bar of daylight. Clem saw matted fur the colour of old hay, a dozen faded black spots and the ribs standing out beneath them; the starving cat paused, baring its fangs with a feeble hiss before slipping back into the gloom.

'By Jove,' he said, struggling to seem unaffected, 'a leopard. What was Mr Inglis's term? *Pantera pardus*. An apt meeting place, I must admit – although this poor puss is rather less alarming than your creation.'

Elizabeth knew she'd gone too far, but was incapable of framing an apology. She would just do nothing, as usual, and let Clem deal with her remark however he chose. 'It lives,' she said, 'as no hunter in Paris will get in the cage.'

She reached for her satchel, fumbling with the buckle. 'I have to return to the Grand. I have writing to do.'

For a moment Allix's packet was face down against the satchel's leather flap. Between the binding ribbon and Elizabeth's gloved fingers Clem glimpsed part of a paragraph, written in English: ' . . . *the sergeant saw me framed in the doorway and attempted to alert his comrades, but my blade found his heart before . . .*' The hand was scrupulously neat, black ink with a faint leftward slope, laid out evenly across the paper. Clem recognised it immediately.

'The letter!' he cried, pointing. 'The bloody *letter*!'

Elizabeth was mystified. 'What in heaven's name are you talking about?'

'The letter that brought us here!' Clem stared at her. She really seemed to have forgotten. 'The one urging us to rescue Han. I'd convinced myself that it was Besson's doing, a bit of well-intentioned meddling – but it's the same *writing*, Elizabeth! *Allix* bloody well sent it!'

Elizabeth frowned; she put the packet away and fastened the buckle. 'I don't see why he would. What could he possibly stand to gain from such a move?'

The scheme fell open in Clem's mind, unfolding like the panels of a map. 'He knew who you were, and that you were Han's mother. He knew it from the very beginning. He wanted to draw you over here – get you caught up in the siege. Get the famous Mrs Pardy on his side. He knew what you could do for him, in the press and so forth. He's – he's been using us all.'

'How absurd,' Elizabeth retorted. 'Your alcoholic indulgences are taking their toll on your reason, Clement. Jean-Jacques couldn't have written any *letter*. His handwriting is next to illegible, on account of his American injuries. He told me that he is forced to dictate his reports to an adjutant.'

Clem became exasperated. 'It doesn't matter exactly who wrote them – they came from the *same damned place*. I'll show you. I still have the letter, back at the Grand. Hell's bells, d'you honestly not see it?'

His mother returned the satchel to her shoulder. 'A good part of your problem, Clement,' she proclaimed, gliding towards the doors, 'is that you have never been able to tell what is important and what is not.'

II

The bath, Hannah's first since her capture, had left her feeling raw, freshly peeled, the chill morning air stinging her skin. She adjusted her kepi, tightened the knot of damp hair at the nape of her neck and surveyed the square. It was another dull, frozen day, but the Prussian-held village of Gagny was turned out in honour of an extremely important guest. The horizontal black, red and white tricolour of the Northern German states had been hung from the eaves of every house. Several infantry companies were arranged in parade order on the frosty green. A small regimental band was parping away before the town hall, playing something that conjured an image of portly couples dancing a waltz.

The stock of a Prussian rifle pressed into Hannah's back, directing her towards three close ranks of prisoners, a hundred of them at least, who'd been assembled for inspection on the far side of the green. This was a surprise: she'd had no idea that there were so many others being held in Gagny. Every other day she'd been brought out here for a half-hour's perambulation. She'd taken the opportunity to memorise what she could of the village's layout, observe its

318

routines and patterns, anything that might prove useful should she manage to work open her cell door or give her ever-vigilant guard the slip. In all that time she hadn't seen a whisker of these fellow captives, yet here they were – men of the line, Zoaves, militia – a full sample of the defenders of Paris. Like Hannah, they'd been permitted to bathe, but were still a scruffy lot, their uniforms filthy and torn and their beards overgrown. Around a third bore wounds of various kinds. Their role that morning, she supposed, was to look defeated, and they were fulfilling it admirably.

Laure Fleurot was the only woman among them. She slouched at the right end of the formation, furthest from the town hall, her orange hair hanging over her face and her hands deep in the pockets of her greatcoat. The *vivandières* had been led off in different directions as soon as they'd arrived in Gagny. Laure had struggled hard against this, thinking that there might be some safety in numbers.

'That's my sister!' she'd cried, bucking against the soldiers' arms. 'You Prussian bastards, that's my damned *sister*! You can't part us, you *can't*!'

Hannah had been prepared for the worst. They'd locked her in a tiny storeroom in the cellar of an occupied town-house, empty save for a cast-iron chamber pot. For the first few days she waited, her ears straining for the scrape of a military boot on the basement steps, intending to use her teeth and nails – and her chamber pot – to protect herself as best she could. No boots came, however; no drunken soldiers bent on violation threw back her door. Neither did anyone attempt to interrogate, torture or starve her. The daily prisoner's ration turned out to be more than a Montmartre resident had in half a week. Her cell's high, brick-sized window was glazed against the weather; a hot-water pipe in a corner even kept her reasonably warm. Her guard had lowered.

319

Another week had passed. Hannah's isolation, the lack of *anything*, soon became tormenting. She was determined not to give up. Jean-Jacques had survived the sortie – she was convinced of it. The only acceptable explanation was that he'd become separated from the 197th on the Villiers Plateau and had fought his way back to the French line. Buried in her storeroom, surrounded by enemy troops, Hannah had to believe that he was alive and free – and very probably out searching for her. It was her duty to rejoin him. She'd resolved to escape from Gagny as soon as she could.

Initially, Hannah hadn't thought that this would prove too difficult. She was in a village, for God's sake, not a gaol. There were no towers, moats, gates or anything like that; a little boldness and she'd be away. In practice, of course, it was not so simple. She was always either locked up or under close watch. They shot people, these Prussians – bothersome prisoners or saboteurs brought in from the countryside. She sometimes heard the rifle reports in her cell. A poorly considered plan and she'd meet her end against a wall with a Prussian handkerchief bound around her eyes.

At a loss, Hannah had taken to sketching on the cell's earth floor with her fingertip. Relying on memory, she composed a series of siege vignettes – guardhouse scenes, the storming of the Hôtel de Ville, Jean-Jacques addressing the Club Rue Rébeval – erasing each one with her coat-cuff as evening arrived. She found herself dreaming of colour: gleaming caterpillars of ivy, cream, russet and jet that squeezed out through cracks in the plaster, blending and spreading to form sunlit vistas of parks and boulevards – modern Paris bustling around her.

Morning would often fail to break in that deadly winter, the black cold of night never fully lifting. Too late, Hannah came to understand why convicts keep tallies of their internment. Her days became a disorientated muddle, drawings in the dirt that were effaced at dusk and gone for ever. Christmas caught her unawares – simultaneously amazed that she'd been imprisoned for so long, and that it had only been three and a half weeks since her capture. All it meant, at any rate, was the smell of roasting meat seeping down through the floorboards, accompanied by raucous laughter and carols sung in German.

Outside the storeroom's high window was a lane, running from the village into the countryside. It was usually quiet, the view of the mildewed wall opposite only occasionally interrupted by a column of marching soldiers or the steel-rimmed wheels of a military supply wagon. With the New Year, however, came a marked increase in traffic. Monstrous artillery pieces blocked what little light Hannah had; shell-carts creaked by constantly. She'd quickly deduced what this surge of munitions meant. Gagny was close to the main eastbound railway, the Strasbourg line; men and equipment arriving from Prussia or the occupied territories passed through the village to deployments elsewhere. Preparations were underway for the bombardment of Paris.

This realisation had jolted Hannah from her torpor. It seemed unfathomable at first, a crime of bewildering magnitude. The Kaiser's men were about to turn the most devastating artillery ever created on Paris, an ancient seat of beauty and enlightenment – and the two million civilians sheltering within it. Unexpectedly, along with everything else, Hannah found that she was worried for her mother. Jean-Jacques and her friends in Montmartre would know how to manage this latest hazard. Clement had left Paris with Émile Besson, floating over the Prussians into another part of France. Elizabeth, though, would be drawn irresistibly into the heart of the barrage.

321

She'd be taking all manner of foolish risks for the sake of her book.

There was absolutely nothing Hannah could do. She paced her cell; she kicked at the walls. This was *her time*. Her home was under attack, *under fire*, and she was locked in a cellar in Gagny. The frustration was excruciating. When on her allotted constitutional, she tried to detect some change in the ubiquitous shell-fire, some slight shift in pitch or reverberation that might tell her whether the onslaught had begun, but without success. Gagny was seven or eight miles from the wall. Held out here she was as good as dead – of no use to anyone.

Hope had returned in the form of laundered flags, drilling soldiers and a general frenzy of cleaning and polishing. Arrangements of a rather different sort were being made, and Hannah heard the word *Kaiser* often enough to be able to guess the occasion. A final royal tour of the line was being undertaken, before the imminent collapse of France and the Prussian victory. At dawn the next morning she was led upstairs, shown to a room containing a bath, towels and plentiful hot water, and left to wash. The visit was happening that day. Here was her chance, a distraction better than anything she could have imagined. She'd bathed and informed her guard that she was ready to be taken outside.

Laure's incarceration had obviously not been as eventless as Hannah's. Her face was bruised and her coat missing several buttons. Hannah's guard stood them together and went to the front of the prisoners' formation. Their eyes met.

'Holy Christ, Mademoiselle Pardy,' Laure whispered, as if they'd only been apart a few moments, 'we really need to get out of here.'

Before Hannah could reply, every Prussian soldier in Gagny stamped to attention. A detachment of cuirassiers swept in from the west, silver breastplates and *Pickelhauben* shining, the hooves of their huge chargers pounding through the village. In amongst them was a carriage, a fine navy-blue landau with its top open; and within was Kaiser Wilhelm, an elderly man in a general's cap, whiskers framing his precise white moustache. Wrapped in a greatcoat and scarf, he had a rather businesslike aspect, like a proprietor touring a factory. A high-ranking aide was at his side; both sat upright, taking in Gagny's modest parade as they were driven around the green to the town hall.

Across from them was a fleshy man in the same white uniform as the cavalry, with a fur-lined cloak instead of the breastplate: Chancellor Bismarck, famed mastermind of the war, responsible for many of Prussia's more nefarious strategies and the resultant suffering and humiliation of France. Hannah could scarcely believe it. What Jean-Jacques would give to be standing here with a Chassepot in his hands! Prussia could be laid low in a heartbeat.

At once vigorously healthy and bloated by indulgence, Bismarck wore a long moustache upon a dogged, jowly face. French cartoons of him depicted a bulbous aberration, a slavering beast, a rampaging, rapacious swine. Like his king, however, the chancellor bore a closer resemblance to a tycoon – a fast-living magnate clad as a cuirassier for a fancy-dress ball. Puffing on a cigarette, slumped in his seat, he appeared profoundly uninterested in the outpost at Gagny, but sight of Hannah and Laure made him lean over the side of the landau for a closer look. The expression he fixed on them was both predatory and strangely playful, as if the three of them were sharing a lewd joke.

'*Voilà*,' he announced as he rolled past, '*les Amazones!*'

A second carriage came behind, larger and less fine, bearing attendants and a couple of lesser dignitaries. Both vehicles pulled up before the town hall. There was a round of sharp salutes as Wilhelm climbed from the landau. The band began a new tune, a lurching, martial number that could have been the Prussian national anthem. Before they'd played a bar the Kaiser had gone indoors, the rest of the royal party hurrying after him. Chancellor Bismarck was more leisurely, pausing to finish his cigarette and exchange a few words with the band leader. He was making a request; as he followed Wilhelm in the music changed again, to an up-tempo hunting song.

The soldiers stood easy. Hot drinks were brought for the cuirassiers, who dismounted and were soon laughing with the infantrymen. A relaxed, distinctly celebratory air spread across the green. The French prisoners were largely forgotten. Their ranks loosened, threatening in places to dissolve completely. A few of them grumbled; someone said '*À bas Wilhelm!*', although not very loudly. Hannah watched the town hall. She could see Bismarck through one of the tall ground-floor windows, in his white tunic. He was making an expansive declaration, his arms thrown open.

'Now,' she said.

Laure snorted. 'You're not serious.'

Hannah glanced about. Her guard was turned away from her, chatting with his comrades-in-arms. No one was monitoring them. She stepped backwards, into the second rank. Laure was regarding her with a mixture of incredulity, amusement and fright, as one might an especially daring feat by a circus acrobat. She wasn't going to be left behind, though, and a moment later they were both at the rear.

Some of the Frenchmen noticed what they were doing. 'Don't,' said a regular with his arm in a sling. 'We'll all pay for it.'

'If you were a man,' Laure hissed at him, 'you'd be doing the same.'

The soldier stayed put. 'Stupid bitch.'

A few yards of open ground separated the prisoners from a tavern courtyard. Hannah knew from her walks that it contained a large stable with a door on its far side. She crossed it in six swift strides – expecting shouts, shots, the pounding of boots. They did not come. The band played on, a good number of the Prussians breaking into song. The tavern was closed up, its windows shuttered. Hannah approached the stable, thinking that it could easily be locked as well, leaving her and Laure cornered in this courtyard. The past ten seconds had changed them irreversibly from prisoners into fugitives. They'd surely be executed.

The stable was open. Hannah rushed past the stalls, colliding heavily with the far door. Her hands were numb, her fingertips tingling; she fumbled with the bolt, unable to get a grip on it. A terrible pressure was building in her chest, making the task many times more difficult – making it impossible.

Laure stumbled into her, all elbows and knees and panicked panting. 'Can we do this?' she asked. 'Really?'

The bolt banged back. 'We're doing it,' Hannah replied. 'It's done.'

Beyond was a crooked lane filled with French peasants, diverted from their usual course through Gagny by the Kaiser's visit. Everyone stared at them; no one made a sound. An old woman pointed towards a low door. This led into a walled orchard, the bare branches of its pear trees dusted with frost. A gate at its end opened onto an icy meadow, past which was the border of a wood. Hannah made a last check for guards. None could be seen. She took hold of Laure's hand and ran.

*   *   *

'I don't like the woods, really I don't,' said Laure, hugging herself. '*Fuck* the woods.'

The *vivandières* were in a hunter's hut, discovered after several hours of wandering through the limitless, misty forest. It was well hidden, tucked in a stand of ancient oaks, and hadn't been used for some time. They'd agreed to shelter there until dark, when there would be less chance of them being spotted. Their exultation at having escaped had long since worn off. Both now saw that the more arduous part of this challenge still lay before them; both also wanted very much to rest. Hannah had eased the door open a few inches, taking care not to disturb the weeds growing over it, and they'd slid inside. The hut was the size of a double bed, and only slightly less cold than the forest. Moss carpeted the walls; toadstools dotted the floor. Above the door a stag's skull hung on a nail, one of its antlers snapped back to a stump.

Hannah stood at the filthy window, watching for Prussians. Laure took this as a good sign, assuming that she was thinking things through – plotting their next step. Her mood began to mellow; she sat down, taking off one of her battered bottines and holding it up to release a trickle of water.

'Everything will be all right,' she said. 'I know it. We're lucky together, Mademoiselle Pardy, dead lucky. Something about you makes up for me in the eyes of God.'

Hannah was weary and cold, and very nervous; she had no time for tarts' superstition. 'What do you mean?' she asked testily.

'We made it through Champigny, didn't we,' Laure answered, 'when all those men were killed. We escaped just then, something few would have dared to try – or got away with.' She rubbed at her bruises. 'And I wasn't so very fortunate while we were parted.'

Her meaning was plain enough. Hannah's impatience vanished. 'Was it the Prussians?'

The cocotte shook her head. She suddenly looked very young; Hannah realised that she probably wasn't even twenty. 'Men of the line. Even guardsmen, a couple of times. They'd get me in the mornings, when we were let out for exercise. Fritz didn't interfere. Didn't much care, I suppose.'

Hannah cursed every one of them. This was what she'd been expecting herself, albeit from enemies rather than alleged comrades, yet it hadn't happened. She'd been closely guarded when walking outside and had been kept in complete isolation. It was as if someone had been trying to spare her – to protect her. It made no sense.

Laure shrugged. 'Nothing I haven't had before. My own brothers gave me worse.' She tugged her boot back on with a shiver. 'Christ, what I wouldn't do for a damned cigarette.'

They fell silent. Hannah felt shame and a tense, directionless anger. She thought of the frequent complaints she'd made about her own upbringing. Elizabeth might have perplexed her, smothered her, annoyed her beyond endurance, but what was that next to *this*? She was particularly upset by the offhand way Laure had spoken, as if what she'd been through was unremarkable – a banal ordeal, part of her earthly lot. It made Hannah want to knock out the window with her fist. Could this ever be stopped? Would their socialist revolution, with all its talk of workers' rule, of federalism and freedom, be able to end such basic human misery? Would a commune? She stared at the floor, mired in troubling reflections.

'We'll get back,' she said at last. 'I think I know where we are. I have a plan.'

Laure was smiling. 'Mademoiselle Pardy,' she said, her tone almost affectionate, 'I'm sure that you do.'

They left the hut at nightfall. Hannah's guess was that

they'd originally fled to the north. Earlier, she'd decided that their best bet had been to move in a broad westwards arc, meeting up with the Strasbourg line and following it back into the city. This had been proving harder than anticipated; she'd grown worried that they were going in a circle rather than an arc, half-expecting the spire of Gagny's church to emerge among the trees ahead. Now, though, the forest's disorientating similitude was punctuated by the flashes of distant explosions. Hannah guided Laure towards them. The ground grew firmer and began to tilt, as if they were rounding the side of a gentle hill. A village appeared between the trunks – not Gagny, to Hannah's relief – clearly occupied, but unlit so as not to attract French artillery-fire; and past this, beyond the artless heaps of the forts and redoubts, was bombarded Paris.

The barrage was being concentrated on the south of the city. Several ranks of heavy guns were sparking up on the Châtillon plateau, lobbing shells over the wall into the dark streets of Montparnasse and the Latin Quarter. From where Hannah and Laure stood, looking across from the north-east, they could see buildings burning near the Jardin de Luxembourg; the flames were sharp specks of colour, lending a pinkish tint to the snow-covered rooftops around them. A railway station was ablaze beside the Seine – the Gare d'Orléans, Hannah thought – the fire lighting up the iron-and-glass hall like an enormous lantern.

'Oh God, my beautiful city!' Laure moaned, turning away, 'I never thought it'd come to this. Damn them, damn them to hell!'

Hannah said nothing, refusing to react to this sight. The most uncertain stage of their escapade had arrived. Sneaking out through the Prussian investment was believed by most to be impossible. Only a couple had ever managed it; a number of attempts were rumoured to have ended before a firing squad. Hannah had persuaded herself that it would be easier going the other way, breaking *into* Paris, but had no idea if this was really the case. Disaster could be close; the luck Laure had claimed for them was sorely needed.

The forest narrowed into a triangle, with a railway bridge at its apex where the Strasbourg line crossed a canal. Somewhere away from the tracks a light was burning. Hannah could see a low parapet of sandbags, but no soldiers.

'We've got to go over,' she said to Laure. 'We'll run – take it in turns.'

They drew closer, moving around a small headland. The source of the light came into view; a lamp was propped on one of the concrete supports beneath the bridge, illuminating a scene of striking stillness and symmetry, the mirror-like canal reflecting the massive iron lattice suspended above it. Standing on the bank, gazing into the water, was a tall, black-clad man. It was Jean-Jacques Allix.

Hannah and Laure laughed; they joined in an amazed, joyful embrace. Salvation was at hand. They were as good as back in Montmartre, telling their story over drinks in the Danton. It was a truly astonishing coincidence. The perimeter of Paris was more than forty miles long; the two siege lines and the no-man's-land between them a tangle of ruins, trenches and redoubts. Hannah had imagined a chance encounter such as this, of course, during the hundreds of hours she'd spent alone in that storeroom. She'd concluded that it was beyond all likelihood, not worth hoping for – but there he was. He'd take them home. Their trial was over.

'Quickly,' said Hannah, 'before he moves on.'

They had to clear a hundred yards of loose woodland and then descend an embankment to the canal path. Hannah began to run, lifting her boots clear of the undergrowth. She was nearly halfway there when Laure grasped hold of

329

her arm, dragging her down into a bed of brambles. The cocotte pointed to the right: a detachment of Prussian infantry was trudging along the canal path, rifles on their shoulders, heading directly for Jean-Jacques.

'Dear God!' Hannah exclaimed, trying to shake off Laure's hand and get back to her feet. 'We must warn him!'

'No.' Laure was adamant. Her grip grew tighter. '*No.*'

Hannah fell quiet. Laure was right: it would be better if they didn't intervene. This, after all, was the Leopard of Montmartre. A trap had probably been set. At any second he would make his move – draw a pair of revolvers and start shooting, or perhaps trigger a hidden bomb. Hannah had read her mother's articles in the *Figaro*. She knew what to expect.

Jean-Jacques was cutting it very fine, though, standing there in the light of that lamp. He must be using it as a lure – the Prussians would approach to investigate, coming out of the darkness, laying themselves open to his attack. They were thirty yards away, then twenty, and still he didn't shift. The soldiers disappeared behind one of the other bridge supports. Hannah realised that he wasn't going to hide from them. He's pretending to surrender, she thought, to get them close, too close to use their rifles – and then the bayonet will slide from his sleeve.

They were around him now, five of them in their helmets and brown coats. Surely he couldn't hope to win against so many. Hannah tried to stay calm, but couldn't help thinking that he might have misread the situation. Was she about to watch her lover die instead of their enemies?

But no; it was far, far worse than that. Jean-Jacques was talking to them. Even at fifty yards' distance, Hannah could tell that he was speaking their language, and fluently. He was speaking German. Stepping back, he made a wide gesture with his arm, then pointed near to

330

where they were concealed. Directions were being supplied; a route estimated.

Hannah blinked. Her beloved Jean-Jacques, the man she'd thought would prove their saviour, was assisting the search party dispatched to hunt them down. Deadness spread through her stomach, up into her lungs, closing around her heart. At her side, in the brambles, she could hear Laure muttering out furious curses.

'It's a mistake,' Hannah said. 'He's – he's tricking them. This is part of it.'

Jean-Jacques gave a couple of further instructions. When he'd finished, the men saluted and began fanning out into the woods.

'There's no damned *mistake*,' Laure spat. 'Christ Almighty, he's *in charge*.'

The forest floor tipped away, pitching like the deck of a ship. Brambles scratched Hannah's cheek; she struck against a tree trunk, crumpling among its roots. A hard, nauseous convulsion shuddered through her. She coughed, rocking forward, her splayed fingers crunching into a pocket of frozen snow.

Laure tore her greatcoat from the brambles and hauled her upright. 'Come on,' she said.

'I – I don't understand . . .'

'You don't need to *understand*.' The cocotte spoke harshly. 'He's a damned *spy*. Can't you see?'

Hannah shook her head. It was absurd. Spies were stooped men in strange hats who lurked around *mairies* and barrack-houses, trying to overhear the conversations of soldiers; or elegant ladies versed in seducing government officials, obtaining secrets in exchange for their attentions. They were not radical orators, or veterans of the American War, or committed socialists hell-bent on revolution. Jean-Jacques had gone into battle against the Prussians, for God's sake

– had killed dozens on those raids of his. How could he possibly be one of them? It was *absurd*.

'That can't be true,' she said. 'It can't. I would have known. Otherwise I am the greatest fool to – to have—'

'You've been *used*, Mademoiselle Pardy,' Laure told her. 'Lied to on a grand scale. It's the way men are: they fuck us and then they knife us in the back.' She peered towards the bridge. 'Of course, this evil bastard of yours has knifed us all. And he'll suffer for it, I promise you. But we have to go.'

Hannah realised what Laure was saying. She meant to expose Jean-Jacques – to throw him open to the wrath of the people. The revelation that a great popular hero of the siege was a fraud, one of the enemy no less, would cause wild outrage in the workers' districts. There would be reprisals; the red leaders, Blanqui, Pyat and the rest of them, would be desperate for scapegoats. Hannah herself would top their list – was she not an untrustworthy foreigner, one of the loathed English no less? – but anyone who'd been close to Jean-Jacques would surely be in danger as well. His former comrades would turn rabid, eager to demonstrate their own lack of involvement and hatred of betrayal.

And then there was Elizabeth. Those articles in *Le Figaro* had plainly been based on falsehood, but they'd made Jean-Jacques Allix famous, transforming him from an obscure rabble-rouser into the Leopard of Montmartre. Mrs Pardy was one of his known allies. The reds would certainly come for her as well.

'Wait,' Hannah said.

Laure studied her, the old contempt returning. 'You're afraid for yourself,' she declared, her voice rising slightly. 'You're afraid for your stupid old mule of a mother. This man has lied to you, to *everyone*, and you are thinking only

332

of the precious Pardy family. Want to plan your way out, do you? How to get back to London?'

'We must be careful,' Hannah said. 'We can't just blunder in and—'

'To the devil with that!' Laure turned to leave. 'This damned Leopard is Montmartre's error, and he is Montmartre's to correct!'

Hannah reached for Laure's wrist, thinking to hold her in place for a second longer; the cocotte pushed her away and their whispered argument became a grapple. Any warmth that had developed between them evaporated. Laure dug at Hannah with a bony hip and then took a swing, her fist driving into Hannah's left eye. It was a good punch; Hannah staggered and tripped, tumbling through a screen of dead ferns into a shallow ditch.

By the time she'd recovered Laure was gone. She looked through the ferns, flinching as she touched her fast-swelling eye. Mist hung among the trees, infused with pale yellow light from the lamp at the railway bridge. The Prussian soldiers were crashing about in the undergrowth somewhere off to the right. They might have heard something – Jean-Jacques might have heard something – and be coming to investigate. This thought made her sick with horror; collecting herself, she retied her bootlaces and buttoned her coat. She had to get out of this ditch. She had to keep moving.

The declaration, a day old and signed by a long list of provisional government ministers, was posted on every corner:

CITIZENS, the enemy kills our wives and children, bombards us night and day, and pelts our hospitals with shells. One cry – To Arms! – has burst from every breast. Those who can shed their life's blood on the field of battle will march against the enemy; those who remain, jealous of the heroism of their brothers, will, if required, suffer with calm endurance every sacrifice as their proof of devotion to their country. Suffer, and die if necessary, but conquer! Vive la République!

Hannah walked on, her arms crossed tightly. This explained the lack of crowds in the avenues, the empty tenements and cafés – and her straightforward passage through the siege line she'd feared would be so impregnable. Another sortie was underway. She'd been alert for mention of the Leopard or any other sign that Laure had got through and started spreading word of their awful discovery, but the few people who stood on corners or outside the *cantines municipales* spoke only of this latest French attack. The sortie was being made westwards, towards the enemy headquarters at Versailles. The defenders of Paris had learned that at some point in the past week Kaiser Wilhelm had been declared Emperor of the Germans in Louis XIV's Hall of Mirrors, to fanfares and great celebration; it was the reason, Hannah realised, for the triumphal tour of the line that had brought the king to Gagny. The Parisians saw this as a direct and deliberate insult, staged to display the continuing power of that which they'd just rejected with such earnestness. Honour demanded a mighty assault on Versailles, the old men on the corners agreed, to let Fritz know precisely what Republican France thought of his new emperor.

'He's done it now, that Kaiser,' they told each other. 'Oh yes, he's pushed us too far this time. He'll see what Paris is really made of!'

Hannah listened with acute disquiet. Jean-Jacques would have been calling vociferously for this sortie, as he had for the first one. His intention from the start had been to get as many Frenchmen as possible sent out before the Prussian cannon. The radical cause, the cause of freedom and the French people, had been exploited to bring about their destruction. And Hannah hadn't seen it, not for a moment. She'd supported him openly and enthusiastically, accepting every unlikely thing he'd presented to her – cheering as this lunatic situation had grown steadily worse. She'd been revealed as what she'd always despised, what her detractors had so often accused her of being: a silly bourgeois girl playing at revolutions, striking a pose, her head as empty as that of any society miss or drawing-room habitué.

In the side streets of La Villette were the consequences. Hannah saw at least thirty children's coffins, pitifully small and crudely made, being carried from the houses of the poor and loaded onto the handcarts that were to take them away for burial. Distraught mothers huddled around them, most too weak for any display of sorrow; sallow and desperately thin, they'd been left to manage as best they could whilst their men went to serve in the militia. These were the ordinary working families Hannah had wanted to help – to liberate from the impoverishment and brutalisation they had endured under the Empire – yet here they were starving, watching their offspring perish from hunger and disease whilst the radical socialists, their supposed champions, urged the continuation of the war at all costs.

Hannah paused on the place de la Rotonde, leaning heavily against a lamppost. She'd been up for more than thirty hours. Following the canal towards Paris, she'd crouched for much of the night at the head of a storm drain, waiting for a chance to sneak by a heavily guarded Prussian position. At dawn, however, the majority of the soldiers had suddenly departed, marching north – to assist with the repulsion of the westward sortie, as she now knew. Slipping into French territory, then convincing a gaggle of bored sentries that she'd escaped from a Prussian gaol and was on her way to rejoin her battalion, had been surprisingly simple.

This meant, of course, that Laure would very probably have got through too. Hannah considered heading to Montmartre to tell her side of things and protest her innocence – but she couldn't honestly pretend that she'd succeed in swaying anyone. Without Jean-Jacques Allix, her influence was negligible. She'd only ever been tolerated by the working people; they'd turn on her willingly. All she could do was warn others who were at risk – warn her family. Clem was gone, thankfully, off with Besson in his balloon. This left her mother. Elizabeth would take Allix's unmasking in her stride; she'd be issuing instructions and conceiving plans within minutes of her daughter's arrival. Hannah was so reduced that this thought brought her relief rather than vexation. She straightened up and made for the Grand Hotel.

The centre of Paris was given over to the ambulance-carts. Perhaps a dozen of them were unloading outside the Grand. Casualties had already been coming in for several hours; Hannah passed through the bloody turmoil of the lobby entirely unnoticed. The door to her mother's suite was ajar. Elizabeth's sitting room was light after the murky hallway, and rich with colour – the kind of colour Hannah had longed for whilst locked up in Gagny. It was *her* colour, in fact: the room was filled with her work, more or less every painting she'd done since arriving in Paris. This was mystifying. Madame Lantier's shed was quite secure. Why had Elizabeth thought it necessary to take such a step?

The portrait, hung in pride of place above the mantelpiece, made Hannah start so violently that she almost knocked over a chair. She took a few deep, steadying breaths, unable to look elsewhere. More than ever she was struck by the picture's vacuity. It no longer seemed so strange. That which she'd been searching for, that which had caused her such frustration, simply hadn't been there. It couldn't be. Jean-Jacques Allix was not a person, not a human being with a mind and a soul and a heart, but a worthless counterfeit. Hannah strode towards the fireplace, flushed with rage, intending to break the frame over her knee and then tear the canvas into a hundred ragged strips.

'Hannah.'

He was standing in the doorway to the bedroom, ducking slightly to fit his head within it. She stopped on the oval rug, caught between the portrait and actual man. One seemed scarcely more real than the other. He couldn't have slept, but you wouldn't know it; that serious, handsome face was freshly shaved and formidably alert.

'You're alive.'

His expression was one of deep joy, mingled with a trace of puzzlement. Hannah went cold; he was *in character*, as an actor might say. It was unspeakably sinister. He was watching her closely, plainly intending to let her reactions show how much she'd discovered during her time outside the wall. Hannah thought about attempting to fool him – pretending she had no notion of what he really was and then using this to steer him into some kind of ambush. To work such a trick, though, she'd have to go to his ambush, return his kisses and hear his false words of concern. She couldn't do it.

'What are you doing here?' she asked.

'I was out in no-man's-land last night,' he told her. 'I heard a Prussian patrol talking of an escape in one of their villages – a *vivandière*, they said. I could only hope it was you.' He looked around the room. 'I had a feeling that you'd come here first.'

Dear God, he was so damned *obvious*. This was almost an admission. A wince pinched at Hannah's brow; she tried to hide it, glancing at the rug, but it was too late. She'd given herself away. He was walking over to her, the joy and the puzzlement quite gone. She darted for the door and he lunged to intercept her, scooping her clean off the carpet. She struggled and his grip became unbearable, stopping her breath; she went limp and he loosened it by a tiny fraction.

'Who have you told?'

Everything was changed. The arms around her were those she'd yearned for in the storeroom at Gagny. Never, though, had they held her like this; it felt as if her ribs were about to snap. His smell was the same, tinged still by the scent of the irises in the windmill, yet what had once been intoxicating now revolted her. This man clenching her to him was not her beloved Jean-Jacques; indeed, Jean-Jacques could not even be his real name.

'What do you mean?' she gasped.

'Don't make this difficult. Who have you told?' His voice, at least, sounded different now, the accent a degree harder – Alsatian shifting to Prussian.

Hannah stared at the ceiling. He didn't know about Laure. She herself was finished, at the mercy of an enemy spy; that which she'd fought to prevent out in the woods was now the best she could hope for. She wasn't going to give this man a chance to escape from Paris and disappear into the Prussian line. Elizabeth would just have to rely on her wits.

'No one,' she said.

His hold relaxed further; then he dropped her in an armchair and went to a window. Hannah couldn't tell if he believed her or not. She looked to the door. There was no hope of her reaching it before he caught her again. He appeared to be weighing his options: a professional adapting coolly to a shift in circumstances. Hannah dug her fingers into the chair's upholstered arms to stop them from trembling. She was determined to keep silent, to match his composure. She would not scream about the love he'd betrayed – faked for the purposes of conquest. She would not level any of the livid accusations that were heaping up inside her mind. And she most certainly would not allow a single tear to be shed.

It was no use.

'How could you?' she asked him, rather more loudly and angrily than she'd intended. 'What *are you*?'

He turned, standing calmly in the grey light. Hannah had gazed into those dark eyes so many times, convinced that all manner of noble feelings could be seen within. Now they seemed inscrutable, beyond divination, malign in their blankness.

'Everything I have done,' he said, 'has been to end this war.'

Hannah almost laughed. 'How you can say that misleading us all, that – that *lying* will bring about—' She stopped. This was pointless. 'What now, then? Do you intend to shoot me? Return me to one of your prisons?'

'No.' He flicked back the curtain to broaden his view of the place de l'Opéra and the boulevards that bordered it. 'We are going to wait for your mother.'

III

Elizabeth rose from the empty ammunition crate she'd been perched on for much of the afternoon. 'We've seen enough,' she announced over the shell-fire, lifting the hem of her dress to nudge Clem with her boot. 'Brandy at the Grand, I think.'

Clem knotted his curtain-scarf and climbed to his feet. There had been a thaw that morning, melting the frozen ground to sludge, but as the sun sank it was turning arctic again. The prospect of hard liquor – of the good stuff from Elizabeth's private supply, imbibed in the comfort of her sitting room – was welcome indeed.

'Hear, hear,' he said. 'Right behind you.'

They left the western terrace of Mont-Valérien, picking their way around its outer wall to the track that led to Paris. The fort, largest and best-loved of the fourteen that encircled the city, loomed beside them in the misty twilight. General Trochu's idea had been that it would serve as an anchor to the sortie, providing the soldiers with a symbol of French steadfastness and strength. In this it had most certainly failed.

The day's action had been focused on the Buzenval

Ridge, the natural barrier between Paris and Versailles and the site of numerous unassailable Prussian positions. It had been a thoroughly depressing spectacle, bloody and futile. From the western terrace Clem and Elizabeth had watched the French battalions slog up the muddy slopes, through the remains of farmsteads and orchards; grind to a halt under a punishing barrage, dropping in their dozens, unable or unwilling to advance any further; and then eventually start to break apart, drifting back down, defeated once more.

As a sign of Parisian desperation – or perhaps in line with Besson's theory about the government's plan to prune the city's reds – the National Guard had been allowed a much greater role than in previous attacks, accounting for nearly half the total force. In addition to their usual heavy drinking, cowardice and insubordination, the citizen-soldiers had also displayed a panicky impulsiveness with their rifles that had led to the accidental killing and wounding of scores of their own countrymen. Clem had even witnessed a band of stragglers blast away at General Trochu's staff after mistaking the mounted officers for a party of Uhlans; at least one had died in his saddle, slumping onto his horse's neck as it galloped off towards Saint-Cloud.

Neither could the militiamen be convinced to remain on the ridge overnight, abandoning footholds for which so many of their comrades had fallen without a thought. To the rear of Mont-Valérien Clem and Elizabeth encountered a swollen river of deserters, inching through the ruined village of Puteaux to the Pont de Neuilly. Elizabeth was soon recognised and the Leopard remarks began. Once again, her Monsieur Allix had been a vocal advocate of a large-scale sortie, with the National Guard as its spearhead; and once again he'd been conspicuous by his absence when the fighting had actually started. Elizabeth put on her usual show of faith. She'd made excuses for him on previous

341

occasions, supplying suitable tales of derring-do to explain why he'd removed himself at the critical moment, and she did the same here. On she chattered, her hands working through their repertoire of Gallic gesticulations, trying to stay genial in the face of queries that ranged from amused and faintly indignant to downright hostile.

'Good Lord,' she murmured to Clem at one point, 'I am not *responsible* for the man.'

Civilians thronged around the gate at the head of the avenue de la Grande Armée, lining the road down to the place de l'Étoile and beyond. They were genuinely shocked to see the heroes they'd cheered out that morning returning to the city with nothing to show but a long list of the dead and maimed. These people, drunk on their own patriotic bombast, had plainly expected the day to close with the National Guard singing the 'Marseillaise' in the courtyard at Versailles. Many women were anxiously inspecting the soldiers as they passed, asking after missing husbands and sons. Clem felt a keen longing for his bed; he'd burrow down among the sheets like a mole, pull the eiderdown over his head and not come out until there was a train waiting to convey him directly to Calais.

'Mrs Pardy! I say, Mrs Pardy!'

A corps of newspapermen was standing in the greenish light of a petroleum lamp, casting questions into the returning militia in an attempt to gather details of the battle. Montague Inglis was on the margins of this group, bent over slightly with one long arm raised into the air. The Pardys stopped and he came to meet them, giving Elizabeth a bow and Clem a quick nod. Little remained of the smooth, adversarial, slightly suspect fellow who'd met them in the lobby of the Grand the previous September. His beard was reaching mad hermit proportions, and his clothes bore evidence of heavy repair. There was a nervousness about him, also – Elizabeth had obviously cut him loose rather against his will.

'Mr Inglis, did you not venture outside the wall today?' she asked. 'Whatever will the readers of the *Sentinel* do, deprived of your first-hand observations on the sortie?'

The journalist laughed, a sad croak from somewhere in his beard. 'That is more your style, Lizzie, than mine. Besides, the outcome of this piece of idiocy was never in doubt. The rabbit, for some unknown reason, decided to leave his hole and scamper about before the stoat.'

Even with everything they'd seen that day, Elizabeth could not let this stand. 'How very like you to pour disdain on the sacrifice of those—'

Inglis lifted a palm. 'My dear woman,' he interrupted, 'I really don't want to run through this debate again. I came to speak with you with a particular purpose in mind – a warning, if you like, to impart to one I still consider a friend.'

Elizabeth's stare said: *Well?*

'There is talk,' Inglis glanced back at the newspapermen, 'of something building up in the northern arrondissements. They say the rappel is being beaten from Montmartre to Ménilmontant.'

'Hardly unusual.'

'Perhaps not, but several of the ringleaders are apparently naming your man – your Leopard. They are claiming that he is a traitor.'

Clem tensed. He'd all but given up on Jean-Jacques Allix. Besson had seemed indifferent to the discovery he'd made in the Jardin des Plantes. Clem got the feeling that he'd already guessed Allix was the author of the letter – that he'd been sure of it from the beginning. Clem himself had not seen Allix since that meeting before the leopard cage, nearly a month ago now. He was beyond reach, beyond investigation, popping up unannounced at the odd ultra rally, but existing principally in the sensational paragraphs of Elizabeth's reports. Clem had imagined many different motives for Allix's mysterious behaviour. Outright treachery, though, alleged by his own people – this was new.

'Inevitable, I suppose,' Elizabeth sighed. 'There is no medium in this blessed city between the Capitol and the Tarpeian Rock: if you do not exist in a state of continual triumph you must be enacting a betrayal. They will rage and rant until he returns from his mission – and then none of them will even have the backbone to repeat their baseless slander to his face.' Her features softened very slightly. 'But I thank you for your concern, Mont. It is always helpful to hear of these little stupidities.'

Inglis bowed again. Clem attempted to learn more about the accusations against Allix, but the journalist had nothing to tell. It became increasingly clear, in fact, that he was in a state of some distress; the Marquis de Périchaux, an old friend of his from the Jockey Club and a colonel in the loyalist militia, had been killed that day near the Château de Buzenval. Inglis had seen the marquis's body being borne into the city, off to his mansion on the boulevard Haussmann. The sight had plainly staggered him. Although capable of great hardness, Elizabeth Pardy was not a hard soul; laying her fingers on Inglis's forearm, she asked him to the Grand for a glass of brandy. He accepted at once, and the three of them carried on towards the centre of the city.

They were walking along the Champs Elysées, almost at the place de la Concorde, when the opening shots of that night's bombardment rumbled through Paris. The Buzenval sortie clearly hadn't affected it at all; it was a different, entirely independent part of the Prussian siege machine. The atmosphere was already turbulent, thousands of civilians and militia thronging in the near-darkness, jostling,

344

arguing and sobbing. As the barrage settled into its bludgeoning rhythm the people let out an enormous, weary groan. Some began to wail uncontrollably; others scaled lampposts and Morris columns, screaming slogans or launching into tirades.

'It really does beggar belief,' said Inglis over the noise. 'These Prussians must have lumps of deuced granite where their hearts should be. They are deliberately aiming for our hospitals and churches, you know. Towers, domes, steeples – the blackguards are using them as targets.'

'It's a crime, Mr Inglis,' Clem agreed. 'A bloody crime.'

The Pardys, of course, had undertaken a full journalistic tour of the bombarded arrondissements. Elizabeth had insisted on it, both to assess the destruction being wrought and to experience what it was like to be under fire; and Clem, reinstated as the default assistant, had been obliged to accompany her. Despite the smashed paving stones in the place du Panthéon and the single hole punched in the golden dome of Les Invalides, the general level of damage had struck Clem as surprisingly light – but the mad fear he'd felt when a salvo of shells had shrilled overhead, cracking and rattling in an adjacent street, had definitely been great enough. It had been another hour, however, an endless, nerve-racking hour, before he managed to persuade his mother to stop conversing with the dazed-looking locals and return to the safer side of the Seine.

'Little wonder that they've murdered so many innocents,' Inglis continued with uncharacteristic feeling, 'so many damned *children*. I went to the funeral, Lizzie, of those poor little fellows from the Lycée Saint-Nicholas. I knew one of their fathers – a big name at the Bourse. The anger at the graveside, the sheer *incomprehension* . . . it was beyond words. That Kaiser is a Herod, a blood-soaked modern Herod, and History will judge him accordingly.'

This incident had occurred some days earlier at a boarding school on the rue de Vaugirard, just by the Luxembourg Palace. A shell had flown in through a dormitory window, killing four young boys as they slept. Righteous fury had swept the city; a great boost had been given to those calling for another sortie.

They were crossing the Concorde now, past the statue of Strasbourg with its lapful of withered garlands. Inglis accepted one of Clem's stale cigarettes, exhaling a long feather of smoke. He appeared close to tears.

'Have you been keeping up with your animals, Mont?' Elizabeth asked, thinking to soothe him with a favoured topic. 'We went to see the elephants slaughtered – but for some reason my foolish son then refused to queue up at Voisin to purchase us a portion of their meat.'

The journalist stayed quiet for a few seconds, squeezing the bridge of his nose and taking another drag on his cigarette.

'Oh yes,' he replied, his voice lighter and a touch forced, 'I certainly had me some elephant. Had to try it, didn't I? Trunk of Pollux, I believe it was, for no less than forty shillings a pound. I went at it like Pickwick's fat boy, Lizzie, but I must confess that I found the stuff far from toothsome – damnably coarse and oily. The stranger the beast, it seems, the worse the dinner. Still, allowances must be made.' He indicated the string of petroleum lamps running from the Concorde along the rue Royale. 'Our cooks are out of fuel, and the solution advised by this blockheaded government is that they use those ghastly contraptions as an alternative source of heat. The chefs of Paris can work wonders with very poor materials, but when they are called upon to cook an elephant with a spirit lamp the thing is almost beyond their ingenuity.'

The entrance of the Grand was the only bright spot on the boulevard des Capucines, dozens of lanterns hanging from its porch to aid the medical personnel passing continually beneath. A terrible scene no doubt awaited them within. Clem had grown accustomed to much about life in besieged Paris, from the hunger and cold to the oppressive boredom; the constant cannon-fire was to him like the ticking of so many clocks. The horrors of the hotel lobby, however, especially in the aftermath of a battle, could never be diminished. He peered apprehensively at the canvas curtains, already hearing the shrieks and the pitiful, childlike whimpers – smelling the torn flesh and exposed organs. *Don't look*, he instructed himself; *just don't look*.

There were three militiamen, perhaps four; they barrelled into Clem, catching him completely unawares, shoving him to the ground and kicking at him with all their strength. Elizabeth was on them immediately, pushing them back and demanding an explanation. From the pavement, he watched his attackers yell and jab their fingers; they were reds, Montmartre men with little brass 197s on their kepis, and they were talking about Allix. Elizabeth protested, delivering her standard defence. Before she could complete it one of them struck her so hard around the face that she stumbled to her knees.

Clem tried to get up. Inglis appeared beside him, shielding Elizabeth and bellowing for assistance. An officer of the line strode from the Grand with a handful of orderlies. There was more shouting and some threatening gestures; and then suddenly the red guardsmen took to their heels, running off across the place de l'Opéra.

Elizabeth was already standing again, a gloved hand laid against her cheek. Without speaking, she made an adjustment to her hat and went into the hotel.

'What – what the deuce was that?' gasped Clem.

'We should get inside,' Inglis said as he helped him to his feet. 'I really think it's wise.'

'What did they want?'

'Blood, Mr Pardy,' the journalist told him. 'They wanted blood. And they will most assuredly be back.'

There was a thin crack of light beneath Elizabeth's door. This was odd; surely nothing left burning that morning would still be alight. Clem was about to remark on this when his mother, who was half a dozen steps ahead, opened it and went through. On crossing the threshold she cried out and dropped to the floor as if she'd been shot. Clem rushed over to her: a stone-cold faint. He glanced up to see what had prompted it and almost joined Elizabeth on the carpet.

It couldn't be true.

Hannah Pardy was dead. She'd been buried somewhere on the Villiers Plateau for almost two months now. Was this some kind of dream-vision, brought on by hunger and an overdose of death and doom? Clem had heard of such things, among the hardy community who still ate their ration in the Grand's dining room. Only the day before a lady had confided to him that she'd heard her pet poodle yapping at the foot of her bed in the night, despite the poor creature having been given up for dinner several weeks before. These, though, were particular to one person. Elizabeth had plainly seen Han as well; Inglis, too, was gaping at the figure across the room.

'Dear Lord,' Clem said.

Hannah Pardy was alive. She was sitting in an armchair in the Grand Hotel, a candle on the table at her side. She wasn't starved, but in every other respect appeared pretty wretched. Her militia uniform was filthy and growing threadbare; her pale skin was marked by anxiety and exhaustion. As she moved forward in her chair, looking with concern at their unconscious mother, he saw that

348

her face was bruised, as if someone had socked her in the eye.

'Is she all right?'

Clem checked Elizabeth's pulse. 'Merely a swoon.'

Hannah's attention shifted to Clem. 'What the devil are you still doing in Paris?' There was conflict in her voice; she was both glad to see him and dismayed that he was there. 'I was told you'd flown off in a balloon with Monsieur Besson.'

Clem got up from the carpet. Allix had lied. He'd let them suffer a devastating grief for nothing. Why had they taken him at his word – and why had he deceived them? What on *earth* was going on? Clem felt a strong need to tell his sister everything he knew.

'We were brought down,' he said, 'by your man Allix, according to Besson – reckons he loosened the stitching of the envelope.' He took a breath. 'There is something very wrong with that fellow, Han, something—'

Hannah slanted her head ever so slightly towards one of the windows; and Clem saw him standing in the shadows, watching the streets below. The situation between them was plain. Han's lover, the famous Leopard of Montmartre, was keeping her in the Grand Hotel against her will.

A gasp from the floor signalled Elizabeth's revival. Before Clem could even look down she was across the room, arms clasped around her daughter.

'My girl, my dearest girl! I thought you were gone for ever – I thought you were lost to me! My sweetest, most precious one!'

Hannah returned this embrace a little awkwardly, unable to match her mother's effusiveness. Things were not as joyous as they seemed. She'd returned from the dead, Clem saw, straight into a nasty bit of trouble.

'Mr Inglis,' said Allix, 'be so good as to shut the door.'

'What the deuce happened, then?' Clem demanded, determined to have it out. 'What's the story here, Allix? Did you rescue her, pray, from some Prussian dungeon? Or just dig her up and breathe life back into the body? Explain yourself!'

Allix turned to the room. Sight of that scarred visage, the eyes so still and evaluating, nearly caused Clem's courage to fail.

'He's a Prussian,' Hannah said. 'He's a spy.'

For several seconds nobody spoke or moved.

Perspiration broke out across Clem's upper lip, tickling in the bristles of his beard. He was acutely aware, all of a sudden, of the closed door behind him.

Elizabeth rose from the side of Hannah's chair, wiped the tears from her cheeks – one a mottled red from where the militiaman had struck her – and fixed her Leopard with a cool stare. She wasn't outraged or mortified; Christ above, Clem thought, she isn't even particularly surprised.

'That,' she said, 'is disappointing.'

Clem couldn't help it; he laughed. 'Had your suspicions, did you?'

'I knew that he wasn't what he claimed, certainly,' Elizabeth replied. 'He couldn't have been. One simply needs to consider the other red leaders – that old pipeclay Blanqui, that posturing dandy Flourens, the idiot Pyat – to realise that this man has no natural place among them. He is of an altogether different stripe. I had imagined that he might be a radical from the east, from Russia perhaps; a true libertarian socialist, an anarchist in the mould of Bakunin, brought in from outside to help this city towards its revolutionary commune.' She lifted her chin. 'To learn that he is only a *Prussian*, however, an obedient servant of the old world, is quite upsetting.'

350

This finally goaded the fellow to speak. 'There is nothing old,' he said quietly, 'about the united Germany.'

'Hell's bells, Elizabeth,' blurted Clem, 'your man is a spy! A bloody *spy*! D'you realise what this means for us?'

His mother gave him a level look – a restraining look. They needed to remain calm. '*Provocateur* is a more accurate term, I think, Clement,' she said. 'The gentleman before us now, Herr . . .'

She hesitated, inviting this person to provide a genuine name. He declined to take it. He clearly wasn't going to tell them anything.

'Our former Monsieur Allix,' Elizabeth continued, 'is a rare creature indeed. Many do not believe they exist. The provocateur is the tool of the most rapacious, the most devious nations; small wonder that Chancellor Bismarck has cultivated them. Men like this one have altered the course of history. They have performed roles that have passed without record – without credit or blame. That is their great skill. Theirs is the hand that angles the lens so that it starts the fire; that unlatches the gate so the bullocks can run wild. I should think that there are men like Jean-Jacques Allix throughout Paris, in all manner of places. There'll be one in the Hôtel de Ville, close to Trochu and Jules Favre; one holed up with the Bonapartists at the Jockey Club; one with the Orléanists, even, bolstering their hopes for a new monarchy.'

The Leopard crossed his arms, neither confirming nor denying any of it.

'Villain,' muttered Inglis. 'I always knew there was something rum about you. Those tall tales of Lizzie's in the *Figaro* – those ludicrous, pantomime politics. I always knew that something was off.'

Clem's mind started to settle – to process this revelation.

Many nagging questions had been answered. This spy or provocateur or whatever he was had been aggravating the divisions of the city in order to weaken it. He'd encountered Han when he'd arrived in Montmartre to embed himself among the northern ultras. Recognising her name at once, along with the singular opportunity she represented, he'd seduced her and won her trust with his show of committed radicalism; and then, when the moment was right, he'd penned that letter. And it had been a stunning success, you had to admit. Only now, with Paris on the brink of capitulation, were people beginning to query him – with the exception, of course, of Émile Besson, his consistent and tenacious enemy. This was why the *Aphrodite* had been sabotaged. This was the secret Allix had been willing to kill for.

Han's face was in her hands. She had it worst of all. Strip away the verbiage about wartime exigency and the fate of nations and the whole affair had the aspect of a loathsome confidence trick. It was maddening to think of what had been done – the liberties that had been taken with his sister's feelings and her person. A true gentleman would insist on fighting a duel over this sullying of her honour, or at least break the nose of the fiend responsible. Clem looked warily at the Prussian. It didn't seem like a very good idea in this instance. Neither could he just turn the scoundrel in. The Pardys had been chosen carefully. Foreigners, and the English in particular, were already considered highly suspect by most in Paris. They were implicated; if caught they'd probably be subjected to the same prompt punishment as the Leopard himself.

Staying in the darkness by the window, the Prussian agent laid out his demands. Firstly, and without delay, he wanted an article published in the *Figaro*: an account of an audacious one-man raid on the northern positions beyond Saint-Denis, designed to hinder the arrival of Prussian reinforcements at Buzenval, that would explain his absence from the attack. He wanted Elizabeth to stress that he held no formal rank in the National Guard, and that the provisional government continued to seek his arrest: appearing on the front line was therefore a serious risk to his liberty.

'I can supply proof of the action,' he added, 'in the usual manner.' There was a trace of irony in his voice. He was referring to the helmets and other trinkets brought back from previous forays – obviously taken direct from the Prussian commissariat.

Elizabeth did not react; she appeared, in fact, to be ignoring him. Some kind of contest, subtle but profound, was underway. She was stroking Hannah's hair, demonstrating more tenderness than Clem had seen pass between them in years.

'Where have you been, girl, for all these weeks, while I was mourning you so bitterly? Were you taken prisoner?'

Hannah nodded. 'They kept me in a village, off to the north-east. I was well treated.' She glared at the Leopard. 'His doing, I suppose. Other girls were not so fortunate.'

'Other girls?' Elizabeth's brow furrowed. 'Do you mean Clement's cocotte – the one Mont and I saw leave with you at the Porte de Charenton?'

The Leopard's eyes were on them both.

Hannah opened her mouth, then shut it again. She looked at her boots. 'No,' she replied. 'We were separated in Champigny, during the battle. I – I don't know what happened to her.'

She was lying. The Leopard stepped towards her, passing before the candle, his shadow sweeping around the room. Elizabeth drew her daughter close, murmuring a warning; but he wished only to ask a question.

'Did she run off at the same time as you? From Gagny?'

Hannah wouldn't answer. She was attempting to remain impassive, to give nothing away, but there was a cruel imbalance here. While she couldn't even call this man by his real name, he knew her with the intimacy of a lover.

'The cocotte is back in the city as well,' the Leopard said, 'and has been telling everyone she can about me for some hours now.' He almost sounded impressed. 'You have killed us all.'

Clem had taken a cigarette from the doctor's jacket; it remained unlit between his fingers. Mademoiselle Laure was alive – alive and in Paris. He might feel those copper locks against his cheek once more.

'Perhaps that is what we deserve,' Hannah said. 'What do you think?'

'Now hang on a minute,' Inglis protested, standing forgotten by the door, 'I don't believe that I—'

'I could try to talk to her,' Clem broke in. 'To Laure, I mean. It might not be too late. We were friends for a while. I might be able to make her see sense – or at the very least slow her down a little.'

Hannah shook her head. 'She won't listen to you.'

'I can't imagine that you'd find her, Clement,' said Elizabeth, 'before it could make a difference, at any rate.'

The Leopard retreated to the hearth, to the boundary of the candlelight, turning around again as he arrived at a new decision. He was standing with his back to that damned portrait; it looked as if he was sneaking up on himself.

'I want asylum at the British Embassy,' he said. 'It should still be secure. Paris is spent. She will fall in a matter of days – and then I'll depart.' He went to Elizabeth's desk. 'I shall write a note informing my superiors of the situation. There is a locker in the Gare de l'Ouest from which correspondence is collected and conveyed to Versailles – if you, Mr Pardy, would be so good as to take it there.'

He took hold of a pen with his undamaged left hand, dipped it in the ink pot and started to write with swift fluency. Clem stared: there it was, the hand that had written both the letter and Elizabeth's Leopard reports. The best ruses, he reflected, were often the most straightforward. Allix had presented himself as a man impaired, and there had been no reason to disbelieve him. Han had seen it too. She didn't move, but the self-control she'd upheld to that point was buckling; she looked as if she'd happily overturn the desk and go at the brute behind it with the poker.

'We'll never reach the embassy,' Elizabeth told the Prussian. 'It's too far. The streets are packed with National Guard, the Champs Elysées especially. Someone is bound to recognise us.'

Clem caught something in his mother's tone – a hint of excitement. Dear God, he thought, she's actually relishing this awful turn of events. She's probably started to construct the narrative in her head: a daughter dramatically returned, a family held prisoner, a mother cast into a battle of wits with an impossibly cunning Prussian agent. You had to hand it to her – Elizabeth Pardy was certainly adaptable. Any ordeal one cared to name was just so much grist to her mill.

'Mont, how about your place? The rue Joubert is a fraction of the distance. No one would think to look there. We'd be safe until morning.'

Inglis pushed up his kepi. 'No, Lizzie,' he answered, 'I will not knowingly help this man. How could I? It would render my life in Paris untenable.'

Elizabeth pursed her lips. 'You are my friend, though, are you not?'

The journalist let out a tired sigh. 'I am.'

'Then I ask that you do it for me. My family's safety is at stake – the safety of my dear daughter, so miraculously

355

restored to me. This man has deceived us most despicably, that I cannot dispute, but I'm afraid we need to ensure that he reaches the embassy.'

Inglis thought for a moment. Unwilling to look at the Leopard himself, he scowled at the portrait behind him. 'Very well then,' he said. 'For you, Lizzie. I must say, however, that my concierge is quite the gatekeeper. I cannot guarantee that he'll prove amenable.'

'He will,' said the Leopard.

Clem returned his unlit cigarette to his pocket and looked at his mother and sister, arranged stiffly around that armchair as if waiting to have their photograph taken. It was up to him to act – to save the three of them. A lightness fluttered through his belly; a hot prickle crawled up his spine. Amazed by his own daring, he took a step towards the door – the Leopard was busy interrogating Inglis, discovering exactly where the journalist kept his apartment – and then he was against the varnished panels, scrabbling with the handle, out in the hallway and at the first staircase. The stairs flew beneath his boots; he jumped down the last half-dozen, nearly falling when he landed, skidding off towards the next flight.

The lobby was a hellish, bloody blur, the air alive with yelling and the dreadful rasp of the bone-saws. Clem raced along its edge and plunged onto the boulevard. Only then did he risk a backward glance. There was no sign of the damned Leopard; he was plainly a lesser concern, of no real consequence to the scoundrel's escape plan. He'd been allowed to get away.

It was a little lighter outside than before, the crowds and towering buildings touched with silver. Clem looked for the source; above was a glorious spread of stars. National Guardsmen, both red and bourgeois, were everywhere. He worried briefly that he might be recognised again and set upon with more effectiveness, but he'd made his move; he could only turn up his collar and press onwards.

It really was too much. The dead brought back to life; the Pardys' position in Paris turned on its head; a close friend – of Han's and Elizabeth's, at least – revealed as an extraordinary and devious foe; and all before he'd had a chance to remove his hat. More than anything he wanted to stop, to smoke a cigarette and think it over.

There was no time. He cut to the left, heading for the northwards diagonal of the rue Lafayette.

They needed help.

IV

The Prussian, the man who was not Jean-Jacques, had returned to the window. He appeared to be monitoring the crowds; Hannah assumed he was waiting for a lull during which it would be safe – or at least safer – for them to leave for Mr Inglis's apartment on the rue Joubert. Focused on reaching the embassy, he'd barely reacted when Clem had taken flight. There was no point in a pursuit; it wasn't as if Clem could damage the name of Jean-Jacques Allix any further.

Hannah wanted to die. She was certain of it. Shame seethed in her; it clogged her veins and choked her heart. She'd bound herself to Jean-Jacques, blended herself into him, and now she had nothing. Her life was founded on deceit, empty, flimsy and improbable, and now it had been stamped flat. The only thing left was death.

'Where has Clem gone, do you think?' she asked Elizabeth.

'To find the cocotte,' her mother replied, 'where else? The little minx has him in thrall. He's been pining for her all blessed winter. His father was the same – easily infatuated. It will burn itself out eventually.'

Recovered from her swoon and everything that had

followed it, Elizabeth was now a model of dignity. Her arm remained firmly wrapped around Hannah's shoulders; her narrowed eyes were glued to their captor. Mr Inglis, the final occupant of that plush, shadowy sitting room, had sat down in a chair opposite them. He was shifting about impatiently like someone being forced to miss the start of a much-anticipated concert; were it not for ageing limbs and rheumatic joints he'd have probably made a break for it too.

'I am hateful,' Hannah murmured, 'the worst kind of fool.'

Elizabeth's hold tightened. 'Do not think that. You must never think that. I will not permit it. You are my daughter and you are *exceptional*. When I believed you dead I almost died myself.'

Hannah scarcely heard her. She looked at the black back before the window. 'He knew exactly what to tell me – how to act with me. Even the way he pretended to be fighting against his feelings. He saw straight away that I was a callow girl with a head full of stupid romantic notions, and he used it to the full.' She put a hand to her face, across her eyes. It was already damp with her tears. 'I didn't suspect a thing, Elizabeth. Dear God, I *defended* him when others voiced their doubts.'

'His actions were those of a thoroughgoing cad,' Inglis declared stoutly. 'Beyond anything I have encountered during fifteen years of life in Paris – the supposed capital of this kind of roguish behaviour. These blasted Prussians really are a breed apart.'

'True enough, Mont,' said Elizabeth, 'but this man is no predator, seducing and deceiving for amusement alone. There was a goal very much in sight.' She addressed the Prussian. 'Tell me – I shall keep calling you Allix, I'm afraid, as I must call you something – was absolutely *all* of it feigned?'

359

Hannah cringed, grasping at the armchair, thinking for a second that her mother was going to talk of love; of intimate matters. Elizabeth was more than capable of it. But no, thank God, she meant the politics, the creed of the International: Jean-Jacques Allix's commitment, stated so often and with such commanding eloquence, to the cause of the workers, to fighting the evils of the bourgeois state, to establishing a commune in Paris and thus bringing about freedom and equality for her citizens.

'It was false, Elizabeth, plainly,' she snapped; she was beginning to sense something like admiration in her mother for this provocateur. 'Dissemblance, every last word. This is a man prepared to urge factory lads and shop assistants onto the battlefield to see through the designs of a king – and employ socialistic doctrine to do it. He is a charlatan, dedicated to a wicked cause.'

Elizabeth was smiling, pleased by this resurgence of her daughter's spirit. 'I suppose that the extremes of opinion are easier to simulate.'

The man turned to them. His efforts to remain detached were faltering again; creases had appeared between his eyebrows, a reliable indication that Jean-Jacques was becoming riled. But this was not Jean-Jacques. The familiarity was misplaced. Hannah glanced away in confusion. How much else of her lover lingered in this Prussian agent? Would he dress with the same precision and care? Would he also refuse all drink but strong coffee and cold water? Would he kiss with the same unhurried passion?

'As I have already told you,' he said to Hannah, 'I acted only to stop the war. My aim was to speed the surrender – to rob the reds of their will to keep fighting. I knew that the sorties would fail, but also that they had to happen. Paris had to be bled. Once the reds were reduced, so we thought, the bourgeois would lay down their arms. It was believed in Versailles that Trochu was only staging a resistance at all because he was afraid that there would be a revolution if he didn't.'

'A fair analysis,' opined Mr Inglis, 'although to be truthful—'

'I desired a rapid conclusion,' the Prussian continued. 'Painless, without occupation or bombardment. There are men close to my emperor who wished Paris to suffer for her decadence and abandonment of Christian morality. I was never one of those.'

This frustration seemed genuine. The siege had not gone as the provocateur had planned. There was no gloating here; no pride in his manipulations. He just wanted it to end.

Hannah wasn't mollified. 'At what point would you have left,' she asked, 'if Trochu had surrendered in September, or in October? Would you have told me, or simply melted away?'

The Prussian didn't reply. 'We must go,' he said, moving from the window. He wouldn't look at Hannah; he clearly wished that he hadn't broken his silence. 'Mrs Pardy, can I trust you to impress upon your daughter the need for quiet?'

Elizabeth relaxed her embrace; she laid her hand on the back of the armchair. 'Will you stay quiet out there, Hannah?'

Hannah hadn't yet decided what she would or wouldn't do. She looked across the room. Against the far wall, between the door and a chest of drawers, were a number of her *café-concert* canvases: Elizabeth had been grouping them by subject. Foremost was a scene from the Danton. Lucien, a dent in the sheen of his silk top hat, was reading a morning paper in a shaft of sunlight. On the stool behind him was Laure, clad in a short-sleeved scarlet polonaise, smoking a cigarette. Drawn loosely, coloured luminously, they appeared to have wandered in after a night in the dance halls. It was an image from a different life entirely.

Her mother leaned in. 'My dearest girl,' she said gently, 'you owe it to yourself to leave this mess as cleanly as you can. You think that revenge will ease your pain, but it will not. You must trust me. The best you can do is start anew. Will you stay quiet?'

Hannah met Elizabeth's grey eyes – eyes identical to her own. The Leopard put out the candle, dropping them into darkness.

'I will,' she replied.

A swell of dirty militia uniforms was blocking the boulevard des Capucines, the guardsmen drowning the humiliation of their latest defeat in gallons of cheap wine. Angry songs were sung and glass was broken; an order to disperse was met with a roar of rowdy, embittered laughter. Hannah realised that they were not leaving the Grand because the time was right, but because it was running out. Whatever was building up in the north would soon be upon them.

'Listen to that!' exclaimed Mr Inglis. 'The people of Paris might be done with Fritz – but by Jove, they ain't quite finished with each other yet!'

Infantrymen had been stationed on corners to keep the more boisterous guardsmen at bay. More than ever, the regulars and irregulars looked like two separate forces – forces that were on the verge of opposition. The Leopard was recognised before they'd even moved out from under the Grand's porch. He'd taken a cloak from a dead Zoave to cover his black suit, but he could not disguise his height, or the four-inch scar on his cheek – or the distinctive English trio trailing behind him. The soldiers began to shout things, asking him where he'd been during the battle, or calling for an officer to place him under arrest.

Elizabeth had remained by Hannah's side, an arm linked through her daughter's.

'This is my fault,' Hannah said to her. 'I should have spoken up sooner. We could have been ready to leave as soon as you arrived at the hotel.'

'You wanted to punish him. That is perfectly understandable.' Her mother looked down the boulevard Madeleine. 'Besides, my girl, they don't have us yet.'

They turned left, heading north onto the place de l'Opéra. There were more soldiers here, queuing in their hundreds outside the military supply depot that had been set up in the opera house. A single petrol lamp burned above the entrance, its sooty glow failing even to reach the edges of the square. The Prussian tried to take advantage of this gloom, but it was no use; within moments shouts of '*Le Léopard!*' were echoing between the opera house and the Grand Hotel.

They skirted the hall at a brisk pace. Away from the square, the only light came from the stars and a low half-moon, cut to a crisp oval by the shadow of the earth. Everything was black or a metallic, bluish grey; above, beyond the columns and domes, the winged statues on the opera house roof were taking flight into a shimmering sky. Two infantrymen ambled into their path, greeting the Leopard with suspicious overfriendliness. He shouldered them aside without speaking.

The boulevard Haussmann was a good deal emptier. Over a mile long, this colossal Imperial thoroughfare was lined with iron-shuttered shops. In front of one of these, just beyond the intersection that connected the boulevard to the rue Lafayette and a few smaller avenues, a crowd was assembling. It was made up of a hundred or so working people, supplemented by the usual contingent of National Guard, and was growing fast. Hannah spotted Laure close to the centre, swigging from a bottle of spirits. She'd done as she'd promised out in the woods. Montmartre had been raised to deal with the Leopard.

The Prussian led them across the road, out of the starlight into deep shadow. They needed to pass through this intersection, only twenty yards or so from the crowd, in order to reach Mr Inglis's apartment. Someone launched into a speech from the lip of a water trough. It was Raoul Rigault, dressed as a militia major – although he certainly hadn't been out to fight on that day or any other. He was stoking those around him for a run at the Grand; a bastion of obscene Imperial inequality, he proclaimed, that should be thrown open to residents from the mills and the workshops. And then he mentioned Elizabeth by name.

'This old *Anglaise*, this Madame Pardy, is the great supporter of the damned Leopard – the Judas of the 18th arrondissement. She made his name in the *Figaro*. She backed up his lies and spun new ones to gain him more followers. She must now be subjected to the same revolutionary justice!'

The crowd bayed, waving cudgels and blades in the air. Someone shouted that they despised the English; that they would burn them all on a bonfire if they could, and dump the ashes into the Seine. There was agreement, and cheers, and yet more extravagant threats – and the man they sought slipped straight past them, escorting his accomplices through the dark intersection. One word from Hannah could have seen the Leopard destroyed. She remembered the promise she'd made to her mother and said nothing.

'We are safe,' whispered Elizabeth. 'My goodness, we are safe.'

They'd almost reached the mouth of the rue Joubert when a dozen pairs of boots hammered from a side street: a party of men with Émile Besson at their front. Clem was among them as well. This was what her brother had fled the Grand to do. The rest were clad in sheepskin jerkins and brimless caps – sailors from the Gare du Nord balloon factory. Several were carrying municipal-issue rifles.

'Stand there!' Besson yelled. 'You *stand there!'*

The Prussian regarded him steadily. 'I will not, Monsieur Besson. You will have to shoot me down.'

Besson advanced – and without warning the two men were fighting in the gutter. They were not as mismatched as might have been assumed. Although smaller by five inches at least and lacking his opponent's broad build, Besson was spurred by fury; head lowered, he drove the Prussian against some railings with wide swings of his arms. Elizabeth went to intervene, endeavouring both to pull Besson off and keep the sailors at a distance. This, of course, made everything worse.

'Dear Lord,' she wheezed, 'you infernally *stupid man!'*

There were cries from the boulevard. Besson's attempted arrest had drawn the attention of Rigault's mob; a number were coming to investigate. Hannah walked back towards them, not knowing what she might actually do when they met. Clem rushed up beside her. She stopped to look at him. Her twin brother had been refashioned by the siege, his form and features trimmed down to the quick. This leanness lent him a new significance. His costume – that shabby green suit, the length of curtain wrapped around his neck, the tall, discoloured hat – belonged on a Westminster thief-master; yet for the first time something in his bearded face reminded her of their father.

Remorse drew around Hannah like a net, swift and tight. It was because of her that Clem had come to Paris; because of her that he'd suffered prison and hunger and who knew what else, and now faced the most dreadful danger. She took his hand. 'I'm sorry, Clem,' she said, 'for leaving you as I did. You didn't deserve it.'

He blinked in embarrassment. 'Oh God, Han, that was all

me. I tripped on a kerbstone, didn't I – went down like the ass I am.' He squeezed her fingers, his forgiveness so immediate that it didn't register in his mind; he didn't even recognise that there had been an offence in the first place. 'You could hardly have come back. Why, we'd have both been tossed in the Mazas.'

This was only part of Hannah's meaning. 'No, I – you don't—'

At least thirty people were now heading in their direction. Hannah turned; Besson and the Prussian were being held apart by the sailors, Elizabeth haranguing in the background. They had him.

'I went as fast as I could,' said Clem quickly; he was apologising to Hannah now. 'I ran the whole bloody way. I wanted to nab him in the Grand. This really is no good at all.'

Hannah collected herself. 'I'll talk to them.'

Clem nodded, moving closer; the twins stood together before the approaching mob. She started to speak – to explain that the spy had been caught and justice would be served. Then they saw him.

'There he is!' someone bawled. 'Traitor! *Traitor!*'

The crowd broke into a charge, running for the Leopard. Hannah was buffeted and barged; she called Clem's name, but couldn't even hear her own voice in the clamour. Hands were grabbing at her, holding onto her – apprehending her, she realised, as one of the guilty parties. She was shoved down, pressed hard against a lamppost. A man threw an arm around her neck and squeezed, trying to work her legs open from behind. The shouting was furious and continual: *'Vive la France! Vive la Commune! Get him! Get the traitor!'*

Suddenly her neck was released – her attacker sent sprawling. She was rescued, just as she'd been on the quay beside the Tuileries; she coughed, struggling for breath, unable to see anything but boots and pavement. A hand took hold of hers, hauling her from the mob into darkness. The index finger was inflexible, a solid piece of wood; and for an instant, without thinking, she was reassured.

They were in an alleyway. Émile Besson was there also, at her other arm. A truce had plainly been called for the purposes of mutual survival; the Prussian and the *aérostier* were virtually carrying her between them.

'Clem,' she said, 'they have Clem. We must go back.'

'We cannot,' Besson replied. 'I am so very sorry, Mademoiselle, but we cannot.'

Elizabeth was in a moonlit courtyard, a long rectangle to the rear of a parade of shops. They'd come around in a circle; they were behind the boulevard. One side was a blank wall, the other a row of padlocked double-doors. At the far end were four broken supply-carts. There was no other gate. They were trapped.

Her mother came over. 'Where is Clement?'

'The crowd,' Hannah gasped. 'Oh God, Elizabeth, I saw him go down!'

'There is hope,' Besson said. 'The sailors will help if they are able. And he is not the one they want.'

The *aérostier* was gazing at her, his hated Leopard all but forgotten. His expression was almost of wonder; his eyes glistened. He too had believed her dead, she realised – had been mourning her while she drew on a dirt floor somewhere beneath Gagny. Right then, at that moment, this left her utterly unmoved.

'Could *you* not have helped him, Monsieur Besson?' she asked. 'I thought you were his friend!'

Besson's dazed half-smile disappeared. 'I will find him, Mademoiselle. I promise you that.'

Shouts were gathering out in the alley; their location had been discovered. They hurried into the shadows, to the nearest set of shop doors. Besson drew a clasp-knife from his jacket pocket and started to force the lock.

Hannah looked around. The Leopard was with them no longer. He'd walked to the centre of the courtyard, into the full glare of the moon. He was standing very straight, calmly tugging the black leather gloves tight on his hands. The urgency that had infused him since they'd left the Grand had disappeared. He removed the Zoave cloak and dropped it by the wall. He was preparing himself.

The Prussian agent glanced over at her. After Hannah's incredulity and grief, and then her agonising anger, had come a straightforward desire for answers. She wanted to know everything about the deception that had been worked on her – the level of premeditation; exactly how detached he'd remained while she'd thought herself in love; how he'd imagined it might end. He seemed to recognise this. His face, previously unreadable, opened up by the smallest amount, the brow lifting almost imperceptibly. He was ready to speak to her.

The first of his pursuers, a gaggle of militiamen, loped noisily into the courtyard, cutting across Hannah's line of sight. They closed around their erstwhile champion, keeping him at arm's length as if containing a dangerous animal. The main body of the mob was directly behind, piling in through the gates, streaming past the doorway where Hannah huddled next to Besson and her mother. A ring of bodies formed around the Prussian, spitting and swearing and promising terrible violence.

Raoul Rigault appeared. He was enjoying himself immensely; this was precisely the sort of thing he'd been hoping for since the beginning of the siege. That his victim was a man he'd recently considered a useful ally didn't seem to bother him in the least.

'We have before us an enemy of the people, citizens!' he

cried. 'An enemy of Paris, of socialism! A traitor to France!'

'I am not French,' the Leopard replied. 'I am Captain Johann Brenner of the Imperial Prussian Army.' He paused. 'I am one of those who have bested France.'

There were hisses and jeers, and the spitting grew more intense; the black coat now sparkled with spittle in the cold white light. The Prussian – Brenner – was goading them, guiding them to an increasingly certain result.

Rigault's satisfaction had vanished. 'You have bested the *Empire*,' he corrected hotly, 'and the Empire only! We have not been *defeated*, damn you, but betrayed – by our coward governor and his band of coward ministers! The workers of France remain valorous; they remain bold; they remain unconquered, furthermore, and will show—'

'I have worked to reduce Paris,' Brenner interrupted, easily talking over Rigault, 'solely by drawing on what is already within her. You must question these leaders, these drunks and lunatics who have assigned themselves the power to command you. You must ask how much blood – how much of *your* blood – they will see spilled to achieve their ends.'

Rigault was scowling now. 'Who the devil are *you*,' he declared, 'to talk of *our blood?* Enough of this! The sentence is death – this foul spy must die, at once!'

'Death!' howled the mob. 'Death to traitors and spies!'

Besson broke the lock.

Brenner went to the wall, offering no resistance. Without ceremony, rifles were raised and fired at little more than point-blank range. Any flash from their muzzles was smothered by the press of smocks and National Guard tunics; the three overlapping reports were almost lost in the cheers. The tall, black-clad man fell dead on the cobbles of the yard, the crowd swarming around his body as if they meant to devour it.

Hannah was in a shop, an upmarket dressmaker's. It was

very dark; there was a smell of lavender and fresh cotton. Naked clothes dummies stood in the slivers of moonlight that crept between the shutters. She fell to her knees and retched, an outstretched palm slapping against the polished wooden floor. Elizabeth and Besson eased her up and on through the shop, towards the boulevard on its other side. Behind them, back in the yard, the mob began to chant.

'*À bas les Prussiens! Vive la Commune!*'

V

Smaller than most steerage cabins, the attic was crammed with mismatched furniture, some of it rather fine; ladies' dresses in a range of sizes and styles; more pairs of shoes and boots than could easily be counted; and a pawn-shop assortment of random semi-valuables, including a large quantity of exotic feathers.

Besson lowered the hood of his pea jacket. 'Much of this,' he said, 'is looted.'

Clem sat up on the chaise longue and adjusted his foot, wincing at the movement of the cracked bones beneath the bandage. He took a sip of rum and then leaned forward to have a good scratch.

'I daresay that opportunities have been taken,' he replied. 'Have you seen any food yet, down in the centre?'

'We have had our share. A convoy of wagons arrived this morning.'

'Dairy has been the big success here. You'd think it'd be a leg of lamb or a minute steak, but no – butter is what the people most want. And milk! By Jove, who'd have thought one could miss it so badly? Yesterday I drank a quart, old man, a bloody *quart*, as if I was a calf long separated from its mother. You could hear it sloshing whenever I moved.'

'Such things are a slight consolation for the people of Paris.'

Clem nodded; what a blabbing blockhead I am, he thought. The official announcement of the armistice – the French capitulation – was over a week old now. The disaster of Buzenval had finally unseated Trochu, and after a frank assessment of the supplies at their disposal, the provisional government had dispatched Jules Favre to Versailles to negotiate terms for their surrender. The bleakest few days of the entire siege had followed. Prussian soldiers occupied the forts around Paris; its inhabitants were transformed from combatants to mere captives, still starving, still freezing, but denied the slightest scrap of hope.

Even the reds had gone into an ominous hibernation. In the wake of the last sortie there had been a final small-scale revolt: Gustave Flourens had been broken out of the Mazas and once again an armed force had marched on the Hôtel de Ville. This time, however, the government response had been rapid and unequivocal. The infantry guarding the building had returned a desultory militia fire with deadly accuracy, killing several of their attackers and injuring scores more. This incident, French regulars shooting down French National Guard, had changed the game. The lanes of Montmartre went silent, and the avenues of Belleville were left to its children, but there could be little doubt that in the red clubs fresh plans were being prepared.

'How's Han doing?' Clem asked.

Besson's head fell. 'She says little,' he replied after a short pause. 'She has been sleeping a good deal. The loss of the paintings was difficult, also, coming – coming when it did.'

'How did it happen? The paintings, I mean?'

'They said they were looking for a spy's accomplice. They

went up to your mother's rooms. The next anyone knew burning canvases were landing in the place de l'Opéra. Troops were summoned to eject them, but it was too late.' Besson looked away, over at a spiral of dress-hoops dangling from a nail. 'I've heard that they paraded a portrait of the Prussian around for hours. Blanqui himself is said to have put a match to it.'

This wasn't surprising. From one of the attic's windows Clem had been able to watch the mob gutting the Danton, ripping out the bar whole and casting the Leopard's fake trophies into the street. That shed of Hannah's had been torn down too, the planks borne off to fuel honest proletarian fires. A campaign had plainly been waged to wipe every trace of the Leopard and his unwitting English accomplices from Paris.

'It'll be better when she can get out of this city.' Clem held up his glass. 'Are you sure you won't join me?'

Besson declined; he would soon be leaving. For a short while neither of them spoke. Without cannon-fire, without street-corner orators, without horses or dogs or cats, Montmartre was deathly quiet. Eventually, an infant cried thinly somewhere below, followed by a splash as someone threw out a basin of water.

'I can get you to the British Embassy,' Besson said suddenly. He indicated his pea jacket – the sort currently being worn by the Parisian police. 'I can procure a disguise like this one. Nobody will think anything of your wound. They will assume you are a casualty of the last battle. It is possible.'

Clem puffed out his cheeks as if astonished; he'd been expecting this. 'Heavens, Émile, I don't—' He stopped. 'I can't ask you to take such a risk. I simply can't. Moreover, this damned thing,' he gestured contemptuously at his foot, 'is rather worse than it appears.' He gave a second's thought to broken ankles and how bad they could be. 'The, ah, the bone pierced the skin, don't y'know. The doctor who came up here to see me said I really shouldn't move it for a month.'

The *aérostier* smiled. He glanced at the feminine items piled around them; he could see the truth clearly enough. 'Very well,' he said, 'but you should really keep to yourself as much as possible. You are known to the ultras, Clement, and they will not forget. The trials of Paris have not ended with the siege. Something else is coming. You must remain alert.'

This was parting advice. 'You're really going, then? Leaving Paris? It seems impossible, old man, that you could exist anywhere else.'

'I must,' Besson said, 'for the time being. I was seen by the reds helping the Leopard of Montmartre escape apprehension. I am French, also, a Parisian; this makes me a genuine traitor. I will be at the very top of Raoul Rigault's list.' He spoke matter-of-factly, without bitterness. 'The last post balloon has flown. The workshops have been closed. There is nothing to hold me here.'

Clem opened his mouth to deliver the stunning argument that would induce Besson to stay. Nothing came. He frowned, swirled the liquor around in his glass and took another gulp.

The *aérostier* got up from his chair. 'I must be off. I should be back at the Champs Elysées before dark.'

'Tell them that I'll return to London after the elections,' Clem said. 'Before the end of February, at any rate. Or March, at the latest.' He hesitated. 'Tell them I'll write.'

A last look passed between the two men. Clem felt an urge to embrace this fellow, this dear friend who'd done so much for his family; rising would be a challenge, though, and might somewhat undermine his claims to immobility.

374

In this instant of indecision the chance was lost. Besson put a hand on his shoulder, uncommon warmth in his eyes; and then he ducked through the low attic doorway.

At the click of the latch Laure's face appeared at the nearest window, tobacco smoke trailing from her nostrils. She'd slipped out when Besson had announced himself, cursing the concierge who'd directed him to them, and had spent the last quarter of an hour perched on the roof. Since that night she'd refused to see anyone save her patient. There had been numerous knocks and shouts up from the street – the *vivandières* of the 197th, Raoul Rigault, one of those painters who used to hang around with Han – and she'd ignored them all. Clem's French wasn't good enough for him to be able to question her very closely about this reclusive behaviour, but it was pretty obvious that she didn't want much more to do with the reds of Montmartre.

The conversation with Besson had given Clem an uneasy feeling – a faint sense of being left behind. Sight of Laure relieved this at once. He pulled open the casement; she hitched up her skirts and climbed in, a cigarette poking from her red lips. Her gown was an iridescent, silky green, well cut and certainly expensive, lifted from God knows where. The cocotte had taken to sloping out while Clem was asleep, returning each dawn with provisions and an armful of swag. A National Guard greatcoat was draped across her shoulders; the copper hair, longer now, was coiled in a loose bun. She sat down heavily in the chair Besson had just vacated, swearing under her breath, rubbing her frozen hands together and then holding them to the grate of their pot-bellied stove. After a few seconds, she noticed that he was staring at her. She leaned over to the chaise longue and gave him a sharp dig in the ribs.

It was almost like an act of penance. Laure had dragged

Clem single-handed from beneath the boots of those set on kicking him to death for the crime of being his mother's son. He'd been insensible, covered in blood, but somehow she'd got him to this garret – owned, Clem later learned, by a friend of a friend long since fled from the city. The following day he'd come round to discover her bandaging his broken foot, looking so beautiful, so pale and fine, that tears had sprung to his eyes.

'Mademoiselle Laure,' he'd mumbled. 'Where the devil have you been?'

She'd turned towards him with distinct irritation, releasing a barrage of words that he'd struggled to understand – although he gathered that he and his family had disappointed her in some heinous way, landing her in a terrible, irresolvable dilemma. Even now, two weeks later, having tended to him devotedly, she still shot him the odd glance of annoyance.

'*Elles vont,*' Clem told her. '*Ma mère et ma soeur.*'

Laure thought about this for a moment, then shrugged and picked up an empty glass from the floor. Peering around for the bottle, she reached across to slide a hand inside his shirt; he jumped at the touch of her icy fingertips.

VI

Hannah looked out at Saint-Denis as it crawled past the window of their carriage. Heavily bombarded in the siege's final weeks, the town was a wreck adrift in a sea of mud. Many of the houses lacked roofs; the cathedral had a yawning hole in its façade in place of a rose window. She caught a glimpse of the statue in the main square, its head sheared clean off. There were harsh voices nearby. Down beside the tracks, a detachment of Prussian infantry was menacing some French railway workers, jabbing at them with their rifle-butts.

'I could tell from the accent,' Mr Inglis was saying. 'Alsatian my eye! It was obvious, quite frankly. That the reds managed to overlook it is a clear indication of how credulous and ignorant they are.'

Elizabeth glowered at him. 'What in heaven do you mean, Mont, you impossible beast? The man spoke French like a native. No one saw through him. Mr Blount at the embassy told me that every officer in the Prussian army has been required to learn French since the early sixties. And the captain was plainly an extraordinary officer. His mastery of that tongue, and our own as well, is really no marvel.'

For a fortnight or so Elizabeth and Mr Inglis had steered their conversation clear of Captain Brenner, to spare Hannah's feelings. In time, though, the boredom of confinement to the British Embassy and the sheer fascination of the subject had rendered it irresistible. One day it had been broached, rather cautiously; now they talked of little else. They'd combed over every detail of Brenner's great trick, from the scar and damaged hand – wounds most probably inflicted during the Prussian campaign against Austria, it was concluded – to the sources of his rhetoric. Her mother always made much of the perfection of the illusion, whilst the newspaperman insisted that he'd been thoroughly sceptical from the start.

The sixteen days cooped up in the embassy waiting for news had weighed heavily on Elizabeth and Mr Inglis, but Hannah had barely noticed their passing. She'd laid out a bed for herself in the corner of a clerks' office and stayed there. It had felt as if she was under the influence of a powerful narcotic. She'd experience disorientating, contradictory emotions; and then, for long periods, nothing at all. France's surrender, once an inconceivable tragedy, meant little. The destruction of her work, even, had been merely another blow landed on someone completely stupefied. Jean-Jacques Allix was written into the best of it, a glaring falsehood undermining those earnest attempts at truth; that the canvases had been burned was almost a relief.

The train rounded a corner and slowed to a long, squealing halt. Outside now was a redoubt, the Prussian flag floating above its walls. Mr Inglis got to his feet. The newspaperman had made it safely to his apartment that night, having fled when the mob charged. So certain did he become, however, that the reds had taken note of him – that he would be dragged from his study and decapitated on the pavement

378

– that he'd joined them at the embassy anyway. He'd written to the editor of the *Sentinel* the same hour that the armistice was declared, offering his resignation from the Paris desk and announcing that he would be returning to London on the first available form of conveyance.

'I'll see what the delay is,' he said, opening the compartment door. 'Honestly, this confounded country.'

Alone with her daughter, Elizabeth began to talk of her book. She'd soon dismissed suggestions that it would have to be abandoned, or even that there would have to be an alteration of subject.

'We are not *French*,' she'd said, 'as the residents of Paris never tired of reminding us. We owe them no loyalty – no consideration of what might offend. Interest in this character, this provocateur of ours, will be intense.'

'You took up his cause, though,' Hannah had pointed out. 'You are hardly a dispassionate voice. Those articles of yours—'

'—were anonymous, my girl. *Anonymous*. Only rumour connects me to them. And I am as dispassionate, Hannah, as the day is long. It is an ideal subject for me. The mystery of it, with so much left unresolved; a man who put us both at such awful risk, who attempted to kill Clement in that balloon to protect his secret, only to sacrifice himself at the final moment so that we might escape. The sheer *nobility* implied by this, despite everything. It is intriguing, you must admit.'

There was one significant change to Elizabeth's literary plans: a marked increase in her daughter's proposed contribution. She envisaged sections narrated by one who'd been in the thick of it – at the Leopard's side. As usual, she'd tried to initiate a bargaining process: a slice of the proceeds, naturally, with the chance of a co-author's credit on the front page if Hannah could bring herself to attempt a likeness from memory – and perhaps, again if she were amenable, a couple of key scenes from the Leopard's astonishing career.

Hannah remained noncommittal. It still seemed ridiculous that she was doing this; it still felt as if she was giving in. But she'd seen Rigault that night, marshalling his murderous mob. No mercy would be shown to her. The despair that had gripped her in the Grand Hotel had lifted: she no longer had any wish to die. She'd let her mother run on for now. A proper discussion of this book could wait until they were in London.

And London, of course, was Elizabeth's other great topic. She'd shown an unheard-of willingness to admit mistakes – what she termed 'the well-intentioned errors of the past' – and wanted to describe how very different everything would be when they were back.

'You are older, Hannah; you have lived a little. Your gifts have developed. You can meet the metropolis on a more equal footing. Taking you to Gabriel as I did that night was utterly wrong. I can see that now, all too clearly. He is far too fragile for one of your robust tastes. But his wider circle really does contain some fascinating people. There's one gentleman I think you'd particularly like, an American painter – quite the wit, and very familiar with these French ideas of yours. I believe he is even applying them to his own renditions of the Thames.'

Hannah shifted in her seat. 'Elizabeth . . .'

'London is changing, my girl. Gabriel's friends talk constantly of setting up their own place – to exhibit foreigners and women and all sorts. If you are astute – if you take the chances offered, who knows what—'

Elizabeth stopped talking; she opened her notebook and began to write. Émile Besson had appeared in the doorway of the compartment. He'd been at the end of the carriage, standing out in the open air, watching Paris sink into the Seine valley. The unmasking of Jean-Jacques Allix had failed to prompt a reassessment of the *aérostier*. Elizabeth didn't trust him; she didn't like him; she suspected him of conservative leanings and a cramped imagination. As he was a friend of Clem's she'd felt obliged to offer him a few days' accommodation in London, but clearly meant to chase him off as soon as she could.

'What is happening, Monsieur Besson?' Hannah asked.

'They are checking papers again,' he replied. 'It is unnecessary. I believe the Prussians enjoy demonstrating their control over us.'

'And this is the city in which we have left my son. Who knows what these tedious occupiers might decide to do next?' Elizabeth laid down her pencil. 'Monsieur Besson, are you absolutely positive that he could not be brought to the embassy?'

Besson had been asked this twenty times at least in the past day, but he showed no vexation. This was how he dealt with Elizabeth; she found it utterly exasperating. 'The ankle was badly broken, Madame. Transporting him would have been difficult, and would surely have drawn the notice of the reds. I judged it too dangerous to risk. Your son is being well cared for, though. You need not worry. He will be safe.'

Elizabeth gave an exaggerated sigh and closed her notebook. Besson sat down, glancing across at Hannah; she hid her smile behind her hand and turned to the window.

Tiny raindrops stippled the glass; a porter shouted something further up the train; and Hannah had an impulse she hadn't felt for weeks, not since the cellar at Gagny. She made a quick survey of the compartment. Her mother and the *aérostier* were at opposite ends of their seat, wrapped in scarves and heavy jackets, four feet of empty upholstery between them. Both

381

were sitting up straight, hands folded in their laps, looking off in different directions. A timetable, out of date and useless, lay on the cushion beside her, its back page blank. Angling it on her thigh, she took a stub of pencil from the pocket of her embassy-supplied coat and started to draw.

Author's Note

Although a work of fiction, much of *Illumination* is based closely on the historical facts of the Prussian siege of Paris during the winter of 1870–71. Mrs Pardy's 'Leopard of Montmartre' was partly inspired by the cult that sprang up around Sergeant Ignatius Hoff, a soldier from the Alsace who attained legendary status among the besieged population for his stealthy slaughter of Prussian sentries – only to be suspected of spying when he vanished during the battle of Champigny (Hoff later reappeared, however, and was exonerated). Hard evidence is unsurprisingly scant, but figures like Jean-Jacques Allix certainly existed. The siege was the culmination of one of Bismarck's most intricate plans; the Iron Chancellor is believed to have flooded the French capital with his operatives many months in advance. It's very difficult to study the calamitous Parisian defence and not conclude that a number of well-placed citizens were deliberately engineering their own downfall.

The *Aphrodite* and her tenacious *aérostier* are inventions, but the wartime Balloon Commission is not. Managed by Félix Tournachon (known as Nadar), Eugene Godard and Wilfrid de Fonvielle, the Commission established a number of factories and workshops across Paris, principally in its disused railway stations. Between 23 September 1870 and 28 January 1871, sixty-six balloons carried out at least 176 passengers and pilots, five dogs, 381 pigeons and around eleven tons of dispatches, including nearly three million letters. It was, as Besson warns Clem, a dangerous business. Two balloons were lost at sea; five were captured by the Prussians, their crews held until the end of the war under sentence of death for spying, although no executions actually took place. At the mercy of the winds, several landed in unexpected locations, such as Holland, Prussia itself and even, in the case of the *Ville d'Orleans*, the heart of Norway – an unintentional journey of almost nine hundred miles. A monument to the *aérostiers* by Auguste Bartholdi, sculptor of the Statue of Liberty, was erected at the Port des Ternes in 1906, but was melted down during the next conquest of Paris by the German army: the Nazi occupation of 1940–44.

Hannah Pardy's circumstances share some similarities with those of the American painter Mary Cassatt (1844–1926). Impatient with mainstream art and the patronising attitudes of a male-dominated art world, Cassatt relocated from Philadelphia to Paris in the 1860s, where she was heavily influenced by the radical naturalist movement that would come to be known, after an 1874 exhibition in Nadar's studio, as Impressionism. The path of her career is basically that which Hannah dreamed of for herself: after a number of successful submissions to the Paris Salon, she was approached by Edgar Degas and began exhibiting with the Impressionists in the late 1870s. Cassatt was no runaway, though; her wealthy stockbroker father did not approve of her chosen vocation but allowed her to pursue it, and both her parents and her sister came to live near her at various times. Unlike Hannah, she managed to remain respectable, residing in the central arrondissements and staying away from the artists' cafés, and she returned to America for the duration of the Franco-Prussian War.

Many other books informed *Illumination*; all errors and distortions are my own. Essential primary sources were the numerous siege diaries kept (and later published) by imprisoned English residents, particularly those of the journalists Henry Labouchere and Felix Whitehurst; the multitude of contemporary English guidebooks to Paris, ranging in tone from impeccably upright to openly salacious; and the novels of Emile Zola's Rougon-Macquart series, which provide a detailed, unsparing portrait of the Second Empire in all its debauchery and desperation. The full list of secondary sources is too long to be included here, but mention should be made of *Paris in Despair: Art and Everyday Life Under Siege* by Hollis Clayson, *Airlift 1870: The Balloons and Pigeons in the Siege of Paris* by John Fisher, *The Fall of Paris* by Alistair Horne, *The Siege of Paris* by Robert Baldick, *Early Impressionism and the French State* by Jane Mayo Roos, *The Painting of Modern Life: Paris in the Art of Manet and his Followers* by T.J. Clark, *Impressionism* by Robert L. Herbert and *Demanding the Impossible: A History of Anarchism* by Peter Marshall.

Thanks are due to Louisa Joyner, Katie Espiner and Euan Thorneycroft, whose expert advice and guidance shaped the novel; Cassie Browne, Alice Moore and the team at HarperCollins; the staff of the British Library; my family and friends, for their continued support and enthusiasm; Kester, for the best writing breaks; and Sarah, of course, for everything.

01747 871333

SP3 6PW